ROBERT – THE WAYWARD PRINCE

Book Two of the Norman Prince Trilogy

Warrior of the Cross
By
AUSTIN HERNON

WAYWARD PRINCE PRODUCTIONS, ENGLAND
Published by Wayward Prince Productions in 2015
An imprint of Upfront Publishing of Peterborough, England.

ISBN 978-178456-225-0

www.waywardprinceproductions.co.uk

While based on historical fact and historical characters, this book is
a work of fiction, but much more can be found on the website at:
www.waywardprinceproductions.co.uk.

Artwork and Credits

Original maps and battle plans by Kathryn Webster
inkandpixelcreatives@gmail.com

DEDICATIONS

For Mandy Irene, patient wife, eternal companion, and supporter.
"Where did you say we were going next?"

For Dea Parkin of Fiction Feedback, still the patient editor and foil
of my wilder ideas.
info@fictionfeedback.co.uk

For Robert II, Duke of Normandy.
How did you fit it all in, dear friend? Your story continues.

Contents

Maps and battle plans.

Prologue.

Chapters.

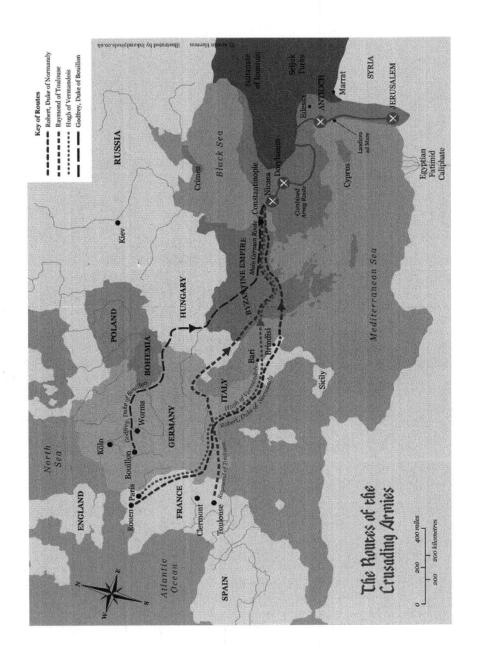

The Routes of the Crusading Armies

Key of Routes

- ▬▬ Robert, Duke of Normandy
- ▬▬ Raymond of Toulouse
- ▬▬ Hugh of Vermandois
- ▬▬ Godfrey, Duke of Bouillon

Illustrated by inkandpixels.co.uk
© Austin Herron

RUSSIA

Kiev

POLAND

BOHEMIA

HUNGARY

GERMANY

Köln

Worms

Bouillon

Godfrey, Duke of Bouillon

ENGLAND

FRANCE

Rouen

Paris

Clermont

Toulouse

Raymond of Toulouse

North Sea

Atlantic Ocean

SPAIN

ITALY

Hugh of Vermandois

Robert, Duke of Normandy

Bari

Brindisi

Sicily

Mediterranean Sea

BYZANTINE EMPIRE

Main German Route

Constantinople

Nicaea

Dorylaeum

Combined Army Route

Black Sea

Crimea

Sultanate of Iconium

Seljuk Turks

Edessa

ANTIOCH

Marrat

Laodicea ad Mare

SYRIA

JERUSALEM

Cyprus

Egyptian Fatimid Caliphate

0   200   400 miles
0   200   400 kilometres

N E S W

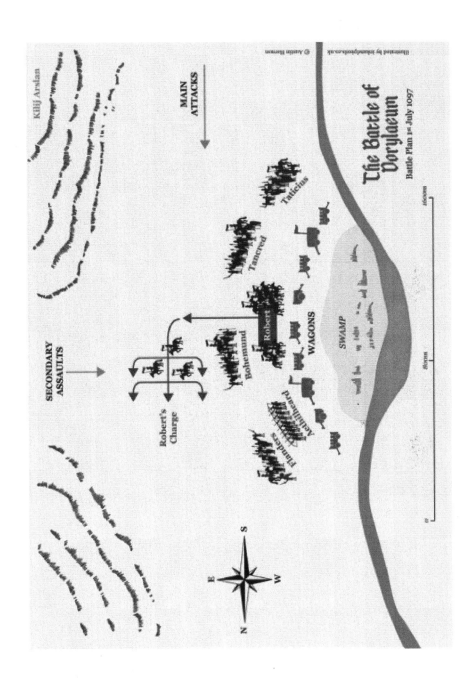

The Battle of
Dorylaeum
Battle Plan 1st July 1097

Kilij Arslan

MAIN ATTACKS

SECONDARY ASSAULTS

Robert's Charge

Bohemund

Robert

Tancred

Taticius

WAGONS

Adhémard

Crusaders

SWAMP

Antioch
The First Deployment
Battle Plan March 1098

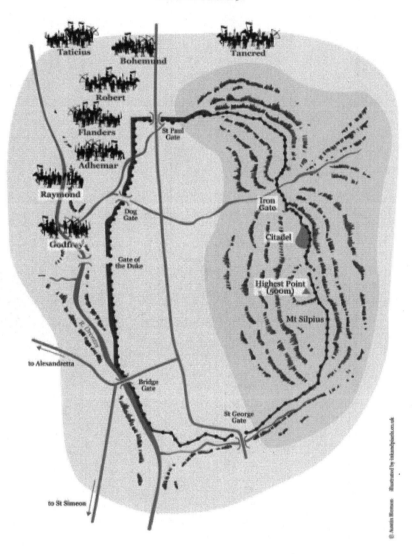

Taticius

Bohemund

Tancred

Robert

Flanders

St Paul Gate

Adhemar

Raymond

Dog Gate

Iron Gate

Citadel

Godfrey

Gate of the Duke

Highest Point (500m)

Mt Silpius

R. Orontes

to Alexandretta

Bridge Gate

St George Gate

to St Simeon

© Austin Hernon   Illustrated by inkandpixels.co.uk

6

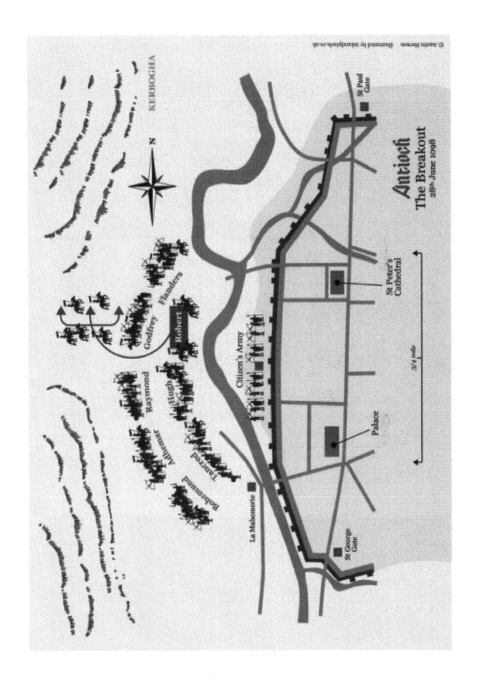

Antioch
The Breakout
28th June 1098

KERBOGHA

N

Godfrey
Flanders
Robert
Raymond
Adhemar
Hugh
Tancred
Bohemund

Citizen's Army

St Paul
Gate

St Peter's
Cathedral

3/4 mile

Palace

Le Mahomerie

St George
Gate

The City of Jerusalem

Robert - The Wayward Prince

Book Two

The Warriors of the Cross

Best wishes

Austin

Enjoy the truth.

Prologue

In the year 1095, Pope Urban II delivered a sermon that was to transform the history of Europe. It instituted the differences between Christendom and Islam by declaring that Jerusalem was in the hands of Moslems, and that as result of this Christianity itself was in dire peril, suffering appalling oppression and threatened by further invasion.

The holy city of Jerusalem had been ruled by Moslems since the end of the seventh century as a multi-faith society but while Urban was at Clermont he received a call for help from the Christian Emperor of the East, Alexios Komnenus, who ruled his Byzantine empire from the ancient city of Constantinople.

Alexios was hard pressed by Islamic Turks and his borders were in danger, so he asked for help from his Christian brothers, even though the Church had long since divided itself into the Latin West and the Orthodox East.

Urban saw an opportunity and labelled the Moslems 'a people alien to God, bent on ritual torture and appalling desecration.'

There was little evidence of this; the governance of Jerusalem had been tolerant and equal-handed rather than one of oppression.

What was clear, however, was that the various Moslem factions, of which there are many, from Egypt to what is now Turkey, were intent on expansion – by whatever means, and it was this that frightened Christian leaders in both West and East.

Urban's solution was to invent the idea of a holy war and he called upon the whole of Christian Europe to 'unite and throw out the savage foe.'

As an added bonus, apart from the liberation of the Holy Lands, he offered the promise of eternal life to all those taking part, or assisting in this perilous undertaking.

The result was overwhelming, if uncoordinated, with wealthy lords, princes, kings and bishops declaring their support, either by bearing arms or by funding the venture, or both – and the common people, with neither funding nor arms, setting off towards the starting point of Constantinople in the hope of eternal life.

By January 1097 the first of the warriors had arrived in Constantinople ready to cross over the Bosporus into Asia, and onwards into Palestine; their ultimate objective, Jerusalem. What follows is one man's experience of the savagery which became known as The First Crusade.

1. A Familiar Passage.

A tumult of noise hit me as I emerged from the darkness of the keep into the bright sunlight. Shocked, I stilled to take in the spectacle. My knights and men-at-arms were lined up to form an avenue of colour and movement, inviting me to process along it, on this, the beginning of our long journey to Jerusalem. At the bottom of the steps, waiting with grins as wide as the river Seine glinting in the distance, were my supporters: Ragenaus, a Saxon warrior of good blood, and the bearer of my banner, Payne Peverel. Payne had been one of those surprises which descend upon men from time to time. When news of my intention to go to the Holy Land had become public, he had come to me from England to ask for a position. I was astonished because he was the brother of the man who, rumour had it, was my natural half-brother by my father's only known dalliance, William Peverel, Payne sharing with him a mother if not a father.

Payne appeared one morning in my great hall here in Rouen and shouldered his way through the crowd, by which I was beset with requests for information and guidance. Standing tall and soldierly, and with a great voice, he carried his greeting above the throng.

'Prince Robert,' he demanded my attention, and silence fell upon those seeking my ear, 'is there room in your mesnie for a member of your family?'

I had never met him or his half-brother, but there was an air of familiarity about the man which sparked my curiosity and I bade him come near.

'You are loud, fellow; what name do you have?'

'I am Peverel, my lord, Payne Peverel. You have heard of me I believe.'

'Approach, Payne Peverel. Let me see you.'

He was a big fellow, of that there was no doubt, and stood a full head taller than me, but he seemed respectful in front of me, so I took him into an alcove while the sudden noise of gossip followed us.

'I nearly met your half-brother once, and I nearly had him killed for his involvement in my brother Henry's dissembling nonsense.'

'I am aware of my sibling's ill-judged loyalties, my lord. But I have come here to declare for you and your cause; will you take me to Jerusalem, my lord?'

I did not hesitate for very long, there was such a strong and instant bond between us I could only assent.

'I will take you, Payne Peverel, on one condition,' I said holding out my hands.

He bowed and let me take his hands in mine. 'Whatever you require, my lord, I shall give gladly.'

'Then you must carry my standard all the way to the holy city.'

His hands tightened around mine; he had the grip of a blacksmith. Then he looked up at me and grinned.

'I am to be the bearer of your own standard, my lord?'

'All the way, Payne Peverel, all the way.'

Today my heart carried the self-same zeal being expressed by the throng, but it also held a cloying sadness. I mounted my horse, held by Ragenaus, and glanced back at the parapet of the keep, hoping from habit to see my beloved Tegwin – she was not there, only a ghost of a memory haunted the wooden rail. It was poor compensation to know that she and our children were safe in England, in the care of my brother, King William Rufus. She would lie in my arms only in dreams as long as this venture lasted and I could return to her caresses once more.

Long before we reached the gate of the outer bailey I could see others of my family and friends waiting astride their mounts, patiently, it seemed. Foremost among them, as befitted a mission of God, was my uncle Odo, Bishop of Bayeux and half-brother to my long dead father, William the Conqueror, and a fighter with him at the battle to wrest control of England from the Saxon upstart Harold in 1066.

Corpulent he was now, and well past his sixtieth year, but still a determined old sod. I hadn't wanted to take him, but as this was likely to be his last adventure, and as it carried the promise of eternal life, I'd been persuaded.

He called out as I approached.

'Nephew: timely, as usual, I see. I have something for you.'

Ignoring his censure, my gaze went to a banner, held by a squire standing beside Uncle Odo. It had the cross of St Peter on it, and three points, the Holy Trinity, flapping in the breeze from the shaft of a lance.

I stayed my horse and stared at that most precious flag.

'Is that the –?' I asked, scarcely believing it.

'Yes, nephew, this is the papal banner, given by Pope Alexander, as a token of his approval for your father's invasion of England.'

'Jesu! Where has it been, Uncle?'

'In my possession, lad, safe in my possession. And now it is yours. Look upon it as God's approval for this holy adventure we are bound on. Sadly, the papal ring also given to your father was lost upon his death; some scoundrel will have it now, no doubt. Here, give the banner to one of your knights.'

I beckoned Ragenaus forward and he took possession of the holy emblem.

'If perchance we fall on this expedition, Ragenaus, that banner will be the last thing to strike God's earth, so guard it well.'

'With my life, my lord, to the last drop of my blood.'

I turned to find Peverel. He held the standard of Normandy, two golden lions on a red background. I had only the faintest idea of what a lion was, but it seemed fierce enough for our purpose.

'Flank me, Payne, for now it begins.'

An odd pair, the Saxon Ragenaus and Payne. Payne had the height it was true, but Ragenaus, with a warbow in his hands since he was ten years old, had the width of shoulder. His legs were not like my tree trunks but they were strong enough to withstand the power he could release from his bow; few men could pull it back fully, and he won many a wager because of it.

Then I stood in the stirrups and made the signal that would cast us into the turbulence of our fate – into the very hands of God. We rode through Rouen accompanied by the blast of trumpets, banging of drums and the shouts of the crowd. With standards and banners proudly flying and the cavalcade behind me, we jingled with splendour and jangled with a grin as we made our haughty way south, no doubt a captivating sight.

As the noise faded behind us and we settled down to a gentle rhythm, I had time to look about and contemplate a little. This was not the only time I had ridden to Italy; the first occasion was when I met the formidable Matilda of Canossa, who ruled in the north, and some of the Normans ruling in the south. Sent by my father to marry Matilda, but then sent by her to tame her southern neighbours, my father's plans went awry as Matilda and I came to a different accommodation, and the Normans in southern Italy descended into a family argument. I had not travelled further, certainly not as far as the famed city of Constantinople, last bastion of Christian rule in the East, and I wondered how we would fare beyond the shores of Italy.

As we travelled I had time to observe my companions. They came close alongside me from time to time and we engaged in conversation. Robert, Count of Flanders was with me. As well as his men and his money, I appreciated his presence as a warrior: fierce eyes, a high-bridged nose and a reputation to match his appearance; he was a welcome asset. Close to me was my brother-in-law, Stephen of Blois, yet him I knew to be more style than substance, his carefully tended beard had more than a whiff of vanity about it. I also suspected that my sister Adela had more to do with his presence on this uncertain adventure than any conviction of his own; she, together with my young brother Henry, were convinced they were the pinnacle of the brood, being born to a king and queen rather than to a duke and duchess like me. Still, they got here by much the same process and their airs and postures did nothing to commend them above me and my other siblings, in my eyes.

Flanders had another reason for going south. Aside from rescuing Jerusalem, he intended to visit his daughter, another Adela; she was married to the Duke of Apulia, the same Roger Borsa whom I might have killed on my last visit to Italy when I had sided with his step-brother the great Bohemund. Adela had attractions of her own having previously been married to King Knut of Danemark; obviously a lady of distinction.

Well south of Rouen we met with Allen Fergant, Duke of Brittany. Of him I had no worries, his beard being that of a man who cared not what the world thought of his style, carrying something of his last repast about it; he was in all respects the image of a lord and warrior, and much proven in battle. Although a man of few words he still had kind words for his former wife, my poor dead sister Constance. All the more impressive given that I knew her to have been a strain for him to live with, being in many ways the opposite of Allen in demeanour and habit, yet no doubt a capable match for Allen's extravagant character.

I had already met Allen some time ago when I was planning this expedition and we had exchanged notes since. Allen was keen to understand my other preparations and questioned me at length as we trotted along.

'So this Saxon of yours, Aethilheard, he has left already?'

'Aye, Allen, with two hundred archers, four hundred horses, and a bulging purse to pay my friend Matilda of Canossa for more.'

'How many horses do you need, Robert? Are you going to start your own war when we reach Asia?'

'I'll be in the same war as you, Allen, but I have heard that our horses might not fare so well on the south side of the Mediterranean – it is reputed to be very hot and very dry.'

'I had not thought of that.'

He waited for a while and then asked another question.

'And these ships you have sent to Cyprus, what is their purpose?'

'Siege engines,' I declared. 'A walled city is not likely to open its gates, even if we ask politely. It might be necessary to persuade them.'

'True. So what's in the ships?'

'Ironworks, shaped timbers, blacksmiths, farriers, other artisans, together with plans, drawings and architects to make sense of it all. We will not want for engines of war.'

'I thought that your devious brother Henry did all the thinking.'

'He thinks about Henry.'

'Uhh! Dangerous. Who's the Goliath carrying that strange flag?'

'Payne Peverel; we might be related.'

'How so?'

'He has a brother, rumoured to be of my father's loins.'

'William strayed? I had not heard of that. And is that Odo wobbling along behind?'

'Surely. You asked about horses, we may need a steady supply of replacements along the way, for that sad creature beneath him seems to have had enough already.'

All those in earshot had a laugh at the corpulent priest's expense.

'What's that, Robert?' he cried from the rear, kicking his over-burdened nag to try and catch up.

'A jest, Uncle, merely a jest. Spare your horse, we will rest shortly.'

I continued to have concerns regarding my uncle Odo. Although he was attended by Gilbert, Bishop of Evraux, he was a great age and it gave me cause to regret that I had not dissuaded him from this two-and-a-half-thousand-mile journey with more zeal. But Odo was Odo, and consumed with fervour for the cause – and the chance of some preferment in Rome – he insisted on coming. I was also aware that the old fox was himself under scrutiny. The papal legate, Father Gerento, was with us, reluctant to leave since his arrival from Rome to help persuade me to take up the holy cause. Gerento, an abbot from Dijon, was well aware of Odo's ambitions, and it was difficult to separate the watched from the watcher in this odd relationship. Still, I thought, we can't have too many priests on a venture such as this, and while they are observing each other they might not miss me at early morning prayers.

After three weeks and two hundred and seventy miles we arrived at Dijon, just short of the Alps, and paused for a few days' rest. Here we would receive and send communications and prepare to cross the Alps.

The next day the first courier arrived in the camp; he dismounted and asked for Abbot Gerento. Shortly a squire came over to me and asked me to join the abbot.

'You have news, Father Gerento?' I asked, or rather made a statement, because everyone knew that there was.

'Indeed, my lord. It may please you to learn that the lady Matilda is at Lucca awaiting the arrival of Pope Urban, and that she awaits your arrival in due course.'

I didn't bother to hide my pleasure and turned to Fergant.

'See, Allen; she awaits us, I can assure you that we'll receive a warm welcome when we arrive. Father Gerento, are we to go to Canossa?'

'No, my lord. Because of the nature of your journey, your *peregrinazione,* the way has been cleared. No need to cross the Alps; bypass them and Milano and go directly to Lucca. There will be suitable accommodation for all your party along the way. Italy is secure and the lady no longer needs to stay out of harm's way in her beloved castles.'

Allen responded. 'That means that the pope has returned to Italy?'

'Yes, my lord. It also means that I must leave you here, I have received instructions for another mission. Prince Robert is sufficiently aware of the route from here, I am certain.'

He looked at me, and smiling risked a comment, 'I am confident that you will be welcomed in Lucca before long, my lord?'

'I expect I will, Father Abbot, I expect I will.'

Odo pulled Bishop Gilbert to his side and remarked, none too quietly, 'I always thought that Robert's return from Italy without Matilda was a bit reluctant, and now my nostrils are twitching.'

'You think there's something in it?' asked the gossiping cleric.

'Robert is no actor when it comes to women; he wears his heart on his sleeve.'

'Tittle-tattle, Uncle, tittle-tattle.' I sent him a withering glance, which he diverted by asking that I gather the leaders together. He had also received news and he wanted to share it.

'Since Urban's presentation at Clermont,' he began once we were settled, 'there have been many who have carried his message abroad, but with false emphasis. There is a monk, named Peter the Hermit, who has caused many to follow him to the Holy Land.'

Stephen asked why this was wrong. 'I thought that Urban wanted as many to follow the cause as were capable?'

Odo pointed out the problem. 'Indeed! But in an organised way. This fellow has gathered thousands of followers and set off to Constantinople without proper preparation. No arms, food or other supplies, no organised structure – only a burning fervour to kill infidels. It is also contagious. Next time we cross a rise, look behind us. We have developed a tail that stretches back to the horizon.'

'I took a look a mile back,' I commented. 'This pilgrimage sounds like a disaster in motion.'

'Indeed,' said Gilbert, 'and there are other unrests.'

Odo revealed that the idea of rescuing Christians in Jerusalem had somehow been interpreted as *from* the Jews; this was not true, but it had been sufficient to spark off a hatred of Jews across Europe and a series of unpleasant incidents, such as riots and evictions, even murders.

He went on, 'The people's pilgrimage led by Peter has gone overland towards Constantinople and is many months ahead of us. This hatred against the Jews is also no part of our venture and Urban wants us to stay clear of it, which we will do if we keep to our plan. But be aware that we may come across the consequences of these issues at some point and we should be careful to dissociate ourselves from both.'

I had a meaty conversation with Stephen and Flanders in which we wondered why it had it been arranged that Moslems, Christians and Jews had somehow come together in mutual conflict in this one spot on earth. We did not find an answer.

I also continued to ponder over the presence of Stephen. He was a rich man; no doubt one of the qualities if not the only one that had attracted my sister Adela, he needed some special quality for the privilege of her bed. He had been a late addition to my party and was boyishly enthusiastic about joining; I suspected that Adela's charms had been withheld until he agreed to secure her eternal life through his accompanying me. Nonetheless he brought some welcome funds with him; he made that plain when he joined me, saying, 'You will not be short of monies while I travel with you, Prince Robert.'

He was one who asked about messages travelling back into Normandy and was assured by me that the lines of communication were in place and would be available for all to make use of. Stephen intended to write to Adela from key points and keep her informed; another of her conditions, no doubt. Also travelling with us was Fulcher of Chartres; he was sent by his bishop, Ivo, and would perform the official task of writing down the events of our passage and remit them back during our journey.

Before leaving Rouen, Adela had worked out a form of dress for the women in the group, one that would enable them to travel as comfortably as the men. That was immediately after she had informed me that there were to be females in my war-band.

'What jest is this, sister? Women!'

'Of course, dear Robert,' she said with the sweetness of iron, 'did you not know?'

'No. Why would I take women? Mind, the idea does have its attractions.'

'You are taking women, dear brother, because there are those who would visit the holy city, and have their sins shriven there. Besides, some of your knights will not go without them.'

'Oh really! And how do you know that, sweet Adela?'

'Because I have made certain of it, Robert.'

She locked eyes with me. She had always done this and helpless I was: to see my eyes staring back at me from a female face, it robbed me of resolve.

I sighed, there was too much to do to start a new argument.

'How do you propose that they travel, pest?'

Having outmanoeuvred me in the matter she explained her plans for those whose piety and determination were stronger than their wisdom: such a journey, such uncertainty ahead. For riding they wore breeches and sat astride their mounts; when it came to making camp for the night, or when coming to a place of *being seen*, they would employ a wrap-round skirt and quickly present the expected image of noble ladies. To this end the routine of making and breaking camp always started with the erection of the ladies' changing tent – and ended with its packing away. What went on in there remained a mystery to us men, but it always seemed to be a highly amusing event for those inside, accompanied, as it was, by much giggling and merriment, and thus a source of puzzlement for those kept firmly out.

We continued along our leisurely way, but when I reached a high point on the road it always increased my anxiety as the numbers seemed to stretch into infinity behind us. I had near two thousand souls in my cavalcade, cavalry and infantry, and a baggage train to match; Allen Fergant and his Brittany people matched me in numbers. But even then, when I could see the end of the orderly lines of our contingent, the unordered mass of pilgrims stretched behind us for miles, with the last ones out of sight. I wondered how many would last the journey.

2. An Italian Winter.

The Alps avoided we soon reached Aosta where more envoys from Matilda met to escort us. They told us that we were only just ahead of Raymond of Saint-Gilles, the count of Toulouse, who had with him a great army of the southern French. He also set off intending to travel across the front of the Alps, but lacking ships like those I had arranged with Matilda, he intended to enter the Byzantine empire through Hungary instead of travelling south through Italy and journey to Constantinople overland. I said a prayer for him; it was a formidable trek through uncertain territory, and I wondered how many of his formation would appear before the walls of Constantinople.

My party left Aosta heading for the Genoese coastline in order to follow it down to one of the important ports in Matilda's Tuscany, Viareggio. This was the sea-port outlet for the walled town of Lucca.

We had set off from Rouen in the first week of October but now, well into November, that was but a memory; we'd been on the road for almost eight weeks and travelled nearly eight hundred miles. Our band was pleased to see the town walls come into view at the head of a valley.

Lucca was a town under a cloud. The *Lucchesi* had sided with the German emperor, Heinrich, and expelled Bishop Anselmo in 1081; he took refuge with Matilda.

When Matilda finally defeated Heinrich at Canossa in 1092, the townspeople knew that they had picked the wrong side.

Thus it was no trivial thing that Matilda had chosen Lucca to welcome Pope Urban back from his proselytising campaign across the Alps. Lucca had been set up as a staging post for the crusading armies; we were all directed there, and the townsfolk were obliged by Matilda and her ruling margrave, Rangerious, to feed and water our weary troops.

Thus there was no cheering welcome awaiting our band when we arrived at the gate, merely a resigned and sullen glance at the prospect of *yet more mouths to feed.*

That aside, when I arrived at the Duomo de St Martino, I was invited to dismount while the rest of my party were guided away to stabling and accommodation.

Passing along the cathedral nave, with a brief stop at the high altar for a blessing by a priest, I was taken on through the gardens at the back and into the private quarters of Matilda.

Grinning like a ninny, yet conscious of the fact that I must be carrying the aromas of eight hundred miles on the back of a horse, I held back from approaching her.

Matilda misinterpreted that. With a scowl she dismissed her attendants, then, turning to face me, asked, 'Has the twelve years of absence made me so ugly that you cannot approach me, Robert?'

My attraction to Matilda, still simmering from my previous visit, reduced me to a stammering youth.

'No, my lady, tis not that. . .'

'My lady? Come here, you dusty prince, now that I see you again I know how much I have missed you.'

We moved together as if there was a magnet in each of our hearts and Matilda buried her head into my chest, breathing in my many aromas.

'Robert, my dear, I have been sleepless each night since you passed by the Alps and drew ever closer.'

I breathed in the sweet smell of her hair and warmed the top of her head with my outgoing breath.

'You felt it as I did?'

'Badly, like a puling girl.' She pulled her head back and looked into my eyes. 'There is no private place here in Lucca; we must wait for that in a different location. I cannot be compromised here – my position, you understand?'

'Yes, I heard about your divorce, how did you engineer that?'

'It was never a marriage; it was an affair of state.'

'I see. I heard that he was younger than you, the opportunist Guelf of Bavaria?'

'Twenty years between us. I had no feelings for him, and he was not man enough to press me into bed. But he was no

23

opportunist, his father pushed him as much as the Church pushed me; it was never likely to be a meeting of minds... or bodies.'

There was an invitation hanging in the air and I thought that I should test the strength of it with a gentle hint.

'Where can we go? We have waited long enough.'

'Be patient, dear Robert. First you must meet Urban, and then when he departs for Rome we will leave for the south. Send your party along behind the papal cavalcade and we will divert to the Via Cassia and stay at Trevignano Romano. It's only thirty miles north of Rome and we can have a few days there.'

'I would like that... we're friends?'

'Best friends. Now!' That was the soft side of Matilda put to one side as the business of Church politics took precedence. 'There will be prayers this evening and you will meet Urban afterwards. Bring your commanders, for there will be a feast. I understand that you have Bishop Odo with you, Urban has asked for him; they've met before?'

'Yes, they hatched the plot to get my brother William involved in this.'

'Just so. Now, if you're concerned about your progress to the Holy Land be comforted, by the time you reach Brindisi it will be too late to cross the ocean and you'll have some time to spend here in Italy. It cannot be with me though, I have much work to do, my love.'

That was too easy an escape and I protested. 'You cannot be at your work all day and all night, surely?'

'Robert, you have no idea how difficult the path I follow is, it occupies me every waking moment and I must plan my time alone. Fear not, my love, my alone time involves you, but it is in a plan. You know how to plan, that is how you are going to succeed in your mission, sì?'

'Sì, amore mio, I have a plan. But politics! What a game.'

'Yes, some game.' She moved closer, we held each other tight, and then she made a little space between us when the pressure in my breeches made itself known.

'Your ardour has not diminished, dear friend. Have you no grey hairs about you?'

'None in public view, or private. We shaved off for the campaign, me and my men; it provides fewer quarters for tiny beasts to reside in.'

She laughed, the giggle of a girl, her eyes sparkled and I would have tumbled her there and then had things been different.

'Now, Robert,' she teased me with her eyes, knowing full well the torment I was in, 'there are baths prepared and I will see you this evening.'

In my eagerness I misunderstood her meaning.

'My lady!' I said in surprise, 'we haven't bathed together before, are you certain that we won't be disturbed, or that it won't become known about?'

Being small, her arms fell naturally around my hips, and her hands fell naturally upon my buttocks, which she clenched and squeezed. With her face buried in my chest I needed to concentrate to hear her next mumblings.

'No, my love, we will not be disturbed, and there will be no reports made about it, because it will not happen here.'

She looked up with a serious expression on her lovely face.

'I know that you're feeling the same as me, but I have enemies, and they have eyes and ears in the walls; where we are now has taken some delicate organising with only my most trusted to guard us. There is much to lose. Even when our focus should be on the liberation of the Holy Lands, there are those who still plot to replace Urban, and I cannot be compromised as his supporter, he needs my help to retain his position. Please wait until we leave this place, then we will have some peace, I promise.'

'Still the Germans?'

'They will not forget that I defeated their emperor, or humiliated him.'

'Yet they're still sending troops to Jerusalem.'

'There are those who do not like the ruling family.'

'Then I agree, I cannot put you or your works at risk.'

We embraced and parted, and I trembled as she left. Our public and private lives must be so far apart as to hurt the heart.

That evening, suitably cleansed, we attended Urban's court. He was surrounding himself with the mighty of northern Europe, who, coming to give muscle to the holy cause, did not entirely believe in his positioning as the leader of this venture. He might have the words to move people's hearts, but this was now a military matter, prayers having failed so far to release the holy city of Jerusalem. Nevertheless we attended in good spirit being quite certain of our impending success in the matter.

Stephen of Blois, Robert of Flanders, Duke Allen of Brittany and me: together we were all dressed in our finest. Odo and Gilbert had also dug out some suitable vestments from their baggage and we made an impressive entrance to the cathedral where Urban was due to lead us in prayers.

At the front, only partially visible through the fug of incense, and suitably shielded by her close attendants, Matilda was sitting in demure majesty, ensuring that none would mistake the fact that here sat the chiefest woman in all of Europe. I made no attempt to approach her, what secrets we held would remain between us.

When the prayers were over, Urban made full use of the opportunity to deliver yet another tedious homily, in praise, it seemed, of his idea of bringing all these magnificent warriors here to one place in order to fulfil his heavenly vision. In the end the message lingered too long and went a little astray, so that the congregation were pleased to hear the amen and were ready to leave but there was another little ceremony before that release came.

A priest came to speak to Odo, who after a word turned to me and asked, 'Where is your papal banner, Robert?'

I looked at Ragenaus and he nodded his head towards the door.

'Will you fetch it for me, please, Ragenaus.'

He went off and I turned to Uncle Odo.

'There is to be a blessing of emblems and the prince of France will also receive a banner of St Peter like yours,' explained the bishop.

'What prince of France?' I queried.

'That colourful youth sitting at the front, that is Hugh of Vermandois, brother to King Phillip.'

As I peered through the fog of incense to try and see this royal brat Ragenaus returned and thrust the lance with the banner into my hand and Odo pushed me towards the front, where the pope was waiting.

I approached, and Hugh turned to give me a glance before he knelt. He was well above me in height and I might have detected a little in-built sneer upon his lips. *Snotty little git.* I knelt alongside him and the pope uttered another well-rehearsed homily as our banners were drenched by a pair of over-enthusiastic priests. My head received a share of the holy water and I grinned at Hugh as we stood up; he smiled a little and seemed less haughty. *We might get on, if he behaves himself.*

'Are you Robert of Normandy?' he asked politely.

'I am,' I replied. He hesitated as if awaiting some kind of accolade, then introduced himself.

'I am Hugh, Prince of France.'

'Then, Hugh, we have a common purpose in coming here. We may meet again.'

'*D'accord,*' he said as I spied Matilda looking at me from her front seat, a definite smirk playing around her lips. I threw my gaze to the heavens and walked back to Odo, my mind on things other than the blessing of banners.

The principal guests were escorted to a grand chamber where the atmosphere became a little less formal and we were able to circulate freely.

Among the movers was Matilda. She gradually drifted in my direction so that after a while we were able to engage in a conversation, of suitably public content, in public.

'Contessa Matilda,' I bowed and almost made a meal of her proffered hand, 'we must thank you for the arrangements you have made to receive us. Here are those who would help us in our quest. Stephen of Blois, my brother-in-law. Robert of Flanders, my cousin, and my former brother-in-law, Allen, Duke of Brittany.'

'Thank you, Prince Robert, quite a family affair I see. It is the least that I can do when you have travelled so far in our holy cause.'

She turned to Stephen and Flanders, neither of whom could resist a modicum of flirting when the opportunity presented itself. 'My lords! Have you found your quarters to your satisfaction?'

Stephen and Robert fell over themselves to claim the hand of this regal power broker. Diminutive, her hair now a fading russet blond, but her eyes still a piercing blue, she commanded the space about her in a way that few men could manage. Matilda could charm and flirt with the best of them – and proceeded to do so. I watched a while in some amusement as the trio did their best to outshine each other in courtly manners.

Looking about the hall I noted that Odo had cornered Urban, *oh well – he has bored us for long enough tonight, I expect that Odo will return the favour.* Then I spotted Payne and Ragenaus standing against a wall, appearing bored. *'What?'* I mouthed. Payne cupped his hands under his chest and lifted up non-existent breasts, casting his eyes to the ceiling. Of course, the hall was bereft of women; only we had the privilege of Matilda. I thought to enquire.

'You seem to be the lone ambassadress for women tonight, my lady,' I said, nodding towards my young men. 'Are there no ladies for my young dogs to talk to?'

Matilda, sharp as a blade, took in the situation at a glance and beckoned over one of her attendants. 'Take those two down to the festival in the marketplace, and keep them safe.'

'*Sì, Contessa*, they will enjoy *la musica*, no?'

'*Sì*, and anything else they can lay their eyes on.' She grinned at me and lifted an eyebrow. 'That big one will be very popular, I believe.'

'Mm, that is Payne Peverel. He comes from the hills of northern England, so not the same as my Saxon archer you'll remember.'

'No, but interesting all the same.' *Capricious Matilda.*

Suddenly I became irritated by my unctuous comrades' efforts to impress the lady and I turned the subject of the conversation to more pressing matters.

'What news do you have you for us, Contessa? Has my friend Bohemund reached Constantinople yet?'

'I've not yet heard, Robert. But no doubt he'll be in the company of Emperor Alexios soon.'

'Huh! That will be an interesting meeting; they were at war with each other not so long ago.'

'True, and who says that they will not resume their squabbling after the holy city has been recovered? There is more to tell. Raymond of Saint-Gilles is marching his French army across northern Italy towards Hungary. Duke Godfrey of Bouillon is leading a large formation of his own troops from Flanders and Lorraine. Some German soldiers have joined him, and I believe that he favours the same overland route.'

My brother-in-law replied, 'He commands great respect in the north, and has lots of money. It seems that we will be well supported, my lady.'

'Yes, Count,' she responded, a little awkwardly as the points of his perfect beard threatened her very eyes. She moved back a little from his too close attentions and replied politely. 'The Lord has provided; we are blessed in our endeavours.'

'And our horses.' I remembered that small point. 'What of Aethilheard; you remembered him from our previous visit?'

'Ah, yes!' responded the Contessa with a light in her eyes, 'and the Saxon prince, Edgar, sent by your father as our wedding guest. Are they all like that in England? I must pay a visit.'

'My lady,' I replied, 'the land is full of blond-haired, blue-eyed warriors with moustaches. You liked the Saxon?'

'I did, he was amusing, Robert. He idolises you.'

'He does? I suppose so. You know how much I trust him?'

'He was carrying quite a lot of your money. Anyway, Aethilheard has gone with some fine horses to Constantinople; I made some good deals and your blond friend has some spare monies in his purse.'

'Thank you. We will need it, I expect, before this matter is done with. You said *some*.'

'Yes, we have a limited supply of steeds suited to the North African climate, I am arranging for more to be taken to Cyprus. They will be kept there in readiness for you; and I am helping you with the costs, to include placing some Genoese ships at your disposal.'

'You honour me, gracious lady.'

It was difficult to keep my hands off her... and she knew it, laughing silently in her eyes. I hoped that her under-linen was as wet as mine.

'Not so, Prince Robert, we both honour God in this matter, and trust in his blessing.'

I nodded, and dribbled, and she went to engage in conversation elsewhere. I caught Stephen studying my face and he made to speak, but I gave him a warning glance, so he swallowed his words and kept silent. There would be no rumours to trouble the lady's reputation, not if I had anything to do with it, but I could not stop Allen, who was not so well informed as to the purpose of my previous visit.

'What wedding, Robert? Have I missed something?'

I pondered for a moment.

Stephen said, 'You might as well tell him, everyone else knows.'

'Tell me what?' the irritated Breton asked.

'My father had marriage plans for me and Matilda. We decided otherwise.'

'Jesu, Robert. You mean you and she have never...'

'No, Allen, by God's bollocks, we have never...'

'*Mon Dieu*!' chortled Flanders, with a snort of derision, 'you are all over each other like panting dogs.'

'Piss off, Rob, someone will hear you.'

But they would not leave the subject and Allen tried again.

'King William sent you to marry the Contessa, and you returned to Normandy bride-less?'

'I heard that he was not pleased, Robert,' said Stephen.

'By God he was not likely to be. What did he say?' probed Allen.

'Quite a lot,' I mumbled.

'Yes indeed, Robert, you went off somewhere just after your return, I remember it being a cause for discussion with your sister,' Stephen added, being helpful.

'Why wouldn't she marry you?' Allen persisted.

I pulled them close, and in a whisper told them.

'Matilda has Normans to the south, Germans to the north, and a reputation to keep inviolate with the Church. Marrying me would not be helpful.'

'God's bollocks,' exclaimed Allen, 'a Norman domain stretching to the Alps? The Germans would not like that.'

'*Mon Dieu*,' added Rob, 'she cannot have men clambering into her bed; the Church is strange about such things. No wonder she will not marry.'

'God's miracles, you are too loud, someone might overhear us,' I whispered in frustration.

'It will only be a blind man, my prince, everyone else can see how you are with her for themselves.' Stephen was trying to calm me.

'Oh, please don't make it worse,' I pleaded.

The trio looked at each other, shrugged their shoulders in unison, and chimed in unison. 'We see nothing, Mighty Prince.'

'Bollocks, you lot. I'm going to rescue the pope from Uncle Odo.'

'Before you go, Robert,' the solid figure of the Duke of Brittany placed itself in my path, 'tell me something. Did your father withhold the crown of the English from you because of this?'

I looked him in the eye. A bit rough was Allen, but sharp.

'It did not help… that's all I know.' I left to find Odo, and in truth, that *was* all I knew.

After a few days, when the great and good had finished with their intelligence-gathering, bargaining, wheeling and dealing – and attempts at flirtation – we set off for Rome in three parties. Firstly the pope and his never-ending retinue, skirts and banners flapping in the breeze, followed by Matilda and her troops, armour and standards flying, then I came along behind with my northern cavalcade with my standard and gonfalon held high – and of all that display of pomp only mine were bound for Jerusalem.

After a few days on the road a messenger came back to us from Matilda: my vessels were in the port of Brindisi awaiting my instructions.

'That's useful,' said Stephen, 'that's one less thing to worry about.'

'That's true,' responded Flanders, 'all we need to worry about is the weather at sea.'

'I've been thinking about that,' said I, and laid out some plans as we rode on towards Rome.

'I want to split into three groups. Stephen, would you go with Allen down to Brindisi and join up with our ships. Tell them that they are to stay there until the spring, when I will require them to move across to Cyprus and wait until I send word to them from the African coast – they will probably be required at a port nearest to Jerusalem.'

'Right! Why?'

'We will not, hopefully, need the supplies that they carry until we have moved off from Constantinople and have discovered the deployment of the Turks.'

'And that we will determine in Constantinople, from the emperor?'

'Exactly. Also, while in Brindisi, see what other ships you can get hold of. We do not know what Bohemund has left us after he crossed the Adriatic Sea to Durezzo. Hire what you can and wait until we arrive.'

'Very well, that has merit; I like the idea of Christmas by the sea.'

'Just so. I also want to know more about Cyprus and the coast nearest to Jerusalem. Find out from the local mariners about ports, landing places and tides. We need to be capable of supporting our soldiers from the sea. The maps show Jerusalem a long way from Constantinople and we need to be sure of our logistics.'

'Consider it done, Robert. This becomes more interesting by the day.'

'Good, it is well that you are so keen. Once we leave Italy it is a venture into the unknown for us, only Bohemund has any experience in the East and he's left already. Rob, can you go ahead to Rome? I shall make a detour before we arrive. Gather what intelligences you can – see if your son-in-law Roger Borsa is there – we will probably need winter quarters within his lands.'

'Really? Will he have forgotten your quarrel the last time you were in Italy?'

'That was Bohemund's doing, I just watched,' said I, thinking that it was true, if only in parts.

'What are you going to do then?' he asked.

'I'm going to stay with Matilda for a few days. She has agreed to support me with her Genoese ships and we have plans to finalise. And do what you are going to do – gather intelligence.'

'Oh! Is that what you call it?'

'What else?'

I caught the glance that passed between them, but they said naught and thought about things for a while before Allen put in a question.

'What's this Brindisi like then? Is it friendly?'

' I don't know, I never did get there on my last visit, but if it's anything like the coast on the other side it will be rather enjoyable.' *As was Gabriella; smooth, and moist.*

'Then I will join you, Stephen. Let us gaze out to sea for a while,' said Allen.

'A good plan,' said Rob, 'and I will see if I can recognise my daughter.' Meanwhile I rocked on my horse and recalled Gabriella, with her warm friendly valleys – shining wet in the surf – and pretty soon started to bulge in my breeches.

When we reached the area of Maglione Sabina, we found an escort of Matilda's knights waiting on the road.

'Is that your intelligence-gathering party, Robert?' asked Stephen.

'Oh, yes, I recognise that captain at the head. He is Matilda's most trusted aide.'

I waved at the Tuscan knight and received a cheery smile and wave in return.

'*Principe* Roberto, welcome to the papal state. We have prepared a campsite for you, and tomorrow there will be another thirty miles to our destination.'

'Thank you, Capitano Aberto, you are most kind.'

'*Principe*, you remember my name.'

He was quite pleased that I'd dragged that one from the vault of my past, and it helped to oil the wheels of friendship – that and the barrel of wine sent out from the village – it was a very friendly night. But time passes and in the morning we were up early, turned out of our sleeping blankets by the freezing cold of the Italian late autumn air.

No time was lost in getting a warm horse between our legs, although I would have preferred something else.

'Right, Rob,' I called, my backside and bollocks warming nicely, 'I'll see you in Rome in a week. Allen and Stephen, we will meet again at Brindisi in four weeks.'

'I'll be waiting,' said Rob.

'Yes. *Addio*,' said Stephen in his new tongue.

'*Sì. Avanti!*' I replied.

'Are you ready, *Principe* Roberto?' asked the captain.

'I am.'

'The Contessa awaits.'

'*Sì, signore,*' I replied with a grin.

I placed myself alongside the Italian and we rode together for thirty miles through the rolling and verdant hills towards our destination. It was by a lake and we paused to take in the view.

'Bracciano, *il lago,*' Aberto informed me. 'Is a volcano, *Principe* Roberto, *spento.*'

I turned back to Payne and Ragenaus to tell them.

'Tis an extinct volcano.'

It was very attractive, now filled with sparkling clear waters.

'Is for special people only, *molto privato,*' explained Aberto.

'What's a volcano, my lord?' asked Ragenaus.

'It's where hell reaches the surface,' informed Payne.

I didn't argue; he might have the truth of it.

On the southern edge of the lake lies the hamlet of Anguillara Sabazia, and nearby on a promontory stands a villa belonging to the Church.

When we arrived our horses were quickly taken from us and we were guided into a courtyard. Built in the Roman fashion, as a hollow square with a garden in the middle, even at the end of November it was still warmed by the late afternoon.

I had eyes only for Matilda, sitting demurely by a fountain with two ladies in attendance.

'My lady, your surroundings are diminished by your beauty.'

'Robert... you have been reading poetry?'

'No, but it sounded better than hallo.'

'Idiot. Come here.' We embraced, forgetting about the spectators, and managing to avoid lip contact we nevertheless indulged in a rib-crushing entanglement before polite coughing penetrated our befogged minds.

She stepped back, a little breathless, and regained her composure.

'Everything is prepared for you and your men, my prince. All the luxuries of this special place are at your disposal. You will be taken to the hot baths, and pleasant rooms await you. When you are ready there is a feast prepared and I am looking forward to your presence.'

It was a very exceptional place, this luxurious, marble-adorned villa; as Aberto told us, 'for special people.' And, I surmised, where special people could be out of the public view, or at least I was hoping so.

Soon I was ready to make an appearance. I was clad in a silken epitoga, loose fitting and very smooth, with sandals. The sniggering and laughter from across the courtyard told me that Ragenaus and Payne had found some amusement in this novel form of clothing. I resolved to appear before them as if I was in every way familiar with both the luxury of our surroundings and the regal attire provided.

'Come along, children,' I commanded from outside their chamber, 'our hostess awaits.' I walked in, surprised at how small it was compared to my rather grand bedchamber; they had two small beds on opposite walls and some sparse furniture, whereas I had a bed large enough to lose a lover in and curtains enough to confuse a man.

'Do we have to, my lord, these things are terrible draughty,' Ragenaus complained.

'Aye,' grumbled Payne, in his deep tones, 'my arse is hanging out in this poxy skirt.'

I needed to take a look, and sure enough the size of Payne had defeated the efforts of our hosts to clad him, the epitoga barely covered his tree-trunk legs above the knees; but they had guessed his foot size accurately and he was wearing a pair of Roman boats, it seemed.

'Well,' I declared, taking a turn, 'mine fits fine, and you are wearing what everyone else will be wearing, so pick up your feet and follow me.'

I needed to turn away quickly before the lurking smile broke out across my face, and I followed an attendant along to the great hall.

There was a long table set with all sorts of fruit and other decorations and it looked very appetising. I was pleased to see that my two were welcomed as honoured guests. My pleasure diminished somewhat when I was shown to the opposite end of the table, a long way from Matilda. She grinned at me and gave a little shrug as I sat down on the chair shoved under me.

Ragenaus and Payne were placed on my right with Aberto between them and opposite was a trio of ladies. It was clear that Aberto and the older woman in the centre knew each other and indeed Matilda introduced her as Floriana, wife of Aberto, and the two young ladies as Allegra and Debora, their daughters.

I remembered my Italian and essayed, 'We are overwhelmed by beauty, my lady; this feast is outshone by our hosts.'

Floriana giggled. 'His words are mixed up, Lady Matilda, but his meaning is clear. *Grazie, Principe Roberto, molte grazie.*'

Then came a warning to dampen the ardour of my two warriors, and make me grin.

'We have invited Allegra and Debora to improve their language skills, Robert,' said Matilda. She had that mischievous smile enlivening her lips, the one which cast away her fifty years and made her a twenty-year-old again, 'their husbands are away on patrol further north.'

The change in demeanour of my two was immediate, and obvious. I gave Matilda a censorious glance and tried to avoid the impending silence with a question.

'Did you meet my uncle, Matilda?'

'*Sì*, he talks a lot. I think that the pope has heard the history of England and Normandy sufficient for the year.'

'Indeed, he talked me into this venture, did you know?'

'I did. Tuck in my friends, see what they have brought us, lamb, chicken, fish, and some greens which you may not have seen before.'

Ragenaus and Payne needed no second invitation and I could see them trying to work out an approach to the beauties opposite them. I suspected that it would be a frustrating evening for them.

'I also heard that your brother, Rufus the king, is paying for your expedition. Is that true, Robert?'

'Not quite, or somewhat, depending on your interpretation.'

'This is intriguing. Tell us more, Robert, but eat, we will not be too formal, and drink – your young men have their tongues hanging out, I see.' Matilda was in a wicked mood.

So in between glugs and chomps I explained the arrangements between my brother, King William Rufus of England, and me, Duke of Normandy.

'We have an agreement whereby I grant him succession rights to Normandy should I not return, and he acknowledges my succession right as heir to the crown of England if he should die before me.'

'That is a big agreement, Robert. But what of Henry, what is his place?'

'None,' was my short reply, 'Father did not grant him any and nor shall we. He may be found something – if he ceases his never- ending mischief-making, but at the moment he can stew in the uncertainty of his own fashioning.'

'I've heard that he is a plotter. Is this not dangerous, *Principe* Roberto?' Aberto was indeed well briefed.

'He has what he deserves,' was all I would say on that subject, and I buried my teeth into a chicken. I realised that there was another cross-table conversation going on by now as the youngsters had found a common language and where chatting away while Floriana and Aberto listened intently to me and Matilda.

Then Matilda probed a little further.

'What of your children, and how is Tegwin?'

'Richard and William are growing satisfactorily and their mother is as...intense, as ever.'

'I know she is fiery. Welsh you see, Floriana.' The lady nodded uncertainly.

'Indeed, the boys are part of the agreement between their uncle Rufus and me. Richard is destined to marry into the Welsh house of Tewdwr, and William has Northumbria pinned to his name. We will bring our borders into order, one way or another.'

'You seem to have things well in control, Robert, but what about you?'

'Me?'

'Yes, you. If, as is said, Rufus will produce no heirs, then you need a queen, do you not?'

'I suppose so.'

Matilda gave me a strange look, as if weighing me up, although what she did not know about me already would be precious little.

'Then we will talk again tomorrow: this feast is almost demolished and I have had little of it,' she said looking at her young guests, their faces all smothered in juices of one sort or another.

The evening went splendidly. Once my young bloods had accepted that the ladies were there only for the conversation, they settled down and we had a few good laughs about the separations caused by language and what to do to recover from a mistake of meaning.

Aberto asked me at length about my plans for the re-supply of my troops once we had crossed into Asia, and I was able to gather a lot more information about how my horses would fare, and other things such as preserving from the heat my supply of warbows and the many thousands of arrows I had despatched in my fleet.

At last Floriana asked to be excused and Aberto rose to escort his family home. My two took the hint, and after thanking Matilda, took their leave for the night, leaving us alone for the first time since we were reunited at Lucca.

The servants stoked the braziers in an alcove at the end of the hall. Although underfloor heating had kept the place pleasant during the cool evening, the flames were a comfort just the same and we settled in opposing high chairs facing each other.

'So have I aged, Robert?' Matilda asked, looking at the fires.

'I suppose that we both have, but you are as I remember you from... what is it? Ten years since.'

'Sì, Roberto, ten years deprived of a man whom I could have loved, if it were not for duty's sake.'

'Duty? An odd word, duty. It robs us of choice, even logic at times, and certainly blocks off the way of the heart.'

We looked at each other for a while, watching the flickering light playing games with our expressions, and then she sighed, as if coming to a conclusion, and clapped her hands.

'You may leave us now,' she said to the shadows, 'you may retire.' The shadows rustled and their sounds died as they drifted out of our ken.

'Are you content, my lady?' I asked after a while, breaking the silence.

'Yes, Robert, I am content.'

'Then should I leave you?'

'Of course. Leave room in your bed for a visitor.'

'As you command, my lady.'

I stood, and kissed her on the head over the back of her chair, before leaving silently for my grand bedchamber.

I came into the courtyard to find half of it in darkness. Only the braziers on the side opposite my chamber were still flickering, and entering I moved to close the carved wooden door, but then hesitated, still uncertain, and left it slightly open in the gloom.

Stripping off I slid onto the great bed and pulled a silken sheet over me. It felt good, and warm, but I lay back thinking and restless. I must have been tired but had not intended to sleep and it was a surprise when I heard the great door thud gently as it was closed. I thought, *wind*, although there had not been any, and then a rustle and a waft of a familiar scent caressed my nostrils, and suddenly I was awake: she had come to me.

There was only a faint light coming through the high narrow window slits above and I could scarce discern her standing by the side of the bed. She wore black, and was almost invisible.

'My lady,' I whispered.

'My lord,' she replied, and cast off her concealing garment.

She was white in the dark, her hair let down in tresses, hardly hiding the dark tips of her breasts. My eyes travelled down to her bush, almost invisible, but hiding the valley at the top of her well-shaped legs; that was a surprise. She was beautiful at any age, and she was perfectly formed.

I sat up and held out a hand. She knelt on the bed and, looking down on me, buried my lips with hers, pushing; I surrendered and slid on to my back.

'*Mio amore,*' she whispered, 'it has been too long.'

Any reply I had was choked off as my mouth was invaded by her questing tongue. She was kneeling over me now and my hands found their way around her buttocks to find her lips, my forefinger slid easily into her and I found her nub with my thumb, hard it was and she responded to my touch, a deep growl almost escaped her throat but the way was blocked and I only half heard it. As my finger moved she became more animated and started thrusting her hips, then she let go of my shoulder with one hand and it went on to my dick. That loosed her tongue.

'Robert! I have not had such a feast for an age.'

She tumbled on to her back and bent her legs. Turning to kneel, I grasped her buttocks and pulled her towards me, onto my pommel-hard penis; she gasped and thrust, and her head went back as I penetrated deeply, with her heels digging into the silken sheets scrabbling for purchase; I fell forward with my arms on either side of her shoulders. She was small, so very, very small, but wild now as she went for her climax, I had no choice but to join her and abandoned all control as we scrabbled and banged our way into oblivion...

'I can't breathe, Robert,' she mumbled from somewhere beneath me.

'Sorry,' I replied, rolling over with her still held close to my chest. 'What was that?' I asked the top of her head.

'That!' she replied, 'was too long in the making. No wonder it is so popular.'

'Popular? Do you think the peasants should be allowed it?'

'I think that everybody should have it, often and every day. Are you ready, Robert?'

'I could be persuaded, with a little help.'

'Will this help?' She moved on to her knees. There was a faint light, moon or dawn, it mattered not, but she thrust her buttocks into the air and with her head buried in silk she stretched her arms above her head.

'See how I surrender my all?' Her voice was muffled, but her meaning was clear.

Moving on to my knees behind her I could see her all, and so could he, hardened again so quickly, hard as the carved bedhead, he quivered while gazing at her offer.

My hands caressed her rump, feeling the gentle curves, then travelled down the crease of her thighs where they joined the bottom of her stomach, I stretched and reached the entrance to her valley, and found her hard nub, she started and thrust back, moaning gently: no words, only sounds, deep earthy sounds. I straightened up and grasping the front of her thighs gently parted her legs and touched her lips with the tip of my solid staff.

It was drooling life's oil, but no less than she was producing. I intended to rub gently at her lips to part them slowly but she suddenly thrust backwards and I slid roughly into her.

'Lively, *principe, allegretto*!' she commanded and I obeyed. Soon the bed was jumping as our hungry flesh demanded its reward, then hearing her quickening breath I deepened my thrusting and fell forward. My groin fitted perfectly onto her buttocks and it all became too much to control as I climaxed, my belly knotted with delightful spasm, and gave her all of the life stream that I possessed before collapsing across her back.

Shortly I rolled over and we lay like spoons, silent yet content, certain of our friendship and caring not for anything else – until I had a thought.

'What was that about?' I nibbled at her ear. 'I didn't expect that.'

She sighed and was quiet for a moment before responding.

'Everybody thinks I am this, or that, always perfect, made of stone... That was for me, that was for my flesh. Now shut up and get some rest, *principe*.'

I was half asleep, dreaming, wondering what the world would have to say if it were witness to our privy life, but then I became aware of the increasing light when she stirred. She pushed back into my groin with her buttocks, but the wooden pole had slipped out of her and all she would feel was warm flesh. I had one of her exquisite breasts cupped in my left hand and gave the nipple a little squeeze.

'Matilda,' I murmured, 'you want something?'

She sat up and moved to the side of the bed, her legs hanging over.

'The dawn is here, *mio amore*, I must go, you understand?'

'Sadly, my love, sadly.'

She cloaked herself again in black and left silently as a whisper.

I did not sleep any more that dawn, but watched and thought as the world woke up once more. Things we want are not always what we get; who orders our lives, who ordains the paths of our existence are rarely people of our choosing.

I must have dozed off, and was awakened by the sounds of splashing and shouts: Payne and Ragenaus had evidently found the baths at the far end of the courtyard. Needing no further encouragement I flung on something loose and went to join them. They were in the caldarium, steam rising from the hot water, so I lost no time in jumping in.

Such luxury! – as soon as I settled my head on the side of the bath, servants appeared with trays of fruit and a flagon of wine.

'Uh! Prince Robert, wine?' shouted Payne, amid the splashing.

'I had little last night. And I thought you were too busy ogling Floriana's daughters to over-imbibe.'

'When we saw that there was no chance of a tumble we took a flagon back to our chamber,' explained Ragenaus.

'Did you have a quiet night, my lord?' Payne was pushing his luck a little.

'Not really, I slept little; I have much on my mind.' Some truth escaped, enough to stop their prying. We were chatting about the next part of the journey, we must have been in there for ages, when a servant entered.

'*Principe*, the lady Matilda invites you to join her by the lakeside, there is food awaiting you, my lord.'

'Lakeside? Is it not chilly out?'

'*Principe*, it is past midday and the sun is warming.'

'Jesu!' I exclaimed, 'we've missed prayers, lads.' And I ran back to my chamber naked, drying off as I scampered between the shrubs, surprising the gardener and a servant girl – who dropped her tray
but did not look away. I grinned at her as I passed and called out, 'Princely balls, you see?' She saw, and made the most of it.

Matilda and I had grown used to the sun shining when we were together; it seemed to be our reward for staying steadfast in our causes, and when I was taken down to the lakeside it was to a warm welcome.

'Robert, you slept well. Come and sit by me and rest, then I'll take you for a walk alongside our beautiful lake before the air cools.'

'Madam, you continue to delight my eyes.' She tittered at that remark.

'From anyone else... that remark would have you on your way, but from you, Roberto, it means so much.'

I sat close to her and our hands touched.

'I see you have not aged since we last departed, despite your many problems. I think I know what it is, Matilda, that keeps you young.'

I gazed into her shining blue eyes, a privilege accorded to few men. They sparkled with amusement as they returned my impudent grin.

'And what's that, my gallant prince?'

'Simple! It's winning; nothing perks up the spirits so much as winning.'

She dug me in the ribs with her elbow.

'Idiot!'

We sat in silence for a while. A servant brought out some wine and we simply enjoyed each other's company, as old friends do.

'There's some sunshine left in the sky before vespers. I have proposition for you,' she said, breaking the comfortable silence.

'Sounds intriguing.'

'I think that you may find it pleasant, as it concerns your favourite pastime.'

We wandered along the water's edge, followed at a discreet distance by a formidable guard of four. Secure she may be – foolish she was not. Matilda had made many enemies in her life and she was not one to become careless.

'Now, Roberto, dearest, you were expecting to see Gabriella again?'

'Well, yes. Your letter told of a child.'

'Sì, and now she has a husband. You must forget her... at least as one of your, er, companions.'

'Where are they?'

'The palace at Salerno; her husband is away with Bohemund.'

'She married well?'

'Sì, she had no trouble finding a suitable knight to take her, and the child to his arms. So you must leave her alone, Roberto, capito?'

'Sì, capisco. He is a fortunate fellow. I thought that you had something else to tell me?'

'I have, dearest, I most certainly have.'

She moved to a large felled tree and sitting down motioned me to join her.

'You know that your father sent you here in the hope of marriage?'

'Could I forget, the scheming sod. You weren't the only one he has tried to mate me with.'

'Don't talk of him that way, he was doing his best. I know about Tegwin and his plans for Wales.'

'There's many who know about Tegwin, but not many who know why. Matilda, what are you leading up to? I know you too well not to spot a plot.'

'Very well: do you want a wife?'

That shut me up. I looked at her with the obvious question in my eyes, but she soon dispelled that notion.

'There is a girl... a very, very suitable girl, from a very suitable background, and she is willing to meet you.'

My life so far had always seen hope and disappointment running hand in hand, and today was no exception. I responded with no obvious enthusiasm.

'A girl? Not you? A girl, do you not think that I am too long in the tooth for a girl?'

'Not me, Robert. That issue we decided on too many years ago; besides I hear that you are still well capable of running with a girl.'

'It seems, madam, that you have very hearing ears.'

Matilda chortled at me. 'Stop pretending! I know that you are flattered.'

'Hmph! What girl?'

'See, you are interested.'

'Stop teasing and get on with it.'

'How does sixteen and suitable to become a queen sound to you?'

'Sixteen! You jest, and a queen? They usually need a king, do they not?'

'They can start by becoming a duchess, can they not, especially if the duke may one day be a king.'

'You are devious! I know where this is leading.'

'To the son of a duke and duchess, no?'

'Who *may* become a king. How long have you been plotting this one, Matilda?'

'About ten years, but someone suitable has become available.'

'Who is she?'

'Her father is Goffredo d'Altavilla, the count of Conversano; he controls most of the lands in the east, in the Puglia district. He is very rich, and the girl is the Guiscard's grand-niece, but she is not yet spoken for.'

'Why, is she ugly?'

'Robert! Quite the reverse, which is why nobody has had the courage to ask. She is quite stunning, and intelligent, and with a will of her own.'

'Why me?'

'Be serious. You are quite a catch, admired by men and lusted after by women.'

'Lust? I prefer love, your love.'

'We have done all of that soul-searching, my love; the crossroads were ten years ago, we agreed the path, we must stick to it. Remember that I've got rid of two husbands; one more husband may be too many for Mother Church. I cannot risk *that* relationship, I cannot offer any ammunition to my enemies. They are also the enemies of the Church, and any scandal will serve no purpose but the devil's.

I looked deep inside Matilda, and saw her sadness; she would see a range of emotions cross my face – sadness, regret, love? Certainly love.

'Ahh, Robert,' she sighed deeply, 'would that there were no tides in life, would that we could swim in our own pool, would that we could live our own lives.'

'I know,' I said, and we sighed in unison. I added, 'Shite, isn't it?'

She shivered in the cooling evening air.

'Hold me, Robert. There is more sadness to be wrung out of our lives yet, I fear.'

'And joy, surely some of that, we have a few days more. Then I suppose I should go and inspect this prize filly that you have targeted for me.'

'You should; you might find a queen, certainly a duchess.'

'Suppose. Has this creature a name?'

'Sibyl, named for a prophetess.'

'I trust that she can see me surviving the next few months.'

A comfortable silence wrapped around us again as we sat enjoying the sun's last warmth, then Matilda spoke.

'There is another reason why you might want to go to Conversano, Robert.'

'Oh, why?'

'Your grandfather is buried nearby.'

'Eh! Robert the Magnificent? I was told that he was in Italy. I never met him.'

'He must have been a pious man, to go on a pilgrimage to Jerusalem when he was so ill.'

'I have not heard him called pious before. Some other things, but not that.'

'Oh. But he must have been a loving man; your father was born of love... was he not?'

'Love? I suppose so. But he had to fight that stigma all his life, love without marriage.'

'It has its attractions, dear Robert, for those who dare it.'

'Sometimes the results are the same.'

The silence took shape as the darkness fell. My grandfather had loved his Herlève, of that there was no doubt, but they were forced apart by the conventions of leadership – the rules. Damn them, rules.

Would I find a wife and a grandfather in this... Conversano. The thoughts of a grave unsettled me and I shivered.

'They should have a fire lit in my retiring chamber. We don't want our extremities to cool, do we, my love?'

'No, I think not.'

We walked back to the villa arm in arm.

'Robert,' she said softly, 'be certain you do not become a target when you meet her, I have heard that her eyes can throw daggers.'

'She needs a gentle hand? I can manage that.'

'Then may I send a message to Goffredo that you will stop by, only to pay a courtesy call, on your way to Brindisi?'

'Suppose!'

'The lady might find your gentle hands interesting.'

Some days linger when they are special, but others seem to gather an uncomfortable pace and go by too soon. When three days go by as if they were one – then they must have been very special.

When the time came we rode towards Rome together, the Contessa and the Soldier, in public the epitome of rectitude, speaking to each other in a correct manner – but the mask slipped a little when the time came to part.

'Robert,' she said with such regret in her voice, 'do not forget, you are not assaulting her fortress, you are there to say hallo to her father, in a diplomatic visit for courtesy's sake.'

'Very well. Will she know why I'm really going?'

'Not officially, unless her father lets it slip, but don't forget she has the brains to work things out for herself.'

'Yes. I'll see you again... when I return.'

'If God wills it.' A tear glistened as it rolled down her cheek, and then she turned her horse abruptly and set off down the road to Rome.

I watched as she vanished into the dust raised by her escort, with a lump in my throat and an empty feeling in my stomach. I wheeled my horse and led my mesnie off on the road to Conversano.

Three hundred miles to see what fate next has in store for me.

3. Christmas in Puglia.

The back of a horse's head loses interest after a while and we spent our time gazing at the scenery, or gossiping. I asked my flag-waving companions about their time at the lakeside villa; truth to tell I had seen little of them since my daring dash from the bath.

'Were you well looked after, Payne?'

He looked behind to where Ragenaus was following.

'We enjoyed the hospitality, did we not, my Saxon friend?'

'Yes, she was very lively. The bed was small though.'

'Oh,' I mumbled, 'I wondered about that.'

'Indeed, my lord,' added Payne in his bass voice, 'my friend and I ended up on the floor, and my knees still hurt.'

'Noisy sods,' came a voice from behind.

'It wasn't me squealing.'

'No, but it was you throwing the furniture around. That bed lacks a leg now.'

'Sorry. You left, then where did you go to?'

'The bath,' replied Ragenaus, happiness in his voice. 'Have you ever sported in the water before, my bed-wrecking friend?'

'No, but it's now on the list.'

'A list?' I was intrigued.

'Sì, principe,' Payne laughed, 'I have a list of things to do before I die.'

'Well you had better start crossing things off soon, Payne, these Turks we're going to meet might have you on a list of theirs,' Ragenaus called out. This was about as close to philosophy as my Saxon standard bearer ever came, but he had the truth of it; with every horse hoofbeat we moved closer to the purpose of our mission, and it was not to share a cup of wine with the enemies of God.

South of Rome we met up with Stephen again and we continued our journey southwards.

'So what's Rome like, Stephen?'

'In turmoil. If this pope thing is settled, it's not very settled. There is armed conflict on the streets, lawlessness abounds.'

'I pray that Matilda is kept safe.'

'She will be, the bandits prefer easy targets. I met with Roger Borsa. He seems friendly enough and has invited us to stay with him a while.'

'That's good, where?'

'A place named Benevento.'

'Where's that?'

'About halfway to Brindisi.'

'Where is Robert of Flanders?'

'He went on with Borsa. They seem quite comfortable with each other and he is going to visit his daughter, Adela, before we cross the sea.

'Good. Let us find Benevento then.'

We set off and it was not long before Stephen's itch demanded to be scratched.

'So,' he began, 'Matilda?'

'Matilda?'

'Is she well?'

'Well enough.'

'Mmm.' A long pause: I could hear his mind busy trying for the next question.

'You were with her the three nights then?'

'Only three.'

'Gathering intelligences.'

'Mmm.'

His hair was now steaming, as if after a summer rain shower.

'And these, *intelligences*, are favourable?'

'Very, she has organised ships, supplies, and horses.'

'Good – but three nights. Did you not talk during the day, Robert?'

'Yes, and at nights, talking, lots of talking. Tell me more about Borsa, I nearly met him once.'

'He mentioned it. He said that you fell out of the sky on top of his defences. How did you do that, dear brother?'

So I told him of my dawn raid outside Melfi... and diverted him from less public matters.

Benevento was a pleasant surprise. It had many reminders of the old Roman Empire, including an amphitheatre, and the grand Trajan Arch, some thousand years old, the two-hundred-year-old Duomo Santa Maria Assunta – and the castle, Rocca dei Rettori, where we found Cousin Rob, and his host Roger Borsa, Duke of Apulia.

'Prince Robert,' greeted Borsa, 'you are back in Italy. How was the journey?'

'Duke Roger, thank you for asking. Italy is fine, as before; the journey was a ball-ache.'

'Indeed, Prince Robert, indeed.'

I observed the duke. He seemed a touch too gentle to me to lead in confrontations – he was known as a studious man – and had fled the field the last time I came close to him at the battle of Melfi.

He coughed, and seemed to prepare himself to say something important. He looked me in the eye to do it.

'I understand that on your last visit you came to call for breakfast with me.'

He referred to that morning at Melfi when I raided his camp on behalf of Bohemund; he had escaped from that slaughter.

'Indeed, Roger. Alas, you were not at home.'

He laughed. 'From my reports that was just as well. I trust that this visit will prove less costly.'

'Times change, Roger, we are on a mission for God this visit.'

'Of course. We will do all we can to assist you on your expedition. Now, what can we do to make you welcome?'

'One of those Roman baths would be welcome.'

'Of course.' He shouted some orders, and soon my weary backside was soaking in the warmth of one of those pleasant reminders of the Roman era.

Roger laid on a welcoming feast. No priests apart from Uncle Odo, his wagging tail Gilbert, and my chaplain Arnulf – but wine aplenty, and my commanders were together for the first time in weeks; it was to be a wonderful night for story-swapping.

Roger led the conversation with a question.

'Have you heard of the fate of Hugh of Vermandois?'

By the puzzled look upon our faces he knew that we were ignorant so he explained.

'There is, unfortunately, some bad news. Hugh was shipwrecked off Dalmatia, and he reached Constantinople with much reduced numbers.'

'He had not many to begin with; his brother, the king, was seemingly sparing with the money he allowed him,' I said, having gained that knowledge from Matilda.

Flanders growled, 'No doubt he talked his way out of the sea. That one has enough opinion of himself to float a mountain.'

We all chuckled at that. The younger brother of King Phillip of France was well known for his overly esteemed view of his own talents.

Roger demonstrated his knowledge of French affairs. 'His vanity notwithstanding, he was advised that it was too late in the year to cross. We managed to avoid him when he passed through on the way to Bari.'

'You were wise, Roger,' chipped in Flanders, 'he has difficulty being in the same room with himself.'

It was a cause for merriment but I worried that more foolish decisions by princes might jeopardise the venture, and subsequent news did little to settle me.

The message coming from the combining of all their intelligences was, to say the least, discouraging. Somehow or other there appeared to be no one in overall charge of this grand peregrination.

'Urban seems to think that a miracle will deliver all these travellers to Jerusalem's gate.' This was Roger's Borsa's observation.

'And the Moslems will throw out the keys and we can all go home sinless?' Allen of Brittany had no time for dreamers.

I had a similar, earthly view.

'It is a worry, if all the armies collide at Constantinople there could be chaos because of a lack of control. I, for one, will not cross the Bosporus unless I can see some order in the matter. Roger, do you know how many are on the road?'

'No, Robert. I know how many Bohemund took with him, and I know how many have passed through here. I can gather the

53

numbers passing across into Dalmatia from Northern Italy, but I have no idea how many are going from Germany across Hungary. I can see that it is now adding up to thousands rather than hundreds.' Roger wasn't the greatest of our supporters, and all this movement was a distraction from his scatty attempts to keep his own domains in order.

Flanders added his own view.

'Does Urban know what genie he has unleashed on us? I've heard the skies in Asia are thick with vultures as they watch the pilgrim road through Syria. Are they to pick the bones of the ordered as well as the chaotic?'

Odo felt obliged to defend the faith.

'You expect too much of the pope; he is no soldier, it is up to you princes of war to find the way together.'

'"Seek and ye shall find, ask and it will be delivered unto you."'

The attention that Gilbert's remark attracted from the princes of war seemed not worth the effort, so he shut up for the rest of the night.

Philip de Bellême wondered out loud.

'Is not Emperor Alexios going to see us safely across the sea at Constantinople, Prince Robert?'

I looked at him thoughtfully. He was a useful youth with bright ideas; he had been with Stephen until we met again after Rome and I had moved him closer to my side as we progressed down through Italy.

'He might! But the signs are not hopeful. He asked for help to resist the Mussulmen but he might not have been expecting a disorganised rabble to descend upon him.'

Stephen had a thought.

'If Raymond of Toulouse, with Bishop Adhémar and his French are moving across Italy into Carinthia, and Duke Godfrey is following the Germans down through Hungary, isn't it going to get a little crowded along that route?'

'Why are you worried about that, Stephen? We are going from Durazzo to Thessalonica on the southern coast, are we not?'

Payne was puzzled. 'Where are these places?'

'I'll show you. Bring my maps, Philip, if you please.'

Philip went off to fetch my campaign maps and we settled down for a war council. The feast was put aside for a while so that we could re-think our logistics to suit the fluid pattern of events emerging. With the maps spread across the table it became easier to discuss the situation.

Roger Borsa showed the routes that he expected the various contingents to pass along.

'Here is Raymond; he will pass along the front of the Alps, north of Venice to Zagreb, and I expect that he will meet up with Godfrey coming down from the north at Belgrade. Can you see that?'

I considered the routes.

'How long will it take Raymond to reach Venice?'

'At his present rate of progress? Probably not till February.' Then Roger thought a little more. 'Actually, with a one-eyed sixty-year-old and a bishop in charge, they might not move that quickly.'

We all laughed, except Odo who took exception to the bishop reference.

'What's wrong with bishops, Roger?'

'They are not known for their warrior qualities.'

I stepped in quickly.

'Not normally! But Odo is not normal... are you, Uncle? He carried a club at Hastings, did you not?'

'Aye!' Odo growled, 'and bounced it off a few skulls.'

'Is that why you are on this journey, Odo? Allen asked, a shade too directly, I thought.

'Among other things,' responded Odo testily, 'among other things, Allen. At my age I cannot take any chances on my redemption, so this journey might help.'

Stephen, changing the conversation, said, 'Aethilheard is well in advance of the French. He will find supplies along the route before they do, so that is not a worry.'

I thought of something else.

'Roger, is it altogether too late to cross over to Durezzo?'

'It is getting close, why?'

'I want to get a foothold over there; in fact I want to establish a camp near to Constantinople. If there are any doubts about this mission, and its leader – or lack of one – I want to know about it before I ever get near to Emperor Alexios.'

'I agree,' said Stephen, 'there is too much going on, and I do not believe that things will just happen – not because the pope *wills it,* anyway.'

'Right,' I said, turning to my cousin Flanders. 'Rob, can you try and get over the sea, and go on to join up with Aethilheard and our horses, establish a camp close to Constantinople?'

Rob eyed me up and I waited. I knew that an answer would emerge in good time.

'I'm struggling with the language here as it is. What do they speak over this *sea* you mention?'

'The Adriatic Sea, but do not worry, Rob,' said Roger Borsa, 'we have arranged guides to meet any soldiers, such as you, crossing over, the emperor has seen to that.'

That perked me up. 'Then there is some organisation, Roger?'

He nodded and Allen added, 'And gather as much information as you can before we ever get close to the place. At least we can keep ourselves in good order if nobody else can.'

Roger responded positively to my idea of an advance party.

'If you go quickly you might find mariners who have not yet drawn up their craft from the water for the winter. And, if you pay enough, they might take you over. But, because they might not get back before spring, you will have to keep them while they over-winter.'

'That's a lot of ifs and buts, Roger,' I said.

'Yes, but you are wise, Robert, I salute you for your foresight. Perhaps it will be you who leads the campaign in the end.'

'Not me, Roger, I care not for the idea. Should we move on to Bari in the morning?'

'I like the sound of that,' said Stephen, 'I have not smelled the sea for a while.'

'I don't mind smelling it,' said Rob, 'I just don't want to be in it.'

Payne had a question. 'My lord, if the general of the French has only one eye, won't he lead them round in circles?'

'No by God!' answered Odo, 'he has a bishop to guide him along the way.'

'Oh! That's all right then.' I laughed, and asked Roger another question.

'How far is Bari?'

'About a hundred and thirty miles; actually it is only twenty miles short of Conversano – if anybody was interested in going there,' he said, an apparently innocent suggestion.

'What's at Conversano?' asked Stephen.

'A castle,' responded Roger.

'So?' said Stephen.

'Nothing, I just thought that I might mention it.'

I said nothing, but thought, *thanks Matilda, some secret that was.*

I was still dwelling on it when later, Roger came up to me in a conspiratorial manner.

'Robert, I'm sorry for that remark about Conversano, it was ill-judged of me, but may I speak directly?'

'Of course, Roger. I'm not offended, just puzzled as to how, or what, you know.'

'I know a lot, Robert. Goffredo's lands are in my domain, and it was me who put the idea in Matilda's head. The problem is that Goffredo is a widower and too old to re-marry, so he has three sons and a daughter to dispose of, and he is terrified of suitors for her, or rather he terrifies them. He hates the idea of losing her and although he knows that she should marry, he doesn't approve of any poor soul who comes anywhere near her.'

'Ah, I see. Matilda said that she was too beautiful.'

'It hurts to look at her.'

'And intelligent, I hear.'

'And cultured,' Roger added.

'And available.'

'To the right man,' he counselled.

'Is that me?'

'Her choice.'

The exchange fell silent for a moment, until Roger made a suggestion.

'Let me come with you, see if I can help: I'll introduce you to Goffredo. Send your main party on to Brindisi. We will call in at Conversano and see whether we shall leave you there for a while.'

I could only assent to that loose-ended proposal, so we agreed on it.

We travelled as far as Bari without Odo or Gilbert. Odo had approached me the previous evening and told me that he had received an invitation to go and visit Roger's uncle, the count of Sicily, in his palace at Palermo.

Odo explained, 'If you are not going to Constantinople this winter, then I will go for a rest in a new place and return to you in the spring. Does that suit you, nephew?'

'Yes, of course, Uncle Odo. There is no hurry to get to the Bosporus, at least until the other armies arrive. Then we can sort out the command structure. Go with my blessing and enjoy the rest.'

'You too, Robert. But beware of tempting eyes, lest they cause you to stray from the path of salvation.'

'Don't know what you mean.'

'Hmph! Don't you really? You will have your chaplain Arnulf to remind you while we are apart.'

Arriving at Bari near the middle of December we found plenty of mariners willing to jingle to the tune of Norman silver, enough to get Flanders and his soldiers away, but not before a tearful farewell for Rob and his daughter Adela.

I stood with the girl and we watched with the others as Rob disappeared over the horizon on his way to Constantinople.

'So how fare you in Italy, Adela?'

'Nicely, Prince Robert. Everything is warmer, they keep the snow on the highest peaks and it is a very pleasant place.'

'You do not miss Flanders?'

'Not in the least. And the winters are quite tolerable, except that the seas can be unpredictable.'

'Well,' said Allen, 'how long does an Italian winter last, Adela?'

'Long enough to let matters develop in the court of Emperor Alexios, I suspect,' I replied for her.

'Aye. And long enough to do some of the other courting, *I* suspect.'

'Don't know what you mean.'

Too many people were now aware of my impending courtesy visit, and nobody was surprised when a message arrived within an eye-blink of our arrival at the port. The invitation was to visit Count Goffredo, and spend the Christmas period in his castle at Conversano.

Somehow it seemed that I was being drawn along a well-prepared path, gently, yet inexorably guided and shuffled along towards... what? I had left home intending malice to those whom I knew not, but now it seems that softer diversions had overtaken my progress.

Before I left for the climb up to Conversano I went to see the others and found Stephen and Allen down by the harbour. They were watching the shipwrights and sailors preparing their ships for the winter. Most had been dragged up the beach and out of the water. These were the ones that Flanders had not taken, the ones that needed repair, those which the owners wouldn't hire out and the ones which had come into harbour after Rob's departure.

My companions were only there out of curiosity, being landsmen they did not come close to such activity very often. But they would be embarking in the springtime, and so had a natural interest in the goings-on.

'Morning,' I said, ''tis cold now, is it not?'

'Aye!' answered Allen, 'worse if your hands are wet, surely?'

'Yes, sod that for an occupation,' said Stephen.

I joined them and watched with interest.

'Yes, at least when we travel by horse the beast provides some warmth. But you have both been across the narrow sea to England, have you not?'

'Aye, in the summer. Castles and hearths are my main occupation in the winter.'

'Yes, Stephen,' I commented, 'but there are better ways to keep warm in the winter than fires, you know.'

Allen laughed. 'Yes, and you are one of the warmest men in Normandy – winter or summer.'

'Aye, and perhaps I will be one of the warmest in Italy. What are you two doing at Christmas?'

Allen replied. 'Not as much as you, apparently.'

The Duke of Brittany had only a fleeting attachment to the art of diplomacy and I wondered how my late sister Constance had dealt with his blunt manners. Ignoring this I made a suggestion.

'I thought that you might stay with Roger. He has a palace atop a hill at Melfi.'

'We know,' said Stephen. 'Is your stay at Conversano to do with winter warming?'

'It might be, or it might be more serious than that.'

'Was your stay with Matilda to do with winter warming?'

Allen had pushed too far, but I held my tongue, ignoring him.

I doubted if Stephen or Allen believed that I had meant marriage, at least I thought not. Here I was, near forty-five years old and not obvious marriage material. Then I thought further; why not? I was fit, the times I spent roistering were well matched by the amount of training I did – and the hundreds of miles I spent in the saddle. I felt good; besides, Matilda had told me that I was lusted after. But by a sixteen-year-old beauty?

Suddenly my confidence ebbed a little.

''Tis but a courtesy call really. I shall probably join you shortly.'

'Perhaps,' said Stephen, 'we need to keep together and plan as the intelligence reports come in. This venture needs a tight rein, Robert. There's too much to go awry.'

'Yes, you're right. I'll be back with you in two weeks, is that good enough?'

'Sounds good to me,' said Allen. 'See you in... where was that?'

'Brindisi, tis further along the coast but has a better harbour, the ships are moving there for the winter.'

They left and I remained fixed to a rock, alone with my thoughts and watching the maritime world going about its business, until a polite cough reminded me that the air had turned quite chilly.

'There is a tavern over there, my lord,' said Payne, pointing along the jetty.

'Come on then, let us test the wine hereabouts. You might find some wenches to play with.'

The next day we left Bari and travelled together until we reached the point, at Polignano a Mare, where I needed to turn up towards the hill upon which sat Conversano. Stephen and Allen needed to travel back northwards a little way to reach Roger's palace at Melfi and he provided an escort. That place held mixed memories for me; the curves of Gabriella, but the bloody carnage my men had wreaked upon Borsa's un-vigilant troops spoiled that vision.

We said our farewells and turned up to the hills. I was determined to impress. Along with Payne and Ragenaus, I took only a few chosen knights and a few of the mounted archers I was so proud of. With my standard and banners flying, men in their most colourful tunics and horses caparisoned in their finest and most regal colourful drapery, anyone would be forgiven if they believed that they were witnessing a prince going a-courting. The addition of Roger's men made for a fine sight.

Conversano lay in the midst of a fertile and prosperous land. Goffredo had carved out a profitable piece of Italy for himself after the Greeks had been banished from the land.

It was no surprise to find the peak of the hill upon which Conversano stood fully occupied by the structures of governance, evidence of a new basilica in construction, and at the very top – Goffredo's citadel, home, palace and symbol of his lordship.

In the afternoon the sun lit up the natural stone and the flags flying from the towers and battlements competed with our own as we toiled up the hill, our horses steaming in the chilly air.

Goffredo greeted me in the courtyard. This extended well beyond the earthen baileys that I was used to. Everything was clean and tidy, the stabling was built in the same stone as the rest of the buildings, and there were none of the usual horse and latrine smells that I was ready to recognise.

'Prince Robert!' he cried, 'we are pleased that you could visit us! What do you think of our castle here?'

'It is fine, Count Goffredo, I am most impressed.'

He turned to my escort. 'Greetings, Duke Roger, thank you for bringing such an honoured guest.'

'Count Goffredo, it is my honour, and a pleasure. He has kept us amused with tales of our cousins in the north, the cold north he tells us.'

'Indeed, cold in the nose and hot in the heart I have heard.'

I laughed. 'Aye, certainly it gets cold, and we find our warmth where we can.'

'Come inside, lords, we have prepared a feast for you.'

Goffredo took me by the arm – as if he had known me for a long time. Indeed he might, as everybody in Italy seemed to know my business.

As we walked up the steps I was much taken by Goffredo's clothes. No woollen cloth for this lord, he wore a gown of finest silk – much embroidered – and against the cold a cloak trimmed with fur – and a fur hat. About his waist was a chased leather belt in which he carried a short sword with an embellished handle.

I'd considered myself to be splendidly presented, but now I could see how the influences of the vivid East had made their mark upon the princes of Italy. If only my brother William Rufus could see the fashions here, he would be mortified; how dull his pretensions would appear against the finery on display in this Italian palace.

We entered the grand hall. It was splendid, with drapes of damask, silken brocades and wall hangings of intricate design. Circling above there was a curtained gallery, at one end of which some musicians were playing.

In the centre a long table was laid out and against the sides of the room were many other buffet boards covered in foods of all description. The room was warm with plentiful candles ablaze and there were many in flamboyant costume, whom I judged to be Goffredo's closest and most important household members.

Goffredo made straight for the top where three young men dressed in their finest were waiting.

'Prince Robert, allow me to introduce my sons Alexander, Robert and Tancred, they have heard much about you.'

'I am honoured,' I replied, 'a splendid hall, so very, er, colourful. Count Goffredo, you are exceeding blessed. May I introduce my most trusted?'

I introduced my travelling companions and eventually found myself sitting at the table picking at the food and engaged in conversation with the old count. His own people, being most hospitable, had spread about the room and were well engaged with their guests.

I did notice a lack of females in the room, but refrained from comment, remembering Matilda's instructions to *be diplomatic*. I did, however, notice the curtains hung around the gallery were twitching, and I suspected that we were being discreetly examined. I wondered if Sibyl was among the watchers.

The next morning when I came down from my chamber I was dressed in a fine silk robe that had been laid out for me, richly embroidered and trimmed with fur. Goffredo knew how to care of his guests – except that he hadn't taken the precaution of waking me for Prime, the morning prayers, so I missed that – again.

'Good morning, Prince Robert. You carry that robe well, we wondered if it would fit you.'

'Good morning, Count Goffredo. Alexander, Tancred, good morning to you also.'

Goffredo explained young Robert's absence.

'Robert has gone off with Count Roger to Melfi; they may catch up with your people before they get there. But too many Roberts can lead to confusion so he won't be missed.'

'Thank you, Count. This is a splendid palace, and warm.' I had noted the warmth in the rooms.

'Yes, we have the ancient Romans to thank for the comfort of underfloor heating, and the land about us is prosperous and well worth fighting for.'

'Ah yes, I believe that you have had some er... discussions with Guiscard in the past about that.'

Goffredo laughed, and his sons joined in.

'That's one way of putting it. Relationships within the ruling de Hauteville family are patchy at the best of times, but sometimes they fail entirely.'

'Quite, I have similar problems myself.'

'So I have heard. Now, after the midday prayer we will have a small meal with the rest of my family. You can meet my daughter, Sibyl; perhaps you would like that?'

'Indeed. If she is as handsome as her father and brothers, I look forward to it.'

I could over-egg the pudding, but I usually carried it off.

After midday I was escorted into a chamber furnished as a dining room. It had a large table in the centre and serving tables around the sides; drapes and tapestries hung all around and high windows admitted the light. On the tables there were many ornaments which glistened as gold or silver. It was a statement of wealth and I was impressed.

Goffredo was standing by a tall, throne-like chair at one end of the table and he beckoned me to come and sit next to him on his right-hand side. Alexander sat opposite and Tancred was on my right, with five places on each side taken up by Goffredo's household or his guests. At the end opposite Goffredo there was another vacant throne, flanked by two vacant chairs.

We sat quietly talking for a while until Goffredo stood up, and, taking this as a cue, the others did likewise. There followed an expectant hush, until, after a slight delay, a trio of women swept into the room, rustling as the shiny silk that adorned them was excited by their movements. Two matrons led the way, the third figure remaining hidden until they parted behind the throne and revealed – Sibyl.

My eyes feasted on her. There was no gold on the table that out-lustred the woman's hair, there were no drapes on the walls that matched the quality of the silks that followed the contours of her body, there was no man in the room that appeared as tall, and there were no waters in the Adriatic that sparkled like her eyes, dark and intelligent.

Goffredo spoke.

'Sibyl, my daughter, you grace us again.'

The young woman returned his smile and then gave everyone at the table a smile – ending with me; she held my gaze for a seeming age, and then smiled.

'My lord, Prince Roberto. You grace us by your presence; may I welcome you to Puglia?'

My mind was working at fever pitch: *sixteen? Sixteen! Matilda said she was only sixteen; that cannot be so... surely.*

I had only partially heard her comment, so engrossed with her appearance I was, but managed a passable response.

'Grace you say, my lady? Not I, there is only one grace in this room, and that is you, Lady Sibyl, and your gracious companions, *un bel trio*, if I may say so.'

I could always come up with something that resembled a compliment, and it pleased the matrons at Sibyl's side at no cost, or so it appeared, and might have achieved a great deal of credit for my cause – if indeed I had one.

Goffredo coughed politely and asked me what I thought about Pope Urban. I did not miss, however, a comment which passed between the ladies.

As they addressed the food on the table one of Sibyl's companions whispered across the table.

'What did he say? That northerner?'

'I think he fancies me,' replied the other.

'He can fancy me anytime he wants.'

'Shsst!' Sibyl hissed at the woman, so she cast her eyes down and attacked an orange in revenge.

Goffredo engaged me in pleasantries for the rest of the meal and I managed to reply to his questions without recourse to Italian. We stayed clear of contentious issues, such as local disputes – the southern Normans being no better in that regard to ourselves; so we discussed harvests, being at sea, the health of my family and the weather. Sometimes I lacked attention as my eyes kept slipping to the other end of the table – and increasingly they were met. Goffredo appeared not to notice and said nothing.

Later, when the repast was nearly finished, Goffredo leaned over to me.

'If the weather is pleasant we usually take a walk in the garden. We would be honoured if you would join us.'

'I would like that. I find many of my favourite activities take place within nature's pleasant spaces.'

'Then you will not be disappointed.'

The ladies prepared to leave the table and the men stood up as they left.

'Come with me, Prince Robert.' Goffredo took me by the arm and led me along a corridor towards an open gate, through which I caught a glimpse of greenery.

'As you see we have made our own privy bailey on this side of the villa. The horses and stabling are on the other side, where you entered through the gate.'

We entered a courtyard encircled by cloisters, as if in an abbey. There were raised boxes filled with various plants and overhead trelliswork carried vines of various kinds. It might be winter, yet the air was filled with heady aromas.

I was impressed and made a couple of circular tours before sitting down to rest and admire the view.

'All it needs is some fountains,' said Alexander.

A different voice responded, clear female tones alerted my ears.

'That would be ideal, Prince Roberto, but we have no water for fountains. It is difficult enough to keep the horses and house supplied up here on this hill.'

I turned at the sound of that voice. It was regulated, deep, and had within its quality a smouldering warmth that made the hair on my neck tingle. The owner was blond, but closer I could see that she had olive Latin eyes in an almond-shaped frame. It was of course Sibyl.

'Lady Sibyl, you favour horses over fountains?'

'Of course. Are they not essential to your life, my lord?'

'They are.' I fell silent for a moment as the girl – woman – came up to me. I was being examined again, this time from very close. I could see her nostrils flare as she sought out the essential scent of me.

'We have come a long way,' I stuttered, 'on our horses, they become as a friend, but...'

She was very near now, daring me to react, to try and touch her. I could smell her essence through the exotic perfumes that danced about her presence; it was becoming dangerous. The others in the garden had started to fade into the background and soon they disappeared from my ken as we practised the ancient art of gentle curiosity, the introductory dance of instinct. Then the moment exploded and the audience came back into my present as Goffredo coughed and spluttered.

'Of course it is horses over fountains, but still it would be nice to engineer some kind of supply up here for fountains, don't you think so, Prince Roberto?'

The question demanded an answer – the woman's eyes demanded an answer. I spoke the words to reply to Goffredo's question at the same time as my eyes gave an answer to Sibyl, they both said – 'Yes! *It would be nice.*'

Sibyl was startled. Perhaps she wondered if she had gone a step too far; this prince from the north had not shied away from her beauty as others had before. I had challenged her to move from her adolescence into womanhood. Seeing the sudden flicker in her eyes, I wondered if I had repelled her. The flicker might have been fear – or it might have been the first awakening of the dormant sexual passion lurking beneath the surface. I wondered if her stomach was calm – mine was not. I wondered if she was experiencing the first thrill of anticipation – if she realised that I had a consummation in mind. And with that thought, I knew I wanted her.

She smiled bravely, and tossed her hair as she turned quickly to engage her lady companions in a diversionary conversation as they walked off along the flowery pathways.

I watched her hips. They moved the fine cloth of her gown as she glided along, white with blossoms embroidered down the skirt. About her shoulders she wore a bolero trimmed with fur to ward off the afternoon breeze – and no hat, none of my women wore hats, whatever the court etiquette. My women spurned the idea of covering up their natural glory, in this case a golden crown of long shining hair and, now that she had turned away, I saw that it tumbled down her back, reaching almost to her waist.

I thought at that moment that whatever plans destiny had for me, they now included this woman. We had joined in a purpose as yet unspoken, and the game was now for the playing.

Goffredo coughed again and brought me back from my dreaming. Goffredo had seen a vision – a marriage: *thank you, Roger, thank you, Matilda*.

'She is a fine child, tis a pity her mother could not see her now.'

I looked at him curiously.

'If her mother could see her now, Goffredo? She would see no child. Open your eyes, dear count, Sibyl is a child no more.'

'No, well perhaps not, I see that. What do you see, Prince Robert?' Goffredo had become emboldened by my obvious affliction.

I was not surprised by Goffredo's boldness. He had status and age on his side, gave no quarter to coyness, and after all this is what he had been encouraged in by Roger and Matilda. But I was reticent – for good reason.

'Goffredo, dear count, I would fail in honesty if I did not remind you of the reason that brought me here. This is merely a transit point in a longer journey, from which I might not return. Some, too many, are of the view that the evil of the Mussulmen will pass as soon as we ask it, but I believe they'll be as attached to their cause just as strongly as we are to ours. They have held Jerusalem for more than a lifetime and they are as likely to give up their lives in its defence as we are willing to die to relieve them of its possession.

'If I had a more than passing interest in Sibyl, I could not speak, knowing what business I must be about when I leave this place. Please see that, if she is not to be hurt, then events must go at a cautious pace. Even if she wished, I could not make more than a friend of her until I am safely returned from my mission. Do you see?'

Goffredo was impressed.

'I have heard that you are a kindly lord, and honourable. May I tell Sibyl of what we have spoken? It would settle her mind if she knew of your regard for her.'

'Tell her, and then if she wishes we can walk together. If that is not her wish then no harm will be done. Yes, please tell her.'

As is normal, the very best of days flew by, and targets on the horizon of life sped towards me at a disappointingly speedy pace. Outside the bounds of Conversano, for good or evil, the world went on at its own pace and the wishes of men would not slow it.

We walked together and it soon became a companionship that might have puzzled onlookers, the forty-five-year-old prince and his sixteen-year-old companion. No one knew what words passed between us, nor would they ever be known because her chaperones were under strict instructions to keep their distance – and nobody disobeyed Sibyl.

She was proud of her father's lands, and after a few days of wandering about, testing each other, she took me to the top of the grand keep. It was easy to see why. Puglia was laid out before us in a magnificent panorama, fertile fields and green trees led my eyes across to the sea.

'What grows here, Sibyl?'

'Everything we need, Roberto. Grain and fruit – the trees are mostly olives; there are cows and sheep, and lots of herbs for flavour.'

'You are blessed.'

'Mostly. Yet there is something missing.' She turned away from the vista and presented her face to me, it had a question contained within its beauty.

'What would that be, my lady?'

'An answer,' she responded with uncertainty.

I began to wonder if the answer was as near as me but turned the conversation; *too soon, Robert, too soon,* I warned myself, *how could she ever consider you*? 'How far is the sea?'

'You like the sea? It is only five miles away. We will ride down, no?'

'I love the sea, it is in my blood. We will ride down, *sì*.'

I had the pick of her finest steeds and we resolved to go the following day.

It was, as she said, beautiful country. The track led through well-tended fields, and although the harvest was in, it could be seen how cared for they were as workers still toiled at the land. There was mile after mile of olive groves and I wondered for a moment what they did with all that oil, although thinking about the meals we had I think I knew the answer to that.

Taking the opportunity one day as we wandered down these peaceful tracks, I broached the subject of my grandfather's grave. Without hesitation she agreed to try to discover from local knowledge where it could possibly be, and that provided a reason to go out even more often.

'You said that you had not met him, Roberto, but what was he doing so far from home, an old man?'

'It's a complicated story. Simply put, he felt that he'd offended the Church while younger and wanted to make amends, so he went on a pilgrimage to Jerusalem. On the way back he fell ill and died at Nicaea in 1035 and originally he was buried there. My father was only eight years old at the time but succeeded him as the Duke of Normandy. It couldn't have been easy for him to survive that burden, and I believe that made him the uncompromising man he was,' I mused, surprising myself with this insight.

'Oh,' she responded. 'You are not *uncompromising*, are you, Roberto?'

I smiled at her before replying, 'I fear not.'

That seemed good enough for her and we rode on a little way, and then she stopped and asked, 'So why are we searching for a grave here?'

'Yes, well. My father wanted his father to be returned to Normandy. The Church granted permission and a mission was sent to disinter and bring his corpse back. The party had reached hereabouts on their way back from Nicaea with the body when news of my father's death reached them so they simply buried it, and left no surviving record of the grave.'

'How sad. Your father must have loved your grandfather.' Sibyl edged her horse closer to mine.

'He loved sparingly, and Grandfather might have been one whom he did. It would be important to William, a bastard, to be loved by his father... wouldn't you say?'

'I would. And your father's mother?'

'Herlève. Beautiful, but the daughter of a tanner. She was very beloved of Grandfather Robert but of course he was forced by the Church and his nobles to give her up; unsuitable to be the wife of a duke, you see. They married her off to a spare count. That's where my father got his two half-brothers from, Bishop Odo and Robert de Mortain.'

'That must have hurt your father! They must have loved their son William.'

'I think so. He was an angry man, always angry. They loved his sister too. I liked her, Adeliza, she was a countess.'

'Was?'

'She died seven years ago, sadly.'

'Oh, I am sorry.'

Suddenly things changed. She reached out, seemingly without thought, and touched my arm. It was a surprise and I almost grabbed hold of her, my horse was close and steady enough.

Instead I held back, saying, 'Thank you, my lady, you are kind. We seem to be a family confused by love.'

She sat silently on her horse, looking at me, her eyes hypnotic, entrancing, causing my throat to dry and constrict. Then, realising that she touched me yet, she withdrew her hand and urged her steed a step or two away.

I knew then that my heart had been given into her keeping.

I did not need to tell Sibyl anything twice, her intelligence competed with her beauty and the more time we spent together the more it hurt not to make that ultimate consummation, but we could not. Now, more than ever, I understood how the demands of convention were stronger than the demands of nature, I understood Matilda's position and I understood Grandfather Robert's, now I was in that situation. We could not bed without the blessing of the Church through wedlock; if Sibyl was to be my duchess then the only way we could bring our love to fruition was to make that commitment to each other before God – but it hurt.

We wandered the hills, and found nothing but dust; no markers, scrapes, caves, or graves – dust to dust, it is true.

Goffredo became a man renewed. Whatever hopes he had constructed for this venture, they were becoming more than hopes. The intelligences he had been sent from England told him that there would never be an heir to the English crown from King William Rufus' loins; if he died the crown would be mine. Whatever I thought of that, Goffredo may well have the future Queen of England under his roof; ambition enough for any man I thought.

I stayed until we were all certain. We agreed that if I came back from Jerusalem I would return to Conversano and see if the lady had waited for me. There was to be no formal arrangement – but if we both felt the same when I returned we might take the next step. I could promise no more than that and she asked for no more from me.

We had an odd conversation not many days before I was due to leave.

It was in the evening sunshine, the half-light just after the sun had dipped behind the western hills. We were quiet in the still evening air, holding hands, so familiar had we become.

'I know the meaning of your name, Sibyl,' I said gently into her cascading hair.

'If you know that, dear Roberto, then you should be careful what you say next.' She turned away from the now lost sun and stared into the darkness of the distant eastern sea.

'Perhaps I am foolish enough to ask more.'

'Then speak the name and challenge the gods.'

'You believe in more than one God? Then I know someone else like you.'

'Your Welshwoman.'

'*Sì*, my Welshwoman.'

'You still love her?' She turned to look at me directly, seeking an honest reply, no doubt.

'I love her, Sibyl, she is the mother of my children, I cannot cast her away. But nor can we marry, that time is gone. I need a wife by my side who none can dispute, I need a princess suited to wear the crown of the English one day, or whose children will when the time comes. Are you that woman?'

'How would I know, Prince Roberto?' She turned away again, hiding the entry into her mind.

'Your name, that's how. It means "prophetess" in Greek, does it not?'

'It does,' she replied in a whisper, 'be careful, Roberto.'

The air was still and the birds had left the dark sky, as if by command, and all the normal sounds of the citadel had ceased as Sibyl gazed into the stygian east.

It was a moment to seize, or perhaps the scent of her had made me reckless so I pressed the point.

'If you can see, Sibyl, then trust me to share it.'

The woman, in a majestic pose, pointed to the east and answered me.

'I see that we will continue this conversation, but... there is darkness beyond which I cannot penetrate, my love.'

I was silent for a moment; *we would meet again, but...*

'You said "my love".' That startled her, and she turned back to face me again, flustered, and there was a tinge of pink on her olive cheeks.

'Oh,' she stuttered, 'did I?'

'If it was not you, then it was some goddess of your acquaintance, I believe.'

We locked eyes. 'Kiss me,' I ventured. She did and we tasted each other for an age – until a polite cough made its way in from the dark, and it was time to move back into the light.

The following morning the noises from outside my chamber bespoke a household preparing for the day. I had slept but fitfully, my mind disturbed by a confusion of imagery, mostly to do with what lay beneath the clothing of my host's daughter.

This was no good. I must put an end to this... speculation, the girl – lady – deserved better than the uncertain future of an ageing warrior, especially when he was about to launch himself and his comrades into the unknown dangers of a foreign adventure.

Rising, I determined to go and eat breakfast but was surprised when I came into Goffredo's family chamber to find only three people in the room. There was but a single table set to dine. There were two of Sibyl's ladies standing to one side by the buffet table – and sitting at one end of the table... was Sibyl, radiant.

'My lord Roberto,' she spoke in that measured way, in a tone which made the hairs on the back of my neck sit up, 'welcome, please sit there.' She indicated the chair opposite her, at the table fully two paces long, and enquired, 'Did you sleep well, my lord?'

I stood at the table and one of Sibyl's ladies thrust the chair into the backs of my legs with too much enthusiasm, such that I sat down with a bump and caused some amusement among those present.

'Pour my lord a drink please, Sofia. My other lady, Prince Roberto, is Julia.' And smiled a smile that made the sun seem dull as I nodded to the other grinning handmaid.

The wine went into the goblet in a shaky stream as Sofia tried to control her own amusement. I shuffled myself into a more comfortable position and lifting the goblet proffered Sibyl a salute.

'Good morrow, Lady Sibyl, you brighten the morning. I must be a wretched sight, I have hardly slept.'

She looked at me and my stomach thrilled at the vision.

'That is remarkable, for I have not slept at all. If you think me radiant this morning perhaps you would like me better when I have slept well.'

'Be careful, young lady, for invitations such as that can disturb a man's imaginings.'

She sniffed, and dissembled an orange before responding.

'Imaginings, my lord? What imaginings?'

'Those which are presumptuous.'

She paid attention to some bread and cheese while Sofia fussed about me and I picked at some grapes. I did not know where to take this conversation any more, I wanted to hold on to her and release her at one and the same time... but how?

'You are skilled at the lists, Roberto.'

That was a statement, not a question – and *Roberto* again. Sibyl was now leading.

'I am also used to winning the joust, with lance, or sword... Sibyl.'

She was looking at me directly, but without any discernible expression upon her lovely face when she surprised me further.

'We have no time for jousting, Roberto, you will leave very shortly, for war, and I need to know your intentions towards me.'

There was a sharp intake of breath from her ladies and I saw them look at each other with disturbed faces.

'My intentions, Sibyl, are to place no burden upon you, my lady, but you are honest and I will return that compliment. I have developed feelings for you, which, ripened as they are in such a short time tells me that we might have a future together... were circumstances different. You are young and I am looking down the back slope of life; you are beautiful yet I lack legs; you are safe and have a future that you can determine while I *might* have a future, but I cannot expect, or indeed ask, that you wait upon that uncertainty. Is that honest enough, my lady?'

She gazed at me oddly and I saw a sadness in her that I had not seen before.

'My lord, you are deceived. People *like* you, you are always surrounded by those who would know you better, whereas I! I am lonely, I am told that I am beautiful yet I cannot see that, what I do know is that it keeps people away; I might as well be ugly for all the good that beauty does me. I have not had an embrace since I was fourteen.'

'Oh, my lady!' Sofia was shocked and the younger Julia gasped.

'How can you say such a thing, my lady? I embrace you every night, do I not?' exclaimed the outraged matron.

'And we hold hands when we are out walking, my lady,' said Julia.

'Oh ladies, I am sorry, of course you comfort me, but it is no substitute for what I long for, to have my own special friend. Do you not see?'

'You mean... a man?'

'Of course I mean a man. You both have one yet none come near me.'

I had become a spectator to this most intimate of discussions, but my mind had been opened: whatever we are on the outside we live within ourselves; ugly, plain, or beautiful, we exist within our body shells and often they belie our true nature.

I coughed, and they turned their attention back to me.

'Ahem. I take it that I am caught up in this search of yours, Lady Sibyl? That you can ignore my age and my short legs?'

'I see you for what you are, my lord, and what I see I like. And as for age? It matters not; I would rather have a shorter time with someone I love than a lifetime with some substitute.'

'Quite a speech. You have thought this through, that is clear.'

'I have, but I knew you before you arrived here, Roberto, you have many friends eager to describe you. Tell me, my lord, how long do you think that you will take to relieve the holy city?'

'Well – my lady. There is no certainty in the matter, but if things go well I expect to be outside the gates by midsummer. I could be back here before winter returns – with the blessing of God.'

'Amen to that.'

I waited for a while to let her digest my little speech, whereupon she returned to the van of the conversation.

'Is it your wish to marry me, Roberto?'

Sofia uttered a cry, 'My lady!' but Sibyl shushed her. I responded.

'It is in my mind, but...' I searched for words to explain my imprudence but she responded immediately.

'Then know that my night was also disturbed by *imaginings*, and although I have not had direct experience of such things, I found them not unpleasant. I too believe that we each know enough about the other to see some future together. Remember my prophecy, my love. Although I love and accept the teachings of Jesu, I also know that the old gods retain some powers, and that you will return.'

Sibyl's attendants fussed about like a pair of clucking hens and we were presented with enough food to feed half the pilgrims in Europe, and as much wine. I fear that we were both emptying our goblets too quickly and I could see her hue brightening. Emboldened by Bacchus, I made what I thought would be a closing statement on the matter.

'If I survive I will return. If you hear of my demise then tell me that you will move on, find someone else. Promise me please.'

'That might be too difficult, Roberto. And do not worry about your age, you look very well, even Sofia says that you curl her toes; is that not true, my faithful one?'

'My lady, you are too bold. What will Prince Robert think of your manners?'

I made my own reply to that question. 'I think them honest, dear lady, and I think them fine, and I think that I am privileged to hear such things from her, at least we all know where we stand.'

I was not to have the final say however; Sibyl had that.

'Very well. We will make no promises except this, that when you return, Prince Roberto, we will resume this courtship and see where it takes us. Will that satisfy you, Sofia, Julia?'

Sibyl received a nod and a bob from both, and therefore the matter was settled – I would survive and I would return, no question.

We went for a walk in the hills later, me and the three women, I outnumbered in the most pleasant way.

'That was the longest breakfast I have ever taken,' I remarked, gazing at the distant sea.

'It was one to remember,' responded Sibyl as we wandered arm in arm across the verdant hillside.

We went down to the sea several times more, but by now it had the greyness of winter upon it. When we went that far we left her ladies behind but always had a troop of horsemen with us; it was not the best of arrangements for a couple seeking solitude, but it was wise. At the strand we would leave them keeping watch from the sand hills that adorn that area, and find a little sandy depression to snuggle into while we talked, and kissed and watched the restless sea... and ignored the rest of the world.

During our wanderings we continued to search for graves, but sixty years had gone by since Grandfather Robert had been interred in this region, and the dusts of time had ensured that no one knew anything about it. It was sad, but there were more immediate things to concern me, that was certain.

We parted after Epiphany. Messages from the coast, items requiring my attention for decision, came with increasing frequency as the year moved forward, so I reluctantly prepared to make my way to Brindisi to join the others.

It was a difficult morning. We stood around uncomfortably, Goffredo babbling on about nothing much while his daughter remained silent, dignified as normal, but the times I caught her glance told me that she would rather that we were alone for this, the next stage of our relationship – or the beginning of it, who knows.

At last I could bear it no longer, so brushing my prospective father-in-law to one side I went over to Sibyl with open arms and she stepped inside my embrace. We kissed, not daring any passion, but our loins touched briefly before she drew back, saying in my ear, 'Go quickly, Roberto, go now, I cannot watch any longer... this mime.'

I kissed her on the forehead, slapped her father on the back and leapt onto my horse – a supreme example of Sibyl's breeding stable – and left.

Unwarlike thoughts dominated, but one thing in particular churned in my thoughts: whatever lay ahead, I would return to this place, my oracle had seen that. My companions fell in behind and sensing my sadness followed me silently downhill towards the sea, sparkling now, as if in spring-like hope, but unable to lift my depression.

My sadness at leaving Conversano wasn't relieved when we reached Brindisi only to receive news about Odo. The bishop had been taken ill in Sicily and died within a few days.

There was an effusive letter from Bishop Gilbert – who seemed to blame himself for the disaster – and a more sober one from Roger, Count of Sicily. They had crossed to Sicily on the count's invitation and while in Roger's palace at Palermo, Odo had been stricken by some ailment and weakened rapidly before sliding into death.

Count Roger had written that he had supervised a splendid burial and that he would erect a tomb in the cathedral of St Mary over Odo's tomb. Gilbert had conducted the ceremony, but he had been so badly affected by his friend's death that he indicated that he would return forthwith to Normandy and play no further part in my mission.

Thus my misery was compounded and I was inconsolable for a while. Uncle Odo had caused me all sorts of problems over the years and his judgement had been suspect at times, but as a man, he had always retained my respect and love, and the loss hurt.

It caused me to wonder how many friends I would lose very shortly, if this expedition we were engaged upon went awry.

During the winter my force had become fragmented, scattered between Bari, Brindisi and Capua. This was because of the practicalities of imposing what was effectively an alien force upon a friendly local population. Normally a travelling army could live off what it could take, buy or sequester, but here because there was no enemy, everything had to be bought – and that included accommodation. All my people had to be supported from my travelling treasury.

The unattached and unfunded did not have as pleasant a winter as the organised armies. Those who were blinded by the aim of this pilgrimage to the practicalities of getting there were left to fend for themselves. Many satisfied themselves with a pilgrimage to Rome and went back to the north, others starved and never returned, some managed to exist as camp followers to the various army groups and remained a nuisance.

Because of the delay in crossing over to the Balkans it also meant that Robert of Flanders was out of touch for the whole of the winter and there was very little in the way of information coming back from the emperor's court, or anywhere in between. We had little intelligence on which to plan the next leg of our journey, so that when it was declared safe to cross the Adriatic Sea we would be venturing into the unknown once again.

4. Towards the East.

When March arrived we prepared to cross the Adriatic from Brindisi to Durazzo, the grand departure to be, symbolically, on Easter morning: 5 April 1097.

When I met up with Stephen, Allen and Roger Borsa at Brindisi we changed plans a little, so I kept my supply fleet from Normandy waiting for further instructions; these vessels were now in the harbour along with the vessels that Roger's efforts had secured for us.

An interesting comparison could be made between ship design from northern and southern Europe; my longship-based *knörr* and the Byzantine *dromon;* both with a heritage in warship design but now adapted for cargo transport.

We were to be transported in the local ships so when the weather appeared settled I despatched my own fleet off to Cyprus as decided, with two exceptions. Of my twelve ships I required a single *knörr* to go to and wait upon me at Thessalonica, where it would provide me with a means of communication in the eastern Mediterranean. The second had been grounded on a rock and was condemned as unsound. It had outlived its purpose and was to be left on the beach, its parts used as spares.

We were encamped along the shoreline, with tents, pavilions and flags proclaiming our presence so none could doubt that here was a formation of some purpose. There was however a distinct difference between my hundreds of men and horses and the thousands of men, women and children gathered nearby hoping for transport across the sea. They were accompanied by many priests and I gathered those together soon after my arrival to speak to them.

'Tell your people that I have no responsibility for them. You were warned not to come south with us, but instead to travel across the north of Italy and down through Hungary to Constantinople. When we leave I will ask the ships' captains to return for you but you must negotiate your own terms for the crossing, I have no money to pay for you. God be with you.'

That statement gathered some angry looks and some hostile mutterings, but my purpose and priorities were clear; I had an army to deliver to the shores of Asia. Pilgrims had no part in the planning of my mission; they must fend for themselves for I could not be diverted.

On the eve of departure, with the fleet of *knörrir* already gone to sea and on their way to Cyprus, the remaining *dromoni* had been loaded with stores ready for tomorrow's sailing. Only my men and horses were yet ashore.

The departure was to be accompanied by a deal of merriment with flags, trumpets, and a grand procession to the quayside where we would receive a blessing. I was chatting with Payne and Ragenaus, finalising the loading arrangements for our horses, when Stephen's squire came dashing up from the harbour.

'My lord,' he cried as he approached, 'come quickly, the pilgrims have gone mad.'

Running down to the harbour, which comprised a horseshoe beach enclosed by two piers, we saw a commotion on the beach opposite.

The unseaworthy *knörr* had been pushed back into the water by a mob of the poor, who were determined not to be left behind. They had waited all winter in great hardship to continue their journey, and now that they could see my ships ready to set sail the hapless pilgrims would not be left standing on the beach.

It was clear to any observer that the vessel, apart from being unseaworthy, was grossly overloaded. Stephen grabbed me by the arm.

'Look!' he cried, 'what are they doing? The captain of our fleet said that ship was fit only for firewood.'

Philip shouted. 'They've got some horses on board, my lord... Fools!'

Stephen shouted to one of Roger's officials.

'Stop them! Make them come back, the ship is unsafe.'

The official shouted instructions to one of Roger's *capitani* and he sent a small rowing boat across the harbour after the creaking vessel.

It was too late. Aboard the creaking ship the two bony horses they possessed had broken loose from their flimsy restraints and were running amok on the deck. The passengers and motley crew panicked and ran to the bows and stern, leaving the animals in the middle. The vessel was now severely stressed – so when it met the first swell in the entrance to the harbour, it quite simply broke in two.

All on board were cast into the winter-chilled waters, drowning before the eyes of the horrified spectators. We were helpless. They were too far out of the harbour to reach in time to save them and we could only stand and watch as one by one the heads bobbing in the waves disappeared from view. Then, when the rescue boats reached the harbour mouth, we watched dismally as the crews began the task of fishing bodies out of the water. Later in the day bodies began to wash up on the beach and the grisly task of gathering them continued. Not many souls were saved and many had perished.

An enterprising priest, upon examining a corpse, was surprised to find that it bore the marks of an injury in the form of a cross. He therefore declared that the soul had been *chosen,* as a sign of divine approval, and that all such travellers would be similarly accepted into heaven if they continued on their way. Much relieved by this prediction the trumpets were sounded, the blessing given, and my fleet set sail later than planned.

When we had cleared the harbour and settled down into our ninety-mile voyage, I turned to Stephen, who was clearly still shocked.

'What was all that about, Stephen?' I ventured to ask.

'I don't know. I cannot see any divine guidance in that event.'

'Neither can I. Do you think it was true? About the crucifixes on the dead?'

'I don't know. I didn't see any, did you?'

'No, but I never inspected the bodies.'

Stephen muttered, 'Do you think it was a sign?'

Philip spoke. 'It was sign of drowning.'

Arnulf clucked at him and muttered a prayer.

'I never did like the sea,' grumbled Allen.

We turned our gaze to the horizon and wondered – while Arnulf of Chocques and Fulcher of Chartres scribbled notes on their parchments.

The landing in the bay north of Durazzo was less than impressive, so it was just as well that it was unopposed.

Back in Brindisi we had disassembled all the baggage train carts and stowed the parts wherever we could fit them between all the other stores. Wooden stocks and rope restraints had been constructed for the horses, and passengers were left to squeeze in wherever they could; it wasn't comfortable but it was only for a few hours, and for the greater glory of God.

We reached our destination to find there were few proper landing jetties and our ships were forced to come as close to the beach as possible to throw most of their cargo into the waters, where it was collected by men who had jumped into the water and half swum, half waded ashore. We ended up with vessels and stores scattered along the beach for nearly a mile. By the time that we'd matched everything up we had been descended upon by local officials, including the mayor, who seemed to think he was the emperor, and a workforce from Alexios' imperial organisation – too late to help.

Their first news was that we had missed one-eyed Raymond's group – he had turned right at Venice, but instead of following the obvious well-worn route into Hungary, had spent weeks wandering down the sparsely populated and unfriendly Dalmatian coast.

They had arrived at Durazzo starving, diseased, and with dead and wounded brought about by encounters with various bands of unfriendly natives along the way.

Stephen looked at Philip.

'Don't you dare say it.'

Philip just smiled, so I said it for him.

'Round in circles, wasn't it?'

'Mmm,' he replied, suppressing a smirk.

'Well!' said Stephen, 'at least Aethilheard's horses would have no competition for fodder.'

'No,' I agreed, 'a one-eyed plus. What else?' I asked the Byzantine mayor, 'what of Bohemund? Has he reached Constantinople?'

'No, my lord,' was the reply, 'he is in camp near Roussa, north of Alexandroupolis, with his nephew, Tancred of Hauteville.'

Allen voiced some suspicions.

'What is he up to? Why has he not gone to the emperor? Are you certain that this southron, Bohemund, is as sound a friend as you supposed, Robert?'

'I don't know,' I answered. 'Perhaps he and his father have tried to take too much land from the Greeks in the past to trust Alexios' intentions.'

'Huh! Some emperor if he cannot guard his domain,' he said. 'What else, fellow?'

'Godfrey of Bouillon arrived at Constantinople in December.'

'Hah!' cried Stephen, 'at least something proper has happened.'

As we made to walk off and get properly organised, the official made one last comment.

'There are reports of a group of strange horsemen. They arrived behind Godfrey, and no one knows who they are.' I looked at him and smiled. 'They are reported as very hairy, with large mustachios, they are armed with great bows and have more horses than they need.'

'Ah! Thank you for your information,' I said happily.

'I wonder if Flanders has reached them,' said Allen.

'Probably. We still have hope then, my friends; we can move a step further. Now mount up and let's see what this emperor looks like, eh?'

I made ready at the head of the column with my knights in close company; the baggage train was protected in the centre of the column with Stephen and Allen's troops bringing up the rear. Archers were sent out riding as scouts. Thanks to the acquisitive activities of our Italo–Norman cousins over the years, the presence of Normans on Byzantine soil was viewed with suspicion, and although under the protection of the emperor, I thought it wise not to leave anything to chance.

Thus with our imperial guides we set off along the Via Egnatia, towards the capital of the Eastern Empire, Constantinople – five hundred miles away.

As is often the case, expecting trouble begat none and the journey became endless day after endless day and those mounted became sick of the sight of the backs of their horses' necks, and those a-foot trudged along watching the ground unroll before them.

I had developed a system to ease the journey of the foot soldiers. With me in the vanguard I took a couple of wagons with sufficient stores in them to set up a camp for the foot-weary, and each evening when they caught up with the riders they would find a campsite with food set up ready and waiting for them: this was a great boost for morale and it led to much quicker march times than was the norm.

This, perversely, did not improve my own contentment, as I filled the time up with doubts of my making; how could I expect Sibyl to wait for me, silly old sod that I was; and then Tegwin kept invading my head in the way she invaded every room she entered, putting me on edge wondering what she was going to do next; she might give someone a tongue-lashing or drag me off by the tunic for a quick purge of the urges. Sibyl did not enter the room like that, Sibyl glided and everyone watched with open mouths. Matilda kept her place. That last meeting was neither expected nor unexpected, it was what it was, natural, a normal which needed no comment. It was by the same token *well planned*. Nothing that Matilda did was without thought, and I wondered if perhaps I was wrong to contemplate marriage to Sibyl; was not Matilda, after all, the natural haven of my life?

All these thoughts were chasing through my head as I plodded further and further away from all the things that I considered important.

Alexandroupolis came and went and we lost sight of the sea for a few days until we came to the shores of the Sea of Marmara, which we followed ever eastward. One afternoon I halted when land came into view on the horizon to our right and called to a guide to explain.

'That is Asia, my lord. The sea appears to block our path but when we get closer you will see the entrance to the Bosporus strait open before us and soon we will see the city of Constantinople.'

'Then tell me when it comes into view.'

One more night and one more day's travelling ensued before that happy event, when he called out, pointing ahead.

'There, my lord.' I saw a headland some miles away. 'That hill is at the end of a promontory. You can make out the great church of Hagia Sophia, the Holy Wisdom; you may know it in Latin as Sancta Sophia. The city is to the left of the church and below, on the water's edge, is one of the emperor's palaces, the Boukoleon. He has a new one across the peninsular named the Blachernae, and he prefers that one, but still uses both. Soon we will see the city walls.'

As we progressed I discerned a line in the distance. It stretched right across before us from the edge of the sea until it disappeared over the far horizon, going who knows where. It became ever more distinct as we neared, and I could see that it was *the* wall. A wall which stretched from the sea and onwards over the hill to our left; a wall which then developed castle towers at intervals; a wall which, when we reached the base, glowered down upon our heads.

We had, at last, arrived at the gates of Constantinople. It was the second week of May, 1097, and the walls were as high as the battlements of Bamburgh castle on top of their dark cliffs, and they stretched out of sight guarding the city.

'The wall of the old Roman emperor Theodosius. Five Roman miles long, from sea to sea it cuts off the promontory and is about six hundred years old,' informed my guide. 'There is another wall within but that is only two and a half miles long. This wall continues around the edge of the sea with its feet in the water so the city is completely encircled.'

I said nothing. I felt very small in front of this depiction of history.

The guide pointed to my right. 'Over there, my lord, you will find your advance party down by the sea, enjoying themselves no doubt. Now I must go and report your arrival to the emperor.'

Looking up at the top of the great wall I supposed that among the many heads peering over it, one of them at least would have sent that particular message. So I headed off down the slope towards the beckoning sea.

There was a great reunion; Aethilheard with hundreds of horses, and Robert of Flanders with most of the news. My advance party proved to be invaluable, they had secured a good site and when the main group arrived we slipped easily into the prepared encampment.

Later, my leaders gathered in Rob's *chapiteau,* a grand canvas hall set up for my use. Tonight we would use it for a feast and a briefing; this was to be a joint event hosted by Rob and Aethilheard.

Rob began. 'There is much to get through and I will let Aethilheard begin. He has had an easy passage, as he will tell you.'

'Aye, Prince Robert, it was better than we expected. You know our route, we were lucky to pass Venice before the French, and had no difficulty finding fodder. It was only when we joined the route down through Hungary at Szeged that we encountered problems. We found that we were following Godfrey of Bouillon, and that fodder had become expensive, and that is where most of our money was spent.

'We lost only twenty animals, but bought some sturdy ponies along the way so we actually have more animals than we started with. Each archer led one of those purchased, which amounts to about two hundred remounts here in Constantinople, and of course what your lady, Matilda, can gather in Cyprus. I have sent my two hundred horse wranglers directly there to take control of the new steeds and start any necessary training with them. Is that in order, my lord?'

'I think that you have done well, Aethilheard. How many languages have you gathered along the way?'

'Not many, but I can point in three.'

We all laughed at that but it was a serious point. If we were to venture beyond the boundaries of Europe we would need to learn some skills in local negotiations, if we were not to lose money in trading.

I looked at Rob.

'Well, Rob, how are you going to amuse us?'

Flanders smiled. 'That will depend upon your sense of humour.'

'Very well,' I replied, 'try us.'

Flanders cleared his throat and shuffled some notes; I could see that he was intending to make the most of it.

'When Godfrey of Bouillon turned up here he was taken straight inside the city to see Alexios, then Bohemund suddenly appeared out of the hills and went in after him. It's been reported that inside they argued with the emperor about who should be the supreme leader. Alexios had his own ideas about that and would not support one over the other. Bohemund, who had previously been regarded as an enemy of Alexios, offered peace and was showered with gifts, and then they all took an oath of allegiance to the emperor. When Raymond arrived he confronted the other two and demanded that he should be the one supreme leader – and refused the oath. It's also rumoured that later, Bohemund tried to get both Godfrey and Raymond to form an alliance with him against the emperor.'

Stephen interjected. 'If all these princes have arrived, then how is it that we seem to be the only ones here?'

'Yes, where is everybody?' asked Philip.

'Alexios feared that there were too many powerful armies near him, and had them all shipped over the Bosporus to get them away from his city.'

'And they went without argument?' I asked.

'More than that, Robert, he gained from them a pledge of loyalty and an agreement that any site they freed from the Turks would become a part of his domain.'

Stephen was sceptical.

'And he believed them? With Bohemund's history of aggression?'

'I don't know, but he reminded them that they were here on the pope's business.'

I responded to that with my own observation.

'Did they remind him that it was he who asked for help in the first place?'

'Well, he showered them with gifts before they left – as a gesture of goodwill... Oh yes. You have heard about Peter the Hermit?'

'And his band of paupers?' added Allen.

'Yes, what of them?' I asked, not entirely interested.

'They went over the Bosporus and got themselves slaughtered. The emperor got the other leaders excited about that and it helped him to get them across to seek revenge.'

'So how long have they been gone?' asked Payne.

'Their horse shit is still warm,' was the response.

'So the hermit is dead?'

'No,' answered Flanders, to the surprise of all. 'He had crossed back over to ask the emperor for more protection. He has joined Godfrey.'

'A clever hermit,' grunted Allen, 'whatever next.'

This was worrying news; a venture such as this needed as its first priority strong leadership. This was not a quality very much in evidence so far, and the fact that the leaders of the largest groups, Raymond and Godfrey, both thought they had the qualities necessary to lead was doubly worrying. Apart from Bohemund, only I had any experience of generalship – and with Bohemund's motives suspect it did not bode well for the future of the expedition.

I looked at Rob.

'Have we come all this way to join an unseemly squabble?'

'I have been thinking about the position for a few days now and may have an approach we can try. There is an invitation from Alexios for you to go and visit him when you are comfortable: let us go and see what he has to say. If I were to ask a question it might be, *why are you not taking charge of the campaign yourself?* He will be the greatest benefactor.'

'That is seemly and just,' said Stephen.

'Seemly my arse,' spat Allen, 'we can do without seemly, we want certainty.'

'Oh! And he won't allow any large groups into the city, they have had enough of northern soldiery – holy warriors or not, they are better in small doses.'

'So what are we going to do with this lot?' Stephen waved his arm at the camp. 'They'll expect something to occupy themselves, and if they're barred from the stews we might expect trouble.'

Flanders had the answer.

'If they want to visit the many fine churches inside the city they may go in small groups. For other, erm, entertainment, the emperor will allow a market and some private tents to be set up outside the walls, with your permission, Robert.'

'No problem, just make sure that the entertainments are clean. I don't want any soldiers going down with drip-dick.'

'Very well,' said Flanders, 'I'll have the *chirurgien* speak to the men and inspect the women.'

There was a polite cough from the direction of my chaplain, Arnulf, who was scuffling about on the fringe of our meeting. I looked at him.

'Was that a cluck of discontent, good priest?'

'We are on a holy mission, my prince. This, er, obsession with the flesh is unseemly.'

'Unseemly!' laughed Allen, 'tis unseemly good, Arnulf.'

'Arnulf,' I said gently, 'these men are about to risk their lives for the greater glory, there will be violence; let them be reminded of gentler things before they die.'

Fulcher took Arnulf by the arm. 'Come, brother, there are things that we do not understand, let us leave these good men to their arrangements.'

And that was the end of that.

'Now, Rob. I want you to set off after Bohemund and the other squabbling princes and get close enough to observe their political dancing – I'll see you when we get over the Bosporus.

91

Allen, will you go with him, cast your gloomy eye over these fellow travellers?'

'By God's bollocks I will, I want to see what we've got ourselves into, Robert.'

'Sounds good to me,' laughed Rob, 'I'm at the forefront again.'

Allen agreed. 'Yes, I want to meet this Bohemund; we'll see who frightens who. I'll keep you a place at the campfire.'

'Thank you, friends. Make certain that it is a peaceful fire and take care. Philip!'

'Lord?'

'You go with the *chirurgien* and inspect the women; you know where to look, don't you?'

Philip blushed a little. 'I'll take advice, my lord.'

'Yes, and while you are about it find out what the proper rates are, we don't want any disputes over fees – and no violence. Any man who offers violence to any woman will be sent home with a squeaky voice.'

'Of course, my lord, I'll brief the captains.'

'Good. Now, about this visit, what shall we wear, Stephen? Robes or armour? What will make the best impression, eh?'

In the end we settled for soft robes with short swords belted to our sides, and no helms – a compromise that sent a message of peace. I sent Arnulf to the head of our procession. He held a longsword aloft as a symbol of the cross and as Ragenaus and Payne waved our emblems, as proud as any, we set off for the imperial palace to meet Alexios, Emperor of the East.

Being next to the sea, and close to an enormous gate, we expected to enter the city through it, but our guide led us up the hill to another gate on the crest. Gate was a poor word for such a mighty construction, more a castle with a hole in the middle than anything. 'This is the second gate,' he informed us. 'The one nearest the sea is the Golden Gate, used only by the emperor.'

'How many gates are there?' Allen asked what everyone wanted to know.

'The wall was mostly constructed in the first years of the fifth century, and there are fourteen gates along its four-mile length.'

'God's miracles!' uttered Payne, 'there are a fair few bricks in this wall.'

We processed through the tunnel of a gate and I began to view my small party as akin to a few ants beneath the feet of Alexios and wondered why on earth he had asked for help in defending the Eastern Empire from the predations of the Turks. This dwarfed anything that we had ever seen in our lives before – and it grew as we entered. Although the walls had a practical purpose defensively, as architecture they would make a lasting impression on any visitor. Larger than any city in Europe, Constantinople cried out wealth and opulence on a grand scale, and left my band of warriors in awe.

Stephen found his voice.

'Robert, you know your father's palace at Caen?'

'Don't! Don't state the obvious,' I said, 'it makes my castle at Rouen look like a wooden hut in a field.'

Payne gave voice to my own thoughts.

'If Alexios controls all of this… why does he need our help? He has more men on the walls than we have brought with us.'

'Aye,' responded Stephen, 'what game is he playing?'

'A big one,' I mused, 'bigger than we had imagined.'

Arnulf thought to venture an explanation.

'I'm not certain, but I fear that Urban's crusade is just the opportunity that Emperor Alexios has been looking for.'

I dragged my eyes away from the teeming wealth of the endless road we were riding along, straight and wide in the Roman fashion, and everyone busy at something or other on both sides.

'What opportunity does this offer the emperor, my thoughtful priest?'

'What we have learned is…' Arnulf needed to drag his eyes away from the front of some houses, festooned with colourful banners, and women peering out of the windows – eyeing up clients perhaps. To remove any doubt one dropped her top and poor old Arnulf nearly fell off his horse. 'Is that… humph, er, Alexios is surrounded by enemies. He may have neutralised some by letting the Christian armies enter his territory. But the Turks are still at his borders.'

Stephen could see the sense in that.

'So if we go and liberate Jerusalem from the Turks?'

'It frees up his army to defend his domain,' said Philip, 'and distracts Bohemund from *his* territorial ambitions.' Young Philip was learning about politics.

'The same ambitions that his father Robert Guiscard was pursuing when he died,' added Stephen.

My own thoughts tumbled around my head. *No wonder William wanted me to marry Matilda. That would have worried Alexios; a Norman empire big enough to challenge him.*

We rode on for another mile along the seemingly endless road named Via Mese, and I churned that idea in my head. Then we topped a rise and the heart of the city came into view. It was dominated by the sight of the great church at the end of the peninsular, the Church of the Holy Wisdom, Hagia Sophia. The stews were left behind as we neared and the houses became grander, each with its own courtyard. When we reached the district of supreme power in that glorious city, with the enormous Hippodrome on our left and the Church of the Holy Wisdom to our front, we paused. From this vantage point we could see the blue seas that almost surrounded the city, and here the full panorama was revealed. It would be difficult to live in a place like this, as its ruler, and not feel important, even special – and concerned lest someone wanted to take it away from you.

After a moment or two of gawping, our guides invited us to continue. 'We go to the palace, my lord.' And we turned away from the Hippodrome and down the hill towards the sea, where we came to an entrance into the Boukoleon Palace.

Riding alongside yet another high wall protecting this private place, we came to another of those tunnel gates and passed through into a cloistered garden, where many gardeners were tending the trees and plants. Passing through another arch we came into a smaller garden and were invited to dismount.

Philip called from the rear, 'There's some people coming behind us picking up the horseshit!'

'God!' muttered Peverel, 'they'll have bags on the horses' arses next.'

The guide remained where he was, and a new, grander figure presented himself. Opulently dressed in flowing silks with a high hat and a golden staff in his hand, he bowed.

'Prince Robert, welcome to the Boukoleon Palace of Emperor Alexios Komnenus. The emperor will be pleased to greet you in his receiving hall. Please follow me.'

From where we were we could see a series of terraces with wide steps leading down towards the sea. As we descended we passed through a series of courtyards, each more opulent than the last, with marble tiles on the floors, frescoed walls, and perfumes emitted by the profusion of plants all around; plants suspended from ropes, fixed to walls and growing in boxes, and tended by dozens of gardeners.

I became uncomfortable; overwhelmed by it all and not at all certain that my clothing was suitable.

Stephen voiced his thoughts.

'I hope that Adela never hears about all this, she'll want some changes at home.'

'Well,' I told him, 'leave the detail out of your letters.'

Standing before a door, which seemed to be the entrance to the receiving chamber, we were asked for our short swords, and it was indicated that Payne and Ragenaus would have to wait here. They were taken to one side where some trays with drinks were offered and I left them quite happy.

Finally we made it inside to the seat of power in the Eastern Empire.

It was a very grand hall. Silks and gold ornaments abounded, the floor was covered with marble mosaic pictures, fountains played amid an abundance of scented blossom and I almost halted to take in the opulence of the place – but a voice called to me from the far end of the room; it was the emperor.

'Robert of Normandy, you are most welcome, come near.'

The imperial court watched closely because this meeting would settle, in public, the relationship being set by the emperor between me and his own administration.

It was settled in an instant, due to Matilda's insistence on diplomacy, and my ability to measure a man.

'Your imperial majesty.' I had not said anything like that before, so I gave him a nod to go with it, but found it difficult not to smile. Something pleasant must have lit my eyes however because he stood up and came down the steps towards me. He was an impressive sight in his trappings, but as we neared I could see that he was in fact a very slight man with a sad expression and a lined face.

'Prince Robert.' The nod of respect was returned by him. He would, by now, know a lot about me from his various sources, and he had evidently made up his mind as to how to deal with me. Now he wanted to get down to business. 'Please introduce your companions. I am certain that I have heard of them.'

So it was that the priests, Arnulf, Fulcher, and Stephen of Blois were brought into the radiance of an emperor for the first time, and made surprisingly proper mumbles, I thought; *well done*.

'I would talk with you in private, Prince Robert, there is much to discuss and I have things to say which are for your ears only. Despite my walls this city seems to leak information. Perhaps we should close the gates to all, except, of course, that I have an empire to rule.' He laughed and motioned us to follow our grand guide.

We were led into another, smaller chamber, and this one was special. As I entered my eyes were drawn across to the far side. It was all windows, great tall and wide windows, all with a view across the sparkling blue sea. Forgetting my manners I walked directly across and peered out. I could see the waters of the Bosporus lapping up against the bottom of the walls and there were ships in the harbour, with a pharos standing tall at the end of a pier. Alexios, now behind me, coughed politely.

'Raise your eyes, Prince Robert, and you will see Asia across the sea.'

'I'm sorry, majesty, it is a rare view.'

'It has its attractions. But over it lies danger, over it lie our problems.'

'With which, imperial majesty, you would appreciate some help, I understand?'

Standing close he fixed me with his eyes. I was examined, I am certain that he was searching for honesty, which, for me, was not a problem.

'You are direct, Robert of Normandy. Let us talk directly then.'

I knew then that we would get some honesty into the conversation, once away from prying eyes.

To begin with we discussed my own journey, as a matter of politeness, but really I think he was probing me, testing to see how far he could trust me. After a while, and some delicious *sherbets*, a new delight to me, he took time to explain about the meetings he had held with my forerunners, and of the agreements that had been made with them.

Alexios wanted assurances about the liberated lands. He made it clear that any of his cities cleared of the Turkish Moslems would automatically be re-absorbed into the imperial domain, and that the question of governorship of those places would be subject to his desires.

He wanted me to understand the distinction between the liberation of an *idea* – Christianity; and the liberation of *place* – a city. These were different in his view, and so he sought my assurances that the principle was understood and accepted by me.

I was not troubled by those ideas, and now Arnulf and Fulcher, overcoming their initial silence, gave voice to their acceptance of this philosophy.

Arnulf was quite clear in his support.

'We can assure your majesty that we came here in support of all our Christian brethren and their liberation from the excesses of the pagans – not in pursuit of lands.'

Fulcher was also quick to grasp the distinction.

'You must know, majesty, that Roger of Sicily has the island settled under Christian control, with Moslem lords as his vassals, and that all can pursue their vision of God as they wish. I am certain that this is the kind of administration that we would all wish for the Holy Lands south of here.'

'Indeed,' said the emperor, 'that is a wise way. It is to be desired that those who are on their way to Jerusalem in advance of you will hold to the same principles.'

Alexios seemed content with our attitude, although reports had suggested that he'd found others, to whom he referred as *the Franks*, particularly Raymond and Godfrey, less amenable, and most especially Bohemund, about whom he himself expressed some doubts.

'You know the man, Prince Robert?' he said, 'and of our history with his father?'

'I know of it, majesty. His father, Robert Guiscard, has invaded your territories in the past.'

'Indeed, and now I have given the son permission to march across them. Do you think that was wise, Prince Robert?'

'Wise, majesty? I know not much of wisdom but I know that it is necessary. Our purpose is beyond mere land, majesty; our purpose is to do with beliefs, surely.'

He looked at me intently. 'Not wise? Robert of Normandy, that is doubtful. It could be that you are too trusting, and that,' he emphasised, 'is a kindness too far for an emperor. There is however one kindness that I hope that you will accept?' He looked at me and I nodded. 'I will give you a team of advisors. You will find that the Turks you encounter across the water have weapons and tactics different from your own. Heed my people's advice and you will learn much, you may indeed learn how to adapt to a different kind of warfare from that to which you are accustomed. Will you accept, Prince Robert?'

'Gladly, majesty, I will take all the help that I can get.'

He only allowed us a few more moments of his time, and although he remained polite, the shufflings of his ministers soon indicated that it was time for us to leave. I was quite happy that I had no different purpose from Alexios. My only intent was the stated one: I was on my way to Jerusalem, and when it was free I would return to Normandy, and that was all that was in my mind when he held out his hand and we parted on good terms.

We stayed within the palace for two weeks more. We were given a team of advisors from the emperor's staff, and took advantage of all the experience and intelligence that they had to offer. This was unlike the earlier crusaders who, we were told, had spent much of their time arguing about whom was to be the expedition leader. As far as I could discover, that issue remained unresolved and, it seemed, we were unlikely to find out until we had caught up with the army already advancing on the other side of the Bosporus.

The biggest problems would occur after we had made our way south from the city of Nicaea, when our main supply routes into Syria and beyond would begin to stretch. The strategy that I had already been planning for, replenishment by sea along the Mediterranean coast, and in particular from Cyprus, was reinforced in my mind. This was the obvious place to site my supply base. Alexios' advisors agreed, and I continued to plan on that basis.

As a small reminder of how complex matters where likely to become once we had crossed into Asia, I was informed that Nicaea was in Turkish hands and that the advance armies were already in the process of attacking that city.

Stephen laughed, 'We are late to the fray, Robert, will there be other cities left for us to attack?'

'God's miracles, Stephen, we only came here to seize the one, how many others do you want?'

'One would suffice, but do we have a choice?'

'I know not. We shall find out in good time, I fear.'

5. Into Asia.

We left the palace and made our way back to our camp by the shore of the Sea of Marmara, about a five-mile trot through the city, and perhaps our last opportunity to witness a civilisation that had its beginnings deep in the mists of time.

From our vantage point we could watch the myriad of ships entering and leaving the narrow waters of the Bosporus. Most were traders by their appearance; Arab, Genoese, some European, and occasionally we watched jealously as multi-oared galleys sped by, no doubt on the emperor's business.

Within two days of our return to camp the transport ships promised by the Byzantine emperor arrived at a landing place nearby. We had lost the sun and the waters seemed gloomy. It somehow matched our mood; we all knew that this was the end of our journey on friendly soil, and that when we landed on the shore opposite we would be entirely alone as we played out our destiny.

Aethilheard was first to embark and eventually we completed the loading of our skittish stallions. They were reluctant to leave the land so we tied them in tight: it was only a crossing of a mile but we could not risk any breaking free. He left under sodden sails with his men standing on the sides of the vessels to keep their animals pacified.

Then we loaded everyone else and soon we were, a fleet of arks, in languid pursuit; very biblical, I thought. When we landed we would be complete as a formation, ready for action for the first time, and the task would begin in earnest. Our first engagement with the enemy now loomed large in our thoughts.

We were put ashore at Civetot, on the southern shore of the Sea of Marmara. This was now safely in the hands of the Byzantines but it was near the scene of that great calamity: the massacre of Peter the Hermit's paupers. News of this hadn't billowed across the sea while we wintered in Italy and it came as a shock when we reached Asia. The pilgrims' remains had been cleared by the time we passed by, but we soon encountered a disturbing scene. To the south of Nicomedia we came upon the remains of the slaughter of the German knights who were supposed to have been the deluded pilgrims' escorts.

The people's crusade had crossed the Bosporus against the advice of the emperor, convinced that their belief in their cause was sufficient protection from the Turks. Then, with a core of five hundred German knights and many thousands of poorly or unarmed supporters, they set themselves up in a camp near Civetot and immediately proceeded to lay waste to the surrounding countryside.

There was no discipline in that horde and no respect for anyone or anything across the water; so convinced of their righteousness were they that they thought they could behave without consequence. Peter, evidently worried about the weakness of the escort, went back to Constantinople to ask for more troops. While he was away there was a predictable response by the Turks lurking nearby, and in October, after several actions, the main body of the German army was trapped and destroyed in a narrow valley – following which the camp itself was set upon by the Turks who in turn laid waste to the women and children who had been left behind.

Alexios told me that he estimated more than twenty thousand pilgrims had met their deaths there.

Now, after three days, we had reached that valley and encountered the detritus of the German annihilation. It was gloomy, and with vultures circling overhead there was an unwelcoming atmosphere. There were steep cliffs on our left and to the right about one hundred and fifty paces of rough ground before the tree line provided any cover. Evidence of the carnage, hundreds of skeletons, lay undisturbed, and none of us thought to count and refute the total of the dead.

'My God!' said Stephen, 'how many of these Turks were there that they could inflict such destruction?'

'I don't know,' I said, 'but we need to be at our best from here on, it seems to be no place for the casual visitor.'

Young Philip said nothing, but gulped and tightened his hand around his sword.

Aethilheard pulled up his horse and called to me.

'Prince Robert, can we stop a moment? I want to look at something.' He dismounted, and leaving his horse with a squire left the track and made his way through the sea of bones towards the trees. The bones were not only of soldiers, many were of their horses; he stood and looked carefully at the gruesome sight, then beckoned.

Stephen got down and walked over to join him. The two had a discussion and returned to the column.

Stephen looked up at me.

'All of the remains have arrows in or near them, including the horses. These knights have been defeated by archers hidden in the trees.'

'Yes,' added Aethilheard, 'those closest to the trees have all died on the spot, they all have the remains of several arrows in among their bones. These nearest the track,' he gestured, 'have certainly been wounded, and if not killed directly by arrows, have been despatched by the sword.'

He walked back and disturbed some of the skeletons.

'See! This one has the skull cracked open by a blade, this one has no arm, and there is a broken blade in the ribs of this one.'

I could envision it; the column of horsemen ambushed from the cover of the trees, many wounded or killed and then the fatal charge towards the trees and the knights mown down by a hail of projectiles from archers whom they would not be able to close with and destroy. Then, when the charge had been decimated, the enemy would have left the cover of the trees to seek out and despatch the wounded. We'd been told that only those lagging behind had escaped to tell the tale.

I was uneasy.

'Archers! It seems, my friends, that they are competent in archery. I was told that they fought mounted, but not here it would seem.'

Stephen expressed his view.

'Probably not for this attack; it was an ambush from the trees, with their horses hidden. But you said that they'd attack as cavalry, in the open.'

I voiced my doubts. 'I need to question Alexios' men again, but we must take it that they are prepared to fight dismounted. If they move these archers independently from their cavalry we must take precautions to protect our riders from their weaponry, or else we will be destroyed before we can sink our lances into their chests.'

When Aethilheard inspected the remains of the arrows, he also measured the distance to the trees.

'I think that they only have a range of up to two hundred paces, and the missiles are quite light, as we can see; they will not penetrate your chain mail from a distance. I think that we can out-range them.'

'Aye, Aethilheard. But what numbers have they?' We all wondered about that.

The Byzantine guide provided by Alexios had been riding ahead but now came back to join us to see why we'd stopped. I asked the questions, and received the answers I'd not wanted to hear.

'Yes, Prince Robert, usually they do fight from horseback, and their army has many thousands of them. You must understand that they are mounted archers first and foremost; they will only come close to an enemy when they have first decimated them. They prefer to catch the enemy in the open and encircle them. They will weaken resolve by riding in a circle shooting arrows into the mass until the time is right for an overwhelming charge, and then they become cavalrymen, as you know it. They are a dangerous foe, my lord.'

That was warning enough, and had been missing from our talks with Alexios' men at Constantinople; perhaps it was too obvious to them. Aethilheard's scouts would now have to operate a wide screen to locate possible ambush sites and be wary of approaching archers. The remaining miles to Nicaea would be very long ones indeed.

There was a sense of foreboding as we rode along and out of that grisly defile; this was not going to be a long horse ride along the coast to Jerusalem, this was going to be an advance against an opponent who could hurt us, and frustrate, or even prevent our advance. I liked it not.

We discussed tactics as we rode along.

'The emperor might not have warned me about their tactics in sufficient detail, but here is evidence of their flexibility; we must not be lured by them into foolish situations and stay true to our own formations. Aethilheard, send out your scouts but keep your main body close to us, you must stay near to our lances and be ready to deploy in support. We must always work together against this devious foe.'

Aethilheard nodded. 'Yes, lord, our strength lies in our close support for one another. The key is in communications.'

'Aye, and we will bring the women into the centre of our formation together with the wagons. From now on they must be guarded from attack at the front and the rear; there seems to be no mercy shown to pilgrims, men and women alike.'

'Yes, lord,' said Peverel, 'I will make the arrangements.'

6. Nicaea.

The region south of the Bosporus was called Rüm, ruled by a Seljuk Turk named Sultan Kilij Arslan. Nicaea was his chief city, which he had held against all attempts by Alexios to gain. It was too close to the emperor's borders to leave in peace and he had cleverly manoeuvred the crusaders into besieging the place as their first task.

Nicaea was a walled city which lay at the eastern end of a twenty-mile long lake and, as such, it was almost impossible to completely seal off, as Alexios was all too aware, and because of the strength of the defensive walls extremely difficult to assault.

By the time that we arrived all the leading figures that had passed through Constantinople were present outside the city walls; I was the last major prince from Europe to join the direct confrontation with the world of Islam.

I was met by Rob of Flanders and Allen of Brittany who conducted us to the area outside the walls that had been already allocated; we were to fill the gap between Godfrey and one-eyed Raymond. This completed the land cordon, but with no boats at our disposal the city was still accessible by water and this remained a serious weakness in the siege.

'Well, Rob,' I declared.

'Indeed, Prince Robert,' he responded.

'What have you discovered?

Allen answered for the pair.

'I have identified twenty languages and six leaders – seven, now that you have arrived, Robert.'

I looked at Rob. 'And how many tongues do these seven leaders have?'

'You are unique in having only the one: the rest are forked.'

Allen made a gesture. 'Careful, these serpent tongues have many ears.'

I snorted. 'Is this a menagerie or a battlefield?'

'Both!' said Rob. 'While the big beasts fight, the hyenas scavenge and the snakes bite ankles.'

Stephen looked about him as if expecting a lion in the tent.

'All this way and it sounds just like home.'

Young Philip was struggling to make sense of it. 'What's going on? What are you all talking about?'

'Tis politics, my young friend,' I counselled him, 'it seems that not everyone is here on the same mission. Explain it, Rob, if you can.'

Flanders made sense of it.

'It seems that Bohemund is harbouring his father's expansionist schemes; he and his nephew Tancred are together in that. Raymond wants control to frustrate their plans while the emperor sits in Constantinople and watches.'

'Ready to pick up the pieces no doubt,' said Stephen.

There was silence for a moment; then I gave out a sigh and spoke.

'What else, Allen?'

'There are some others here looking for some pickings; mercenaries.'

'Huh!' exclaimed Stephen, 'a false purpose, I believe.'

'It is,' responded Flanders, 'they are a nuisance and can be bought for the price of a loaf.'

'What do you mean?' asked Philip.

'Their loyalty is as fleeting as their full bellies. They tour the camps promising fealty, then do it again elsewhere. There are some well-armed knights at that game; who knows if they will stand and fight if it comes to it.'

I asked, 'Are you suggesting that we should keep our own formations? Not get mixed up with the other groups?'

Rob looked at me. 'I wasn't, Robert, but it's the best idea I've heard so far.'

'All right, we'll go and see what these various princes have to say for themselves. As a matter of interest, how is this siege going?'

He perked up a little; there was positive news among his doubting.

'Not too bad, we've had one engagement and then the city's governor returned to find us at his gates. He was chased off, but he might be back.'

'That was Sultan Arslan, was it?' asked Stephen, 'the one who destroyed the German army?'

'The very same. It seems that his easy victory over Peter's wanderers gave him the wrong impression and he got a bloody nose when he turned up here. Beware their archers, Robert, they sting.'

I looked at Aethilheard and received a half-smile from him.

'Let's see how a full arm of metal-tipped ash will suit their guts,' suggested the Saxon.

Rob told us more about the squabbling Frankish princes.

'There is a sort of war council, but the only thing they've agreed on so far is how to share the spoils; the treasures and booty.'

'What do you mean? Are they petty thieves to scavenge about defeated towns?' I was annoyed.

'They say that it will help to pay for the war.'

'I thought that Alexios was paying for it?'

'He is, but these venal princes want a bonus.'

'All right! Enough of this, I have heard enough. Where is this council held?'

'In Godfrey's camp, nearby. He holds the east wall, Bohemund has the north and Raymond is to the south.'

'Is it a coincidence that I am next to Godfrey, Rob?'

'No, not entirely.' He hesitated. 'I have chosen it for you; I judged that you might be happier with Godfrey over the others. Change it if you want but it would be difficult, with everyone settled in their camps, you see. '

'No, it suits me. I know Bohemund from the past, and like him... as a man. But I know of his ambitions and I want no part of them, they remind me too much of my father's.'

No one responded to that remark. Probably only Stephen and Rob knew what it meant anyway, and they kept silent.

'What about Raymond?' asked Philip.

'Yes, well, I don't want to go round in circles either,' was my flippant reply. 'Seriously, I believe that he's just a bit too old for all this, the action here is merely a beginning. I remind you all of that: there is a lot left in this venture, believe me.'

Fulcher coughed, and held me by the arm. 'Prince Robert, may I remind you of something. This is the place where your grandfather Robert died and was first buried, before your father sent a party to collect his body from the church of St Mary, within the city walls. He was to be taken back to Normandy.'

'Yes, Fulcher, I know about that. I will visit the church when we enter the city.' I told him of my searches in Conversano, but not about anything else.

Although Flanders had spoken of a fractious command structure, the fact was that much had been achieved since the demise of Peter the Hermit's hopefuls. The road that we had travelled down had been developed as the main supply route and supplies were flowing along it in adequate amounts. This was just as well, because the multitudes gathered about the walls of Nicaea were estimated at about seventy thousand souls; we soldiers, some Byzantines and many more pilgrims, all expecting eternal salvation for our trouble.

Soon I received an invitation to join Godfrey and the others for the next great council. This would be presided over by the papal legate, Adhémar of Le Puy, the pope's nominated spiritual leader of the venture.

Godfrey had set up a pavilion to shade the delegates from the sun. It was open-sided apart from one end which was closed off and had various charts and maps suspended against the canvas wall.

As I made my way inside I was greeted by the unmistakable roar of Bohemund.

'Robert! You randy old git, welcome to Valhalla.'

It seemed as if the giant had grown even more since last I had seen him. Control of the hair on both head and face had been abandoned, and his shoulders now seemed as wide as he was tall.

'Bohemund! Have you found happiness here?'

'I have; my sword is wet with blood and we sleep well together. I hear that your sword has tasted another maiden, is that true?'

'No tis not, she remains as I found her.'

'What ails thee? Have you lost desire in your dotage?'

'My touch remains sensitive to a lady's desires, but this one is different. This one I intend to have as my wife.'

'Hah! A wife! Congratulations, Robert. Will not the fair Matilda be disturbed by this? I fear, of all the Italian candidates I had a wager on her... You have cost me money, you bugger.'

'Bugger I am not! And keep your money in your purse, along with your other valuables. And have a care how you refer to the Lady Sibyl, she is high in my affections.'

I wore no smile on my face when I made that remark and Bohemund was sufficiently sensitive to recognise that a line had been drawn.

'Robert, good prince, I wish you well. We all wish you well.' He threw out his arms to embrace me and was shortly joined by the gathered leaders. They all expressed their good wishes to me, a prince of Normandy – and perhaps a little envy that at forty-five I was contemplating marriage to a sixteen-year-old maiden: *here was a man to admire.* I preened like a straw-heap cockerel.

Adhémar called the council to attention. Marriages interested the Church only insofar as their dynastic consequences – he did not wish to see the conversation degenerate into the embarrassing subject of sex.

'My princes! May we turn to the business of the day?' and having gathered them in, commenced with an attempt to enumerate our armies. 'Welcome, Prince Robert. Now that you are here it is time to evaluate our strengths and define our responsibilities, do you not agree?'

'Not before I have met with the good duke, Godfrey.'

Another voice, resonating with authority, imposed itself upon the gathering; Adhémar spluttered and made a bow in the direction of a grand fellow sitting in a grand chair at one side of the pavilion.

'Duke Godfrey of Bouillon, I surmise,' I took the initiative from Adhémar. 'You have the advantage of me. Some time to settle, I see,' said I, looking at his chair.

'Hah! Robert the wit, I have heard of your sharp tongue, I hear that it amuses the ladies.' He smiled, not unkindly, so I took the remark as a friendly opening. 'I had heard, Robert of Normandy, that comforts would be in short supply on this side of the Bosporus, so I decided to bring this old friend along with me so that I might have some relief from the aches of journeying. What d'ye say, young prince, eh?

'I say very wise, Godfrey; what else have you brought to ease your carcass?'

'Oils, unctions, and a soft saddle. We must talk, Robert, later. Get on with it, Adhémar, get on with it.'

'Yes, Adhémar, do that.'

The second command came from an old fellow with a high pitched voice sitting on the opposite side of the pavilion. I presumed this was Raymond, although nobody bothered to introduce me. I thought to go and visit him later, I needed to know what this band of travellers was made of; the tensions were all too obvious. It was not very encouraging.

They all nodded as Adhémar took a parchment from his clerk and spread it upon the table.

'The tally is seven thousand five hundred mounted knights, with thirty-five thousand men-at-arms. These are the numbers which you have reported to me. In addition, Prince Robert has some two hundred mounted archers within his command and as far as I am aware this is the only such force at our disposal... is that true?'

I nodded but qualified the figures.

'The two hundred refers to the most skilled; there are also about two hundred horse wranglers – handlers gone to Cyprus with replacement horses. These are at various stages of archery skill but will be fully trained and increase the numbers available. I was also given horses by the emperor that we can use in a scouting role.'

'Humph!' snorted Bohemund, 'that is more than he gave us.'

Godfrey ignored that remark and expressed his satisfaction at my position, then added, 'We believe that there are a further thirty thousand ancillary troops, lightly armed but mostly inexperienced, which also includes the wagonners, artisans, engineers, cooks, shit-pit diggers and putters-up of tents. Then there are innumerable priests, poets, seekers after eternal life, wives, harlots and hunters of fortune among the camp followers. But you, Robert, by God, you are ahead in this, we had not expected the Turks to use the bow to such effect, they have caused great damage. Perhaps you can return the injury?'

'Perhaps we can,' I agreed, 'there is a need to look at tactics. I assume that Alexios did not mention the matter of the Turkish archers to you? Can I remind you that archers played a great part in my father's invasion of England, on both sides? I was not there but we have been working on the issue ever since, the idea of swiftly moving archers in support of the heavy knights is a matter of some practice to us.'

Bohemund growled.

'I still like the crash of horses into flesh, it is most satisfying.'

'Aye Bohemund, it is... if you can get near enough without becoming pin-stuck like a hedgehog.'

Bohemund brushed down his chest as if ridding himself of a plague of spikes, but he knew the sense of my words.

Old Raymond fixed his eye upon me.

'Can I send one of my captains to meet your captain of archers? I have heard that he is Saxon, is that so?' His voice cackled like an ageing hen, and I wondered at the wisdom of his joining this undertaking – although I knew that he was rich beyond my dreams and probably added something to our assets.

'That is so, and he is a true friend of mine; we have been together for many years now. You may all seek him out for he is very experienced in the subject of killing knights from a distance.'

That quietened my audience for a bit and gave me the chance to take a look round the tent.

Sitting to one side were two Greek noblemen from the court of Alexios; I had been told about them. The first was Manuel Boutoumites. He travelled with Godfrey as an advisor. The second, named Taticius, was a Byzantine general, a eunuch and also a skilled and brave warrior. He was also, unfortunately, short of a nose, which had been cut off in some earlier action; that particular shortfall was covered by a silver plate. He brought with him some two thousand Byzantine troops to boost the numbers gathering outside the beleaguered city.

The Turkish citizens, peering over their walls, should have been seriously worried by now, especially after the rescue attempt by their great sultan, Arslan, had failed.

As the tent had grown quiet, Boutoumites took the opportunity to engage me in conversation.

'Prince Robert! Have you seen the Turkish archers in action?'

Boutoumites was an impressive figure. His fine robes betokened one who was high in the esteem of the emperor, and his finely trimmed beard betokened one who was high in his esteem of himself; nonetheless I held no opinion of the man... yet.

'No, I have only seen the results of their work, near Nicomedia.'

'Ah yes, but do not be distracted by that action, they prefer to work in the open, on the plains. I would like to see your men and speak with your captain – Aethilheard, was it?'

'Of course, he is outside.' I gestured and he left to find the Saxon.

The rest of the council were discussing arrows, but Adhémar recalled them to their present task.

'Duke Godfrey!' he called, 'you have a plan to end this tedious siege?'

'Yes, Adhémar, the riddle is solved; we will attack the fortress from the sea.'

Godfrey looked pleased with himself and sat back awaiting the obvious response.

Bohemund fell into the trap first.

'Hah! The sun has boiled Godfrey's brain: by sea, hah!'

Some laughed, some shifted in their seats wondering what it was they'd missed.

Flanders made the next move.

'Godfrey, the sea that laps at the feet of the fortress is a lake, is it not? Twenty miles long and seven miles wide.'

'Yes! But, we will *portage* some boats across the hills and attack them across the water.'

'*Portage?* What's portage?'

'To carry the boats overland.'

Godfrey stated it simply because it was simple; to completely surround Nicaea, we needed to blockade the walls whose foundations lay in the waters of Lake Askanian.

'Do you not see? We have tried mangonels, which cannot throw rocks either very big or very far; they have ballistae inside the walls, which are bigger and deadlier. We have tried to approach the walls under a *vulpus*, which collapsed, and then a *testudo* to sap under the walls, but that didn't work either. We are reduced to hurling captured Turkish heads over the walls with our pathetic mangonels and yet still we are outside the gates and it is time to try something new.'

Some of the lectured got a bit sniffy by Godfrey's assault on their efforts, but they couldn't deny the truth of it. We could stay there till doomsday, sweating in the sun, while the Turks laughed at us and bathed in their private lake.

Godfrey pressed his point. 'We know that they are receiving supplies by night over the water, so let us use the water against them and bring this boring farce to a swift end.'

There was a lot of muttering and mumbling until I suggested something.

'It can't hurt us to let Godfrey have a chance with his plan. Let him have that chance and take a break from this frustration.'

Bohemund cracked first.

'Well, if this is Godfrey's plan, let him take it on; it was he who promised to capture the city for Alexios "as we were passing," if I recall. Let me know if you need any help, Godfrey, and good luck with your land boats.'

'That is not the whole truth, Bohemund, as you well know. We cannot leave this garrison in our rear; it sits astride the supply routes.'

I was going to introduce my supply-by-sea plans, but lost the moment as the other leaders latched quickly onto Bohemund's suggestion.

They agreed too easily. If Godfrey owned the plan and it failed, then they could all say, *I told you so,* but if it succeeded then they would be a step closer to Jerusalem, at little or no cost to themselves.

Godfrey was pleased, and gestured for me to leave the tent with him. I followed, trailed as usual by my banner-bearing shadows. Of the two, Payne seemed to be attached, so close did he attend me, and at times he blotted out the sun; still, that might be useful if it became any hotter. Ragenaus was not always so obvious; he was difficult to spot at times but always anticipated my needs and appeared as if from nowhere when I wanted him. I was pleased with the two as they had become good friends, and it made things easier for me to manage with such support.

Godfrey told me that he had already set things in motion, and then he took us to see Boutoumites, with whom he had already agreed the outline plan. Taticius was there, which gave me an opportunity to study him. His few remarks, in a very nasal whine, were nevertheless honest and sensible and I found him likable. We had a short discussion and the trio revealed that the Byzantine pair were going to carry out the water-borne invasion of the city. Godfrey would remain here guarding his interests; he was not about to leave Raymond in sole charge.

Boutoumites said that he needed Alexios' permission to do this, and I reasoned that the emperor was now not far away on this side of the sea, although their reluctance to confirm this told me that everyone in this venture was playing their own game.

'What was all that about, my lord?' asked Payne when we left Godfrey.

'That, young fellow, was about as revealing as it can be, about the relationships between these lords we're travelling with.'

'They don't trust each other, Payne,' voiced Ragenaus, 'they all want to be in charge but none of them has much idea about what to do next.'

'I thought that Godfrey said that it was his idea to take to the water,' answered Payne.

'I doubt it,' I said. 'What does Godfrey know about invasions from the sea? The Byzantines are masters at it. If anything Godfrey has been manipulated by our Greek friends.'

'Greek?' questioned Ragenaus.

'Aye, Greeks it was who took over the old town of Byzantium many years ago,' I told him.

The next day I asked Aethilheard what he had discussed with Boutoumites regarding archery, and we set about planning defensive and counter-offensive tactics for use against the Turks, if, or when, it came to confrontation in the open.

Messages came back from Boutoumites in Civetot telling us that the plan was going ahead and that Alexios' shipwrights had now turned their skills to wagon-building, and when they had completed that task they would load their boats onto the new wagons. Then, drawn by oxen, the boat-laden wagons were to set off for the far end of Lake Askanian, a journey of twenty miles from Civetot.

The accompanying force was commanded by Boutoumites. They reached the lake on 17 June 1097, and were kept in a bay only a mile or so away from the city, out of sight. Messages were passed and it was agreed to co-ordinate the assault with a land offensive the very next day; this had now taken two months to prepare and I prayed that it would be successful. We, being cavalry, could only stand and watch.

That morning the appearance of a fleet of unexpected vessels coming down on them, bearing strange banners and flags with warriors blowing horns and shouting, unnerved the garrison, so they let Boutoumites and Taticius into the city by the watergate and negotiated a surrender.

It was a triumph for Alexios. The pair appeared on the battlements in front of us and raised his banners; they had the city, and Sultan Arslan's treasury, safely in their hands.

We never set foot within the walls.

Alexios' cunning had clearly triumphed. At little cost to himself or his troops he had seized Nicaea. Before that several hundred soldiers had died in their futile attempts to breach the walls – and yet they were left with nothing. I thought it unwise, and that he might regret the action later. Inside the city, Boutoumites and Taticius now controlled the Turkish garrison while the far larger Frankish army outside the gates stewed in frustration. It did not augur well for future cooperation between Alexios and we Normans, or the Franks.

If the Frankish leaders were pissed off by this obvious piece of duplicity, their men were doubly so. After so many futile deaths and injuries, they had been looking forward with relish to getting inside and looting the unfortunate city. Deprived of that income they were in open revolt. Alexios, working through his network of agents within our gathering, became all too aware of the situation and resorted to a tactic that was all too familiar to his northern guests – bribery. He simply dished out money, giving away copper coins to the soldiery to calm them. During this distraction the Turkish garrison was allowed to quietly disappear into the night.

The next council of princes was called by Alexios, now camped nearby. I worried that he might lack the powers of persuasion to stem the tide of resentment which had built up over his actions, but I prayed that he would weather this storm because of our holy mission. I walked to his tent in the company of Godfrey, who intended to make his feelings known.

'This is an affront,' he bristled on the way, 'I was supposed to take the city with those boats.'

'Ah well, dear Godfrey, the tides of war and all that.' I grinned at him and he stuck his sword into the ground and twisted it with venom. 'Think on, friend,' I cautioned, 'the emperor is still the commander-in-chief; if he takes a tactical decision then who can gainsay him?'

'True, Robert, true. But if he thinks that I am going all the way to Jerusalem suffering his tactical decisions and becoming poorer by the mile, then he can think again.'

'Then we had better decide on who is to be the general in the field. At the moment we lack a command structure.'

'Humph!' was all I got in return.

If Alexios was to maintain the upper hand, then bringing the squabbling princes together seemed to me a dangerous step; far better to keep them apart, I thought.

When we were all assembled in his camp at Pelekanum, arranged to display all the power of an emperor in its grandeur,

Alexios deployed his considerable skills as a diplomat and managed to avoid a direct confrontation over the siege of Nicaea. He simply stated that we were honour-bound to hand over the city if and when we had taken it, and that goal had been achieved without bloodshed, which was more than *you* Frankish princes had managed so far: end of argument.

His next brazen move was to invite us to renew our oaths of allegiance to him – Raymond, who had somehow avoided this subjection at Constantinople, also found himself a reluctant participant.

'You are all part of the same grand venture,' he stated with all the authority of an emperor, 'therefore you should all be assured of each other's commitment.'

That was clever, I thought, and said so to Allen. 'He has imposed a unity on us. Now everyone has a common cause and oath – like it or not.'

'Aye, he's a clever bugger right enough.'

'And well within his rights, Allen, this is within his territory.'

Then, with the initiative firmly in his grasp, Alexios persuaded the leaders into agreeing the next strategic move – neutralise the city of Antioch. Held by the Turks it lay in our path but might be unwise to leave in our rear as we moved towards Jerusalem.

We agreed a plan of advance. This was to split the army into two groups because of its size, and Alexios gave us some advisors, including Taticius, who could bring only three hundred or so knights with him as the Byzantine foot soldiers were staying behind to garrison Nicaea.

Sensing an opportunity to separate me and mine from the mutual animosity of Raymond and Godfrey, I turned to Allen.

'I'd prefer to join Bohemund now I've had time to see the conditions here; he has more experience in these parts.' Allen nodded so I went over to the giant.

'Can we join you? We have some special skills that you might find useful. If you and I combine our forces we will be approximately one third of the army, will we not?'

'Aye, Robby, I'll be happy in your company,' he said tensely, 'I trust not those two to agree on whether tis night or day. Tell me more about these archers of yours – they are not carrying crossbows, I see.'

'No, I favour the English and Welsh warbows, not the crossbow. They fit my tactical purposes better. I'll tell you more later.'

'Welsh?

'Indeed, friend, Welsh. Let me tell you how the Roman legions fared when they came under the spell of the Welsh bowmen.'

'I look forward to that. Taticius, though? He looks too much like the emperor's ears to me.'

'Yes! That's one thing he's not short of.' Bohemund could hardly stop himself laughing. 'What now, Bohmey?' I asked with a grin.

'It would be too much for me to go off to war with one-eyed Raymond and a eunuch with no nose.'

I saw his point – too many missing orbs.

We fell against each other for support as we staggered away from the grand pavilion of the Emperor of the East.

We were still giggling like girls when Godfrey caught up.

'What in Hades is up with you two maidens?'

Bohemund answered, 'Me and Robby want to revise the order of march, and we don't want to go with Raymond.'

He explained why but the joke slipped by Godfrey as he thought things through.

'I agree. You take the smaller part of the army in advance, and we will move the main force along behind you on a parallel route. That will cause the Turks some puzzlement while they try to work out how many we are and what route we will follow.'

I pointed out that he had agreed to two equal formations.

'Yes, but Alexios pushed us into that. As he's not advancing with us I think that we can decide for ourselves, and your idea is better.' He looked up at Bohemund. 'You and Robert go together, you work well with each other, and take Flanders with you. It will give you the smaller part of the army but it will be more manoeuvrable and you can respond with more flexibility. Take Taticius with you and keep him near, I will have Boutoumites at my side.'

Bohemund added up the forces.

'So you will have your brother, Baldwin; Cyclops Raymond; snotty Hugh of France; and Robert's brother-in-law, Stephen. What about Allen of Brittany?'

'I need to talk with him, he will decide for himself,' I said.

'Yes, if you take the lead we can shadow you from the north on a parallel path. Keep tight communications and we should be safe.'

Bohemund looked at me.

'Yes, I'll accept that. I'd rather have No-balls than One-eye with us, we can keep an eye on his ears.'

The laughter gained control once more, and Godfrey thought it worth a chortle until I said to him, 'Mind you take care of my brother-in-law Stephen. If he comes to harm it's you who'll have to tell my sister.'

'Jesu!' said the startled Godfrey, 'the Conqueror's daughter? I don't want that, you keep him.'

I glanced behind as we set off for our camps. Godfrey was watching with a puzzled expression, perhaps wondering what he had done by agreeing to combine the talents of the shortarse, the giant and the eunuch.

As we wandered along I looked up at Bohemund.

'Now look at what you've done. We could have gone to war with one-eyed Raymond, and instead we're lumbered with nosy No-balls.'

'Shh! don't let him hear you, he might be upset.'

'You think his hearing works then?'

The giant supported himself on my broad shoulders as we staggered along the way, he wiping the tears from his eyes.

There was one final twist to this turn of events. I told Allen of Brittany what we wanted and asked him to go with Godfrey.

'Why can't I come with you two? What are you plotting?'

'I don't want to be entirely ignorant of what Raymond or Godfrey is up to. Go with either, but we need to know what their plans are if they're different from what they're telling us.'

Allen grunted, thought a little, tugged his beard a lot, and then gave out a sigh; I supposed that he'd reached a decision.

'Good plan, Robert. I'd prefer Godfrey, at least I'll know who he's looking at.'

With humour winning the day we were as satisfied as it was possible to be, and so set off along our much interrupted journey.

7. Confrontation on the Hoof.

By the tally our formation now consisted of two thousand cavalry, plus my two hundred mounted archers, and eight thousand foot soldiers; there was also a considerable baggage train with thousands of assorted pilgrims; men, women and children. More children than we'd set off with, it is true, but life goes on.

Thus organised we set off on the next part of our journey to Antioch. I was slow to move off that morning as I had a series of messages to prepare and despatch before leaving Alexios' camp, so lagged behind Bohemund somewhat – but no hurry because before them lay six hundred miles of an increasingly sparse countryside, in an increasingly hot sun, with decreasing water sources and ever lengthening lines of supply: any sane man might not have attempted it, but when on a mission for God – all is possible.

The column had travelled southwards for about fifty miles following a river valley towards the place known as Dorylaeum when trouble came our way near Bozüyük.

On the evening of 30 June I came up to Bohemund's position. He said that his scouts had spotted movement in the hills ahead – which was why he'd made camp. We discussed matters but held off sending word to Godfrey until we knew for certain what lay ahead and instead sent out piquets; they would observe all the possible routes into our camp and warn us of any night-time activities. Periodic reliefs were tasked and the rest of us settled down for a good night's sleep, ready to move on before the dawn.

Our position had a swamp on our right, within a loop in the river; our western boundary. To our left was a scrubby, open area of about half a mile which extended to steep hills; it seemed secure enough, at least until the dawn arrived.

Movement was spotted on the horizon to the south and we began to form a more secure defensive position and sent word back north to inform Godfrey: *we have encountered the Turkish army*.

Our wagons were moved into a semi-circle around the edge of the swamp. The horses, supplies, and non-combatants began to move behind the protection of the wagons, with the swamp and river guarding their backs.

Taticius and his men were placed to the south of the swamp, together with Stephen to safeguard that boundary and watch the river. Flanders' group provided the same protection to the northern edge.

Ranged some two hundred paces from the front of an inner half-circle Bohemund was placing his foot soldiers, his *militis;* they would have a frontage of half a Roman mile. Their shield wall would be supported by Bohemund's *balestriere,* but I considered their rate of fire pitiful compared to my war bows. His cavalry under his nephew, Tancred, was evenly spaced along the length of the infantry defences and I stationed Aethilheard's archers directly behind Bohemund's central position. We completed an inner defensive circle with wagons on the east and the river on the west.

I was holding my cavalry together directly behind Aethilheard when Taticius sent a messenger along the line: as he passed each commander he cried out, 'The forces of Sultan Kilij Arslan!'

Our prime enemy had turned up and it was not long before they made their first move.

There was the sound of thunder in the distance: horses. Then from out of the valleys to the south a cloud of rising dust heralded a stampede of horse-borne archers, they were in loose formation, as if a swarm of bees. Harbingers of death, they galloped towards us at speed. Even after being warned, not all of the rag-tag pilgrims had found shelter behind our lines. Typical of ordinary citizens, and not understanding the urgency of the situation, they continued to mill about getting themselves organised, dragging totally useless items from off the baggage wagons, and made easy meat for the onrushing Turks. By the time these stragglers recognised the danger it was too late and the galloping archers began to pick them off – making targets of their backs as they fled behind our protective lines. Riding by, unleashing a storm of arrows into our shield walls, the Turks rattled us and were gone in a few moments leaving behind carnage and panic among the unarmed Christian pilgrims, and not a few casualties among our armed ranks. This was worrying.

Bohemund had no time for those too slow to take cover as instructed but rightly concentrated on completing his own defensive lines.

Then a second wave galloped down upon us, unleashing yet another arrow shower upon our heads. This screeching horde of Seljuk Turks were bent on revenge for the loss of Nicaea, and on our destruction.

Then, without direction, and unwisely, Tancred led his cavalry out from behind the defensive lines to engage with the Turks as they thundered back down the valley. His disordered men proved easy meat for the loosely formed pagans. Unprotected by our archers and having no coordinated formation, Tancred's men fell, stricken by arrows loosed at them from all sides. The Turks did not seek to engage with hand weapons, content instead to use their bows at close range to deadly effect.

We watched in helpless frustration as wave after wave of the enemy flew by first in one direction and then, reforming out of sight in the dust, returning from the other direction to unleash their deadly hail upon us, taking a dreadful toll especially upon Tancred's men, the disorganised cavalry trying desperately to stem the tide of death in front of the infantry positions – the open ground to our front became littered with the silent dead and crying wounded.

I rode up to the fuming Bohemund.

'What, in God's name, are they doing out there?' My fury erupted at the carnage to the vulnerable horsemen scythed down before us.

Bohemund, incandescent with rage, shouted back.

'It is useless, they ride by with a handful of arrows and can release a dozen in the time it takes to pass by, then they return with another handful of death,' he screamed to make himself heard as yet another wave passed us and the air was filled with the hiss of the deadly missiles.

I screamed back at him. The noise was terrible; apart from the screeching Turks, my ears were assaulted by those horses and men being struck and pinned, and especially by the screaming pilgrims, women and men, trying to hide behind the wagons – it was distracting but there was naught to be done about it.

'We have to hit them with a co-ordinated charge; I'll go and get organised. The next time they pass by, open your lines and I will ride through and make ready to face the next wave.'

Bohemund shouted his consent, and passing orders to his dispirited infantry, sent urgent signals to get Tancred's men back behind his lines.

Soon I had my captains gathered. Protected by a wall of shields and bellowing to make myself heard, I told them quickly what I expected of them.

'Aethilheard, move your men inside the northern sector of the shield wall and keep them safe behind it; when you see that I am ready you know what to do: bring down their horses, and give us a chance to get to grips with them.'

'Aye, my prince, we will prepare them for your lances.'

I faced my captains of cavalry. 'We will go forth from here in two conroys. The next time the Turks go past by we will line up across the valley and watch them disappear into the dust. I will be in the centre of the first conroy; Tancred, bring your men out and line up behind me. You must watch our deployment very carefully and try to match it. We will meet the pagans as they come back down the valley, as we lose our momentum bring forward your line to support us. Do you see your task?'

'I do,' replied the angry youngster, 'leave some for my sword, if you please, Prince Robert.'

'I will,' I promised the perspiring warrior, although I wished that he had the training that my men had undergone. I knew that I needed his troops as a back-up but prayed that I would not.

Mounting my by now decidedly jumpy stallion, I raised my lance and faced my men.

'You wanted to go to Jerusalem, yet we are only halfway there, and these Turks would prevent you. Are you going to let them?'

'NO!' came a great shout from my warriors, such to set the pilgrims off wailing once more.

'Then remember your training, remember your formation, and remember your God – and his son – who died for our salvation, and whose city is defiled by these abominable pagans. Let us about our business. ARE YOU WITH ME?'

'AYE!' came the response, mighty in its fervour, then another great shout, 'Victory for Christ.' And soon we were lined up behind Bohemund's defending screen, assembling into two columns, and I felt the excitement building.

The stallion between my thighs, feeling the frustration of a morning of doing nothing, began to tremble; he knew the signs of impending battle and was reacting. It would be so all along the line of beasts, their ears pricked back and their skin shivering as they dug at the ground, anxious to be off. Here was a mighty weapon about to be unleashed; menacing horseflesh, ridden by men filled to the brim with the spirit of God's purpose. Something titanic was about to happen: this is what we came for.

On the crest of a hill overlooking the valley I could see Arslan and his high command. They were watching, no doubt confident beneath their flags and calling trumpets, no doubt certain that their horsemen would roll easily over us, as they had those hapless pilgrims and those German knights months before.

As the next attack flew by from south to north and disappeared into the dusty distance I rode out from the security of Bohemund's lines and stretched my cavalry across the width of the valley.

Turning to face north in two lines with mine at the fore and Tancred's behind, we formed into ten conroys of ten knights. This was not a normal deployment; I was about to test my theories for the first time in earnest. If I was wrong I would probably die knowing it.

I knew that Arslan's horsemen, in the dust and out of sight, would have turned, replaced their handful of arrows, and set off to come back at the trot, preparing their bows as they advanced.

Anxiously standing in my stirrups I took a look about me to make certain that everyone was ready in their allotted formation, that the lines were straight and the lances held high.

'What say you now, Payne,' I shouted, 'you still want to carry my banner?'

He grinned, it was not pleasant. 'I am, no other.'

'Ragenaus?' He did not answer, instead he stared ahead, waiting, his knuckles white around the shaft of his lance.

I struck him on the arm and he turned, with wild eyes he mouthed, 'What?'

'Ready?' I shouted. He nodded assent. We were ready.

My heart pounded fit to leave my chest as I saw that all was ready and that there was no way out of this save victory or death. I had not been in action like this for years, and this was making me sweat. I breathed deeply, steadying my own disturbances, and then made sure that everyone could see me before I secured myself into the saddle and took a firm grasp on my lance.

Now, settled in my centre, I checked again to left and right and looked over towards the shield wall to see Aethilheard behind it, waving at me from atop his horse. He would see the whole battlefield from there and I trusted him to give us his total support. Then I waited with trembling hands, always that over-excitement before facing death, waiting... waiting for the moment to release my own onslaught against the Turks. I had the best by my side, and hoped that their youth would prevail over their fear. On the outside flank of each of the conroys were placed two experienced knights, and I knew that they would perform their task of holding their formations tight together.

The tension was stomach-churning and the smell palpable, horses farted and shat themselves, no doubt a few men would begin to wonder how metal entering their chests would feel – too late now.

The drumming of hooves came at us down the valley – they were returning – dust rose anew in the distance and soon they could be seen, with a quickening pace they came at us again and the thunder grew ever louder, trembling the very earth beneath us, then they started to shout and scream and even though they were still a half-mile away the noise funnelling down the valley was frightening.

I nodded to my flag-bearers and lowered my lance to an angle, starting the trot. Right across the frontage the first of my two lines moved forward – one hundred horsemen– disciplined and determined, advancing as one with Aethilheard's men on our left flank waiting their time to loose their cloud of death.

If Arslan was watching closely he might begin to wonder at the contrast between the uncoordinated stampede of his galloping horde and the seeming calm in my lines. Only one philosophy was going to win this encounter: whose version of God would prevail?

My judgement was now crucial and at last I lowered my lance to the horizontal, and couching it tighter beneath my elbow, triggered the next stage of the action.

The onrushing Seljuks, seeing me to their front, loosed off their first volley but most of the arrows went over my head and fell between my line and Tancred's. That was their first error – they had misjudged the range because I had begun my move forward at the optimum moment. I saw Aethilheard give the signal and from behind the shields a forest of arrows lifted into the air and began their death-laden journey towards the nearing Turks. We were only one hundred paces apart as the hail of metal-tipped missiles flew at the oncoming Turks; if they had seen the action it mattered not because it was too late as the yard-long arrows struck them full on, penetrating heads, chests and horses' throats.

By now I had developed tunnel vision, my focus limited to a target group of the enemy directly to my front.

'Tighter! Tighter! That banner!' Their bannerman had not fallen, he was now my target; my screamed instructions drowned out the screeching babble of the pagans and the Turkish banner-carrier became the single most important sight in the world. Payne and Ragenaus pulled their horses even tighter into mine and I felt the familiar bone-crushing as our legs and knees became squashed by the violent galloping of our panting steeds – I prayed that the youngsters would remember to aim their lances as we closed upon the enemy at an uncontrolled speed.

Before the Turks could loose another shot at us, their formation – such as it was – was decimated by the airborne deluge; the surprise had worked perfectly and those behind the forerunners found themselves tripping over their fallen comrades and their thrashing steeds.

Those at the front, who had ridden under the missile shower, could now see that there was no way past us, the valley was filled from side to side with my onrushing cavalry and they began to panic – slowing and turning they became practice targets for our metal tips and were the ones who felt the full weight of my Norman cavalry crash into them; my line overwhelmed them at the full gallop and the weight of our tight-knit formation carried all before it.

I took my man full in the throat and unseated him; the weight of the doomed man hung on the lance for a blink before it was dragged down. It almost wrenched out my right shoulder before it broke in the ground and I almost flew over his horse as mine hit his steed with its shoulder.

The deluge of blood pumping from the perforated man drenched me; mixing with the snot and saliva thrown back in my face by the panting warhorses it caused me to lose my grip on the slimy lance, so saving my shoulder from too much harm, and my horse almost went down as it stamped upon the belly of the fallen steed of my target.

Immediately, the charge slowed, there was too much debris on the ground; we were now treading in piles of dung and offal, men and horses pierced and disembowelled. Some Turks were still active and I unsheathed my sword and looked for the next target. Their bannerman had gone down but I was faced by another, his hate-filled eyes had singled me out and I knew that only death would halt his purpose. High in his saddle with a curved sword above his head he skidded and skipped over bleeding flesh to try and bury his blade in mine. Screaming hideously he made to strike; my shield went up to divert the blow as my longsword blade buried itself, point first, into his lightly armoured stomach. I felt the clang of his blade resonate as his horse squashed my knee and he fell onto the ground, to be trampled by Ragenaus in close attendance.

The battlefield now turned into a melee as riders sought out targets for themselves, and increasingly had to chase and catch them as the Turks lost the will to face us. Thoroughly demoralised they tried to turn and escape back up the valley of destruction. It was futile, for as my men began to tire, Tancred and his force, eager to seek revenge, began to bypass us and continued to chase after the retreating enemy: they soon gave up the chase as the fleeing Turks outpaced our heavier mounts but we had won, the field was ours, archers and cavalry had combined to sweep the pagans aside, thank God.

It was vital that we did not pursue the Turks at this time, and I signalled a return to our defensive positions. This was the ending of the agreed plan and it was well executed.

Arslan must have witnessed the disaster in full. When the storm of arrows had fallen upon his men they had brought down so many horses behind the front runners as to cause absolute chaos and the Turkish charge had lost its momentum. Then, when his front line had melted like snow before the Christian charge it allowed us to get in among the milling Turks who had lost any cohesion and were easy victims to the heavy Norman swords.

Ragenaus, along with me, had lost a lance, but I was proud of them all, fine young warriors.

As we trotted back towards our lines I noticed some bloodied ornament pinned onto Payne's lance, near to his handhold. It was a shoulder – with the arm still attached – and a bow still gripped in a vice of death by the frozen hand, torn off by the violence of the strike. I pointed at it and grimaced. The mighty Payne had been oblivious to it, but then thinking it an unwelcome souvenir, stuck the point of the weapon into the ground to leave it standing upright, a gory pointer to the way back for our returning comrades following along behind.

When we neared the defensive line Aethilheard rode up grinning like a ninny.

'Did you like that then?' he laughed, eyes ablaze in some manic fire.

I hardly heard him, he seemed to be outside my red madness, and my brain was barely functioning outside of savage necessity. I turned my gaze upon my friend and, seeing me, he backed off with shock on his face. I led my successful cavalry back behind Bohemund's pikes and shields: we found no respite there.

Arslan had signalled for another strike from the south, and while I was recovering my senses another wave of Seljuk Turks came charging down upon our shield walls.

Although half a dozen men were injured, we had none killed and now I needed time to reorganise. Bohemund was holding the centre successfully, but the Turks were concentrating on the south side of the defence and while we reorganised we could only watch as the defenders did their best to repulse their attackers. They were hopelessly outnumbered, and it was clear that there were many hundreds of those damned archers galloping by and loosing off their missiles into the soft targets behind the metal lines.

I recovered shortly and regained full control of my thoughts, and though my limbs were still trembling with the after-effects of the first action I was ready to return. I looked to Bohemund to see where he wanted me to deploy next.

Our position was in turmoil. The thousands of unarmed followers were cowering behind the wagons; they had themselves covered with storage bags and bales taken from the baggage carts to ward off the Turkish arrows zinging to earth around them. The marauding archers had made the terrified mass behind the lines of well-protected soldiers the prime target and dozens were transfixed by the plummeting shafts: light they might be, but at this range they were effective against un-armoured pilgrims nonetheless.

Then a cry for help went up as a concentrated effort was made by the attackers on the south side and they came at the wall with lance and sword to grapple hand to hand. Such was the press that they made a breach and Taticius was pushed back towards the centre.

Bohemund signalled to me, and acknowledging the problem I mounted and, taking five conroys with me, charged straight at the milling Turks. Two hundred paces to cover and as we closed we could see that they had reached the wagon line and were busy with an indiscriminate slaughter: men, women, and children were falling under a close-quarter onslaught with spears and sword – the blows of a ruthless enemy – *no mercy* the philosophy. *So be it!* I thought as I bore down on the screaming and uncompromising evil in front of me. Once again the light Seljuk cavalry proved no match for the weight of we Normans on our destriers, and it crumbled before us.

Selecting targets, as before, the tyros at my side made their new lances count as their un-blooded weapons were plunged into foreign flesh. We soon found ourselves in another melee, with sword-strike and counter-strike all around, but this time it was the weight of our weapons that gave us the advantage. The Turks fell under our heavy metal, which proved too much for them. I stood high in my stirrups to crash my weapon upon their heads and soon we over-ran the enemy and those who had penetrated Taticius' defences were reduced to meat. As the last twitching body was despatched to whichever god he wanted to visit I looked closely at my men. This time we were all covered in blood; whose was not discernible but most of us seemed unharmed, if mightily raging.

I called them in again to regroup. This time I had lost three knights. It was a warning not to engage the enemy at such close quarters and in loose formation; the outcome was less certain, and I could not afford to lose men indiscriminately.

Bohemund's centre was picked out for the next attack.

Tancred's remaining cavalry were now proving burdensome. His knights and horses, disorganised behind Bohemund's lines, were too large a target for the Seljuks racing past once more, and many were receiving hits. I galloped across to him and instructed him to place the horses behind the wagons in the swamp and support Aethilheard's archers behind the front line. Here they could cover them with their shields and armour and allow them to return the Turkish arrows with less harm.

Two more pagan assaults failed because the heavy English arrows were knocking over Seljuks with ease. Arslan again changed tactics, returning to a frontal assault against the shield wall to try and penetrate with swords and lances. Our situation was desperate and we could not keep up this resistance. I wondered if Godfrey would ever appear, I wondered if our messenger had reached him.

Bohemund now had Tancred on his left and Tancred's brother, William Marchisus, on his right, both off their horses now and ready to fight near their uncle's side. His banners marked him as the commander, and I watched as the giant waited behind his front lines and the wild horsemen thundered once more towards him.

The Seljuks loosed off their first volley, and then some leaped from their horses, drew their swords and began to scream, wild-eyed, as they covered the final few paces, galloping full tilt into the metal line across their front. The crash was deafening and the line bowed, and then parted, letting some still mounted Turks through; several horses received arrows in the side and fell screeching in the noisy chaos, and as their riders struggled to break free of the thrashing animals, Tancred's dismounted knights fell upon them without mercy and slew them as they struggled.

The breach was soon blocked by twitching flesh and Bohemund's men stood firm behind the steaming wall.

Further along, Bohemund found himself faced by a dozen of those who had penetrated the defences and, grinning broadly, he started to swing his giant's sword at them. The first blow cleaved a man from shoulder to hip, and then, as he struggled to pull the weapon from the jerking flesh a figure came flying through the air over the spouting body, a sword held high ready to strike down upon Bohemund's head – such was the strength of the Norman that he was able to withdraw and raise his weapon in one movement to thrust it up into the chest of the flying figure to impale it on the blade. They met eye to eye for the first and last time as the Turk was held briefly on top of Bohemund's bloody hilt.

Hearing a scream to his right from a familiar voice he turned to see William pinned to the ground by two Seljuk spears. Too late to save the youngster he nevertheless distributed retribution with a hate-filled heart, slashing the head off one unbalanced Turk with a swinging stroke and immediately burying the point straight through the other's belly with the returning thrust; it met the air on the other side of the victim's back.

I watched as Bohemund stood to find that his section had despatched all those who had breached the wall – but at a terrible cost. His face was an awful vision from hell and I knew that there would never be any mercy shown from now on. I waved encouragement to him; he returned the gesture but spat on the nearest Turkish corpse and dug his blade into another to emphasise his hardened attitude.

The safe area was becoming filled with the writhing wounded, corpses being left where they lay; some of the bolder priests had left the comparative safety of the wagon shelters and were attempting to administer aid to the dying. Of more immediate use, some of Tancred's now horseless cavalrymen had formed a supply chain under the guidance of their sergeants and were keeping the archers supplied with arrows, and the men at the barriers supplied with new lances or pikes, and water.

My own troops had lost some cohesion and my task now was to reorganise to keep up their fighting effectiveness. We were now the only operational horsemen left and we made three more rescue assaults to support the hard-pressed lines. Behind, it was becoming increasingly desperate as the ground filled up with human and equine blood and bodies. In front of the steadfast lines of defence it was now very difficult to move because all the fallen were being shredded by the passage of the thundering hooves; the ground was treacherous and the Turks had no footing to close upon our wall any more. This improved our defences as it made an assault on the position hazardous. There would not be many complete bodies to bury from in front of Bohemund's defences.

Just before midday the Seljuks withdrew again, no doubt to reorganise for their next attack, and we, exhausted, did likewise.

I made my way over to Bohemund's position and joined the leaders gathering there.

'Robby!' Bohemund grasped me around the shoulders. 'This is a busy day by God!'

'Too busy for me; I hope he has noticed.'

'Who?'

'God!'

'Bollocks to him. How are your numbers?'

'Not desperate. I've lost six knights, five archers and nine horses. There are some wounded.'

'God's miracles! I am not so well placed. I think that your cavalry charge was a shock to them, you were fortunate in that, perhaps they will be watching you the next time – and those archers! God's bollocks, Robert, what about them? Frightening. They got off two volleys over your heads before you hit the Turks. My *balestriere* would still be on their backs loading a second bolt when Aethilheard's second wave struck.'

I smiled, but it was not the time for a discussion on results. There was much more to do yet, and Bohmey wasn't listening anyway as he gasped out his next instructions.

'We need to spread our strength across the front and consolidate the reserves. Will you continue to command the reaction forces, Robby? Hold them in reserve and only commit them as a last resort. Watch keenly where we are in most trouble and leave me to command the front line.'

'Surely,' I replied, 'I have little else planned for the rest of the day.' So I went off to reorganise.

I was tired, and talking to my men I could see the weariness in their eyes. I wondered if Godfrey would ever turn up – then visions of Sibyl interrupted my thoughts, I so wanted to survive, and these damned Turks were not going to stop me.

The interval of quiet stretched further into the day and we wondered what new horrors Arslan was planning for us. If help did not arrive soon we would become too exhausted to fight and death was inevitable. But then, as the sun began to sink in the western sky, it seemed that God had tested our resolve sufficient for the day.   Bohemund shouted and pointed towards the hill from where Arslan had commanded his army. It was empty, devoid of movement; they had given up and gone. Then came a cry from our northern flank; more movement. This time shining metal and then familiar banners appeared on the horizon: Godfrey had arrived to finally thwart the sultan's desires.

A quiet fell upon the valley as the noises of war fell into silence. Men suddenly felt drained of all energy and slumped down where they had been standing – all save the small parties led by priests who were attempting to tend to the wounded.

Godfrey rode up to where I was standing with Bohemund.

'My God! What vision is this?'

Soldiers, infantry, archers, and cavalry alike were sitting on the ground back to back for support, and if they had not moved when he approached they might have been mistaken for piles of offal in the shambles, such was their state; covered in blood and guts.

Tancred snorted.

'God! God's vision! If this is God's vision, what then, is the devil's?'

I looked up at him. He had tired eyes in a bloodstained face, and I supposed that I was the same. I had seen too much that day. I was tired deep inside, exhausted by the efforts of the past few hours and exhausted by the emotional drain of the sights before me. This had been no tourney.

'Hallo, Godfrey, you are just in time for Vespers... you know I never miss evening prayers.'

Aethilheard laughed. 'Prayers? Prayers you say, it will take more than prayers to atone for this charnel house.'

Godfrey stared at me.

'My God, Robert! Are you harmed?'

I cast a bleary eye on our rescuer.

'Your God is it? I hope that he is pleased with this day's work.'

A voice behind Godfrey spoke. 'Oh he will be, noble lord, he will. Let us give praise for the despatch of these devils' spawn.'

I looked beyond Godfrey. There was a monk of sorts, shabby, raggedy, but animated; he was the only happy person in that damned valley.

'Jesu! Godfrey, who's that? What's that?' I said, glaring at the madman.

'That, Robert, is Peter the Hermit,' replied the duke apologetically, 'he has attached himself to my group.'

'Well, tell him to shut up, else I shall detach his tongue from his head.'

Bohemund spoke for us all, and the lunatic took the hint and scampered off crying out praises to the Lord.

The conversation stuttered somewhat and no one seemed to know what to do next. These northern lords had been in many a battle but this one outstripped our parochial affairs and made them seem as petty squabbles.

To his credit Godfrey assumed the leadership, and with his un-bloodied contingent started to organise the clearing up of the battlefield.

He got the exhausted warriors moved off to a resting area, the wounded to a place of succour, and then started the digging of graves and the identifying of bodies.

Most of us slept through the remainder of the evening and the night. When I awoke the next morning it was to the smells of cooking, the sound of the priests as they led prayers, and the chatter of Godfrey's men, still toiling at the grisly business of gathering bodies, or bits of them, for the cleric's attentions.

I met Bohemund at the nearest cooking pot and we were soon joined by others. We sat down and ate without enthusiasm, or conversation, until Arnulf and Fulcher came up.

Arnulf touched me on the shoulder.

'My lord, how are you this day?'

'Better than the last one, my fine priest. What news do you have for us?'

'Godfrey has scouts out and it seems that the Turks have gone. Fulcher has made an assessment of the casualties.' He looked across to the cleric.

'Yes, my lords, I have made a tally. There are about four thousand Christian bodies to be buried and two thousand more wounded.'

'Jesus!' Bohemund spoke his first word of the day.

'Shall I go on, my lord?'

'Please do.'

'Our best estimate of the Turkish dead is about three thousand.'

Godfrey had joined us and heard the rest of Fulcher's report.

'Most of our dead are unarmed pilgrims, nearly four thousand souls; they had little protection from the arrows. All of their dead are warriors, they died fairly in battle.'

'Not so!' Tancred cried out, 'not so, they shot over us and targeted the pilgrims... that is not honourable, that was not *fair*.' He spat the word out as if anxious to get rid of it.

Stephen agreed. 'I saw that too, Tancred.'

'We all watched *that*, Stephen, we all saw that,' confirmed Bohemund, 'but they had cause to regret that tactic when they came within the arc of my sword.'

'Yes, Bohmey, we saw you create a space around you; did you enjoy your harvest?'

Bohmey bounded to his feet as he declaimed the enemy, rejuvenated at the memory of his personal charnel house.

'Harvest! By God's bollocks there are a few Turks who will harvest no more. I trust that their women will lie fallow until their wombs shrivel up.'

I spoke next.

'It is plain, my friends, this is a war of creeds. Support one side or the other then you are a soldier, armed or not: all will be victors or vanquished... There are no spectators in this bloody affair.'

After a while Godfrey spoke again.

'I sent Adhémar over yonder hill, he received a surprise. Arslan's main camp is just over the rise; you almost marched straight into it.'

Bohemund was astonished.

'How did our scouts not find it then, Tancred?'

'Our scouts are dead. We sent them ahead along the wrong valley. We need to pay more attention to this screen that Robert always has about him. He wouldn't get caught like that.'

I kept quiet as Godfrey continued.

'There is some good news, however. When the Turks spotted Adhémar on the horizon they all fled and left their supplies

behind. We have gained baggage animals, camels and horses, and –
'

I laughed. 'Camels! Camels, what in God's name are we going to do with camels?'

Flanders, who had also been attracted by the food, chipped in.

'You can ride them, carry things on them, harness them to the wagons, or eat them.'

Taticius, who had joined us around the pot, although he would not have detected any smells, spoke up in his adenoidal tones.

'Prince Robert, you can ride them and carry things on them, but they won't pull wagons and they are too valuable to eat.'

'Yerrs,' said Godfrey uncertainly. 'There is more: Arslan also left his treasury behind, there is much in the way of gold and silver. He has paid for his defeat, in fact, in more ways than one.'

Later, recovering my wits, and rid of my blood-drenched garments, I had a conversation with Bohemund and Aethilheard regarding the Turkish archers. We were sitting in the sparse stream of the river trying to scrub off the smell of gore.

I said to the Saxon, 'Did you see how they acted? How they were able to fire so many arrows in such a short time, Aethilheard?'

'Aye! They have a technique strange to us, they carry a dozen arrows in the hand that holds the bow so they can nock and loose very quickly.'

'Yes,' agreed Bohemund, 'and the bows are shorter than ours. They can turn and fire them from all angles – from front to rear – even when they are galloping away, they can still fire at targets behind them... very dangerous.'

'Yes, I saw how they worked. I watched one archer ride past and loose twelve missiles as he went by. We cannot allow them the advantage of such tactics, we must break them up.'

'As you did, Robert, as you did,' spoke the admiring Bohemund.

Aethilheard nodded and made a considered addition.

'I will gather all of the bows and missiles from the fallen Turks. I intend to put them to use.'

'Good!' said Bohemund, 'and bring back all of our unbroken arrows, I can see that archery is going to play an important role in this war, we need all the shafts that we can carry.'

I nodded at my chief of archers.

'Mark his words, Aethilheard; we need a flexible response, do we not?'

'As we have discussed, my lord, as we have discussed.'

Bohemund seemed puzzled at that remark. 'You have already thought on this? I think that I need to keep you two close by me.'

I merely grinned at my Saxon friend.

Three days later, with one-eyed Raymond now joined, our army resumed its journey to Jerusalem. We left the Turkish dead to the attentions of the vultures: a gesture to mirror *their* treatment of the dead from Peter the Hermit's misadventure, and a signature for the future. No quarter, no respect, total war – in the name of God.

8. The Road to Antioch.

We now travelled in three columns, one behind the other. We'd decided to stay together and not split our strength. We had been near disaster at Dorylaeum and we were fortunate that a third, my third, of the army had not been wiped out. We also had the pleasure of Hugh of Vermandois. He had asked to accompany me and Godfrey was glad to see the back of him. 'He knows nothing about everything,' complained Godfrey, 'see if you can teach something about anything, please, Robert.' I sent him to Flanders, he might find a use for a spare prince of France; I had more pressing matters to consider. I was in the leading column with Bohmey but we had only travelled for two days when the scouts brought back some disturbing news; Aethilheard came to me with it.

'There will be no supplies from the land ahead of us, my lord. The Turks are burning and destroying as they go, we must cross Phrygia with what we have.'

'Thank you. Come with me, let's find Taticius.'

The Byzantine was plain in his response to my question.

'It is bad, my lord, there is nothing for two hundred miles now that we have left Dorylaeum. The ground is arid and very hot during the day and very cold at night, it is a most unpleasant region. We must reach Ikonium before there will be any respite.'

I conferred with Bohemund and Godfrey but as there seemed to be no other way we set off to face the perils of the high plains of Phrygia Major.

It was worse than my imagining. Although the country had changed when we crossed from Constantinople into Asia it had been a gentle transition, until now that is. When we came out of the hills we were faced with wide open rolling plains upon which nothing grew – years of war had wiped out all attempts at agriculture and the people had long ago fled the land for safer places. Arslan's ravaging policies had made the devastation complete; what we carried was what we had to survive on until we crossed into a friendlier environment.

The weakest of the European horses were the first to succumb to the extremes of climate with some dying of heat exhaustion. Then the people started to collapse. The elderly and infirm, despite surviving the assaults of the Turks, found the scorching sun and freezing nights more unforgiving enemies.

Women collapsed and were left behind. The vultures would find bonus flesh in their bodies when they picked out the embryos of their unborn babies.

I ordered my men to walk as much as they rode to spare the horses. Without the cavalry and the archers we would be vulnerable – especially if we were caught out here on the open plains. Taticius' words hung heavy in my thoughts; we would be easy prey to the normal tactics of the Seljuk Turks, encirclement and death. Soon everyone was walking to give the surviving warhorses every chance to reach the beckoning mountains ahead. The remaining oxen pulled the wagons; the camels and Arabian ponies, spoils from Dorylaeum, carried such dwindling supplies as were left.

Our column now stretched back for several miles. Those at the front were gradually leaving the halt and the sick, the disenchanted and the lazy far behind. Raymond's force was out of sight behind us as we plodded wearily onwards. I expected him to find our stragglers a hindrance when he caught up with them – I doubted if he could spare them any succour. Our only priority now was to get as many fighting men off this abominable plain and I determined to keep our column moving as a unit: if the Turks attacked now we too would be food for the vultures.

Each day the sun came up to do its killing and our only shelter was the ever-present swarms of flies, come to feast on our smelly bodies, encased now within dust-caked clothing. Weary travellers looked eagerly towards the south each morning to see if the mountains had moved any closer; it seemed that for days they never did. The column took to collapsing by the roadside when the sun was at its highest, dragging blankets off the wagons to form sun shades. Our priests were the first to stir when the heat began to fade. Urged on by their holy zeal, Fulcher and Arnulf began to say their prayers and gradually we all rose to our feet to join them

141

and begin the weary trudge once more. We were forced to ration the water supplies to a few sips during the day. We were travelling from mean watering place to watering place, but Taticius was concerned that the Turks may have poisoned the wells, so we needed to keep a reserve of the precious liquid until we knew that the next water was safe to drink.

One night when the sun had gone down I insisted on continuing the march to make the most of the cool evenings, and then in a fit of divine wisdom I realised that this was the way, and as long as Aethilheard's men could discern the trail and see no signs of the enemy we carried on... Slowly – relentlessly – we made progress through the cool nights and slept through the heat of the day.

Then, on one joyous morning, as the sun lit up the sky we beheld the longed-for peaks. Spurning our daytime sleep we continued, and they appeared to gallop towards us, promising hope of harbouring water in the shadow of their foothills.

Not all those who plunged into the waters of the first river that they came across were destined to survive. The final few days of dehydration had ensured madness when ample water again presented itself to the frantic travellers – and they drank themselves to death in the shade of the cooling waterside trees.

Fulcher and Arnulf recorded it so: 'And eight hundred have died on the journey in the last month.' This depressing news I told them to keep to themselves.

'Aye, Robert,' said Allen, 'we are all going to die, but we need as many live bodies to get to Jerusalem as possible, so do not dishearten our travelling companions.'

'Jesu,' grumbled Bohemund, swatting flies with his cow-pat hands, 'let us all die in foolish hope. I hate little things.'

After a discussion we decided to stay in the hills for a while to recuperate. The area was fertile, safe, and quite pleasant.

Soon, when Godfrey was feeling fresh, he decided to have a day's hunting and went into the hills to find some game. Unfortunately the game found him and he was severely mauled by an enraged bear.

Later, I went with Bohemund to see him in his tent.

'You missed the attentions of Arslan,' said the giant, 'how did you manage to attract the attentions of some poor animal?'

'The animal in question was as tall as you are, but had talons of iron... see!'

He pulled back the sheet lying across his chest.

'Shit! It seems that your animal had a handful of arrows,' said I, surveying the deep gouges across the victim's torso.

'It feels that way. We need to discuss our next move, but I would appreciate a few days' rest first.'

'Of course,' I replied, 'it is comfortable here and ahead there's another desert to cross. We'll move when you're ready.'

'Thanks. As soon as I can get on a horse we can make progress.'

'We will,' said Bohemund confidently, 'but it will be more certain if you take a few days to recover, then the journey will not bother you so much.'

Godfrey agreed and we went off to prepare a plan for the next stage of the journey.

Well recovered after the rest we left the hills and after a short stage in mid August we came to the place named Ikonium. It had been in the hands of the Turks, but when they learned of Arslan's defeat, and the approach of his vanquishers, they acted prudently and left.

The next target was the city of Heraclea, and this was where we met a Christian population – these were Armenians, proud, independent, and fed up with being ruled either by Byzantines or Turks: our arrival was seen as liberation and we were made welcome.

Here we needed to make a strategic decision. The Anti-Taurus mountains barred our way to the south and entry into the region of Cilicia – which we needed to traverse before we finally turned towards Jerusalem. There were two possible routes. One went north into Cappadocia and skirted the mountains before turning south – and one led straight through the mountains in a narrow defile known as the Cilician Gates.

There were other factors which, I agreed with Bohemund, needed discussion, and we called a conference.

Bohemund began, mostly because he had a prepared speech, and nobody could stop him.

'We have come through many trials to get this far. God has smiled on our endeavours and brought us to this point. We are the ones who have been chosen to complete this holy mission and bring relief to the city of Jerusalem.'

Stephen and I shuffled a little at this grand address. I prayed that it might remind all the leaders present of our true mission. I reserved judgement upon the man who had spoken, Bohemund's deepest motives still troubled me, but I said naught.

Bohemund said more.

'We are still far from the final objective and there will be more obstructions placed in our way before we reach the holy city. One of these is the city of Antioch.'

Godfrey joined in supporting Bohemund; he was recovering fast and was determined to maintain his position as one of the leaders, if not *the* leader of the expeditionary force. Raymond of Toulouse was still making no secret of his own ambitions in that regard, and with Alexios now many miles to the rear there was no longer any restraining hand on the personal ambitions of these great lords.

'Yes,' I said in support, 'it is as Bohemund says, we have a long way to go and although we could bypass Antioch, if it could be taken it would be better not to leave it in our rear.'

Bohemund nodded at me to continue, knowing what I had in mind.

'It is not only the threat of an Antiochene garrison left in our rear that we should consider, it is the lines of supply that we are stretching; they would also be threatened by that garrison. It's also time to remember that the sea comes into play once we have left the mountains, and when Antioch is behind us. It will become the main means of supply, and if Jerusalem will not surrender to us we can't besiege it without heavy equipment that, as we could not carry with us, must be brought by sea.'

144

Raymond was not much of a strategist, in fact he was not much of a thinker at all, and he seemed puzzled at my mention of the sea.

'What has the sea to do with sieges? Surely we are in the desert and Jerusalem is in the desert, is it not?'

Godfrey gestured to Taticius – who produced a map.

'You see, Raymond,' he said, spreading the map before the puzzled duke, 'Jerusalem is quite close to the sea, it is only thirty miles away from this port of Azotus Paraliyus, it would be easier to support our operations by sea rather than bringing supplies by any overland route.'

'Yes, yes! But we have no ships.'

'I have.' They looked at me, and Flanders confirmed the fact.

'Yes, Robert has.'

Godfrey and Raymond had nothing to say, not wishing to reveal that they had given this aspect of invasion so little thought, no doubt. They would not know of my arrangements with Matilda, or of the maritime plans laid by me when in Brindisi.

'I have a fleet waiting at Cyprus.'

Godfrey became very interested.

'What for? Why Cyprus?'

'Look at the map, Godfrey. Cyprus lies central to all the areas we have been wandering through. In Lemesos I have the metalwork for heavy siege engines, armour and weapons, thousands of arrows, farriers and blacksmith's tools – and with the ships are carpenters, shipwrights and other artisans; all we need are the ports to operate from and we can have more certain lines of supply.'

Bohemund and Stephen watched, quietly amused. We who had recently tasted battle were now feeling superior to those who had turned up late, and not yet been blooded.

Bohemund blasted on.

'We have been made welcome here and I suspect that there are many of these Armenians who would join us and support us in our quest; I want to make this region a firm base for the support of our further operations – Robert wants a port, and there is a way that we can achieve both objectives.'

Now Godfrey's manner became wary. He was mirrored by Raymond who was much more suspicious of anybody attempting to seize the leadership: but both men held their tongues, for now anyway, and Bohemund went straight to the plan.

'I don't want to take this... rabble,' he waved in the direction of the pilgrim's camp, 'through the Cilician Gate – a narrow pass through the mountains. We would be vulnerable and may end up in a bottleneck, perhaps even stoned from above. But! I want to take control of it. I will send Tancred into Cilicia, he will recruit what Christians will join us and see if he can get hold of more horses. Then we'll try to take the Turks by surprise and seize the port of Tarsus.'

'Is this what you want, Robert?' asked Godfrey.

'We need a port, tis true, but one closer to Antioch would be better. Nevertheless, if Tarsus can be taken without undue effort then let us take it. I think it is vital to our success, both at Antioch and later at Jerusalem that we give ourselves as many options as possible.'

Stephen nodded his support and Allen muttered, 'Then get Robert his port, addle-heads.'

'Then I agree.' Godfrey missed Allen's remark but was quick to see the advantage. 'We will go north around the mountains, recruiting and replacing lost horses – I had not known how poorly my fine steeds would perform in these conditions. I will send my brother, Baldwin of Boulogne, with you to accompany Tancred on your recruiting cavalcade through Cilicia.'

Raymond made an effort to impose some authority, asking me, 'Would you take the lead around the mountains, Robert? I admire your strange mounted bowmen; they are exceedingly useful as scouts.'

As this had been our intention I nodded and the matter was settled. On the way back to our lines I sighed and shook my head.

'What?' growled Bohmey.

'Tis like herding chickens.'

'I'd like to knock their heads together, but your way is less tiring.'

'True,' I replied, 'very true. Has Tancred left?'

'He should have. I want Tarsus and it will take Baldwin at least another day to set off.'

'I hope we're not storing up trouble for later,' I said.

'That's what I came for, Robby, trouble.'

I rode on for a while in a cloud of gloom. Visions of Sibyl distracted me as I pondered our progress; we had stumbled our way thus far, but how long would God's goodwill endure?

'Aethilheard,' I called, next time he came near, 'come and cheer me up. We will talk about our ladies.'

'And our children,' exclaimed the annoyingly ever-cheerful Saxon.

Aethilheard stopped me with that remark, and Sibyl faded as Tegwin's dark eyes occupied my vision.

'Oh yes,' I agreed, 'and our children. Let us talk of your two, sweet Rowena and young Alfred. I wonder if they are keeping up with the news in England.'

'Surely, my lord Robert, they must have access to the king's correspondence. I hardly imagine a messenger will arrive at Westminster or Winchester without the lady Tegwin being soon at King William's side, demanding to know its contents.'

'You are right, my friend, nothing will escape Lady Tegwin's attention.' I smiled at the memory of Tegwin, feisty little sod that she was.

'No,' ventured the probing archer, 'including Italian enchantresses, I suspect.'

'Oh, you heard about that?'

'You did not expect *that* to remain privy long, my lord?'

'No, you bugger, but I did not expect to discuss it today either.'

He smiled, and we rode along in contemplation a little more until I said, 'What do you think Tegwin will do, Aethil?'

'Mmm,' he mused, 'there are two possibilities, my lord.'

'Only two?'

'Aye, only two, as I see it. She will either have your balls off with a blunt knife, or –'

'Or?'

'Or she'll drag you off by the ear to the nearest bedchamber.'

I was left to ponder my options while he wittered on about Rowena and Alfred. Occasionally my boys, Richard and William, came into his ramblings, and it was good to hear him speak of them, but I could not help but be distracted by the problem of Tegwin. He was good company, my Saxon, loyal, fierce, and the best father a woman could have for her children. So the time went by pleasantly enough, mostly, except for...Tegwin.

Bohemund got his trouble the very next morning when he witnessed Baldwin's men, drawn up ready to depart.

'Robby!' he shouted at me as he galloped towards my lines.

'What?

'That sod Baldwin, he's taking five hundred, and Tancred left with only three.'

'I said that there'd be bother.'

'Well,' responded the angry Bohmey, 'I'm sending another three hundred.'

So yet more troops were detached from Bohemund's force to chase after Baldwin, who was chasing after Tancred, who was chasing Turks.

There was a grunt from behind me as Payne made clear his feelings.

'What manner of idiots have we taken up with, my lord?'

'Pious ones, Payne. Very holy and ambitious ones, I fear.'

Bohemund glared at Payne. 'Your squire has too much to say, Robert, he needs to curb his tongue.'

'My squire is a knight by right, and a friend, and he has no need to curb his tongue.'

The two big men sized each other up, each bristling with ill intent, so I stepped between them and said quietly to Bohemund, 'This is not helpful, friend, save your anger for the enemy ahead, for there are none here.'

Another grunt, another parting glare, and he went back to his lines to organise his second detachment.

'Easy, Payne,' I cautioned, 'I have need of your services.'

'Sorry, my lord, he is a noisy sod.'

'True, but let us get on with the task.'

The next part of the journey went remarkably to plan. From Heraclea to Caesarea, the Armenians either joined us or made supplies available, and we gained many allies along the road. Any Turkish garrisons we encountered were deserted by the time we reached them – Arslan's defeat had proved to be a massive propaganda success, and any resistance was only token.

Eventually we arrived at the town of Coxon, on 7 October; it was here that we reached the end of the mountains and turned south again towards Antioch.

Raymond became ill and took to his bed for a few days. We used the opportunity to rest, and Raymond, presumably driven by the desire to continue as a leader, made a quick recovery.

He was now full of fervour and insisted on continuing, 'to go and occupy the city of Antioch.'

The final part of the journey around the Taurus Mountains held a sting in the tail. After leaving Coxon to head towards Marash, we came to a precipitous pass; a narrow trail with sheer cliffs on the left and a seeming mile-high drop on the other.

Our guides informed us that it was 'unavoidable'. So Aethilheard led off in single file and we followed with a little distance between us. Although it was frightening at first, I soon lost awareness of the abyss on the right as I concentrated on guiding my horse, which at times hesitated as the ground before his hooves crumbled and stones hurtled into the void. I worried about those following and prayed that the path would hold up as they traversed the mile or so of danger. When we reached the floor of the valley it was still so narrow that we needed to carry on regardless, because to stop would have caused a blockage and extra danger to those behind.

I caught up with Aethilheard when the valley broadened out.

'Jesu, Lord Robert, that was shite. Did you hear the cries behind us?'

'I did, do you think some fell?'

'I heard a woman scream,' confirmed Ragenaus, 'it seemed to last an age.'

'Poor souls,' was all I could offer as I signalled to go on, wondering how many had fallen to their deaths along that treacherous path to heaven.

When we reached the town of Marash, in mid October, the journey lingered in the mind like a bad dream. The latter part was worse than my Alpine crossing when I first went to Italy to see Matilda, with the arid desert almost beyond description, and it had been crueller for those who followed along behind me.

When all who had made the journey safely were gathered together, Adhémar told us that between Constantinople and Marash, half those who had left Europe had died one way or another. He had gathered information from all sections of our host and the story he had to tell was distressing and depressing in the extreme. Warriors killed in battle certainly – but the non-combatants were mostly lost through disease, starvation and exhaustion; in particular across the plains of Anatolia where sunstroke, heat exhaustion and dehydration had taken their toll. I might have suspected it, but it was at the rear of the procession where the rate of attrition was highest; as the weak fell back they could only watch helplessly as the ever-shortening tail disappeared into the dust ahead of them. Those whose loved ones had fallen could only wait to die with them as the vultures circled overhead – there were many couples who left the earth as intermingled bones, to be found by those following the detritus trail of God's warriors.

There were no burials for the laggards; no graves, no stone cairns to mark their end-place; only the queues in the skies marked the point of their demise, and those aerial queues diminished in time.

Nevertheless, it was expected by those still living that dying by any means while on the crusade would betoken the same atonement for sins as being killed in fighting, and so we pressed on in faith and hope towards our mortal destiny.

Once out of the mountains, Godfrey's group took the lead followed by Raymond. Bohmey and me had been asked to form the rearguard, but even with numbers severely reduced the cavalcade still stretched over three miles. This was yet another suspicious move and I wondered at Raymond's complacency in allowing Godfrey to lead without argument. He had a reason, I was certain, but what?

Aethilheard said that my mind had been unsettled, and that was true: whose had not? But Raymond's silence bothered me still.

Now we were travelling down the eastern side of the Tarsus Mountains nearing the Belen Pass, known as the Gates of Syria. This is where we expected to meet up with Tancred and Baldwin: it was a surprise when we found only Tancred waiting for us with his three hundred men, and not in a happy mood.

He came straight to Bohemund, who after a few words with him sent for me.

'You'd better hear this, Robert; there is treachery in the air.'

'Hallo, Tancred. Where's Baldwin? And where's the three hundred Bohmey sent after you?'

'Rotting in a gulley as far as I know; the little turd is pursuing his own ends. Those three hundred are dead, slaughtered in their sleep.'

'Right! Let's hear it.' Bohemund gave some orders for the security of the camp and we went and found a place to settle and listen to Tancred's tale.

'We got to Tarsus and the garrison looked as if they would resist, so we sat outside the gates all day and must have worried them because someone came out to treat. I said that we were the first of many, and that the town would be left unharmed if they handed it over.'

I asked, 'Had Baldwin caught up with you?'

'No, not then, but I didn't know he was coming behind me till he turned up.'

Bohemund nodded. 'Yes, sorry about that, I hadn't known how many he was going to take until after you left.'

Tancred continued.

'Yes, and there's more. The garrison commander agreed to surrender the town and placed my banner on top of the citadel. We didn't enter the town because I gave them permission to stay under my protection, or to leave if they wished. Either way they would come to no harm.'

'That seems fair to me,' said Flanders, 'it would help our reputation as fair dealers in the region.'

'Just so,' responded Tancred, 'but then Baldwin turned up, and he decided he was unhappy with the arrangement. He accused me of grabbing the town, and then demanded that I should agree to share it with him... so I refused.'

'What argument did he use?' I asked.

'He said that there was an agreement to share spoils equally among all the crusaders.'

Bohemund thought for a moment. He was after all one of the leaders who had submitted to that agreement.

'Yes, but that was where we had all played a part in the winning of the spoils. We shared Arslan's gold because Godfrey and Raymond had arrived before we were all dead. It's clear here that Baldwin played no part in the winning of Tarsus.'

'Well, he thought that he should have joint ownership, and he didn't leave it there. He made secret contact with the garrison commander and told lies to get him to change his mind.'

'What lies?' asked Bohemund.

'He said that you were not to be trusted, that you would sack the city and impale all the soldiers and citizens. That he should only trust Godfrey – who would care for them.'

Stephen was annoyed.

'As you said: a little turd.'

Bohemund remained remarkably calm and asked Tancred if there was more.

'Then they threw my banner over the wall and let Baldwin into the city.'

'What next?' rumbled Bohemund, controlling his anger.

'So I left. He had more men than me and he had the citadel. The Turks seemed happy to remain in his protection, what else could I do?'

'You did right, young cousin, but what happened to the three hundred?'

'Aye!' said I, 'the missing three hundred, where are they now?'

Tancred paused to gather himself. Bohemund proffered him a flagon of wine, which the youngster gobbled at gladly, then told us more.

'I moved east and found the town of Adana. It is Armenian and had just thrown out the Turkish garrison; they were pleased to see us.'

'Flanders asked a question.

'Is this a revolt against the Turks in the region? Is it general?'

'It seems to be so; the Armenians are very keen to take control of their lands and are willing to help us.'

'We've found that too,' said Bohemund.

'The ruler of Adana is called Oshin. He was very helpful, and a canny dealer, he offered to lead us to easy pickings in a town called Mamistra. He also offered me two hundred of his men to help to take it off the Turks; he said it was the most prosperous trading centre in the area.'

Bohemund's eyes lit up.

'You had a fight?'

'No, Uncle, no fights, the Turks pissed off when they spotted us coming. We were welcomed into the town with great celebrations by the Armenians; we had a grand time. Lovely women.'

'Women! What's women?' gasped young Philip, his bollocks hanging low no doubt.

'Yes, yes,' said Bohemund, remembering, 'but what about the three hundred?'

'Oshin received news and shared it with us. Your three hundred arrived after we left; Baldwin would not let them into the city, so they made camp outside to consider things. That very night some of the Turks who had remained left the town to creep up on the camp and slaughtered them as they slept.'

Bohemund stood up, his face glowing with rage. I was still sitting on the ground and I felt the light from the sun darken as I came under the shadow of the fuming giant. Looking up I saw Bohemund's unruly locks outlined by the sun's rays: *if this is not Odin then it must be his brother.*

A mighty bellow came from the enraged giant.

'Where is he? Where is the little turd? I'll separate his parts; where is he now, Tancred? He is meat.'

Tancred stood up and reached up to take his uncle by the shoulders.

'Not yet, Uncle. Not yet, I haven't finished yet.'

'Finished! NO, it's not finished yet.'

Bohemund took a deep breath then walked around this circle of friends – twice – before taking another breath and sitting down. He glared at everybody; they all found something of interest in the distance, except me.

I looked Bohemund in the eye, and let him have it.

'Leave revenge aside for now, let the matter lie; we'll hear Tancred out and then see how to deal with the matter.'

I received a growl in reply, but the volcano sitting opposite subsided – it would erupt later, no doubt.

'Go on,' I instructed Tancred.

'We received word that Baldwin had left Tarsus and was on his way to Mamistra. It was said that his men had quarrelled with him over the massacre – but not before they had taken revenge on the remaining Turks; they slaughtered them all. Now, making the best of it, he has left some of his men inside and has declared it his possession.'

Flanders spotted the flaw with that logic.

'So he believes that he can own it?'

Bohemund muttered, 'He owns naught.'

'Is there more to this labyrinth of treachery?' enquired Stephen.

'Yes,' replied Tancred, 'he came to Mamistra, and set up camp nearby on the river. Some of my men went over and started a fight with them. Some got hurt, but Baldwin's men were outnumbered, I had the two hundred Armenians with me, and I called mine off.'

'So where is he now, nephew?'

'Gone off on some scheme of his own. They say he has formed an alliance with some local ruffian of ill repute. Who cares? *I* should own Tarsus; my banners have flown above the citadel.'

Tancred was both pleased with himself and outraged by the actions of Baldwin, and so he should be.

Bohemund's mood was not improving, but the outside world was starting to impinge upon our thoughts again. Leaders must lead and we still had some way to go to reach Antioch. By now Godfrey and Raymond would be well ahead of us – who knows what they'd get up to if left alone for too long.

Bohemund stood up.

'I will discuss Baldwin with his brother, Godfrey, when we catch up with him, of that you may be certain.'

Allen asked, 'Can I come? My sword pines for blood.'

'Then sharpen it, Brittany, make it ready,' I answered. 'You may need both edges in this morass of treachery.'

9. The Walls of Antioch.

We came up to Godfrey's encampment, some twenty-five miles short of Antioch, to hear that Raymond had despatched an advance party in the command of one of his senior nobles, Peter of Roaix, 'to reconnoitre the city'.

We joined the other leaders to confirm the strategic plan for the city's capture.

Taticius, who had travelled with Godfrey, attended as Alexios' representative and to provide us with the necessary intelligence. He produced detailed maps, and outlined the latest situation from his spies within the city walls regarding the Seljuk numbers and disposition. He spoke of only about five thousand troops to defend the city.

'And how many miles of wall?' I asked, puzzled. The numbers were suspicious.

'Five or six miles, Prince Robert,' he answered.

'That is not enough to defend the city,' said Allen. 'You said five gates, the citadel and a population of uncertain loyalty; we could take it with an attack at the five gates.'

'Perhaps,' I responded, 'but we'll lose valuable lives and it may not be necessary. They could not leave the city undefended and follow us if we moved on.'

I asked if he was certain of his information, where did it come from, and he explained that the city earned its money from trade, and that the gates were always open for traders, and spies, during the day, and firmly shut at night.

'So will they not admit us as traders, General Taticius?' Bohemund had recovered some of his humour, even though dark thoughts were lingering regarding Baldwin.

The Greek grinned at him and gave a remarkably girlish giggle at the thought.

'Go and knock, Prince Bohemund. If you return with your head on your shoulders we may all be allowed in.'

'That's no, I believe. Let us go and see this trading outpost and see if we can change the governance of the place.'

This was Godfrey at his commanding best. I felt that I should support him while keeping my options open, so I agreed.

Then Raymond made a mistake.

'I heard that the city was ready to surrender, general.'

'You heard wrongly, my lord, do not rely on rumours.'

So that was why Raymond had sent his man, Peter; he had hoped to take possession. I nudged Bohemund but we held our tongues; that was information for later.

Truth to tell, I was bothered a little by the idea of laying siege to the place, unconvinced about the strategic necessity and keen to get on to Jerusalem. However, I could see that the tide of opinion was against me at the moment so I resolved to make the best of it.

I took Bohemund and Adhémar out of earshot and engaged them in quiet conversation.

After some discussion it was decided that we would agree to not leaving this fortress city lurking in our rear as we advanced to Jerusalem. I still had some doubts but acquiesced, and it only remained to agree the objectives and responsibilities so that we could proceed. We re-joined the council and I settled down with Bohemund to listen to Taticius' briefing.

We had agreed beforehand to ignore his distinctive vocal delivery but still gave each other a dig in the ribs as the dark-skinned Greek began. Bohemund kept his laughter level down by glaring at Godfrey from time to time and I wondered how long I could keep them on amicable terms.

Taticius called our attention with a polite cough. I was fascinated by the silver nasal plate he wore to cover the missing nose, it seemed to be very expensive, so well chased it was with elaborate decorations.

'We are here at present,' he pointed on the map to a town called Baghras. It was north of the great lake of Antioch and controlled the route to the Belen pass, now in our rear. 'This is the first strategic point and we should garrison it to ensure that the pass remains secure.'

'Aye!' said Tancred, 'the Cilician gates and the Belen pass are key to maintaining our supply lines back to Constantinople.'

I thought about my ships but kept quiet.

'Indeed,' responded Raymond, his eye fixed on nothing that I could determine, 'it is better than the route we took, that was too far.'

'But necessary,' growled Bohemund. 'We have gained many allies through our journey around the north.'

I felt the bristling atmosphere in the tent and waved Taticius on.

'The next point to secure will be here,' he pointed at a town to the east of the lake called Artah. 'With this place occupied you will have a secure frontage of forty miles to control the northern routes into Antioch and the road east to Aleppo.'

Godfrey tried to ignore the withering glances from Bohemund and expressed his satisfaction with Taticius' comments.

'That lake makes the frontier easier to patrol. Is it the water supply to the city?'

'They use it, but there are wells within the city walls.'

That was a key point if it came to starving the garrison out.

'Now, my friends, the city.' Taticius drew attention to the map. 'It is built along the west-facing front of this saddleback mountain; the northern peak is named Mount Staurin, and the higher peak to the south is called Mount Silpius. To the west a curtain wall runs from the slopes of Staurin, out to the river Orontes, and southwards until it turns east once more to ascend the slopes of Mount Silpius.'

'Jesu!' A voice from the back – Philip had just joined us and was astonished to be confronted by the scale of the problem, presented in such a graphic way.

'How long is the wall, General Taticius?' he asked.

'About five or six miles long with hundreds of towers along its length. There are only five gates and two bridges over the river – oh! and the final defence is a castle on the top of Mount Silpius. There is a cathedral here, near the Dog Gate – and there is this,' he pointed to the saddle between the twin peaks, 'the Iron Gate. It leads into a steep gorge through to the desert plain in the east, but is difficult to reach.'

Adhémar pushed forward, the idea being that he should present the finer details as the most neutral person available, apart from myself. I nodded to the bishop as his cue to begin.

He made it simple. It wasn't a complex problem; along the walls there were only five entry points but we had nowhere near enough men to blockade each of them without being hopelessly separated from each other, so he suggested that we form a cordon at the three most important gates, thus seizing control of the north-eastern corner of the city.

'What about the other two, down here on the southern side of the wall?' Allen of Brittany asked.

'We can do nothing more than send out patrols, Allen,' answered Godfrey. 'It is not ideal but winter approaches and we must prepare ourselves to survive that, during which time we can take note of the city's defences and look for weaknesses.'

The leaders tacitly nodded assent. But I knew for certain that each and every one of them was trying to see where the flaws were, and what advantages lay in adopting such an approach. Receiving no objections, or affirmations, Adhémar continued.

'Duke Godfrey, can you take up a position that secures the Gate of the Duke, and control the road to Alexandretta?'

'Robert has lost hope of the port at Tarsus –' Bohemund coughed loudly to ensure that everybody knew that that was the fault of Godfrey's brother, Baldwin – 'however, there is the one at Alexandretta.'

I nodded, and although Raymond still wasn't convinced about the efficacy of sea routes he agreed anyway.

'My lord Raymond,' said Adhémar, 'will you move in front of the wall by the Dog Gate? Lord Bohemund, will you block off the St Paul Gate? Prince Robert, with Duke Allen and my lord Flanders will fill in the northern corner between you and my lord Raymond. It only remains to determine who will garrison Baghras?'

'I will.' Taticius grabbed the route back to Constantinople.

I dug Flanders in the ribs and he responded, 'I'll take Artah.' Nobody was quicker, and nobody made any objection. Bohemund looked at me and smiled, this was just how we wanted it. He even let the reference to the failed expedition to Tarsus go by without further reaction: things were coming along nicely.

My alliance with Bohemund had given us total control of the northern walls of Antioch, and the major part of the city, which lay just within them.

Bohemund displayed his contentment with the situation on the way back to our lines.

'Well done, Robby, that was a plan well executed. By controlling the northern approaches we have the ear of the emperor, the voice of Taticius and the balls of Bohemund to work with. What say you?'

'I say that you can work with your own balls: I'm content with mine. But I'm happy to stay away from Raymond and I'm pleased that you resisted the temptation to antagonise Godfrey: what was it he said to Fulcher?'

'Yes, he wasn't pleased with Baldwin, although he mentioned that his wife had died. Still, that didn't excuse his actions at Tarsus so he's sending Fulcher to find him and see if he can bring him back.' Bohemund added with a grimace, 'If the scurvy twat does come back he'd better stay away from me.'

Back in our own lines we prepared for the siege of Antioch, not that anyone, other than me, had put any thought into preparing for the siege of one of the largest and most defendable cities on the shores of the Mediterranean. But first, there was a bridge to capture.

I advanced, having regained the leading position, to see that there was a lake on our right, and a river, which came from the mountains to the south. It ran towards us before turning right across our path; here there was a bridge that crossed the river before it headed off down to the city. The river was named the Orontes, and ran in front of the great walls of Antioch before reaching the sea. Taticius described the bridge as *Djisr el-Hadid* – the Iron Bridge.

'They make a lot of things from iron, Taticius,' I commented.

'They have the skill, my lord, and these are places well worth defending. I understand that you still make stronghold doors from wood.'

'Some. It depends how permanent they are, or how long they have been there, but you are correct, mostly wood.'

'Please note, my lord, that you will not burn down the Iron Bridge, nor the iron gates which defend Antioch… you will need a different approach to that problem.'

Just another worry along the way to the eternal gates, I mused, then sent back word to Godfrey that I was making plans to seize the Iron Bridge and outlined the part that I expected him to play.

Aethilheard's scouts went forward and they brought back a report from their first sighting of the enemy. They were indeed holding the Iron Bridge; it could be closed by two iron-bound doors set in stone gatehouses. Estimates put the defenders at about seven hundred.

I had replaced my lost horses by demanding spares from the other leaders. 'Give them up,' growled Bohemund, 'he knows better how to use them than we do.' So the replacements were forthcoming.

Aethilheard was the eyes and ears of the force, with most of the ponies, and I could still assemble an assault force of three hundred cavalry with another hundred in reserve.

Having heard the reports from Aethilheard and now knowing the disposition of the Turks and the layout of the ground around the bridge, I gave my orders and made ready to take it from the enemy.

It had been months since our last encounter. All the privations of the horrible journey over desert and mountains, and all of the deaths we witnessed along the way, now surfaced in a terrible rage against those who had caused it – the Turkish guard on the Iron Bridge were about to receive a visitation from the hounds of hell.

I told Bohemund my plan.

'I will ride upstream, well out of view of the bridge, to where the river shallows, and find a crossing point, then we will return on the other side to attack the bridge from the direction of the city. At midday you will march towards the bridge to distract the defenders and we will fall upon them from their rear.'

'God, Robby, thou art a devious little sod, have you no shame?' Then he poked me in the ribs, before crushing me against his expansive chest.

'Shame is a luxury we can ill afford on this venture,' I gasped, before pushing him away, 'or crushed ribs either.' He laughed; it may have been heard in Antioch.

The defenders knew of course that we were heading their way, so it was no surprise to them when the first shining helms and lance tips appeared in the distance, and they prepared themselves for the expected assault. They were, however, facing in the wrong direction when we fell upon them from behind.

This was not a co-ordinated cavalry charge; the ground was very rough, but there was not an organised enemy before us, they were behind prepared defensive walls, on the other side of the river, facing the wrong direction and open to attack from the rear. For me, the target was those on this side of the river manning the gate and on top of the twin gatehouse towers. I galloped towards the bridge and we were upon them before they knew it. I buried my lance in the first surprised defender who turned at the sound of my hooves. Then out with the sword and standing in my stirrups I laid about me like a madman. The defenders were pressed against the closed gate and fell before the onslaught as my men ran amok. Allen in particular, trying to swing his sword, posed as much danger to our men pressing forward as to the Turks he was enthusiastically chopping down.

The action did not last long. The confused and terrified troops not on the bridge were frightened out of their positions and scattered within moments of our appearance. Many disappeared into the undergrowth and reed beds along the riverbank.

The defenders in the towers cast down their bows in the hope of an honourable surrender, and I was content to disarm them and herd them together for a little lecture.

They were lined up so that I could take a good close look at them; I wanted to see this ferocious foe and examine their dress.

None would face me; some fell on their knees and bared the backs of their necks, evidently awaiting the final blow.

I said to Aethilheard, 'See these killers of women and children; do you judge them brave, my fierce Saxon?'

'No, my prince, I judge them fortunate to find you merciful. Watch this,' he commanded one fellow, with his eyes a hand-span from the pagan's terrified orbs – whether the captured man understood the words or not, he surely understood what happened next.

Taking up his bow, Aethilheard stood squarely in front of the man and drew it with an arrow nocked – everyone could see the power in the Saxon's shoulders as he stood like that for a seeming age, smiling, without effort. Suddenly he turned and picked a target, loosing the missile. It disappeared in a flash of feathers as it sped towards a tree some two hundred paces away. It struck the middle of the bole and penetrated fully two hand-spans.

Aethilheard grabbed the Turk by his neck, and almost throttling him with the power of his grip propelled him over to the tree to witness the power of our weapons.

'See that?' he growled, shoving the terrified fellow's face into the tree bark. 'Remember that when you get inside your city.' Then he dragged him back to face me again.

'Go and tell them in Antioch,' I said, eyeing each of them, 'that Robert the Norman is coming. Tell them of the colour of my metal.'

These were valid siege tactics. Because there was no question of surprise in this instance – everybody in Asia knew we were on our way – the purpose was to terrify and disconcert the defenders, though we had not yet arrived before the gates. The knowledge that we would do so soon was a good start to the operation.

I set up camp by the bridge and was joined by Bohemund.

'Enjoy that, Robby lad? You looked good from where we were.'

'Yes, Bohmey, actually I did, it was very satisfying.'

Indeed it had been. The fright of Dorylaeum had faded and, hardened by the extremes of Anatolia, I had developed a steely

163

humour; if they had fallen before my lances twice now, they would surely fall again.

So now we had secured another key point along the way. Next we went on to throw a cordon around the city.

On 20 October 1097 we renewed our journey and set off down the road to Antioch. The mountains which it occupied had been in view for some days, but today the city itself would come into our sight.

As I crested the last rise, I stopped, and my column was brought to an abrupt halt by my astonishment. Here was the city, founded fourteen hundred years ago in the time of Alexander the Great. Begun by General Seleucus and named after his father Antiochus, it had been a major city of the Roman Empire and had survived many earthquakes and attacks upon it. Now it was to be visited by the military might of the north in the name of our God. *In nomine Dei*; may he have mercy upon the souls of its citizens.

'Jesu!' exclaimed Stephen as the scale of the place became apparent, 'do you think we have brought sufficient in numbers?'

Bohemund looked stunned – this was no map, no daubs on a parchment; here was a walled city laid out in front of us in all its geographic glory and historical significance.

He looked across at me. 'Well!'

'Well what? It still only has five gates.'

'Thank you, Robby, I wish that I could diminish all my problems with such ease.'

'I learned it off my father; he was good at the diminishing game.'

Stephen nodded vigorously. 'Aye, he was. I couldn't get it off with your sister when he was in the castle.'

'I couldn't get it off with your other sister even when he was dead,' grumbled Allen.

I laughed. 'So tis true, Constance was a reluctant bride.'

Allen sniffed and mumbled something but said naught.

'Talking about getting it off,' added Ragenaus, 'I wonder what hospitality lies behind yonder walls.'

'A smile with a knife in its teeth I shouldn't wonder. Come on, we might as well get on with it.'

So saying, Bohemund prodded his mount and we went off towards our next impossible task.

As we wandered along behind, Stephen remarked to me, 'Are you thinking what I'm thinking?'

'I'm thinking that we may be here quite a while.'

'Does it bother you?'

'I've got a seventeen-year-old waiting for me in Italy.'

'Whereas I've got your sister waiting for me in Normandy.'

'What's wrong with my sisters?'

'They have too much of their father in them.'

'Bugger, isn't it?'

'Do those walls seem to be getting higher to you?'

'Jesu Christus! Yes. The closer we get the taller they become.'

'Have you brought a ladder?'

'Not with me.'

'Do you think that they will open the gates?'

'No.'

'What are we going to do?'

'What would we do at home, Stephen?'

'Set up camp outside and bore them into submission.'

'Quite! Christmas in the sunshine, that'll make a pleasant change, won't it?'

'If you say so, Robert... There seems to be a pleasant spot over yonder, should we occupy it?'

'Suits me, dear brother-in-law, suits me.'

We found that Taticius had not been exaggerating in his description of the fortified city: the walls were indeed taller than five men, with over three hundred towers set into them. The river formed another obstacle, it would be folly to get stuck between the walls and the river – and arrows would fly a very long way when loosed from the top of the walls. Also, the city would never be truly occupied until the castle on top of Mount Silpius had been taken.

Having expected Raymond to pass us when we halted to make camp, I was surprised when he failed to do so. Instead Godfrey rode up next.

'Where's your friend, the count of Toulouse?' I shouted.

Godfrey came over to where I was wrestling with some pavilion ropes.

'Careful who you name as my friend, young Robert. The silly old sod has gone round the back of the mountain, to see what lies behind, I think.'

'That's not a bad idea; he can have a look at that iron gate pass while he's there.'

'It's not a bad idea, but I'm not going to tell him so.'

'We need him and his money, Godfrey; be gentle with him.'

'Humph! Ever the diplomat, Robert, ever the watcher.' He smiled kindly, and even though I'd increasingly questioned the motives of these lords, I thought that Godfrey might be the most honest of them. Still, time would tell.

'I'm off to find the Gate of the Duke. I hope that it is as pleasant as these olive groves you've secured for yourselves.'

'Indeed, Godfrey, I wish you luck in that quest,' I replied, returning his smile. He had a parting remark, cast over his shoulder.

'And don't let your lot cast their rubbish in the river. I do not wish to be offended by the sight of your discards floating by my camp.'

I grinned, but he had a point; we needed to make the necessary arrangements for sanitation within our formations.

When Raymond elected to make a detour down the eastern side of the mountains to find Peter of Roaix before rounding the southern end to take up his position, it messed up our intentions to move into position smoothly, but I supposed that the watching Turks would find it amusing as we marched about in apparent confusion before them. *Well done, Raymond.*

Godfrey made his way down the western bank to take up his position opposite a central gate.

After a few days, we Normans had our section of the wall secured with defensive positions built, Taticius guarding the way back to the Iron Bridge and the mass of pilgrims encamped between us. Godfrey had built a wooden bridge opposite his gate, the conveniently named Gate of the Duke, and Raymond had eventually raised camp in his position.

Then we all settled down to see what the Turkish garrison commander, Yaghi Siyan, would do next.

Waiting by the river, in among the figs and olives, we were tempted to think that this besieging venture was not such a bad occupation after all.

Taticius came to see me after a few days. He trusted me, or rather he trusted me because he had been told to by Alexios. I seemed to have been judged the most honest in my purpose, and as I had demonstrated my worth on the battlefield, it was me that Taticius chose to work with.

I took him along to talk with Bohemund; there were some things to settle.

'So, Taticius, what is this Turcoman, Siyan, likely to do next?' Bohemund asked.

'He will wait,' replied our Greek, 'he has time to watch you all drown in the winter mud. He will send spies in among you, and listen to your men moaning and their stomachs groaning. Then he will send to his allies and tell them about your strengths and your weaknesses and one morning you will wake up in the mud and find your blankets peppered with arrows, your few horses gone, and your women ridden to death by a whole regiment: if you wake up at all that is.'

'Cheerful sod isn't he?' said Stephen, who like us all didn't enjoy the reference to Christian women being raped.

Bohemund looked puzzled.

'Mud! What mud? Where does mud come from in this sunshine?'

'It will change, the winter will bring it about. The peaks will have snow on them and the valleys will flood, but it will not snow down here... it will rain.'

I confirmed it. 'I have heard it said, it will rain and the wind will make it feel cold: we should prepare for it.'

Bohemund did not need much persuading; he had spent too many nights campaigning in Macedonia, but he had not been expecting cold weather so far south to be a factor, but then he had not been expecting to find himself in a siege situation.

He sighed and asked Taticius, 'Is there anything of hope then?'

The eunuch laughed his nasal laugh.

'Of course, my lord. Siyan has only five thousand men inside the walls, and in that,' he said, pointing at the citadel, isolated on the shoulder of Mount Silpius. Although it was all of two miles away from where we were standing, we could feel the eyes of its towers staring down at us.

'That castle is practically impregnable, and it has its escape route through the mountains behind, the Iron Gate.'

'How many iron gates are there?' I enquired.

'Two,' Taticius replied, 'you captured one on the bridge, but you will not ride a horse at the other, the path is too steep. Note the city at this end of the enclosure; it is populated by Syrians and Armenians – mostly Christians. The enclosure between the houses and the mountain slopes is scrubland, you could march your army about within the walls and no one would even notice.'

'I intend to, but what is your point, Taticius?' asked Bohemund.

'His point, Bohmey,' I pointed out, 'is that Siyan has as many miles of wall to defend as we have to attack – but with far fewer men, and a potentially hostile civilian population which far outnumbers his garrison.'

'Ahh! I see it now. Would they revolt, Taticius?'

'They might if you paid them enough, most of them just want to get on with their lives. Whatever happens between you and Siyan they are merely spectators, and will only gamble on taking sides when they can see a likely outcome.'

'I see,' Bohemund responded, 'what now, Robby? What do you want to do?'

'I am questioning our purpose in this siege. Now that we know the strength of the garrison, it surely will present a negligible threat to us if we move on. Let us remain here until spring and then depart; I came here for Jerusalem, not Antioch. But for now tis time to test my maritime supply lines. I will move down to the coast and bring in the supplies for you; you must construct a safe camp to overwinter within, a palisade with watchtowers and a keep – winter quarters for all. As well as shelter for you it will show the Turk that we are not ready to move on, worry him a bit more.'

'Very well, Robby. What do you hope to achieve?'

'I will secure the ports of St Simeon, and Laodicea ad Mare, and set up communications with Cyprus. From there I will send you timber, and artisans to build your forts, and institute lines of supply to keep you fed throughout the winter. Stephen will protect the roads; Aethilheard and Allen will protect Stephen. We will require as many horses as you can spare to move the supplies up from the beach. Then I will set about finding replenishments and horses from along the coast, and perhaps bring in some of my own steeds from Cyprus.'

'Yes, Robby, but you can't leave me without cavalry, you have shown their value lately only too well. Take any palfreys and anything else with four legs that you can find, but not a single destrier from me.'

Taticius remembered something.

'There is a port west of Laodicea, called Baniyas, it's famous for its trade in timber. You will need to go there, it's also rich in comestibles.'

Bohemund was pleased and could hardly wait to stuff *his* new plan up the noses of Godfrey and Raymond. Adhémar also took advantage of the plan and asked if I could get him over to Cyprus – there he hoped to meet with Alexios' Christian leader, Governor of Cyprus and nominal Patriarch of Jerusalem, Manuel Vutomites, and conduct 'some Church business,' as he put it.

All my early planning was coming to fruition; the long delaying meetings with Alexios and the messages which I sent across the seas to Italy and Cyprus were now paying off.

Together with Stephen, my mesnie, and Taticius, we rode the twenty miles downhill to St Simeon. When the sea came into view I could see that my ships were waiting; ten vessels as arranged, moored in the estuary of the Orontes river.

I was greeted by my fleet commander, Artus of Caen.

'Prince Robert. I had hoped I was in the right place, it is a little isolated here.'

'Artus, greetings. You have done well to find this spot, I congratulate you. You've not put any supplies ashore, I see?'

'No, my lord. We are watched, I wouldn't risk losing anything.'

'You did the right thing; we will secure the area before anything leaves the ships.'

The estuary was not ideal as a port, especially for the larger vessels that had sailed from Normandy. The beach was exposed and it would be better if the ships could sail upstream a little, beyond the first bend, and beach there to be safe from any winter storms.

As we'd descended into the river valley, I had spotted a defendable area not far from the sea, so Stephen went about the business of constructing a palisade to make it safe to live and work in, while I questioned Artus for any news.

Together with Adhémar, we quickly assimilated the strategic position along the coast and worked out the best plan to support the siege inland at Antioch.

While we worked on the plan Stephen was directing the unloading of the ships. First, the construction timbers, and the artisans needed to begin the fortifications. Then the component parts that would be quickly turned into wagons. When the wheels were on, the wagons were filled with supplies, timbers, metals and weapons, and the strange tools belonging to blacksmiths and wheelwrights were transferred. The ships were emptied as the wagons filled, until the wagons could hold no more, but as the vessels still held most of their cargoes the supplying of the army waiting outside Antioch was going to be a very repetitive affair.

On the hills surrounding the estuary Aethilheard's men cleared the area of the curious and the dangerous. No spectators would be allowed to linger and report back our dispositions or operations – to whoever would want to listen.

The short November day was soon over and I gathered my staff about me in the newly erected pavilion, lit by tapers to illustrate the newly drawn maps hung on the sides.

'We are here,' I pointed to St Simeon. 'Forty miles south is Laodicea... here, and across the sea is Cyprus, which is one hundred miles from Laodicea, and one hundred and thirty miles from where we are now.'

Philip, looking at the maps, asked, 'That is why Cyprus is so important?'

I grinned at Artus and he agreed with enthusiasm.

'It is central and key to our efforts to support the army. It lies within the dominions of the emperor and within easy reach of Italy, Constantinople, and the whole of the Mediterranean coast. Wherever the armies are, in relation to the coastline between Antioch and Jerusalem, we can re-supply them from the sea.'

'Yes, and ships are our best means of communication too,' added Stephen. 'What are the plans for tomorrow?'

'Tomorrow I want you to start moving the wagons up the hill and return empty as many times as you can. We'll see then how long it takes to empty the ships. And I want some of the vessels fitted out with stalls for twenty horses. As for me, I intend to sail down to Laodicea and attend to the defences. Artus informs me that there are Genoese ships waiting there but they're feeling insecure in the midst of the land of the Turks. They need some encouragement so I will take two hundred men-at-arms.'

Taticius looked at me querulously.

'Genoese! I heard rumours, Prince Robert, but how are they here?'

'I arranged it with my friend, Contessa Matilda, before I left Italy. It was confirmed with the emperor before I left Constantinople that they can pass within his dominions in support of our great cause.'

Adhémar said nothing, but might have wondered what else I had *arranged* to surprise him. Suspicions abounded in the camps of the Franks.

I expanded my plans.

'When the first ships are emptied and readied we will leave. You carry on, Stephen, and transfer all the supplies up to Antioch then you can send the other vessels down to Laodicea after me. I'll organise more supplies to come up from there on a regular basis.

Hold this beach secure whatever you do, it is vital to our operations.'

'I will, do not worry, Robert, I will.'

Adhémar remembered why he was present.

'Prince Robert, will I be travelling with you in the first ships to leave?'

'Yes. I will get you on a passage across to Cyprus as quickly as I can. I intend to make a regular service across the sea part of the supply lines. But remember it's winter, and we can only move when the weather permits us.'

It being late, and a little cold, all those not on guard were keen to get some rest and I joined them. I slept but fitfully as rain fell at times during the night, and the gentle surf lapping on the beach disturbed the peace; eventually I dropped off and if any of my tired men woke before dawn, I heard them not.

I stirred early, my thoughts all a-tumble, and, wanting a piss, left the pavilion to empty my bladder into the sea. Shortly, as the eastern sky began to lighten, I became aware of a figure standing at the edge of the sea. It was Adhémar.

'Bishop Adhémar. You are about early today.'

'Yes, Prince Robert, I could not sleep for thinking. Ah! Here comes Arnulf. Good morrow, Arnulf; I have been thinking.'

'Thinking? It seems to be a common problem. Does the idea of the sea journey disturb you, bishop?'

'No, Arnulf, not that. It is that these sands, this beach, that small village over yonder... these are places where Paul of Tarsus strode, where he preached the words of his master, Jesu Christi. These are blessed sands. Here, and now, I feel as close as I ever have done to the word of God. For the first time on this perilous journey I feel that I know why I am here.'

I stood quietly for a while before saying, 'It was a thousand years ago, bishop.'

'Yes, but I feel it... Believe me, the shadow of Paul still falls across these sands.'

I spotted an opportunity for a bit of peace and asked Arnulf, 'Would you like to go to Cyprus with Adhémar?'

'Oh, can you do without me, my prince?'

'I'll manage. Tis a rare opportunity to see the island of Aphrodite.'

A shadow of doubt passed over his countenance with the reference to earthly matters and I thought I had spoiled my chance of losing my shadow for a few weeks, but curiosity won and he accepted.

Then the present world broke into our reverie; men coughing, horses farting, the rattle of metal armour and cooking pots, and then the sun high enough to illuminate it all – another day dawned in an alien land.

Later, we set sail southwards to reach the second port in my plans, Laodicea. This was to be my centre on the mainland as much as Cyprus was my link to Europe. Laodicea provided better shelter for the ships we were using; St Simeon was too exposed to the winter storms. Alexandretta was too far north and when we got away from Antioch it would become of little use in supporting operations at Jerusalem.

Reaching Laodicea, an established port since Roman times, I found a dozen Genoese ships, loaded with the supplies of war and ready to sail. After greeting them and giving them reassurances, I despatched them to St Simeon for Stephen to deal with. After reinforcing the meagre garrison with my detachment of men-at-arms, I left in a *knörr* to inspect the next port of Baniyas.

This was where I hoped to augment our sparse timber supplies with locally sourced wood. Our plan to confront Antioch's walls with a line of donjon and bailey fortifications was now underway; the Turks had not yet witnessed the Norman approach to a siege but they would not have to wait long.

As the year matured and the winter turned wet it rained most of the time, but as it was essential to maintain supplies our mariners found it difficult to keep up the pace. The biggest problem became the wear and tear on the ships. Usually they'd be laid up for the winter to allow essential repairs and maintenance to be carried out; this year I wanted them on the water and they suffered because of it; sails, rigging and sailors' hands all began to fail and it slowed down the passage of supplies. Young Philip struggled to keep his parchments dry and became quite protective of them, but they were important, all those lists. So were the letters intended to go further, back to Normandy and Brittany. No doubt their contents were not entirely credible and I looked forward to the day when I could assure any recipient as to the accuracy of those reports, just as I looked forward to telling Sibyl – although I went through periods of despairing that I should ever see her again – or Tegwin, or anyone else who mattered to me.

We were hard pressed to keep up with demand, but the hardship at sea was as nothing compared to that of the forces on the land with food supplies very low.

Adhémar returned from Cyprus, and leaving Payne and Ragenaus behind to control things I took Philip and accompanied the bishop back up to St Simeon to discuss his visit, and for me to see how Stephen was coping with things.

'I hope that you enjoyed your time on Cyprus, Adhémar, because things are not very comfortable outside the walls of Antioch.'

'No sign of surrender then?'

'No, it's getting messy up there. Stephen sends to me that there is regular contact between the Christians of the city and our forces. Traders are allowed out of the gates to set up stalls and they go back inside at night. Bohemund thinks that some of them are spies.'

'He is probably right, why does he allow it?'

'Stephen thinks that Bohemund has bought some of them and they are spying for him. He says that some very strange people have been visiting Bohemund and he may have some plot of his own in play.'

'That, also, is likely. What else does Stephen think?'

'He says that the Turkish horsemen pour out of one gate or another from time to time, loose off hundreds of arrows, and bugger off back inside. Raymond and Godfrey are losing men and horses daily but they cannot follow the Turks because they are back within the walls before they can react.'

'What is the horse situation?'

'Not good. We continue to lose warhorses, replacements are thin on the ground and I may have to bring ours over from Cyprus. What have you learned from there?'

'Your horses are fine. And the emperor will continue to support us, but I only have the promise of the governor of Cyprus, Vutomites, to provide such supplies as are sent to him by the emperor, and there is no suggestion of troops being sent to support us.'

I thought about that for a while before voicing a dark thought.

'Alexios intends to let us capture Antioch and then garrison it with his own men. Then we go off and capture Jerusalem.' I looked at Adhémar very closely. 'That's the way of it, is it not, Adhémar?'

'I fear you may be right, my prince.'

'Then if Bohemund is doing some plotting of his own, it would hardly be a surprise, would it?'

'No. I'm cold, is there no shelter from this never-ending rain?'

I continued to regard Adhémar; something was not quite right.

'What Church business was it that took you to Cyprus?'

'We sent joint letters to the heads of Europe, Vutomites and myself, asking for support – Antioch will need a bishop.'

'What's that to you?'

'As will Jerusalem,' he replied, ignoring my question.

'You are not going to start another row between Rome and Constantinople, are you?'

'No, not when the situation can be mutually beneficial. Jerusalem is a long way from Constantinople.'

'Antioch is nearer and closer to Alexios' domain.'

'It would be a convenient arrangement. Does it bother you, my prince?'

'No, I have little interest in the politics of the Church.'

I looked away, over the side of the ship to observe the grey sea, then the sodden sails and the miserable seamen; it added to my gloomy mood. *War is simple,* I thought, *tis the flies around its arse that bother me.*

'Stephen should have a fire to warm you; we won't be long now.'

I set a limit on this conversation. More plotting, more manoeuvring for position. The carcasses of Antioch and Jerusalem were in the jaws of jackals before ever we had them in our control.

At sea the sails were wet, the hawsers hard to handle; the sea's surface was spattered by the rain and progress was slow. The captain got the crew to row now and again – as much to warm them up as to help speed the vessel. We reached St Simeon eventually, and as we entered the estuary, Adhémar was surprised to see how much progress Stephen had made in protecting the beachhead. A palisade now formed a defensive perimeter in the shape of a semi-circle with several watchtowers built into the wall. The palisade's ends were footed in the water's edge, and its defences were completed by the river itself.

They had also built quays, so it was safe to service the ships as they arrived full, and departed empty.

We were greeted by a miserable-looking Stephen, who conducted us to shelter and warm food. When we were settled he asked me about our current consignment.

'What have you brought us this time, Robert?' he uttered, without much enthusiasm. I could see how tired he was.

I gestured towards Philip, steaming by a fire and cramming his mouth with chicken.

'Philip has the lists. Have you got your requirements for the next consignment?'

'Yes, it is mainly for food, and more shelters, and I've included firewood. People are becoming ill in the wet; even the strongest have ailments of the chest. We are weakening as the winter goes on.'

Adhémar tried to cheer him.

'We've made the necessary arrangements with Cyprus for supplies, and more will be available, but it is the shipping – Prince Robert will tell you.'

I nodded. 'We are held back by the weather, our ships spend too much time in port to keep up with your demands. If we had more vessels, could you handle more through here? Do you have sufficient men and horses to increase your baggage trains up the hill?'

Stephen sighed and showed his fatigue.

'No, by God's miracles, we could not. There are twenty thousand to feed and we cannot do it with the present rate of re-supply.'

Adhémar asked about local foraging. We had expected to undertake at least some foraging, perhaps by purchase or perhaps by force – it was normal practice.

Stephen could only disappoint us again.

'No, it has proven too costly. Every time we send out a party they are attacked before they can lay their hands on any meaningful supplies. It seems that there's a Turkish base somewhere close by; Bohemund is going out with Flanders soon to find and destroy it, and try and prevent these ambushes.'

Adhémar tried to bring some cheer to the evening.

'Well,' he said with enthusiasm, 'at least I can take them good news in the morning about the supplies from Cyprus.'

Stephen looked at him with bleary eyes.

'Yes, bishop, no doubt, but news won't fill their bellies.'

'No, of course,' he replied, quite deflated that his news had not been better received. So he tried a different tack. 'How is Lord Godfrey?'

'Poorly.'

'And Raymond?'

'Poorly.'

'Who is not ill?'

'Bohemund, Tancred. This is a young man's war, bishop; nobody will be cured by it, but more will surely become ill.'

Stephen's attitude shocked Adhémar.

'Have faith, my son, we are being tested, it is beyond our reasoning... The Lord's intent is to test our commitment: have faith.'

Stephen stared into the embers of the fire just outside the tent doorway, but kept his thoughts to himself. After a while he mentioned that Bohemund would like to see me.

'Why? I have enough to do down here.'

'I think he wants your advice. He respects you greatly, you know that?'

'I suppose so, but I cannot spare the time. While this wet weather lasts we can move the ships, if only slowly; if it turns stormy we'll be stuck in port. Besides I must keep Laodicea safe. Give him my regards and explain for me.'

'I will,' Stephen agreed wearily, but perhaps thinking that my refusal would not go down well, tried again.

'I suspect that he is seeking your friendship... some support from you, confirmation that he's doing the best. He is becoming isolated from the others; their illnesses are leaving him as the natural leader. You know what would happen if he felt there were no constraints upon his actions?'

'Yes, Stephen, I see it, but if that is the way we will achieve one leader then it can only be better than the situation at present, where everyone is in charge. Just leave it, let him know that he has my support, if from a distance; I'm needed down here.'

Stephen nodded. He also had enough to do, his supply line up to Antioch was attacked on a daily basis somewhere along its length – he was in a war of attrition, and it was extremely wearing.

Adhémar said nothing. He knew what his goals were – it was just a question of positioning: pick the winning faction and all will fall into place. *I, also, am weary, but of these seekers after glory – pah!*

Things were better back at Laodicea. I returned to find Payne and Ragenaus on the jetty grinning like ninnies.

'What ails thee?' I demanded, 'what's so good about this eternal strife that we're in?'

'Well... my lord,' Payne ventured, then shuffled, but could not remove the grin.

'We have got a pair of housekeepers, my lord,' blurted out Ragenaus.

'Housekeepers! What, a pair of old crones? How much are you paying them, how are you paying them?' I asked.

'Erm, we are not paying them, lord, they turned up at our billet and more or less pushed their way in,' Payne informed me.

'Yes, and they are not crones, my lord,' added Ragenaus.

'Oh really?'

'Yes, my lord,' said Payne, still shuffling, looking for approval, 'and their names are Naomi and –'

'Ariadne,' proclaimed Ragenaus.

I looked at them, a pair of children at that moment, with new toys. 'I take it that they're not past fifty then?'

'Er,' stuttered Payne, 'nor twenty, my lord.'

'Very well, I suppose you couldn't bring yourselves to turn them away.'

'No, lord,' they responded in unison.

'Then remember that if there are any children they remain your responsibility. Now what has arrived in the port since I left?'

The matter was settled but it had revived my own thoughts, tumbling images of Matilda, Tegwin, and Sibyl – *Jesu! My life is a mess.*

The year turned into 1098 but there was little to celebrate, as I found out when I next went back to St Simeon.

Stephen was looking even more depressed and morose than before.

'Hallo, Stephen,' I ventured a greeting as I stepped off the craft. 'You look pissed off.'

'That's how well it's going. What have you brought me?'

'Weapons, arrows and spears.'

'No livestock? Horses?'

'Some, they're still on the horizon,' I pointed to the sails coming up behind. 'Not much use for war but they will carry and pull wagons.'

'Palfreys?' Stephen brightened. 'Better than naught I suppose. What's that awful smell?'

'It's from the second ship.' I pointed at the one which was just scraping along the jetty. ''Tis sheep.'

'Sheep! God's bollocks, Robert, sheep! What can they carry, for Christ's sake?'

'Nothing, but you can eat them.'

'I suppose… Why did you not bring just the carcasses?'

'They keep better alive; slaughter them here. Don't make so much fuss, Stephen, they're becoming very expensive. Actually anything useful is becoming very expensive. If Alexios wasn't providing some money we'd have been on our way home long ago.'

'Home!' A wistful expression came across Stephen's face. 'I could do with home right now. I can't get anything right for that lot up the hill, they think I'm holding back on them. In fact they blame you for the shortages, they say that you're enjoying a life of luxury and debauchery in your seaports.'

'Some hope. The only things shaggable in Laodicea are in that boat over there, and I eat the same as I send you here. Be assured, there is no luxury in this accursed land. Now tell me about the siege.'

I wasn't about to tell him the truth about Laodicea; the quays and sailors' hostelries, the Roman baths and the solid forts standing guard over the place, and especially about the private villas with extensive vineyards and views of the bay – and housekeepers. *I might take him there one day*: a thought to salve my conscience.

Stephen turned, and we walked up the beach a short distance. A watery sun had appeared and it made the day a little more cheerful. We sat down on the sand. Stephen gathered his thoughts and began to brief me.

'There have been disasters. Bohemund and Flanders set off on a foraging mission. They took men, cavalry, such as we have, and infantry enough for the task, but they were ambushed and lucky to escape.'

'Anything more?'

'Yes. While they were away the Turks sent out a raiding party from the city. More casualties, and more horses lost. Adhémar lost his banner in the fighting and the Turks flew it from the city walls. Imagine, Adhémar's banner, a likeness of the Virgin Mary, flown upside down by the Turks, what insult is that?'

'Christ have mercy. It grows worse by the hour.'

'There'll be little mercy if we lose this one, Bohemund has ensured that.'

'Why so?'

'When he returned from his raid and heard about Adhémar he took the heads off his Turkish prisoners and had them catapulted them over the walls.'

'No mercy?'

'None. So the Turks returned the gift with a barrage of Christian heads, it was unseemly.'

'Merciful God, what a mess. Give us guidance.' I stood and paced along the sands for a while, then turned and said to Stephen, 'I should seek to bring some order into this sad adventure. First I must go back to Laodicea and bring back my mesnie. I need to reorganise the defences there to operate without them and place someone in charge of the supply operation. Tell Bohemund that I'll be back before the end of the month.'

Stephen nodded his assent and cheered up a little, the thought of having me in support, backing him up among the squabbling Frankish princes had helped.

'Have you brought any wine with you, Robert?'

'Yes. Go and get the fire ablaze, I'll be back shortly.'

Stephen faced the sea, and raising his arms against the sky, shouted to no one in particular, 'Shite! Bollocks to you all! Tonight I am going to get pissed, sod it.'

I joined him. Since seeing Payne and Ragenaus' 'housekeepers', two girls who had found their way from Constantinople, I had been filled with a yearning for something better, something that I had lost from my life. If so much was not now dependent on me I might have jumped on the next ship to Cyprus and said bollocks to it all. Instead I got pissed and awoke on the heaving sea – having been loaded as cargo onto the empty vessel – then proceeded to empty my cargo over the side for most of the voyage. Serves me right, I thought, but that yearning had not gone overboard with the contents of my stomach.

Three weeks later I returned to the beachhead at St Simeon, together with my mesnie, having dragged my two protectors from their housekeepers' attentions. I found Taticius waiting for me.

'Greetings, Taticius. Where is Stephen?'

'The Lord be with you, Prince Robert. He is up the hill with Bohemund. I have taken command here while they sort out the operation, and there is much to be done.'

'I see. How goes the siege?'

Taticius' eyes glinted on either side of his shiny plate; he uttered an adenoidal snort that betokened an adverse view of *the siege*.

'It is not a siege, it has ceased to be a siege; it is now an encampment before the walls.' I wasn't certain as to his meaning but held my tongue, awaiting further explanation. 'We do not have sufficient numbers to ensure that the gates are closely guarded, and we are only sending out foot patrols to try to control those moving in and out of the city.'

'No mounted patrols?'

'Not many, we have very few horses and those are held in reserve. We can only hold two gates secure, the St Paul and the Dog Gate. Godfrey has put a wooden bridge over the river opposite the Dog Gate now and he can chase back any marauding Turks, and everyone has wooden palisades and towers to take refuge in when necessary.'

'How many are left?'

'In all you still have about twenty thousand mouths to feed, but only about five thousand are military and less than five hundred are mounted.'

I suspected that the situation would be less than ideal... *but this is unsustainable; in a few weeks, when the weather improves, the Turks will roll all over us: it must be changed.*

'We need assistance, Taticius. Will you go back to the emperor? If he wants Antioch he will not win it by sitting on his arse in Constantinople.'

'I agree, my lord, I just needed someone to say it.' He hesitated before making a suggestion. 'When we arrived here,

Prince Robert, you wondered at the wisdom of this siege, and thought of leaving here in the spring. Is this still on your mind?'

I had no difficulty in confirming my thoughts in that regard.

'Yes. It has changed my planned support; it has altered to supporting this siege instead of going along the coast to support the attack on Jerusalem.'

He looked worried. 'The emperor is hoping for the return of Antioch. Are you going to try and persuade the other leaders to press on?'

'I doubt that I will succeed in that, Taticius, they seem set on this prize.'

'Then the sooner it is done the quicker you can get on.'

'I suppose so.'

But doubts ran around my head. We had diverted ourselves in our prime purpose for the obvious gain of the emperor. But what could I do? It was pointless leaving with only my men; to achieve our goal would require everybody to de-camp and move onwards. I must wait for a suitable time to boot them up their backsides.

Taticius pressed home his desires.

'Can I have a ship? I'll leave my command here to my deputy and go to Cyprus; I'll see what more I can squeeze out of Vutomites. I should find a Byzantine ship there and I will send despatches back to Constantinople to request more help.'

'Go safely, Taticius, may God speed your passage.'

'Thank you, Prince Robert, but I'll care for my passage myself.'

I grinned. He'd not lost his sense of humour, despite all his other losses, and I went to make the necessary arrangements for Taticius before travelling up to Antioch.

I found very little of encouragement when I arrived. In the three months since we arrived, the disposition of the forces before Antioch had changed little. They were concentrated into three armed camps, watched over from wooden keeps protected by wooden palisades with battlements to fight from, but they only stretched between the Gates of the Duke and St Paul.

To the north of the palisaded camps was the area occupied by the pilgrims; it was vulnerable. Although protected to the front by the army, on one side by the mountain, and to the other by the river, our commanders could only spare a minimal of troops to guard its northern rear. A cynic might argue that the civilian camp provided a valuable cushion for the army in case of attack.

Altogether we now occupied an area of about two square miles outside the city. To an observer, the size of the city dwarfed the size of its would-be occupiers – and it would take a huge victory of faith and of hope over reality to think that we would ever reduce it to subjection. The Turks must have sneered at us every morning when they viewed our pathetic array. Quite why they had never come out from behind their walls and destroyed us I could not understand; as a siege it was a miserable effort.

I rode towards Bohemund's position outside the St Paul Gate – my approach had been reported.

'Robby!' the familiar voice boomed out at me from half a mile away.

'Oh God,' I groaned to Philip, 'he sounds really weak.'

'We could have done with him in that fog two weeks ago, he could have kept us away from the land.'

'Stephen and Flanders are with him, I see; quite a welcome.'

Whatever policy differences lay between me and Bohemund, it didn't break our friendship – that would have to be tested in stronger ways to be set aside.

'Greetings, Bohmey, it seems an age since we parted.'

'Aye, and in a different world I fear. Come inside, Robby, there is much to discuss. Have you brought any horses?'

'Not many, their cost is beyond my purse.' That was not entirely true but my horses were for the relief of Jerusalem. There seemed little point in wasting them on a siege.

'That is the truth, Robby; we are being held to ransom here, is that not true, nephew?' He looked at Tancred who nodded glumly, before adding, 'Raymond has established a fund to re-horse as many knights as possible but the merchants are bleeding us dry.'

I completed my greetings to Stephen and Cousin Robert.

'You two look tired.' That was a simple statement of fact.

'Yes, Robert,' said Flanders, 'it is a wearisome business... and it goes on without end.'

'It would end soonest if I could bury my sword in someone's head.' This from Duke Allen, who arrived from his position in time to hear us whinging.

'We need to gain entry first,' said Bohmey, fingering his pommel.

We dismounted and settled down to exchange information. We were a very select group, with no one to represent Godfrey or Raymond – this was to be a very Norman parley.

Bohemund, not being one to mess with courtesies, went straight to the point.

'I'm minded to tell those two that I'm going to pull out of this shambles.'

'Are you?' I asked in a neutral tone.

'No,' he said, with a grim smile, 'I have come too far, and gained too little – and there is something else.'

The crafty lord beckoned us nearer.

'Two weeks ago, Robby, we caught one of the Turks out on a night raid. He was anxious to return to his family and offered us information to gain his release.'

I wondered exactly how anxious the prisoner had been, or how he had been *persuaded*.

'What information?'

'It seems that guarding the watchtowers is a family affair. Each gate is controlled by a family head. Our prisoner thought that his patriarch would open the family gate in return for his son's release.'

Stephen nodded. 'It seemed too good to be true.'

Flanders agreed. 'It was.'

Bohemund went on.

'We made arrangements to release him at the gate but it remained shut and we were showered with rocks from above.'

'Aye,' said Robby, 'we heard later that Yaghi Siyan had taken precautions and replaced the family with another, so that idea was a failure.'

Something was puzzling me.

'How do you know all these things? Have you spies inside?'

Bohemund laughed out loud and was joined by the others.

'Spies!' he roared, 'spies! The place is thick with them, by the balls of Beelzebub! Every merchant sells donkeys for horses' prices and takes note of your health as he does it. All information has a price, Robby, and it works both ways, so the merchants get paid twice: once by the Turk for chatter and again by us for tatty asses.'

'It's not that simple though,' Flanders chipped in. 'They get paid to tell us things, and we pay them to tell the Turks things, so now nobody knows what the truth is. Except that the merchants grow rich on lies.'

The conversation had gone off in a direction of its own, so I asked, 'What has this to do with *something else*, Bohmey?'

'What?'

'You said that you had *something else* in mind.'

'Ah yes, something else indeed. I have developed a relationship with someone who has the ear of someone else.'

I wondered if this was likely to go on much longer, I was losing track of who was what, and the introduction of *someone else* might finally lose me in Bohemund's wilderness.

'You see, Robby, dear friend, we will use treachery to gain access. We are going to buy our way in.'

I wondered why we could not have arrived at this point earlier – but still.

'I see,' I said uncertainly, 'and when is this to happen?'

'Soon!' said the giant, 'we will be ready soon.'

They might have been, but the Turks had been hatching plots of their own, and they were ready sooner than Bohemund.

News came the following morning, 'A great host is approaching from the east.' This was reported by our scouts. A sense of urgency took over and we convened to decide on a course of action. Bohemund's previous grand plan went unexplained as we hastily contrived a response to this new and immediate threat before going to a council of war with the other leaders.

This was the first move by the Turks to relieve Antioch, and because of the improving weather, had been expected. The advancing force was reckoned to be about ten to twelve thousand

186

strong, and led by Ridwan of Aleppo. They were camped near Harim, twenty-five miles to the east.

Bohemund led the discussion. It was clear that neither Godfrey nor Raymond had any ideas other than forming a defence where they stood. I needed to ensure that more imaginative solutions were explored.

Bohemund was to make frequent references to the maps that I prepared for him.

'This is where Ridwan has advanced to,' he pointed to Harim on the map. 'It's about eight miles south of Artah, which is still held by Flanders' men.'

Robert of Flanders nodded proudly. 'My banner still flies there.'

Bohemund continued, 'We think that Ridwan will attempt to take the Iron Bridge that Robby captured, so I suggest we base our plan on him taking that route.'

Godfrey wanted to know why.

I responded.

'Because it is the easiest for him. His intelligences will tell him that there are only a few holding the bridge, a small guard from Taticius' force, and there will be little resistance, they can only fall back and warn us. Besides, the route through there is the quickest and easiest for him to take.'

Godfrey went over to the corner where Raymond lay quietly in the fetid gloom. He was sweating profusely, an attendant mopping his brow. He was asked a question but all that Godfrey got back was a moan and a weak wave of a hand.

Turning back to Bohemund, Godfrey posed a question.

'Why don't you want to make a stand here?'

'Ridwan will be expecting that, there will be no surprise. There's no tactical advantage in allowing the enemy to plan for the expected. I want to do the unexpected, see if he can plan for that!'

Bohemund must, like me, have sensed that he would win the day for our Norman plan if he persisted. I hoped that he would resist revealing the sting in the tail for long enough to get it accepted.

Godfrey thought that he had spotted a flaw in the strategy of taking the fight to the enemy.

'Are you to surrender this camp to the city Turks, then?'

'No, it will be defended; the siege will be maintained.'

'You intend to mount an aggressive expedition *and* defend our present position? God's miracles, that will be clever.'

Flanders grinned.

'Then clever we'll be, good Godfrey... or die in the failure.'

It was at that point, I think, that it came home to Godfrey that the momentum had accrued to us, but because he had no serious alternatives to respond with, and no energy to argue with, he decided to agree; possibly to let us take the blame for the approaching disaster – or take his share of the glory if we lived. He may have been wise for the moment. Neither he nor Raymond were fit enough, nor young enough, to take on these ambitious young Normans.

'Tell me your plan then, Bohemund,' he said in resignation.

'We go out and attack them; I need every horse we can muster. I intend to defeat the enemy in the style of Robert of Normandy, the ground will be of our choice and suited to the use of cavalry in the manner of Robert's past successes.'

'Why does not Robert go? How will you defend this position?'

'We've agreed that because the major part of the defence of this place will be in the hands of your infantry, supported by Robert's archers, he will command here and retain all the archers. I will take their horses to augment Tancred's cavalry.'

'What about Stephen and Flanders?'

'They're coming with me; I need their knowledge of Robert's methods to make my plan work.'

'I'm staying with Robert,' added Allen, although unasked. 'My sword senses blood nearest to Robert.'

Godfrey went over to the pale-faced Raymond and consulted for a while in whispers before he returned to face us.

'If we agree, what will be the price?'

Bohemund drew himself up to his full majesty and fixed Godfrey with a fierce glare.

188

'If you do not agree, Duke Godfrey, the price will be extermination – and I will not agree to that.'

'What do you mean, not agree?'

'I will not stay to be slaughtered.'

Adhémar was astonished. 'You would leave us?'

'I came here for success and have waited too long for it. I will not agree to fail.'

Tancred, who had been waiting silently in the background, now added the killer blow.

'If you have no other plan, my lord Godfrey?'

Godfrey looked across at Raymond – he simply nodded weakly.

'It seems we have little choice, Bohemund. Robert, are you confident?'

'I am, and there is work to do, Godfrey. Besides, we have wasted too much time outside this poxy city, I want to move on.'

I was short with Godfrey, unusually so, but I could see little use for further discussion.

Godfrey gave a little sigh.

'Very well, let's be about it then.'

Bohemund left after dark; he had no intention of allowing the Turks on the walls to count his riders – it would not have taken very long, in the event there were only about nine hundred – to face twelve thousand – still, they had faith.

I set about explaining the desired troop disposition to my new subordinates. I showed how the borrowed foot soldiers would be backed up by archers – and I was able to produce more of those than Godfrey's brother Eustace and Bishop Adhémar had expected.

Captured weapons had been brought together, and the knights with no mounts, and others, had been trained in the use of the Turkish bows.

The briefing was going quite well until I came to explain how the unarmed pilgrims, including their women, would be part of the deployment. I was explaining how they would be utilised to provide support behind the lines – I wanted them to bring water, attend to the wounded, and replenish supplies. There was a silence when I asked about the numbers available, including women.

After an embarrassed silence Adhémar told me, 'There are no women left in the camp, save the ladies of lords.'

I was perplexed.

'What do you mean, bishop?'

'They have been banished, for their sins of fornication.'

I was astonished.

'Did they fornicate on their own?'

'No, of course not, but they tempted men to join them.'

Payne Peverel made his presence felt with a blast from the marquee doorway.

'My prince!' he cried, 'I have discovered that most of them were married and were forcibly separated from their husbands for this banishment.'

My mood changed, and there was anger in the air.

Peverel said more. 'They shaved the women and sent them around the camp before despatching them to their fate. Fortunately a lot of their men went with them, but they were lost to us, my lord.'

'Whose idea was this?' I almost whispered.

'Fulcher of Chartres'. He persuaded the council that we were unsuccessful in our mission because of the sin among us, and that we must be purified.' This was Adhémar's weak response.

I did not often succumb to anger – but this was beyond reason.

'So where are these sinners now?'

'Cast out into the desert, who knows? We also fasted for three days, to be certain of our purity.'

'Fasted! God's miracles, fasted! I thought you were all starving up here, I've spent the last three months trying to feed you all... And you have been FASTING!'

Adhémar opened his mouth to reply but did not draw breath before I filled the air with rage.

Now, bishop, and all your miserable fellow priests, let's get this straight; I did not invite these pilgrims along on this God-blessed journey, your pope did that and seeing as how everyone on the road has his and God's blessing, they will all be treated the same. And while I'm at it let me remind you, you bishop born of a woman, that Jesu himself was born of a woman: would you cast out the blessed Mary with such disdain? I think not! Now I charge you, Adhémar, get out of here and go organise a recovery party to bring back the bodies and souls of men and women from the peril which your ill-conceived logic has cast them into. Now go before I take my men and leave you standing on your own in this poxy desert.'

Arnulf gasped and grasped my arm. 'My prince, be not so hasty, I beg of –'

'Not now, Arnulf.' I turned away and left the tent, frightened of my own anger. I did not return for a while, by which time Adhémar had made himself scarce.

Arnulf came to find me, and speaking gently, reminded me of the task in hand. He did not seek to justify the actions that had just been described. A wise man was Arnulf, because my opinion of churchmen had ebbed like the tide on a wet beach.

Persuaded, I returned to my friends and issued a command to Philip.

'Go after that bishop. Tell him to stay here and pray, and then take a patrol into the desert, find those poor wretches and bring them back here. They are sisters of the blessed Mary and will not be sacrificed on the whim of some twisted thought.'

I knew full well the fate of Christian women captured by the Turks; systematic rape followed by decapitation was the pattern.

The Gods of Islam and Christianity were at war and the idea of *respect* had been trampled into the bloody dust of the desert.

My simmering fury found an outlet the following day – 9 February.

When the Turks noticed the absence of horses in our lines, they opened the St Paul Gate and sallied forth to attack our positions.

It had not taken Philip long to locate the banished, cowering in some miserable grove within sight of our camps, knowing not what to do or whither to go. They were soon brought within the three palisades, those with husbands reunited, and organised to support the pending attack. Adhémar was with Godfrey at the Gate of the Duke, he would not come near me for a long time, while Godfrey's brother Eustace commanded Raymond's position at the Dog Gate and the north-west perimeter outside the Gate of St Paul was in my own hands with Allen by my side.

In front of the St Paul Gate there was open ground to manoeuvre upon, so the enemy chose to concentrate their efforts upon my position, and I was ready for them.

Standing upright on the battlement of the wooden keep, I surveyed the preparations; close by me, and much more mature than when they had set off on this momentous journey, were Payne, Ragenaus, and Philip. My flags, nailed to the very top of the position, were flying defiantly, as we watched the first advance of the Turks.

Beneath us, and sheltered by the sturdy wooden walls of the palisade, were our rescued women.

Also sheltering behind the sturdy palings were our knights, soldiers and archers, all watching for my signals. This was our favoured defensive ring and I prayed that the other two compounds were as well prepared – and then they came.

Spewing out of the gateway three abreast, the deadly Turkish archers urged on their snorting beasts and closed down upon our defences with great speed. My first signal saw a shower of death unleashed from behind our wooden walls. First, the longbows sent off their armour-piercing shafts to descend upon the heads of the advancing Turks – striking man or horse, they broke up their order but the bulk of their numbers charged on and soon unleashed a storm of arrows of their own. They flew over the outer palisade and began to strike the keep – it sounded like the rattle of a hundred drums and made the structure shake. At the same time those of my men with the Turkish bows, using a lighter shaft, let loose on a flatter trajectory, again taking out horses and riders.

'Jesu!' cried Allen, peering over the battlement when the Turks had passed, 'the walls look like a hedgehog.'

'Aye,' I replied, 'we'll stay curled up inside here then.'

Most of the riders survived, and having loosed their missiles, turned and regrouped some distance away. This was their expected tactic and we had witnessed it before at Dorylaeum. Again they galloped past and took casualties, but there were few casualties behind our protecting timber; our preparations had been too complete.

Then they tried a new tactic. When the next riders sallied forth their archers were carrying flaming arrows. As before a lot were downed, but many survived our aerial barrage and let loose their fiery missiles. Most were aimed to land within the outer paling and again started to strike the inner keep, where some, still aflame with an incendiary grease, started to scorch the wooden walls. The area of the inner bailey began to fill with noxious fumes and several women left the shelter of the palisade and ran towards the keep to try and douse the blaze. Risking injury, I leaned over and shouted to them to return to the safe zone at the bottom of the palisade.

'Wait there!' I shouted, above the screeching Turks, 'wait until I tell you.'

I gestured to one of my captains, crouching low behind the battlements. 'Go down below and wait behind the postern door. Gather blankets and what water we have, and when I signal, go out and douse the flames. The women will help.'

He climbed down the ladder together with three others and I waited as he prepared. As the attack faded and the surviving Turks returned to regroup inside the city, I shouted, 'Now!' and watched as the flaming arrows were removed from where they'd pinned the fire to my wooden walls, and those timbers burning were extinguished.

'Have you ever seen a flaming hedgehog, Allen?' I laughed as I peered over the top at our peppered timbers.

It was difficult to see down there now and only those on top of the keep knew for certain what was going on outside. For seeming ages we repelled the burning attacks. This was not going to be an easy victory; the city garrison seemed to have an endless supply of horses and archers and they returned time and time again. In the intervals between charges, my women scampered about the compound dousing flames and collecting the spent Turkish arrows, which they carried to our men waiting behind the palisades. In a virtuous circle the Turks were providing the ammunition for their own defeat – some arrows were re-ignited before we sent them back so those who came too close were rewarded with a fiery response from their own flames.

In this artillery battle there was only going to be one winner: we who were sheltered by the wooden walls. When the fruitless slaughter came to an end I was left to survey, as best I could through the smoke, the field of Turkish dead and dying scattered all around my position.

They closed the gate mid afternoon, and when some time had elapsed and the smoke cleared I could see that our other positions had survived, and they too were decorated by the dead and dying enemy. When I judged it safe I sent men out to bring in as many enemy horses as could be caught and purloin as many Turkish weapons as were worth salvaging from the blood-rinsed battlefield. All in all it had been a profitable day before the walls of Antioch and quite against our earlier expectations.

In the evening, as the light faded, the gate opened again in front of my position and, under a white flag, parties of litter-bearers began to emerge. I was content to let them collect the bodies – these were now quite naked. All accoutrements, weapons, jewellery and other personal effects had already been removed into the besieging strongholds and I saw no point in a vindictive attack upon these unarmed carriers; they were probably Christian anyway, pressed into service by their Turkish overlords.

That night messengers arrived from Bohemund. He had triumphed over the numerically far superior army of Ridwan, and was on his way back; I knew that there would be some glorious tales coming back with them and was eager to listen to their recounting.

Bohemund rode through the night, and in the morning his arrival signalled an end to such niceties as I had given the vanquished; instead he unbundled many sacks of Turkish heads and placed them on spikes along the front of the city walls.

'How did you fare?' I asked when he had done with his grisly task.

'I had them on ground of my choosing,' he grinned. *I knew it, he had listened to me.* 'Their vanguard came to me up a valley, I took them in a charge and they turned back.'

'Good, and next?'

'I had squadrons hidden at the sides, behind the crest. As the vanguard turned in confusion your men swooped down upon the main army; it was a goodly rout.'

I thought that he had pushed fate a little too far.

'You brought the leading Turks on to your position and they fell into your trap?'

'Aye!' boomed he, 'and when we hit them from the sides they lost control, we killed most of them as they tried to run away.'

'Taticius has foretold this; they do not like confined spaces, they prefer the open grasslands. But this was well done, mighty one, it was a bloody matter. How do these Turks select their battle commanders? There is an arrogance about them, is there not?'

'We are fortunate, Robby,' he replied, 'they have learned little. If we catch them right they are crushed beneath the weight of our charge.'

'Then pray that they remain in ignorance, for all we have in advantage is our wit, we will be surely overwhelmed if they take some time to think.'

'Oh, be of better cheer, Robby, that was another victory.'

'Surely, and we must find you and your men a safe spot to celebrate. I expect that those priestly scribblers over yonder will be sending messages of your success back to Rome and Constantinople.'

Bohemund looked to where I had pointed. There was much scrabbling in chests for the implements of news. Parchment and pens appeared like magic after each such event; I felt that the eyes of everyone across the sea were watching us closely: no escape from prying eyes here, too much depended on our success.

He looked with ill-disguised contempt. 'Aye, as if they could write us into Jerusalem.'

195

And with that he shouted for one of his captains to dish out some of his precious money on over-priced wine from the ever-lurking merchants.

It was a great victory, but the doubts lingered; how can the Turks remain dim for so long? The winds of fate were now blowing coldly against the city of Yaghi Siyan – perched high above in his towering citadel, his rescuers now vanquished, he must have been feeling extremely isolated.

Next Bohemund shouted an order and from within his ranks some foreigners rode out, well dressed and clearly of high rank; perhaps even Turks.

'Robby, my friend, come and meet somebody new.'

'Who are they?'

'They, my stout warrior, are Egyptians, ambassadors from the Vizier, al-Afdal.'

'Who? Where?'

'The Fatimid caliphate of Egypt,' he said proudly, as if he knew what he was talking about. 'Now listen –'

I interrupted. 'Where did you find them?'

'They turned up to watch our progress, they witnessed my victory.'

'Egyptian spies?'

'Friendly spies, they are Moslems of different sect, known as Shia, and they do not like the Turks who we are fighting.'

'What sort of Moslems are the Turks then?'

'Sunni,' he said, smirking with his knowledge.

'Sunni! Shia? How can there be two kinds of the same?'

'We have two Churches and more popes than we know what to do with.'

I was becoming accustomed to the illogical in my life.

'Oh! Like that. Will they help us?'

'In a way; they won't fight their Moslem brethren on our behalf, but nor will they help them, or hinder our cause.'

'I see, that's good... I suppose.'

I was beginning to smell a plot. *How has Bohemund met with these Egyptians? He was in a battle hundreds of miles from Egypt! And yet he finds ambassadors in the desert: how very odd.*

196

'So what are they going to do?'

'They will go back to Egypt and tell the Vizier how successful we have been, and ask him to keep his ships away from the coast, so that we may get on with our just cause.'

'They will cede control of the eastern sea?'

'That's exactly what I mean, Robby. No interference, and no assistance to the Turks against us. We are sending envoys to state our intentions directly to their ruler.'

'I like that. Well done, Bohmey. What else is in your mind? You are up to something more, I can tell.'

I was accustomed to the way Bohemund worked at things in his circumfluent way, and knew that there was something else.

'Just wait a little longer, Robby. We'll be done here soon and I will call a council before long, but I just need to put the final piece in position.'

I held his gaze for a moment: *how far to trust him?* But he was bold, and there was more amusement than deceit in his eyes, so I let it go.

'Fine. Introduce me to your Egyptians; I've never met one before. I think that I smell something odd in the air.'

He laughed, but not too convincingly, I thought.

I got nothing out of them, of course; being diplomats they were only there to make contact and report back to their ruler in Cairo. They repeated what Bohemund had told me but as I had much to do I did not spend a lot of time with them and left them as soon as it was polite to do so. Wondering, of course, wondering.

At the beginning of March we received word of the arrival of a Genoese fleet at St Simeon; this was expected, but only by me. It was reported as the largest seen there since I'd taken control of the port.

Bohemund wanted to go down and take possession of the cargoes but Raymond got wind of that and insisted on accompanying him to ensure that the war supplies were distributed evenly.

Recently, conditions along the route had altered considerably. Despite our victory over Ridwan we had lost absolute control of the southern end of the city near the St George and Bridge Gates. The hills were alive with Turkish patrols and I suspected they were preparing for another assault, but our scouts couldn't find their main force if that were so. The road to St Simeon was more dangerous as a result and because of the risk, we organised a properly constituted armed convoy to bring up the supplies in one journey.

I had the vanguard, with Bohemund bringing up the rear. We were sniped at, arrows descending out of the blue sky, all the way up until we neared the Bridge Gate, at which point we were subjected to a serious attack from within the walls by Yaghi Siyan's men.

The supply train was badly mauled and I was hard pressed until Bohemund arrived with his limited cavalry to help me drive them off. Then Godfrey, who had been left as camp commander, came down on the Turks from the direction of the camp and they became squeezed between our two groups. Realising the position they'd put themselves in, they attempted to return to the city, but the Bridge Gate became chaotic and was blocked by fallen troops. Our men ran amok once more and indulged themselves in a systematic slaughter of the helpless Turks. They eliminated all who had come out through the walls to attack us but we still lost three hundred foot soldiers and two cavalrymen.

The bishops and priests hailed the victory as proof that their cause was indeed blessed; the victorious commanders cited the victory as yet more proof of their military superiority. The Turks lost large numbers of their defending force and took a serious blow to their morale.

Bohemund and I knew that we were still pushing good fortune – that we had been involved in yet another example of the dangers of a fractured command structure. We determined that we would demand closer control and coordination of any such adventures in the future.

There was an after-note to this battle. Outside the St Paul Gate there was a ruined mosque with a burial ground, and this was the place where Bohemund had chosen to use his newly arrived building supplies and construct a stronger fortification.

Formerly, he had allowed the Turks to bury their dead in that spot, but the next day he had the bodies disinterred and found that they'd been buried with gold and other valuables, another godly favour, some would say. Then he sent the heads to the emissaries from Cairo, as a gift for them to count and take back with them as a chilling message to Egypt. To the garrison in Antioch it was yet another blow to their morale – and a portent of their future. To me it was a blow to my friendship with Bohemund – I liked it not.

Bohemund raised a fortress around the mosque with rock towers, stone walls and ditches and named it *Malregard*; a disturbing sight for the defending Turks. At the same time another fortress was raised to seize control of the crossroads outside the Bridge Gate. Command was given to Raymond, now recovered enough to accept it, although he still looked ill to me, and he named it *La Mahomerie*, in honour of the Virgin Mary.

One way or another, by luck, sacrifice, or divine intervention – the noose was ever tightening about the throat of the city of Antioch.

The sun had started to make more frequent appearances, and as it became warmer so the atmosphere in the crusader encampments improved. This was especially so in my camp, where normal relations between men and women had resumed – the priests and zealots were wise and made no comment. The fact that I had defended my compound with the assistance of women caused them some agony no doubt, but success is success and not to be sniffed at if it aids the greater cause.

I became increasingly concerned about Stephen; he looked ill and had no life about him. One morning in March, as we sat together in the warming sunshine, I asked him about it.

'Stephen,' I said gently, 'you seem remote from us, does something ail you?'

'Robert, I am weary in body and spirit, I have an ague and shiver like a crone... there is no energy in me.'

'I have heard that is not uncommon in these parts. Who knows what infections lurk in the rivers and swamps we have splashed through.'

'Aye, I long for the cool streams of Normandy.'

'You said that you are poor in spirit.'

'The things we have seen, and done; I am weary of it. It seems a long way from holiness.'

'I've not noticed you've been slow to draw a sword.'

'Perhaps not, but this flaunting of heads, the dishonouring of fallen men, it seems shaming to me... And to blame women for our ill fortune, that is a step too far for my liking. There is no logic in it and I like it not.'

'The priests think it appropriate.'

'Huh! Men who know not women, who know nothing of their gentleness; what qualification is that to pronounce from?'

'I know not. They have mothers, just like Christ, have they not? They must have been strange creatures to have affected their sons in such a way.'

'Is it sacrilege to speak thus?'

'Anything that upsets the clerics is called so by them, and they don't like to be upset.'

Bohmey and Flanders came along at that point, and settled down to join the conversation.

I'd been about to seek out Bohemund, and so took the opportunity to test him with a proposition.

'Bohmey, it is time to bring this matter to a head. Nobody came this far to sit outside of Antioch for the rest of his life. A lot of them want to go home.'

'I know. I'm working on it, I have contacts inside the city, and we are waiting for the right moment. What more do you want to do, Robby?'

'Accelerate things... make them happen.'

'How?'

'Until now we haven't fully closed off the city, and it has been able to trade for supplies from one gate or another; now that we have the new forts in place we are capable of doing it.'

Flanders was enthusiastic.

'Yes, we have forts outside most gates. The garrison has just come through a winter; supplies must be at their lowest. They've been beaten every time they've attacked us and the relieving force failed. They're at their most vulnerable since we came here.'

Bohemund nodded. 'It's true. My contacts tell me that they're at a low ebb. The garrison has lost one third of its strength, they cannot afford to make any more sorties to raid us and keep men along the length of the walls. What do you want to do, Robby?'

'Build another fort outside the St George Gate, piquet the Iron Gate to the rear of the citadel on the hill, and cause all of the traders approaching the city to do their business with us. Starve the whole city, civilians and garrison; make them want to let us in.'

Flanders agreed. 'I like it. Will the others agree?'

Bohemund snorted. 'Please themselves, I'll do it without them anyway.'

I reined him in.

'Easy does it, Bohmey, it will be easier if they cooperate. Don't forget Raymond is carrying that considerable treasury with him, and if we're to buy up all of the incoming supplies we need his money. Think on it carefully.'

'Mm. What about Godfrey?'

'If he feels that you would support him in his desire to be lord of Jerusalem, he would probably support you in becoming lord of Antioch.'

That flummoxed the mighty man.

'What do you mean, Robert? How do you know my intentions? I mean, have I ever said that, or anything like it? And who said that Godfrey wanted the lordship of Jerusalem?'

I looked him in the eye. 'You started all this spying business; it seems that you've created a useful habit. You don't deny your ambition then?'

'Humph!' was the immediate reply, and he took a sudden interest in scraping a little rust off his scabbard.

My reliable cousin, Robert of Flanders, took up my cue, and ignoring the busy giant opened up the speculation to public view.

'If we keep those two Franks apart, Robert, and at odds, it will suit our purpose better.'

Bohemund stirred and fixed Flanders with his gaze.

'This is too mysterious for me. State it plainly, what do you mean?'

'If Godfrey and Raymond both want to be king of Jerusalem, as rumour has it, and none of us do, then as long as they both need our support to achieve their goal, they will support us in things that they have little interest in. Keep them divided by seeming neutral, but support them both as long as it suits our needs, see?'

My northern cabal watched as Bohemund churned our suggestion around in his mind – it had to fit with his own scarcely concealed plans for mastery of Antioch, and eventually it did.

'Devious buggers!' he exclaimed, 'let's bring the council together.'

The noose was completed and the grip tightened. Raymond was persuaded to fund a new castle at the St George Gate which was quickly built by Tancred – imperceptibly we Normans were starting to lead in the taking of Antioch – while Raymond and Godfrey were positioning themselves for the main prize of Jerusalem.

Worried about neglecting my port, and matters being quietly under control outside the city, I decided to go back down to the coast for a while leaving Bohemund to contemplate his future prize and get on with his scheming.

Before I left I held a briefing at which I explained my plans and preparations for the next phase of the operation.

'I am going to see to our supply lines, they need to become more flexible to support us after we've left this place. I intend to identify suitable ports nearer Jerusalem and see how we may build them into our plans. Robert of Flanders will act on my behalf here.'

After the gory episodes outside of Antioch, the sea strand was a nice place to strip off the foul-smelling clothing and engage in some welcome de-lousing – including removing my hair, thought to be the best solution. In a time of hardship, such simple things are the substance of happiness to a soldier.

Thus I left Stephen in this pleasant state at St Simeon as I boarded one of my remaining *knörr* to pay a visit to Laodicea. I took Philip along. He was acting as my secretary, my own scribbling skills being limited, and he would document my requirements, instructions and supply listings, and continue to get the deluge of letters home across to Cyprus and beyond. The world of Payne and Ragenaus seemed to brighten up considerably when I told them we were going back to Laodicea, and I prayed that their housekeepers had not found new bedchambers to keep tidy.

The port was busy, but it wasn't long before someone hailed me from the shore. I looked him over. He was about forty years old and tall and dark with a full beard; he wore a loose robe with no sign of any weapons about him. There were two soldiers attending him, and they appeared capable of keeping him safe, at anytime, anywhere.

The picture that I presented to him might not be recognised by those back home. The privations of the last two years had melted all the fat off me, and my face, seen in reflections, was so lean as to make me appear older than my middle forties. Despite the temperature, I wore a mail coat over a linen shirt, and always, a sword and knife at my side. I had been told by others, including Bohemund, that my eyes, set in a skin burnished by the sun and wind, were frightening to behold. Perhaps that would warn most people to stay away.

The Byzantine, for that is what he was, swallowed, coughed, and made to introduce himself.

With a short bow he began.

'Prince Robert, I am Aiolos, an emissary from the Emperor Alexios: I bring you his greetings.'

'Ah! From Alexios: I return your greetings.'

I jumped ashore and strode up closer to the man.

'I suppose you want to know about the siege at Antioch?'

'We have intelligences, my lord, but a view from you would be much appreciated.'

'I see.' I could tell that this notable would not appreciate the hospitality of a harbour-side tavern. 'I lack a place of privacy here.

Perhaps you would come to one of the forts up there.' I pointed to the rocky edifices above the town.

'No need, Prince Robert; we have made arrangements to accommodate you in a villa nearby. If you would honour us with your person, that is?'

'I think that I might oblige you, Aiolos. Have you a rank?'

'Not as you have, my lord, but my family is well thought of at the emperor's court.'

'A diplomat?'

'Indeed, that is my privilege.'

'Then lead on, Aiolos the Diplomat, and let us see what we can find to pass the time of day with.'

Accompanied by Payne, Ragenaus and Philip, I was escorted to a pleasant villa just outside the city and led into a coolly shaded courtyard. Sherbets were provided by a servant and we settled down for a comfortable résumé of the war.

Aiolos began. 'We understand that at present the situation is one of improvement, and that you are moving closer to assaulting the walls.'

'You are well informed.'

'Indeed, Prince Robert, we have eyes.'

'Then you do not need me to explain the situation.'

'Not in detail. However, we would like to know your intentions after you have seized the city.'

'My intentions are to move as quickly as possible on to Jerusalem. That is what we came here to do… is it not?'

'Indeed.' He hesitated, searching for the correct words no doubt. 'You have no plans to become the ruler of Antioch?'

'I haven't.'

'Nor anyone else?'

'I am not aware of any.'

'I see.'

I knew that this was a game, an effort to discover whether or not the Franks would keep their promise to turn over any captured towns to the emperor – but as Bohemund had not admitted any secret plans to me, I could, for the time being, answer honestly. I decided to take the initiative.

'The emperor remains fully supportive of our endeavour?'

'Indeed, my lord. He is closely interested, and prays a great deal for your success.'

'Then perhaps his prayers could include the manifestation of some useful supplies. Since your representative Taticius left, we have noticed a slowing down in your assistance.'

'I am certain that we can assure you of the fullest support.'

'And when will this support become fulsome again?'

'If you will provide a list of requirements it will be at sea before the dawn lightens the sky.'

'That soon?'

'Just so, and your supplies will be on their way from Cyprus within three days.'

'Including my horses?'

'They may take a few days longer, but be assured they will be sent.'

'I am most grateful, and heartened by your continuing support. We will succeed in this only if Christendom remains united behind us. I am sure that the emperor will understand the importance of his continuing contribution.'

'We understand fully. I will convey your thoughts directly to his imperial majesty.'

'Pray also carry my good wishes to his majesty.'

'I will, and with all haste. Now, my lord, may I offer you the hospitality of the emperor? I am to ensure that all comforts are available for you and your party in this place for as long as you require.'

'You are not staying?'

'No, I must prepare to leave; but this place is secure and you may relax for as long as you wish.'

'Thank you, and pass on my thanks to the emperor.'

'I will. Good night, Prince Robert.'

When the envoy had gone Philip looked at me and smiled.

'If this villa is Roman, do you think, my lord, that they have any of those hot Roman baths in the place?'

'I don't know, but I intend to find out.'

I beckoned over the man with the sherbets but there was a polite shuffling from the other two and somehow my instincts knew what it was they were thinking.

'Did we pass your billet on the way up the hill, Payne?'

'Indeed, lord.'

'Were there any signs of life?'

'Only eyes at the apertures, my lord,' added Ragenaus.

'Were they housekeepers' eyes?'

'I believe so, my lord.'

'Then you should go and see if they have kept the place tidy. Return in the morning and attend me, if you please.'

'Aye, my lord,' they called in unison as they scampered out the door.

The servant with the sherbets came over and bowed.

'We have arranged something for your comforts, my lord; please follow me.' It occurred to me that he had heard, and understood, our conversations, and I resolved to warn Philip that we had our own personal spy in the villa, sherbets and all.

He led us across the courtyard and into some chambers at the back of the villa, where there were indeed baths and steam rooms.

After throwing off our clothing, we slid, opposite each other, into the warming, relaxing waters.

I had almost slipped into sleep when I sensed someone enter the room behind me. With that presence came a waft of perfume and the sound of shimmering silk, and without opening my eyes I knew she was female. My head was resting against the side of the bath on a pillow; I kept my eyes closed but knew that she had come to stand behind me. I heard the slither of silk, probably from letting her garment slide to the floor, and then I felt her feet slide down my sides as she sat on the edge of the bath and placed her hands on my shoulders.

She eased me forward so that my shoulders nestled against her knees and her hands began their work. I heard the clink of glass as she unstopped a phial and oiled her hands, the smell reaching my nostrils, bringing with it a great calm, and then felt the firm touch of her fingers as she explored the knotted muscles of my shoulders.

'Ahhh!' The noise just slipped out of me as the tensions began to fall away. Then – I heard Philip gasp, as if astonished, and I opened my eyes to see what was amiss and saw that Philip had a woman behind him exactly as I had – but that she was black. Startled, I glanced to my side and saw to my own astonishment that the legs wrapped around me were also black, or very brown; we were in the hands of Africans.

'Prince Robert!' Philip gasped out, 'what shall we do?'

'I don't know, I've never been here before.' My penis broke the surface of the water as my body floated upwards.

'Hallo,' I said to the glistening head of my phallus, 'I haven't seen you for a long time.'

'Who?' cried Philip, nearing panic.

'My dick, you prick, what's yours doing?'

'Oh God,' exclaimed the young knight as he realised what was happening to his extremity, 'what shall we do, my lord?'

'You can do whatever you like; I know what I'm doing.'

Saying which, I reached up behind my head and pulled a squealing bundle of ebony flesh into the pool over the top of my head.

She surfaced and turned towards me smiling – such white teeth – she straddled my thighs and placing her hands upon my shoulders drew her nipples across my face. They were almost black and likely to put my eyes out so sharp were they.

I looked into her eyes, and asked, 'What are you named, my dark beauty?'

She responded in some tongue that was mostly sibilants, but it sounded like 'Sassie', so that is what I called her. She made an attempt at 'Prince Robert'; she was very well briefed.

Never mind what she said – the look that passed between us was enough, it was the universal knowledge that men and women possess as a natural talent, one which makes the ultimate communication a language that needs no words.

Then she manoeuvred her body and I groaned as she slid her wet tunnel over my throbbing shaft; I only gave one thrust before my belly heaved and she received the pent-up store of my life fluid, kept waiting deep inside me for such a release.

She cast her head back as she felt the heat of the jet strike deep inside her and laughed out loud. She said something to her accomplice, but it was beyond me.

When my senses returned I looked over towards Philip, but all I could see of the other girl was her glistening wet back. Her head was buried deep in Philip's groin and his eyes were focused skywards.

'What's she doing, Philip?' I enquired.

'I... don't know,' he panted, 'either she can hold her breath for an impossibly long time... or, umph! Or she is breathing through my dick.'

My companion, seeking to distract me from the activity on the other side of the bath, now stood up in front of me to reveal the splendour of her body. She gazed down at me as I took in the sight. A proud head, breasts that were mostly nipple and a muscle-defined stomach. Her nether lips were barely concealed by her short curly hair, the water drawing a line there, but I could see that her thighs were muscular and she appeared well enough equipped to drag any remaining life out of my hungry body. I drank in the beauty of this glistening Naiade and she watched as I started another erection. Leaning forward, she bit my left ear, took hold of my hands and, urging me up, led me off to a side chamber where she drew the curtains behind us.

I was in for a busy night.

The next two weeks went by in a trice. During the day we were in a frenzy as I dictated scrolls of instructions and lists to keep the supplies moving northwards, and dealt with the myriad of questions and problems that beset us. In the evenings it was just as frantic. Philip and I both knew that this was but a brief respite before we must needs move back to the squalor of Antioch. Perhaps I should have had the occasional twinge of regret, or visions of other faces waiting for me elsewhere, but now was here and nothing else was certain and I tried not to let such longings put me off attending to my black beauty.

Two weeks later, with my semi-permanent erection becoming painful, we were enjoying fresh fruit and wine in the bath when the manservant entered.

'My lord,' he uttered gently as he bowed, 'there is a message from the harbour.'

'Tell me,' I mumbled, replying through a grape.

'Your ships are ready to leave now, as you required.'

'I see. How is the wind?'

'It seems set fair for St Simeon.'

'Very well.' I looked up at the windows, high in the walls; the sharpness of the light was already fading in the sky. 'Tell them we sail at dawn, and be sure that we are wakened. Thank you.'

That was the end of the conversation, as the servant went off with my response to my fleet captain and I advised my young knight.

'Make sure that you leave your Sushi –' Sassie and she were sisters it transpired – 'something to remember you by. You might never see her again.'

'My lord, I will do my best... as you command.'

We managed to reach our *knörr* by daybreak, but did not see much of the voyage as we curled up out of the way and slept our way back to St Simeon. The light was fading when we stepped ashore, which was useful, as no one was able to remark upon the bags under our eyes. I made my way to Stephen's tent and settled down to exchange news.

'We're receiving supplies daily now, thanks to you, Robert.' Stephen made an attempt to be positive.

'Thank you. I think that the emperor has realised that we cannot do this without his help, but it is little enough, I think he could try harder.'

'Well he started it all, he should have planned it better.'

'Oh yes, of course. He might have assumed that the Turks were going to give up and go away... I think not.'

'No, that's an assumption too many. There is disturbing news from the north; some great overlord is rolling towards us. The rumour is that he is gathering a multitude as he comes near.'

'Multitude! How many is a multitude?'

'That's the worrying thing; we cannot get close enough to make an assessment. Our scouts go out and the desert is alive with his advance parties, only small groups have been seen but they are everywhere.'

'Think you that it is a bluff, or a serious army?'

He shrugged. Whatever the truth, it was worrying enough for me, and I could see that he was still down in spirit. 'What else?'

'The governor, Yaghi Siyan, has turned to beheading prisoners, then hanging the bodies from the walls.'

'Jesu!' I crossed myself, 'what honour is left in this place?'

'Not much. Is it our mission to bring honour to this pagan land?'

'If that is what we get with Jerusalem, then so be it.'

'Bohemund thinks that Siyan is exceeding desperate.'

'It seems so.'

'He has no supplies and needs to hold on until this Turkish army arrives, so by executing his prisoners he ensures that his men fight fiercely. There will be no mercy if we get inside.'

'When! we get inside.' I looked Stephen in the eye. 'Be assured, Stephen, this thing is about to be settled, if we don't get inside we will be trapped against the walls and exterminated. Believe me, it won't be very long before our fate is decided.'

I prayed that Stephen would find hope. He had his men to inspire, but if he showed doubt they might lose heart. Perhaps I shouldn't have said it, should have invented some untruth to bolster his spirit instead.

As I rode up to the city I could see that activities outside had altered considerably. It was now better organised, with the army groupings gathered closely round improved forts. There were training grounds set aside and the horsemen, together with the foot soldiers and archers, were practising their skills and formations. All intending traders had been allocated market areas and instructed to keep strictly within the boundaries – they had a choice; trade with us at fair prices, or go away: this was the new order of things.

I sought out Flanders, and after a few words we went to see Bohemund.

'The two Roberts! Your return is timely,' he said quietly, looking at me.

'Come and sit close.'

I sensed that there was something in the air – Bohemund speaking below a bellow was a significant clue.

He started in a conspiratorial manner.

'Robby,' he said in what he considered to be a whisper, 'we need to move things along quickly. The Sultan of Baghdad has sent a general, named Kerbogha, he has gathered a force from all over Persia to destroy us in front of the walls of Antioch, and ensure that we never see Jerusalem.'

I met his troubled gaze.

'I have heard that they are too numerous to count, it is true then?'

'They are more numerous than the flies around a cow's arse.'

'That many?' said Flanders.

'Aye, that many,' replied Bohemund, becoming louder, and then reverting to quiet – for a moment.

'I want to take action now: sod Raymond. I have things in place. Will you join me?'

'In what?' I asked, not happy at excluding the other leaders.

'I have bought us entry to the south wall, and my contact is ready to help us enter over the parapet.'

'Who is it? Why the change of heart?'

'He is an Armenian named Firuz. He is worried that if we are annihilated outside the walls the Turks will exterminate all Christians left inside.'

'Then he has a point, it is unlikely that this Kerbogha is coming all the way from Baghdad to preside over a Christian city.'

'I agree,' said Bohemund, 'and he has lodged his son with me for assurance, but we need to act swiftly before the knowledge begins to leak, inside or outside the walls. I want to go tonight.'

'Die tonight, die next week; what's the difference?'

'A week,' croaked Stephen.

'No,' hissed Bohemund, 'live tonight or die next week.'

His eyes sparkled in a way familiar to me; *in his head, Bohemund was already on top of the city walls.*

I cast the final die. 'What's the plan?'

I was to have no direct role in this desperate bid to invade the city, Bohemund made this clear.

'I will lead the silent invasion over the wall, and it is time that Godfrey and Raymond did something other than huff and puff. They will assault the city through the gate when I have opened it up to them. You, dear friend, will hold your cavalry back in reserve, although I doubt they'll be needed inside the narrow city streets. Your main task tonight, Robby, will be to brief Raymond and Godfrey when I have gone. They must prepare to assault the gates as soon as I have them open.'

I could only agree. It was Bohemund's plan and I had a part in it, but he had given me little time to go and engage the other leaders. I needed to think of something compelling to say.

In the late evening of 2 June 1098, a detachment of cavalry and infantry left Tancred's location outside the Gate of St George.

They headed off down the St Simeon road for all to see, and disappeared behind the hills. Once out of sight they were to halt and begin a special preparation, well known to me and my men.

The horses would be stripped of all equipment and put out to pasture – they were no longer needed. The men would make ready their weapons by dulling all the shiny bits with mud, and protect all metal parts with cloth bindings to prevent them rattling and banging together. They were to prepare themselves for a night action to be undertaken in total silence.

By the time it was dark they would have fed from the cold rations which they took with them – there would be no fires – and then they would settle down to get as much sleep as possible. They would be awoken by watchmen when it was time to commence the final assault upon the city of Antioch.

Bohemund had planned carefully, and I knew now that he had been making contacts and preparations for this action for at least a month. And now I needed to go and brief Godfrey and Raymond.

'Is he mad?' was Raymond's first response.

'It is brilliant, if it works,' was Godfrey's.

'You will support this, Godfrey?' asked Raymond.

'Of course, Raymond. But be mindful that it will give Bohemund the freedom of the city, it will let him roam around inside the walls as he pleases; you are aware of that?'

'Unfortunately I am, but if it gets us inside... I have little else to offer.'

'Well spoken, Raymond,' I said by the way of encouragement. 'Godfrey, listen carefully, for this is what you must do, and quickly.' I issued Bohemund's instructions to the letter and prayed that we had left enough time to prepare for our part in his grand plan. How it unfolded, I heard the next day.

When all was at its quietest, when the night was at its darkest and when human life was at its lowest ebb in sleep, and sentries dulled by inaction, the raiding party made its way to the base of the wall, beneath the tower controlled by the Armenian, Firuz.

It was well up the slope, well away from the St George Gate, wherein the guard would be.

They found a rope ladder, lowered from above, which allowed the first of the invaders to make their silent way to the top of the wall. When safely up they only needed to wait quietly until the dark ramparts filled with warriors climbing behind them.

Once ready they were led down the wall by Firuz, towards the St George Gate. Those guards who were found in the minor watchtowers were killed swiftly and soundlessly as death spread downhill; the manifestation of the silent reaper.

On the ground outside the wall a group of soldiers mirrored the progress of the assassins at work on the walls above their heads – they had a special job to do. When the sentries in the last minor tower had been despatched, those outside the wall appeared at the base of the main gate and made their presence known to the guard above. Being thus distracted the Turks made their final and fateful mistake: engaging in insults with the foolish

Franks below. The first that the guards knew of the presence of the Christians upon the wall was when, peering over the walls at the fools taunting them below, they felt the killing steel of Norman swords penetrating their ribs.

The surprise was complete, and the party waiting outside the gate was forced to stand back as Turkish bodies rained down from above. Soon the gate was open and the main invasion began.

It was then that I witnessed the remainder of that day's fateful action. As the troops of Godfrey and Raymond moved forwards out of the dark, the non-Moslem citizens, acting on a signal, laid hands on their hidden weapons and joined in with our men on a systematic slaughter of the Turkish garrison. Before long all the main gates were thrown open by citizen-led assaults from the inside, and no Turk would be left alive outside of the mountain top citadel. When day dawned it was this position alone which was left occupied by the former rulers of Antioch.
But before long the invasion fell into total disarray as the personal intentions of the Christian princes were exposed for all to see.

Bohemund seized and placed his banner on the highest point of Mount Silpius, opposite the towers of the citadel, while Raymond seized the Bridge Gate and the nearby Palace of Antioch.

Those leaders, busy staking claims to the major sites within the walls, lost control of their troops who proceeded to loot and pillage all else they could lay their hands on. I waited outside the city for word from Bohemund in vain. Eventually I decided to enter and we found ourselves in a shambles.

Discipline had collapsed. There were dismembered bodies lying everywhere, Turks by their clothing, but also some civilians, Turkish collaborators perhaps, who had been butchered in a similar fashion. I wondered what their transgression had been to lose all within sight of victory. The smell of blood hung heavy in the air and there were still sounds of distress all around us to assault the ears. The months of pent-up fear, both inside and outside the city, had resulted in an explosion of hate, or revenge or primitive bloodlust – and I wondered if I wanted to be a part of it. As we wandered through the city my men were stunned into silence, and I could find no words to offer them any kind of comfort.

Eventually we found Adhémar, who was similarly distressed, and then we attempted to find the leaders and prevail upon them to regain control of their troops.

Late in the day a major prize was brought before Bohemund – the head of the governor, Yaghi Siyan. He had been caught outside and paid the ultimate price for failure. Yet the citadel still stood defiantly. Siyan's honour on that fateful day was saved by his son, who had managed to retreat to and safeguard the citadel. Without it we could not make the city completely secure.

On the morning of 4 June I awoke to a shout. Panic rose in those still left outside the walls and they made haste to shelter within them. The first of Kerbogha's troops had come into view and the city was yet again under siege. The besiegers were now the besieged.

Our success had placed us into a mess of our own making. The tactics of starving the citizens into a state of mind that made them compliant in the final assault meant that we were all trapped inside a charnel house, with little hope of supplies from the outside. We were facing an enemy so numerous that they really could encircle the whole city, including the covert rear entrance of the Iron Gate.

We quickly burnt our wooden forts, excepting that of La Mahomerie – which as it controlled one of the river bridges, we would attempt to hold. Then we retreated within the city walls; any arguments about who owned what would have to wait.

Adhémar, determined to redeem some of his lost authority, called a council to discuss our position and we gathered in the basilica of St Peter in the north of the city.

The bishop looked about him to confirm who was in attendance. He had originally intended to lead prayers for our success, but was now faced with the prospect of raising morale in the face of our new predicament.

'I do not see Stephen of Blois, Prince Robert; where is your brother-in-law?'

'I know not,' I replied, 'it has been a confusing time.'

'I have seen him, my lord.' A knight, Philip de Barneville, made a hesitant statement.

'Where?' I asked.

'He went off along the road to Alexandretta some time ago.'

'What! Who was he with?'

'A few of his knights, my lord.'

Bohemund raised an eyebrow in my direction – but said nothing.

I heard Flanders swear under his breath, but say naught out loud.

There was an embarrassed silence. Nobody voiced the thought, *treacherous coward,* and Adhémar broke into our unkind thoughts.

'Let us pray for his soul and trust that he can be led back to the path of righteousness once more. Brethren, let us join together in thanks for the progress of our mission and pray for God's guidance in our future endeavours...' He droned on for too long as usual, but I welcomed the diversion. I was shocked, and angry, and looking at Flanders I could see that he had an expression of contempt on his face: *who wants to know a traitor?* It would be a short list.

The first engagement with the enemy was a disaster, and a reminder of known enemy tactics. A small group of thirty or so Turkish archers was observed approaching the river by the Gate of the Duke. Young Barneville, being brave as well as young, gathered fifteen of his knights and set off out of the gate to engage them.

The Turks turned and fled, but they led the eager lad into a trap – three hundred more poured out from a hidden canyon, and jubilant with their luck chased down the luckless lad – he was unhorsed by an arrow in the back, captured and decapitated along with his fellows in front of hundreds of horrified spectators lining the city ramparts to watch.

The Turks displayed his head on a lance to taunt us – such a fate was waiting if we failed.

I was saddened and deeply upset. I had known Barneville since he was a boy, and thought highly of him; now a moment's indiscipline had cost the poor soul his life. This was indeed a costly lesson – as Bohemund reminded those gathered together at the funeral in St Peter's.

'We are trapped in this shitty place. If we want to break out and survive we should plan a means now and make it soon – delay will only weaken us. Because we cannot defend all the walls our only hope of success is to face them outside and pray that better tactics will win the day. I will discuss with you how the main body of the army should be deployed, but for now we should hand over all the cavalry into the charge of Robert, for he, above all, understands their use and the tactics of the enemy. To make the most effective use of our remaining few horses they should be combined into one effective force and given to the most experienced commander – are we agreed?'

The final question, coming with the force of an English sea storm, brooked no dissent.

I was now the army cavalry commander, but when I assessed my new force it amounted to the piffling totals of two hundred and fifty experienced men and horses. There were about four hundred captured Turkish horses waiting to be trained, and about two hundred semi-trained wranglers to bring up to standard – as we had just witnessed the first of the advancing Turks in action, it was hardly a hopeful situation. My best asset was still my archers, almost intact in strength, and I now determined to increase their numbers.

Before another day had passed it became time for Cousin Robert to display his mettle. Kerbogha had quickly overwhelmed the Byzantine outpost at the Iron Bridge north of the city, Taticius' former command and the scene of the first skirmish for the city, and set up his main encampment two miles away where the Kara Su River met the Orontes. His next objective was to remove the obstruction of La Mahomerie; Flanders was given the task of defending it.

217

Although Raymond had been quick to claim possession of the siege fort, it seemed his interest waned a little when it came to holding on to it in the face of an enemy. Because of its size, Flanders could only fit two hundred soldiers into it, but was shortly faced by the two thousand which Kerbogha had sent to clear it out.

Robert of Flanders held firm for three days – we watched as they came under sustained attack by arrows and returned as many missiles in response. Losing La Mahomerie would allow the Turks unrestricted access to the land between the river and the city walls.

Rob's men held it with dogged and savage resistance. Eventually it came down to hand-to-hand combat, using their swords, lances, and a dwindling supply of arrows. But the position became untenable and difficult to re-supply, so on the night of 8 June he set fire to the place and retreated behind the city walls.

I received him back inside the city with open arms.

'Well done, Robert, well done, you have won us valuable preparation time, they'll hear of this in Normandy. You'll be a hero.'

'I hope to survive to enjoy the honour,' replied the tired and bloodied warrior. 'I'm knackered, Robert.'

'You and your men stand down for a rest. I'll call for you if I need you, but you'll be brought up to date with our position when you are recovered, Rob. Thank you, thank you all.' With that I needed to leave and get back to organising and preparing for the expected assault; there was little time for celebration.

The situation worsened very quickly. Kerbogha, with his superior numbers, was able to control the mountains and reach the citadel via the precipitous path through the Iron Gate and bring reinforcements into it. We were trapped, with annihilation fast approaching.

It was at this point that the ambitions of Bohemund bore fruit. Frustrated by his failure to seize the citadel on the first day, he had set up a position on the highest point along the long ridge of Mount Silpius to the south of the citadel. By doing so he controlled the route up and down the mountain in the south of the city and effectively blockaded the ancient citadel.

Both sides now glowered at each other across the valley waiting for the next move.

Within the city walls, Godfrey had the northern sector with the St Paul Gate, and Raymond held the sector between the Gate of the Duke and the Bridge Gate, leaving me and mine free to roam about the southern end of the enclosure.

After another day of inaction on top of the mountain, Bohemund scrambled down the scree slopes for one of our Norman strategy meetings.

'How are we to improve our situation, Robby?' Bohemund grimaced at me as he asked what he thought an unanswerable question.

'Oh! That's easy,' I replied.

'I knew that it would be,' interjected Flanders, still plump with pride after his gallant action at the La Mahomerie bridge, 'but could you just remind us of its simplicity?'

'Yes!' I responded, 'we do the unexpected.'

'Very good, Robby. Now do you see it, Flanders?' said the unusually patient Bohemund, 'the solution lies in simplicity, and Robby is about to explain it to us, aren't you, my fine friend?'

'Yes. But first we need a miracle.'

'Fine, Robby, fine,' said Bohemund without hearing me out, 'but perhaps there isn't time for that. In the meantime, Robby, go down to your training grounds and keep producing cavalry mounts and archers. Flanders, take responsibility for the wall from the Bridge Gate to the St George Gate and I will keep the citadel in check.'

'Very well,' said Flanders. 'Then what?'

Bohemund looked at him as if he were deaf.

'Did you not hear your cousin, Flanders? We wait for a miracle.'

'Oh! Of course. Tell me, Robert, how often do miracles come about?'

'Generally about every two hundred years or so, but do not worry, dear cousin, we are due one shortly.'

'Ah! Then I'll tell the men, should I?'

'No, Flanders,' said Bohemund, 'not yet. We haven't yet decided on the exact nature of the miracle, and my friend, the Duke of Normandy, has yet to arrange it.'

I thought that my friend's faith in my divine power was quite touching.

'Yes, I'll work on it while I'm training horses. I'll pray for some divine inspiration.' Then I left to work on my own miracle, that of turning horseless Saxon archers and horseless Norman knights into riders of Turkish steeds – as well as to produce the miracle I believed necessary to rejuvenate our tired army.

Bohemund experienced the very worst of times atop his precious mountain. The pressure became unrelenting as his men were subject to a series of attacks across the lofty mountain saddle. Yet his main strength lay in holding the highest point of the mountain, well above enemy heads in the citadel – this gave him an advantage and it was difficult for the Turks to engage his position. Nevertheless they tried for fully three days and nights, but they were beaten by the logistics of supplying the citadel. The site had little water and could not sustain the numbers that Kerbogha needed to sustain the pressure on Bohemund – and so he was forced to withdraw his men from the stronghold.

During the same period, Flanders was experiencing the strains of command in a different way. Having been successful in defending a static position, he decided to go out on a raid himself. He exited the city from a small postern gate in the wall, and attacked a Turkish camp that lay close by.

The result was mixed. Flanders was successful at first, but the action attracted such a fierce counter-attack that they were forced back to the gate – which, being small, would not admit them in all at once. Many were crushed as they attempted to gain entry or slaughtered from behind by the enraged Mussulmen.

I was annoyed and called him a fool, and forbade any more such ventures, brave or not; we could ill afford to waste life or arms.

It also provoked a renewed assault upon Bohemund's position as the Turks, repulsed upon the mountain top, came round it to attack our section of the city wall in several places at once.

While it was difficult for them to gain a foothold on the wall itself, nevertheless they came in such numbers and for such a long period that we went without proper sleep or rest for many days and nights.

On top of it all, we could expect no help from other parts of the city because Raymond and Godfrey were in similar situations. It was then that more desertions took place. Some – terrified by the constant pressure and noise – went over the wall on ropes one night. We only became aware of this at daybreak, when we found a line of stakes outside the wall – topped by Frankish heads.

Desertion quickly became an unpopular idea and any waverers returned to the wall as defenders.

Meanwhile down behind the wall in the area of the St George Gate, Aethilheard was wrestling with the difficult problem of incorporating the Turkish horses into the Norman way of war. Hugh of Vermandois had been pestering Flanders for a more prominent role, 'one befitting my status,' and he wanted to meet my Saxon. He had altered during the past year, we all had, and I thought it time to give him a chance. Aethilheard was not impressed, remembering him as an arrogant young know-all, and gave him such a glance as should have struck the Frenchman down.

'Come with me, Aethilheard.' I took him to one side and spoke to him calmly. 'That young fellow has changed his demeanour considerably since being thrown into the general melee of war. He is eager to watch and learn from those skilled in such matters. Take him on as a trainee and perhaps we will fashion something useful from him.'

'Very well, my lord. Can I send him back if he's useless? I have no time to waste.'

'If he is useless, tip him over the wall. Now then, Aethilheard, come and greet the French prince properly. How goes the training?'

'God's blood, my lord, we are struggling. These animals have been raised to a task different from what we need of them.'

I knew that, I had been watching for a while. I set him a question.

'Do you remember Grentmesnil, in Leicester?'

'Yes, but that is a long way and a long time off. He had a way with mounts.'

'Yes, and we're going about this in the wrong way,' I said. 'The horses are what they are – trained in a certain way. It will be quicker to get the riders to adopt their ways to the horses than the other way around.'

'That makes sense,' he agreed readily.

Hugh nodded. 'I too can see the sense of it. How is it to be achieved, Robert?' Hugh had newly discovered the art of asking questions rather than offering opinions.

'We ask the horses,' said I. 'Offer them a rider and see if they will accept him; if not, offer another until we match as many animals and men as possible.'

'Ye-es!' Aethilheard had some doubts, 'I can't see them performing as our destriers do.'

'No,' said I, 'that will not be possible. But if it gets more archers and others on horseback, we will have a few more options.'

Hugh agreed. 'We have none at present, Robert; options are rare luxury in this chaotic place.'

So we retrained the riders to mount and ride in the Turkish fashion. Then they matched riders to horses that would accept them. Some riders tried out several horses before they could be matched, or broke too many bones and gave up on the idea that the horses could be used as destriers in a cavalry role.

In the end it was accepted that some of these foreign animals would be utilised singly, or in groups loosely, to carry commanders, archers and messengers about the battlefield. The few genuine warhorses left I would retain within my own control and hold them ready to perform the task that they were trained for – and in which they'd be most effective: that of the shock cavalry.

Elsewhere, in a moment of madness, Godfrey attempted Flanders' raiding tactic out of the St Paul Gate and lost two hundred men in the process.

'We are in the company of idiots,' I fumed, 'such a stupid waste can only give confidence to these swarming flies outside the city. Will they not listen?'

Thus I was forced, together with Flanders, to climb up to Bohemund's position and rescue him; I wanted him back down the hill to insist that he take over as the army commander.

We found him completely surrounded on his hilltop, but our arrival, huffing and puffing from the climb, saved him.

There was no secrecy about our approach, we could be seen toiling up the mountain, and I confess that I missed a horse between my knees. I had about two hundred similarly breathless, erstwhile archers, cavalrymen, and assorted *militis* with me, and it was the infantry who engaged first and began to chase the Turks back around the sides of Bohemund's position, while we climbed up to join him. When we reached his position on the top of the last rise we stopped to regain our breath. We were behind Bohemund's front line and they were engaged in hand-to-hand fighting.

Bohemund was ready for us and I could see him organising his men, he was engaged all along his position but he pointed me to his centre and I saw the opportunity.

I signalled that we were ready and he waved us forward. Charging like berserkers we ran through his lines – two hundred unorganised loonies in an uncoordinated charge. We fell upon his attackers, galloping down the slope as one shambolic mass, albeit horseless, and running straight at the horrified Turks. My momentum gave me no opportunity to think and I simply swept down my long blade upon the first head to appear in front of me, then as I went for another I tripped and fell forward, ploughing the hard scree with my nose and feeling the point of my blade entering flesh. A body fell on top of me, pinning me to the ground. I was drenched with blood and struggled to free myself from the twitching victim.

Ragenaus cried out as I tried to get to my knees.

'My lord, are you hurt?'

'No! But get this meat off me.'

223

Payne used his lance, buried in the dead man's chest, with my banner at the end of it, to lever the corpse off me and I was able to stand up.

'Thank you, Payne. Keep my standard flying if you please!'

I sought out my next target but they were all in flight, scrambling up the slope towards the citadel, unwilling to continue the engagement. This was a mistake. My infantry were at their heels and as the terrified men scrambled up the steep hillside their pursuers swiped at their ankles; incapacitated they fell to the ground on their bellies with their backs exposed, inviting targets for sword and lance. It was an opportunity swiftly taken and not many Turks were able to reach the safety of the citadel. The ensuing slaughter was fit reward for the effort we'd made in getting up there, I thought unkindly.

Finding a convenient rock I sat down, my head spinning. Bohemund came across.

'God's bollocks, Robby, you left that a bit late,' he said, grinning through his gore-splattered face, 'could you not have set off earlier?'

'Piss off, you dim monster. Could you not have chosen the sea strand to fight upon?'

'I like it up here, the stench of the city does not reach these heights. Besides you can see the sea down there, if you peer hard enough... if you can see past the end of that Taticius-like nose.'

'Yes, I can, and before I lose any more bits, and if you have done with my services I am going back down, nearer to it, if you don't mind. The air is in short supply up here. Besides, you are needed down there.'

With the situation in the city fully explained, Bohmey agreed to come straight back down as soon as he had reorganised his siege of the citadel, which was still occupied by what stubborn Turks were left.

I stood up and waved my sword to gather in my men and set off down the mountain. My breathless shock troops followed gladly, pleased to be going downhill, and, grateful, no doubt, to resume their proper roles.

When I had gone about a hundred rocky, boulder-strewn, scrambling paces, I heard the merry giant calling after me.

'Thank you, Robby. I owe you a favour.'

'Uh!' was my grateful reply as I slipped and scraped my backside on the unforgiving scree. 'Bollocks!'

That action was followed by more desertions, and then there was a disturbance in the sky. A comet was seen, and taken as a happy portent by the Christians so it cheered them up, but as it was viewed by the Moslems in a similar vein the cheer was short lived.

Beset on all sides and approaching famine, the surviving citizens and their northern guests, were, I judged, in the final stages of defeat when my predicted miracle occurred – not before time.

In the north of the city, where Adhémar was positioned, a story began to circulate concerning a divine intervention.

A man from Provence, a pilgrim named Peter Bartholomew, had approached Bishop Adhémar with a story that told of him being beset with visions. The same vision had appeared to him while he was in different parts of the Holy Land and it concerned the lance that had penetrated the side of Jesus on the cross: Peter said that the lance had been buried in Antioch within the confines of the basilica of St Peter, and that the location had been revealed to him in his visions.

Raymond, present when the bishop was told this, became most agitated, so full of energy and zeal that he insisted they should go and dig it up. It was uncovered in the spot forecast by Peter and presented as proof of divine intervention in support of our just cause by the enthusiastic Provençal lord.

As it had been foretold, I was not entirely surprised.

Soon there came a distinct change in the mood of the place. Once the full story had been made public, as by the will of God, the attacks on the walls and sorties from the citadel stopped, and we were able to take some rest and recuperate. Raymond was certain that this lull was entirely due to the presence of the holy lance, and urged his fellow leaders to take offensive action against the Turks immediately.

Although appearing pleased by this renewed enthusiasm, Bohmey and I counselled caution and refused to be pushed into premature action. Instead we got together to see how close we were to a state of readiness for a breakout, and to bring this hopeless situation to an end.

Once again we gathered together for a select war council. We were near to my training ground and we simply stood together in the open to talk. Flanders started the inquest.

'What does Raymond want us to do?' he asked.

Bohemund responded with a curled lip.

'Run out of the gates and impale ourselves on Turkish swords.'

'He thinks they would be warded off by their lance?' asked Allen.

'I do not know whether or not the Turks believe in its unique qualities,' I said cautiously.

Hugh had attached himself to Bohemund. 'I would learn more,' he'd told me, and Bohmey agreed to take him. Now he wanted to contribute. 'I have heard that Adhémar believes it to be fraudulent.'

'Why so?' asked Aethilheard.

'Because he knows that the real lance lies within Constantinople, in the care of the emperor.'

'I said that we needed a miracle.' I reminded them of that point, quite smugly.

'Yes,' said Flanders, 'let the clergy argue, it is not for us to question.'

'Very well,' said Bohemund, 'if it is divine intervention – and it is a divine war that we wage so can we not expect some divine help?'

'Of course,' I responded, 'let us make the most of it.'

They all found that easy to agree with. If the Lord had found a way to give some assistance – perhaps even a way to indicate his approval – then it was not for us to question his chosen method.

'Good,' said Bohmey, seizing the opportunity, and my hint, 'let us see how we can make best use of this to help us break out of this prison. We cannot stay here, the position is untenable, we must break through the Turkish lines if we ever want to reach Jerusalem. Apart from riding out to face them, what else is there?'

Hugh came up with an answer.

'We could try diplomacy.'

This suggestion had resonance with me. I had experiences of Hugh's brother, Philip's view of diplomacy – it usually involved handing over vast sums of money.

'To buy our way out?' Aethilheard was thinking the same.

'I expect that he has riches enough without our poor pittances. What else can we offer him?' asked Flanders.

'Do we know what Kerbogha might want?' asked Hugh.

'Simple,' I replied, 'he wants in.'

'And we want out,' said Flanders, stating the obvious.

'Aye, out of here,' chimed in Aethilheard, 'this place was not our target.'

'Indeed,' I responded, 'but after the people of the city helped us to gain entry we cannot, in all faith, leave them to the mercy of the Turks. We cannot leave without guarantees for the safety of the Antiochene, and unless we can be assured of that we cannot go on to Jerusalem.'

'Only Alexios can guarantee that,' said Flanders, 'and where is he?'

'Somewhere between here and Constantinople,' I said. 'I wish that I could get to the coast, to my ships.'

Aethilheard said, 'But he must know our predicament?'

'Well, if he does not arrive or send troops he will lose this city. And us.' Flanders had uttered a truth which confirmed something in Bohemund's mind.

'I don't intend to lose it,' he stated bluntly. 'Nor do I intend to fight for it unless I am to retain it after it is won.'

For the first time someone had actually come out and said that they had an ambition and purpose beyond the relief of Jerusalem. Bohemund wanted to establish a Norman territory beyond the Balkans on the mainland of Asia Minor. He was not going to hand Antioch over to the Byzantine emperor.

There was silence while we went through, in our heads, the implications of Bohemund's statement.

Surprisingly it was Aethilheard who spoke first.

'Then it seems to me, Lord Bohemund, that you have created a double-edged sword for yourself.'

Bohemund glared at him and growled, 'What do you mean, Saxon?'

'I mean that if you will not join in this fight then you are doomed along with the rest of us. You cannot win it alone; you need us as much as we need you.'

'I don't know what your problem is, Saxon.'

'It is this, Bohmey.' I needed to make it clear. 'You have stated your intention to break your oath to the emperor, and keep Antioch. We will not join you, and neither, I suspect, will Godfrey or Raymond if they find out.'

The atmosphere had changed back and forth in an instant. Bohemund had seized an unexpected initiative only have it wrested out of his grasp by the odd man in the group. The others might have struggled to state the obvious – but the Saxon had no such qualms, and had put it simply, and well – Bohemund could easily isolate himself.

Flanders stated his position.

'I have no wish to own Antioch: if you have, then keep it. But if you will not assist me to get to Jerusalem I will leave by the back gate and you can get on with it yourself.'

Hugh concurred.

'I will take my Frenchmen with Flanders. I came not here for Antioch, but Jerusalem, and my sacred promise will only be fulfilled by that accomplishment. I could not face my brother King Philip if I failed in this.'

It had become an impasse.

They looked at me but I asked them to wait and left the circle to speak with my chaplain, Arnulf. As we two returned to the training ground the sounds of the wider world around us intruded. To the northern end of the city, two miles away, the sounds of

228

conflict could be heard faintly on the wind; Godfrey was evidently busy. Nearer were the sounds of my panting horses and breathless riders.

'Practise, practise,' called Aethilheard. 'Do that manoeuvre again,' he shouted at the exhausted riders, then returned his gaze to Bohemund.

Arnulf whispered in my ear. 'You must grasp this, my lord, the fate of Jerusalem hinges on this next moment.'

I nodded and turned my gaze towards the expectant group of leaders and spoke to them loudly from where I was standing, and without embellishment. Arnulf remained in close attendance.

'I will help you to win your prize, Bohemund... and then I will leave you. If this place is of more importance than your sacred vows then you will need to sort it out with your conscience... and Alexios.'

Arnulf stirred behind me, preparing to have his say.

'If this earthly prize attracts you, Lord Bohemund,' he looked directly into the warlord's eyes, 'then it would be wise to keep it within your heart, it would be unwise to distract the others from their task.' He meant Godfrey and Raymond – he meant that Bohemund should not broadcast his intentions until the city was safely won.

'It is an offer, Bohemund,' I confirmed. 'You keep your intentions privy until the way is clear to Jerusalem, then we will leave you. If Godfrey and Raymond want to argue with you about the stewardship of Antioch afterwards, then you can face them on your own. Your choice, Jerusalem or Antioch, what is it to be?'

'Antioch.'

Bohemund wanted nothing else so we agreed; he would help us break out and then retain the city for himself. An unwise choice, I thought, and it would further diminish our numbers, but the fellow had made his decision. Then we turned to discuss the battle plan. The atmosphere had cooled, but I remained polite and the others took their cue from me, yet somehow honour had left the field – or rather, if there was any honour left in that place it had received a death blow.

They gave me a further two weeks to complete my battle plan and prepare my cavalry, after which we would march out of the city and give battle to Kerbogha's massed pagans. All or nothing – win or die.

By 25 June we were ready to involve the others in the scheme. It was helped by the fact that both Raymond and Adhémar were too ill to argue – Raymond was having a convenient relapse, and Godfrey could not offer an alternative.

Bohemund was the most experienced, and I wanted him to be in overall command, so it was he who presented our plan. Godfrey took some persuading, being keen to be seen taking a leading part, and he came up with a potentially disastrous battle plan. He wanted to march out on to the plain over the river and face Kerbogha's multitude in the traditional manner, with formal lines. I soon put a stop to that idea.

'That!' I declared firmly, 'would be Kerbogha's plan, to isolate us on the plain where we would be annihilated. This is their favourite strategy from when his people lived on the great plains of Asia; they will encircle us then ride around us, shooting arrows until we are all made holy.'

'Hah!' cried Bohmey, laughing, 'that's a good one, Robby – holy, ha!'

Godfrey, crestfallen and tired, simply said, 'Set out your instructions, Bohemund. Let's get on with it.'

'Very well. We will use a plan based upon our experiences at Dorylaeum.'

'Where you were nearly annihilated,' retorted Godfrey.

'We were only half an army,' smirked the giant.

'And now we are half a starving army, how is that an improvement?'

'We have a secret force to assist us now.'

'I see,' snorted the bemused count, 'and where is this force?'

'All around you, look.' I waved my arms at the travelling pilgrims and recently freed citizens wandering about, and at a knot of men standing to one side. 'There are the local leaders, they want to help, they will join us outside the walls, I have asked them.'

Godfrey looked, and saw, and asked, 'But they are not trained, Prince Robert, surely they will not fight; besides they have no weapons.'

'They have incentive, dear Godfrey. And there is no shortage of weapons, we have Turkish curved swords and Turkish short bows at our disposal by the thousands, and they would rather die outside the walls, fighting, than inside being hunted down like trapped rats. They will fight.'

'My God: a miracle.'

'They are very numerous at present, Godfrey, and very welcome. Give thanks to the Lord,' said Bohemund. Although I thought him a little more pious-sounding than normal his words were in keeping with the moment.

'Right,' I said, 'let us get these eager lambs organised if they want to retain their city, else we will all die together trying.'

We set the day in June – we would go forth on the morning of the 28th, and whatever the outcome the gates of the kingdom of heaven awaited us.

Adhémar had recovered his health, sufficient to reveal a new idea, given to him in his fever. He asked for the assistance of the women. *Jesu! Another miracle,* I thought.

On his instructions, and after a search of the city for suitable cloth, they presented us with a pile of red crosses, fashioned from all sorts of materials.

'Wear these, you fine warriors,' he declared outside St Peter's. 'Wear these badges to affirm your commitment to the cross of Jesus, for now you are warriors of the cross, crusaders in the name of the Lord.'

Although a lot of those present were never warriors, their commitment to the cause had impressed me over the past few days and I knew they would die a glorious death – or triumph over the enemy. So be it.

This was the morning. I watched as the sky lightened behind the citadel on the mountain top and it was thrown into dark silhouette, while the valley below lay concealed in darkness.

I moved down from my camp, set on the mountainside, and came into the city streets. I was to exit from the Gate of the Duke, there was a long avenue leading to it and it was filled with troops. First I encountered the armed citizens and pilgrims near to St Peter's Cathedral. They would exit the gate last, but they were already standing in their squadrons, three ranks each; shield carriers, sword bearers and archers, drawn up as if they had been in the role all their lives; and quietly, as instructed, with their captains, chosen from their natural leaders, standing proudly at the front.

I heard them whisper as I rode with the Saxon squire Oslac down the slope, passing them by: 'Tis Robert of Normandy.' And a few, not so quietly, 'Lead us to victory, good my lord.' 'God and Robert, lead us, brave prince.' Laying it on a bit thick, I thought, but gave them a cheery wave, and wondered how they would react when the first chest was pierced by an arrow, or the first head rolled off in front of them. Still, the chance for that discovery was not far off – and now unstoppable.

In front of each squadron a priest was standing, clad all in white with that red cross stitched to their chests. They were all mumbling prayers of one description or another. Five squadrons were so arrayed and somehow I took heart; even if they were never engaged by the Turks, surely their numbers would give them a fright. I prayed so.

Deep within the shadows inside the monstrous walls our main forces were now deployed in their allocated positions. Silently they had walked; no marching, no thud of hundreds of feet in unison – all movement eerily silent. My next encounter was with my own cavalry. Payne, Ragenaus, and Philip already had them standing by their mounts.

'Morning,' I greeted them cheerfully, 'are you rested?'

'Well enough, my lord,' said Payne, 'and yourself?'

'Too well, Payne. On my own, unfortunately.'

The trio giggled nervously. A poor jest, but it was difficult to be witty at such a moment.

'I am going down to the gate. I'll watch from the battlements. Follow Godfrey's men when they start moving, I will join you when you reach the gate. Whence the day will have begun in earnest, my friends: God be with you.'

'And you, lord,' was the chirpy response that I received. *They seem in good spirits, I pray that they survive the day.*

Next, I met Godfrey himself. His was to be the last regiment to take the field. As I approached I could see that he too was wearing a white surcoat embellished with the newly stitched red cross over his armour.

'Morning, Godfrey,' I uttered quietly. 'Nice day for blood-letting.'

He looked upwards in exasperation. 'It was, Robert, it has started to rain now.'

'Ah! So it has. That will be the holy water sent by God. I've been expecting it. Why are you wearing that white surcoat and red cross, Godfrey? Your belief in this venture has faded, has it not?'

'Perhaps, but needs are pressing this morn, and we need unity of purpose, do we not?'

'Indeed, and I expect mine to be mired in red by mid morning.'

'Let us pray that you will survive to remove it, Robert. God be with you.'

'And you. Watch the signals closely; we need to keep control out there.'

'Surely, my friend, surely.'

Then, one by one, I passed the squadrons that Raymond had agreed to contribute. He had agreed to send a detachment to the citadel to release those of Bohemund's men who wished to fight alongside their mighty leader, but Raymond himself lay, once again, in a sick bed at the bottom of the hill; no miracle cure for this ageing adventurer.

Then I reached the gate, and Flanders who was occupied but waved a hand in greeting as I stopped to dismount. He came over shortly.

'Robert, what are you doing here? Your squadrons are at the rear, surely?'

'Indeed, Rob, but there is time to watch young Hugh prove himself. Come with me and we'll watch from the battlement.'

Hugh, with his special squadron of shock troops, archers and swordsmen, would be lined up behind the Bridge Gate; they would exit the city first and upon their shoulders hinged the success of the day.

The fates of Antioch, Jerusalem, Byzantium and the Christian world was about to be changed.

Just before the first fingers of light illuminated the trampled earth inside the gates, men began to shout and horses blow and whinny. Commanders were performing their final checks before the Bridge Gate was opened. Everyone would be in their allotted formations in their allotted places by now.

Before the main force could exit, Hugh had a task to perform; the first objective was the bridge and the burnt-out fort of La Mahomerie.

We ran up the steps at the side of the Duke Gate to witness the first event planned for this crucial day. Craning our necks over the wall we could see the bridge in the distance, nearly three quarters of a mile away, and watched for the first signs of action.

Bohemund was in overall command and would give the order to release the hounds of hell upon those defending the bridge. Then, the first signs of movement; cries from along the wall reached our ears as the actions that Hugh's men had practised were now put to the test.

Coming out through the gate at the trot they split into three troops of thirty men formed into two lines each. The front fifteen consisted of knights a-foot, and men-at-arms with spears, lances and shields; the second line of fifteen, being close behind them, were the archers, and the task of the first line was to protect them. As the first line spread across the front of the gate the archers began their deluge and those Turks on and around the bridge were forced to take cover, meantime the left and right troops ran to the sides and halted to allow their archers to loose, whereupon the centre advanced thirty paces on the run and recommenced the aerial bombardment – the result was a continuous hail of arrows upon the Turks position, initially from the centre and then from the flanks as the three troops closed upon the bridge with frightening speed.

Those guarding the bridge were given no chance of responding and when the deluge halted they looked out to find the infantrymen upon them, as the foot soldiers thrust the blades of their weapons into the unfortunates' flesh. The infantry spears were fearsome enough, but a lance hurled through the air at a distance of ten paces would penetrate your chest, whether it was cast from the back of a horse or from a knight on foot. It could pin you to the wood of a bridge through your armour, and your dying eyes would witness the progress of the thrower as he passed you – drawing his sword in pursuit of his next target.

As soon as we could see that the bridge was secured I scampered back down with Rob Flanders to mount our horses. I watched him trot out, followed by Raymond's captains and Godfrey's men, and then took my place at the head of my cavalry to follow them on to the battlefield.

At the Bridge Gate, the archer squadron under Aethilheard would exit behind Hugh. They were mounted on a mixture of available horses, some Turkish and some bought. Their task was to turn left and gallop south to protect the rear of the main army from those Turks besieging the St George Gate. Behind Aethilheard would be Adhémar, and finally Bohemund.

Now was the day begun.

Flanders' men left the city, crossing the Duke Gate bridge and marching along the riverbank to a pre-set position with their right flank next to the river. Next came those of Raymond's men not engaged on the heights; they trotted off southwards and would join up with Adhémar's troops in the centre of a great arc made whole by Godfrey's contingent. We had planned a semi-circle of steel with the river at our back from which to face the Turks, and now they could be seen, watching from a distance. I thought them fools to let us set out our chosen formation, but thanked the Lord that they lacked the wit to stop us.

When that great semi-circle was completed by Bohemund's men coming out of the Bridge Gate and over the bridge, I led my cavalry along the riverbank and halted behind Raymond's lines. Next came Tancred out of the Bridge Gate, and formed up behind Adhémar's lines. Thus I was ready, secure in the protected ground, to respond to any eventuality; holding two bridges and facing all directions from which the Turks could attack. Our rear, between river and wall, was vulnerable, but already the wall near the Duke Gate was lined with those citizens and pilgrims unfit to face the enemy on the ground. All those who could pull a bowstring, man or woman, were equipped with Turkish bows liberated from their armouries, and stood on the wall ready to loose their arrows upon any Turks foolish enough to attempt to ride down that narrow field.

This was indeed very similar to the position we held at Dorylaeum, and I was extremely surprised that the Turks had not attacked us at our most vulnerable, during the time we were forming up. Now we were at our strongest – and we still had more waiting in the city ready to deploy.

Hugh and his men, recovered from their sortie upon the bridge, made their way behind Godfrey's lines together with those archers given to him, and prepared to protect the foot soldiers in front of them. The whole army front was now composed of a shield wall, backed by knights a-foot and protected by a third line of archers, mostly with Turkish short bows, standing behind them. I had a reserve of archers, trained to the English bow and protected by infantry with shields, at my disposal. Meanwhile Bohemund was busy re-instating the defences of La Mahomerie, bringing wagonloads of rocks from within the city to fortify it as his command position; from here he would control the battlefield.

When I had questioned his choice of position, he'd replied, 'This is where I shall fall, defending the final bridge, for if they reach here the rest of you will be dead.'

My cavalry was sectioned into three squadrons of sixty horse with Allen of Brittany commanding on my left, and young Philip de Bellême on my right. He had been promoted simply because I was short of captains after our long struggles, but we were as well prepared as we could be. Our entire frontage was hardly three quarters of a mile long, but eager to die for the Lord. And then we waited.

Restless, frightened men; men anxious to kill somebody, anybody; men thinking about home; horses catching the excitement, pawing the ground at one end and fouling it at the other, men farting in response; everyone, calm or scared, sweating onto their saddles: a very sweaty, smelly place was the plain before Antioch that morning.

We did not wait very long. Firstly, horsemen appeared in the hills before us, more than a mile distant, and observed our comings and goings. Then they also appeared from our right, in the direction of Kerbogha's main camp near the Iron Bridge.

After a while a party bearing a white flag came down the valley opposite, an embassy no doubt, and were permitted to ride to Bohemund's position. The priests out in front of our battle lines waved their banners angrily at the Turks, and then set to leading the troops in prayer as a gesture of defiance. *Let them look*, I thought, *they might not want to attack us if they can see how determined we are.*

After a while a messenger came over to me from Bohemund's position.

'Prince Robert, my lord Bohemund says that they want to fight twelve knights to twelve of theirs to decide the matter; winner takes all. What say you, my lord?'

'Tell Kerbogha that we prefer the contest between his army and ours, and tell Lord Bohemund that I do not trust Kerbogha and there is too much to lose if I am right. All or nothing, all of ours against all of his, the day is set.'

The messenger looked at me oddly then galloped off back to Bohemund, three hundred paces away. I watched as the message was delivered. Bohemund waved at me and his banner was lifted, the game was on and the embassy galloped off madly into the distance.

How long before a response, I wondered.

They made the first move, but it did not come from the direction of Kerbogha's camp.

From the valley before us, over a mile away, came a multitude of horsemen. Their screaming echoed across the valley and bounced off the city walls, so that we might think they were attacking from all sides. Before they reached our position they formed a ring in front of Godfrey's lines. Circling, they rained arrows onto his defences; our newly trained archers responded but were outnumbered and I feared for the result.

A message from Bohmey arrived. 'Take them out, my lord urges you, Prince Robert,' the rider gasped.

I nodded to Ragenaus. 'Go and instruct Philip to do his duty.'

The Saxon sped off down the line and soon Philip was leading his squadron towards a gap opened for them between the lines of Raymond and Adhémar. Turning towards the circling Turks, Philip, at the gallop, cut into the formation and began to lay into them; his cavalry now inside the Turkish circle found them easy meat and unprepared for such an unlikely visitation. Suddenly most of them broke off and began to gallop back towards the cover of the hills.

I thought, *do not follow them, Philip, do not...* and then I was screaming, to no avail. 'Messenger,' I called for one, 'fetch them back, they must not follow, bring them back.'

I was anxious, for this was a famous trick, to pretend to run and then lead the pursuers into an ambush. I watched as Philip and his men disappeared into the valley, chased by my frantic messenger.

'Pray, Payne, pray for Philip.'

It wasn't long before our prayers were answered and our horsemen came charging back down the valley, not led by Philip, although I could see his banner bringing up the rear. They came for the gap, slowing down as they approached, and I saw that many were wounded and they were short in numbers.

Philip was among them and came straight over to me, his face showing signs of shock and the back end of his horse festooned with arrows. When he halted in front of me the beast slid down onto its rear haunches and keeled over, leaving its erstwhile rider standing on the ground in a state of disbelief.

'It was an ambush,' I shouted with some anger.

The lad nodded, crestfallen as I hurt his ears. 'You were warned not to pursue; learn from it, lad. Now go and see to your men and send me word of your casualties. This day is not yet done and we can afford no more foolishness.'

He went off as bid at the same time as a messenger from Bohemund arrived, pulling up and sending a shower of sand and pebbles into my face.

'Lord Bohemund requests you deal with them.' The rider pointed up the plain towards Kerbogha's position.

I looked. More than a mile away to our right they were forming up across the plain – now it was my turn.

'Ready, Payne?'

'Aye, lord.'

'Then let us be about our business. Wulf,' I shouted to Aethilheard's senior captain, 'take them behind Flanders' lines and watch.'

The Saxon nodded and shouting orders ran off with his English and Welsh archers towards Flanders' men. They had a surprise in mind for our opponents.

Digging my heels into the beast's bony sides I moved towards the gap through which Philip had retreated a few moments ago. This time we would form up properly and the Turks would feel the weight of our half-starved and borrowed steeds. Oh happy thought.

We lined up with my right flank hard against the front rank of Godfrey's men. I could see Flanders and he waved, wishing no doubt that he was with me; my left flank was nearer to that unfriendly valley, and I knew that we were vulnerable from that direction, and we should move forward to be protected by the foothills beyond; *get on with it then* said the voice in my head and I increased the pace. The Turks were coming at us at speed out of the dust of their passage. Time was fleeting and I stood in the stirrups. 'For God!' I cried, and lowered my lance.

There was little time and Wulf's heavy arrows were already darkening the sky from behind Flanders' lines to strike the forerunners. I picked my target and forgot all else as I aimed my lance at him. We were near collision point when he loosed his last arrow, it bounced off my helm but then my lance was through his chest and torn from my grasp as we passed. Lifting my sword out of its scabbard I raised it in one motion to strike at the next target to appear out of the dust. I struck down and his shoulder parted from his neck and I was drenched in a stranger's blood. Spitting it out and near gagging I found myself in a frantic melee, with swords, arrows and lances as likely to strike friend as foe.

Two more strikes brought two more Turks to the ground, but then I was almost hurled from the saddle as someone crashed into me. I turned to find his hairy face upon my shoulder, but it distorted with astonishment and the grasp that the fellow had about my neck loosened as Payne withdrew his lance from the Turk's side and he crashed to the ground alongside my horse's hooves – once more I was saved from behind by Payne's misuse of my banner lance – another crash to my left as Ragenaus despatched yet another intent on removing me from the earth, saved again by Ragenaus' attention to his duty... I felt quite important right then.

'Thank you, Payne, kindly raise it high again,' I commanded. 'We will consider having it permanently red, seeing as you're so pleased with that colour.' Grinning, I took a look around me, not afraid, not worried any more I searched for death, but the spectre was diminishing.

Those Turks still horsed were heading back towards Kerbogha's position, their enthusiasm spent for the moment, and my men were despatching their wounded, clearing the field of survivors.

Shortly I gathered them in and led the way back behind Godfrey's lines. Bohemund's messenger arrived, as expected.

'My lord sends his compliments, Prince Robert: well done.'

'Thank you,' I replied, 'is your lord comfortable in his nest?'

'He is well, my lord. I believe that he is about to give the Turks another fright.' The man pointed towards the Bridge Gate.

I looked over and saw an astonishing sight. Only half a mile away the gate was open wide and from it spewed forth... a band of musicians! With trumpets sounding and drums beating, it heralded a procession of priests leading out the first squadron of our citizen army. Three squadrons went to the right of the bridge and two to the left, although wisely they kept on the wall side of the river. I did not doubt their commitment as much as I was uncertain as to their skill at arms, so was pleased they took such care.

Now we were fully out, with no more in reserve. What would Kerbogha do next? We did not have long to wait. Another message from Bohemund.

'They are retreating, my lord, will you clear up the field?'

'Tell your lord, gladly,' I responded and set about this new task with a lightened heart. We again had the day, with hardly any casualties and the Turks sent off to think again. Oh blessed day.

I sent instructions to Allen. 'Chase up the plain and see how far the Turks go; do not engage but return forthwith if they offer a fight.'

Then to Philip, 'Go onto the battlefield and gather in as many horses as you can, and ask the lord Godfrey if he will send out his men to retrieve as many weapons as they can lay hands on.' We needed everything to help us along our way to Jerusalem.

'Now, Payne Peverel.'

'Yes, good my lord?'

'You see that river behind us?'

Aye, my lord.'

'What say we test its depth and cleanse ourselves of this vile stench and gore?'

'I say, gladly, my lord. Gladly.'

Godfrey, Flanders, and Allen of Brittany had disappeared into the distance for some time when a messenger came back. He came upon me dipping my feet in the cool waters of the Orontes River.

'They have fled, my lord, the Turks are gone.'

Then he continued on to Bohemund's post. Soon his signal flags were waving and the citizen army began to file their way back inside the city walls. Our squadrons were ordered to rest where they stood and food was taken out to them on wagons. The day had accrued some peace.

I decided to take the cleansing bath I had promised myself and stripped off those offending, blood-soaked rags and plunged into the river. It felt good; even though its cool waters came a long way down from the mountains, it was refreshing enough yet outside of Antioch to provide a cleansing bath. The water further in was colder than at the bank but it was worth the initial shock and we soon became used to it and found in its cathartic qualities a kind of renewed baptism. After initially submerging I moved back towards the bank to sit in that warmer, shallow water only up to my waist, with my head and shoulders exposed to the June afternoon sun: I was not contemplating moving.

We were near enough to the bridge to see Bohemund at the centre of many scurrying messengers, and his captains coming back and forth to report to him. After a while he came over, followed by Aethilheard's captain, Wulf – evidently confident there was no longer any threat to our position. Suddenly I felt a chill, the waters were no longer so pleasant: *why Wulf, where is Aethilheard?*

'Robby,' said Bohmey, altogether too quietly, and with no celebration in his voice.

'What now, Bohmey, is an easy victory not enough for the day?'

'It was not that easy, Robby, I have the casualty lists.'

'Oh. How bad?'

'Not too bad in numbers. Hugh lost twenty men in the assault on the bridge, that zealous lad of yours, Philip, lost twenty cavalry in his mad moment, and...'

I looked up as Bohemund hesitated. 'What?'

'Your Saxon Aethilheard, I'm afraid... sorry. He had a sharp tongue, but he was a fine warrior.'

Bohemund didn't need to say any more. *Shit! What am I going to tell Rowena? The children, how am I going to tell Rowena? Tegwin will be upset to hear that death has come so close.*

'Did we lose many archers?'

'Five,' replied Wulf, with no joy at so little lost.

We sat down on the riverbank and said nothing for a while. I suddenly felt tired, sick of it, sick of the killing. I sighed.

Bohemund tried to cheer me up. 'There is good news, Robby. Kerbogha left his pavilions in a hurry, they have set the earth afire over the hill, but Godfrey has gathered in much gold and other treasures. It will go into our fighting fund. Plus many horses, and weapons by the wagonload, and much food for us and fodder for the horses; we will eat well tonight. We have made a profit this day; it will help us on our way to Jerusalem.'

'You are coming then, big boy?' I asked for confirmation.

He did not answer that, so I left it hanging. He would tell me when he was ready.

His next statement concerned more earthly matters.

'Are you wearing anything under the waters?'

'No,' replied I, staring up into the sun-blessed heavens, 'why do you ask?'

'No reason, except... except that the riverbank has filled up with women, they have come to help clean up the wounded, and wash the dirty linen.' He laughed. 'Some are heading over here.'

'Jesu, shoo them away,' I said.

'Can't do that, my naked warrior, I have duties to attend to. Where is your squire?'

'Further along. He seems to be in the same predicament.'

'Oh dear, a naked prince with no protectors. Be afraid, Robby, a girl is looking over here. I'll see you later; we must talk about our next move.' Then he left me... *dog's turd!*

The girl he had referred to did indeed come over here. I tried to ignore her, watching the folk across the other side of the river cavorting, playing, washing clothes, with warriors washing the dirt of the day off.

A shadow fell across me. I heard the rustle of her dress, sensed her presence.

'My lord.' A soft voice, deeply accented, and confident, but wary.

'Beware, maiden, I am not seemly.'

'My lord, there are plenty of unseemly men to look at.'

I looked about me, she was right; the river was full to overflowing with them. Then I cast my head back to see where the voice had come from.

She was fully a woman, although not very old, with long black and curly hair.

'What is your name, girl?'

'Rachel, my lord.'

'And how old are you, Rachel?'

'Eighteen, my lord.'

'What do you want, Rachel, who is eighteen?'

'To help, my lord. All of the women have come out of the city to help our saviours.'

'I see.' I turned a little to view this 'helper' as much as I could without losing my dignity.

'So where is your man, Rachel?'

'He was killed at Nicaea, my lord.'

'I'm sorry, Rachel. I have lost friends too.'

'Yes, lord. It has been a bloody business so far, and you are still covered in it.'

'I am? Where?'

'Your head and shoulders are caked in it. I can remove it, if you permit, my lord.'

'Very well, my breeches and other things are in a pile behind you, if you could manage to wash them too...?'

'I will, my lord, but first your head.'

She was good, gentle but firm; using a wet cloth she teased the blood off my head then set to work on my shoulders.

'Ahh! Jesu! That is good,' I exclaimed as she set about relieving the knots bunched up in my shoulder muscles. 'You have strong hands, Rachel.'

'I didn't before I set off on this journey, but now pushing and pulling wagons and chopping firewood have made them so. *Là!* Am I hurting, my lord?'

'No, quite the opposite, I am most grateful.'

'I'll see to your linen now, my lord,' she said and began to beat my clothes against the rocks of the riverside while I contemplated my next decision.

Truth to tell, my shoulders were not the only part to feel the results of her ministrations, I was also stirring below the water as life returned to my old friend, his curiosity aroused. Who is this, I felt him ask.

My mind made itself a decision. 'Come round here where I can see you, Rachel.'

She stepped around in front of me. She had her skirts tucked into her waistband, showing a shapely pair of legs. I looked up into her face. Soft brown eyes, set in a sun-kissed skin, and a mouth which had mischief in its curves.

'You are French, from your speech,' I declared. 'You know that I am not?'

'I know who you are, my lord.'

'I see, so why choose me to help?'

'You have a reputation, my lord; I have heard stories about you along this journey. I was curious.'

'I am a curiosity?'

'In a way, my lord. You are frightening, yet I am not afraid.'

'You need not be.' We looked at each other for a brief moment, it didn't take long; we both wanted the same thing, why hide it?

'I've heard that there is food enough for a feast tonight. Would you join me, Rachel?'

'*Oui*, I would like that, my lord.'

'Mmm. My name is Robert.'

She moved closer, I could hear her breathing. That fellow between my thighs threatened to break surface and I leaned forward slightly to keep him under the water. Placing her hands on my shoulders she gently kissed my forehead. 'Robert,' was all she said, gently, a mere whisper, but with the strength of a howl.

I rallied; this would need to wait until later.

'Ragenaus!' I shouted, although he and Payne were only about three paces away, and watching the play.

'My lord?'

'See to my armour. Rachel will see to my clothing, and then when you are ready bring her up to my billet. We will eat together tonight. Wulf, you are appointed commander of archers. Rachel, my breeches if you please.'

She scrambled up the bank to where they were drying and slipped back down holding them out for me to take. I expected that she would look somewhere else when I stood up, but she was a bold one, and held the things open as I left the water and stepped into them. Her face was very close to the dangling beast and because my undergarment was damp she helped to pull it over my hips, and then, while I was tying the strings, she stepped back and gazed into my eyes, grinning her gamine grin. The day had brightened in spite of the dying of men and the setting of the sun. I walked back up the hill to my billet dressed only in breeches and a sword over my shoulder. When I had delved into my war-chest and donned what was left of any decent clothing, I felt quite, quite hopeful.

That evening, with the sun replaced with burning braziers and cooking fires, my mesnie assembled for a feast. My captains had been among our squadrons to make certain that all the men were catered for, and there seemed to be no shortage of women who wanted to join them – Christian men being in short supply within the walls of Antioch, I surmised.

There was Ragenaus, Payne, and Philip. Wulf, now chief archer, enjoined by invitation with my other captains. Arnulf was present, although he spent his time trying to avoid looking at Rachel – who had become the centre of attention. Not surprising as she joined fully with the conversation, although sitting, as she was, on a log with her legs akimbo, she would have dragged the eyes of any man towards her.

Somewhere, hidden within the depths of the city, merchants had liberated their stocks of wine – the prices reflected its scarcity – but on that night they managed to dispose of their entire stock I was sure.

We had a jolly time, and later there were attempts to drag information out of our principal guest.

'So, my lady,' pried Wulf, 'who was your husband, sadly killed in the service of our Lord?'

'He was a noble knight, in the service of Hugh of France.'

'Hah!' exclaimed Ragenaus, 'that is enough to get any man killed.'

Her eyes flashed and I tried to calm the talk.

'Hugh is err... impetuous, but he is brave, if young. He will learn.'

'My husband, he was brave. He died defending the prince.'

'Then perhaps the prince should be caring for you, dear lady,' interjected Arnulf, clearly wanting rid of the girl.

'I care for myself, priest,' she retorted. 'I choose whose shelter I seek.'

That shut him up, and he left soon after, muttering prayers as he went. I doubted if Rachel was in them.

It was time. I saw her face reflecting the firelight, it was greasy from the half of chicken that she was demolishing, one hand pointing a chicken leg towards the depression where her skirt had dropped between her thighs. She looked up, her teeth glinted at me and that grin, that greasy, shiny, dripping grin, took hold of my emotions. I nodded my head back towards my billet doorway and she gently closed her eyelids in acceptance. We did not want to wait much longer and as Rachel said her goodbyes and left without fuss I made a closing speech.

'It has been a long day, my friends, and we all should get some rest, there is much to do in the morning. I will say goodnight.'

'Aye, lord, a good night, and much to do,' quipped Wulf, eyeing Rachel's legs.

'I thank you all,' I said, ignoring this. 'You have performed well today, I am proud of you all. May God speed us on our way and remember our mission. Tis not Antioch we sought, but the holy city. Tomorrow we will plan the next part of our journey of salvation. Goodnight all, and God's blessing be upon you.'

The light never quite fled the night in June, and when I followed Rachel into my billet it did not take long to see her. To my surprise my truck bed, a device of folding wood and canvas, had been stacked against the wall and Rachel was on the floor, lying on a pile of hay, covered in a fine sheet. When she had made these arrangements I knew not, nor asked.

'We would not fit together on that *petit lit*, Robert.'

'You intend us to fit together?'

'*Oui*, I have decided, I want you in the state that I found you in today.'

Truth to tell, I was not wearing much more, having only added a linen shirt to the breeches I had worn to walk up the hill, so it did not take much to return me to my mother-born state.

I knelt down beside our straw pile and pulled back the sheet. She was as naked as me, even in the dim light; beautifully, fully, and offering-all naked. She giggled a little as my eyes wandered down her body, lifting a knee a little, but not completely hiding her dark bush. She was full-breasted with dark nipples and my lips first sought them out, to enliven them. She gave out a little gasp as I ran my teeth across the hardening tips, then I smothered her noises with my lips and our tongues met so as to enflame our desires.

She opened her legs and I knelt between them, holding her hips. She grasped my dick and pulled it towards her, and then with a sudden demand cried out, 'I have waited too long.'

I plunged into her as all control departed; this was urgent, this was needed, this was the remedy for all the frustrations of the last few days of dark despair as we bucked and plunged into the delights of ecstasy and release as stomach-churning spasms ended the frantic hungering to accompanying sounds of joy. We were together in that, without any practice, *a goodly partnership* was my first rational thought. After a short while she gave out a little squeak, a small voice somewhere underneath me.

'I can't breathe, Robert, you are heavy. *Merde*.'

'Sorry,' I said as I rolled off.

'Where are you going, prince? We are not done yet.'

She was right, we were not, Jesu! She had an appetite for love such as I hadn't experienced for a long while; too long. We coupled throughout the night, on and off, rest and play. Then too soon the dawn made its unwelcome return, and a new day had begun.

'My lord.' Ragenaus was outside. 'Food, my lord… for two.'

Rachel was lying face down, but naked. I scrambled around until I found the sheet and cast it over her lovely shape.

'Come in, Ragenaus, what have you there?'

He entered tentatively, and placed a wicker basket on the ground, struggling not to notice my companion.

'The lord Bohemund has requested that you attend his meeting, my lord.'

'Yes, when will that be?'

'He said that it will begin when you arrive, my lord.'

'In that case tell him not to start without me.'

Ragenaus sniggered, he knew my humour well.

'I will, my lord,' he answered, and left.

'Rachel.' I squeezed her buttocks and they clenched obligingly.   'There is food. Tis morning.'

'What is it?' She asked.

'Cold chicken and bread,' I responded, looking at the basket.

'I'd rather have hot cock,' she replied from deep within the straw.

'Then you shall have both, my lady,' said I, slowly pulling down the sheet.

I staggered out, properly dressed, near mid morning. Rachel helped me back into my mail coat. I asked her what she was going to do next, hoping that she would stay, knowing that she should not.

'I will go back to the French camp; I expect they will find me a husband,' she said wistfully.

'You mean a man? A guardian?'

'No, Robert, a husband. I fear that I am too important to be a sergeant's chattel.'

'Oh. Who are you?'

She placed a finger across my lips, and then whispered, 'Rachel. We might meet further along the road. Go and see to your supreme commander, he has need of you.'

'You heard?'

'Your knight is not the quietest of men.'

'Very well, my lady: Rachel.'

I kissed her and we parted with a smile. I wondered how we would react if I met her in some court somewhere in the future, if I lived that long. A strange thought crossed my mind: *I seem to be gathering too many lady friends to die. Too much sadness would come from that; I must therefore survive*. That settled I headed for the slope.

By the time I got halfway up that damned mountain to see Bohemund, I was ready for the knacker's yard.

I found my chaplain, Arnulf, there, he had gathered a congregation around him on a plateau, and with my arrival he began a service giving thanks for our survival and offered prayers for the souls of the departed.

Glad as I was for the rest, apparently I did not appear to be much of a victorious commander, as Arnulf pointed out.

'My prince,' he said after prayers, 'why so glum? You have given us a great victory.'

'Yes, Arnulf, but at what cost?'

'Perhaps there is a cost to all great achievements. We can see that the Turks suffered the more grievous harm, and it was a wondrous sight to behold.'

'What was?' I seemed to be still numbed from the previous day, or was the night too strenuous, and I was only half listening to my concerned chaplain.

'The charge,' he said, with wonder in his eyes, 'from the walls we could see it all. The valley was full of onrushing Turks, and then you set off towards them, a pitiful few in the face of hundreds. Then when you struck they seemed to melt away as snow in the sun. It was a miracle, my lord.'

'No, good priest, it was not a miracle. Miracles are good; that was carnage, and the only thing melting away was the lives of men.'

He shut up for a moment, giving me the chance to ask what I hoped was an obtuse question.

'Who was Rachel, Arnulf? I have heard of her in the Bible, have I not?'

'Indeed you have, my lord, she is someone to stay clear of, a great beauty, a temptress to bring a man down.' He looked at me oddly. 'You haven't fallen for such a woman, have you, my lord?'

'No, Arnulf, not fallen.' *Risen more like*, I thought.

'Where is Bohemund? He asked me to come up here.'

'He is at the very top of the mountain, my lord. While you rested things have happened.'

'Bollocks! I'm not going up there. So tell me, good priest, tell me the news.'

Arnulf told me of other events since the battle. He told me that some leaders had been busy in other ways.

Bohemund left the field immediately after he had witnessed our success. He went directly to the summit of Mount Silpius and threw Raymond's men off.

The Moslem commander holding the citadel, an emir named Ahmad ibn-Marwan, had witnessed Kerbogha's shambolic advance down on the plains below and was only too keen to surrender the castle. He had quickly accepted Raymond's banner to fly above his towers, but, when Bohemund returned, Marwan just as quickly tore it down, exchanging it for one of Bohemund's, and it was this red banner that now flew on the heights above the relieved city of Antioch.

Raymond took umbrage at this and his troops grabbed the palace, which lay within the old city, as his headquarters. This was watched with some dismay by the other leaders and they immediately sought ways to resolve the situation. The hard-won victory and the main purpose of the expedition had now been reduced to an undignified scramble for personal advantage. I was wearily unsurprised.

With the way to St Simeon and the routes back to Cyprus and Constantinople open again, news of the triumph of Antioch would soon reach Europe, and the ears of Alexios. I wondered what would be made of it without an accurate report. I instructed Philip to write to my brother Rufus, to Tegwin and to Sibyl and tell them of my survival.

Godfrey called a council on 3 July. The leaders elected for a period of peace, saying that it was now too hot to march on Jerusalem. I thought that wasteful but I told them that I'd go back down to Laodicea to prepare my supply lines for when they decided to move. Wulf, Payne and Ragenaus, newly knighted for his bravery, were to remain here to train as many horses as possible, then bring them along the coast when they had matched as many men and horses as they could. Philip was to remain and manage communications.

I took Flanders along with me. He deserved a reward for his stout efforts, and, as I explained to him, 'I am sure that you'll enjoy it in Laodicea. You will see that the emperor has made every provision for our comfort.'

'I am grateful for the rest, Robert. It is harder arguing with these unholy French than fighting the Turks.'

'Aye, tis true. I did not want to remain here for so long but circumstances dictated that we did, and it hasn't turned out all bad, has it, Rob?'

'Mm, perhaps. When Alexios gets the idea that Bohemund fancies himself ruler of Antioch there will be consequences, I'm sure.'

My mind galloped ahead. I was looking forward to some more African adventures. I wondered what Rob would make of grappling with ebony flesh, I presumed that he would not turn down such an opportunity – *we shall see*.

10. A Summer of Contentment.

When I arrived at St Simeon it was to receive a gloomy report from Artus regarding the state of his fleet.

'These vessels, my lord, are nearly done for, they have sailed too far and carried too much in the pursuit of your wishes; we need to have them out of the water and give them some attention.'

'Show me.'

I went about the fleet and saw for myself the leaking hulls, frayed rigging, torn sails, and worn and creaky fittings.

'What should we do then, Captain Artus?'

'If we can get them all out of the water I can scavenge the best bits, and then see how many serviceable craft we can make up from the parts. Even so, those that can be refurbished might not make it through another winter. You need to see about a replacement fleet to support you on land.'

'Very well, Artus, perhaps I can solve this problem for you. I am leaving a small garrison here to hold the port. We need to move our focus further along the coast to support our operations. Leave them your best ship for communication, and we will take the rest down to Laodicea and work on them during the summer.'

'Thank you, my lord, that is the answer I was hoping for.'

Approaching Laodicea our sails would have been spotted on the horizon so by the time we reached port the quayside was thronging. It was also clear the noisy spectators were expecting me, the Duke of Normandy himself, the hero of Antioch, so I had been told, on one of the ships.

After the battle outside Antioch, I had appointed a new youngster to attend me because the status of Ragenaus had risen so much. The new lad was Oslac, who had been with the much-missed Aethilheard, and advancement had presented itself earlier than usual.

It was the case that, in my mesnie, it was likely to happen sooner rather than later, as was an early death.

Laodicea was all a-buzz, it seemed that the whole of the Latin world now wanted a part of this spectacularly fortunate expedition. Ships from all over the Mediterranean had congregated in the port looking for work, trade, or other opportunities that might present themselves. A successful army was usually the focus for purveyors of services of all kinds, and Laodicea was no exception.

On the voyage from St Simeon the new squire had been busy with my attire. He had found clean white linen for my shirt, and clean breeches, and spent time with a mixture of sand and oil to make my metal gleam. So! Here I was, resplendent in helm, sword and chain-mail coat, all glistening with oil in the sun, and made illustrious by my new white surcoat with a red cross – our symbol to signify a crusader. I could see that Ragenaus and Payne had taught the youngster well.

I was not usually one for pomp and ceremony, but I understood it, and could put on a show when it was necessary. Today one was of those occasions and I would not disappoint the crowd – now cheering as they spied me, all primped up.

An armed guard, together with a gaggle of officials to complete the welcoming party, had already lined up before we touched the jetty.

As I stepped off the creaky deck an elderly man came forward.

'Greetings, Prince Robert. I am Argyros, the emperor's representative.'

'Greetings, Argyros. Where is Aiolos?'

'He is summoned back to the emperor and bade me give you his congratulations on the splendid victory at Antioch. For my part I am full of admiration for the achievements of you and your companions. It augurs well for the rest of your mission to Jerusalem.'

'Indeed. Thank you, Argyros. Are you empowered to speak for the emperor?'

'I am, Prince Robert, here are my letters.'

He handed over a roll of parchments which I passed to Oslac.

'I will read them carefully; there are matters that we need to discuss...'

'Of course. You must be in need of rest, food perhaps. Allow me to escort you to your villa.'

'Thank you. Is it the same as on my last visit?'

'Indeed, if it suits you, my lord.'

'Does it have the same facilities?'

'They are both awaiting your return, my prince.'

'Then the same place will suit me fine, lead on. Come on, Flanders, our food awaits.' *Aye! And on a black platter methinks.*

'Lead on, Robert, I could eat a goat.'

Rob looked at me oddly as I suffered an attack of the sniggers; *goats he wants, perhaps he can be tempted with a different dish.*

When we reached the villa the manservant was waiting with goblets of wine to wash away the dust.

'What is your name, fellow?' I asked.

'It is Erastos, my lord.'

'Very well, Erastos, is the bath prepared? I haven't had one since the last time I was here.'

Rob was puzzled; he hadn't known that I'd been in this place before.

'Last time you were here, Robert? When was that?'

'Oh! You know? The last time... when I came to organise supplies.'

'You didn't mention villas.'

'Didn't I? It must have slipped my memory. Oslac, you may go with Erastos. I shall send for you if you're required, I expect that Erastos has suitable quarters prepared for you.' The servant bowed and led my lad away.

We were walking along the cloister towards the bathhouse when Rob came back with another comment.

'I saw you washing in the river outside Antioch, what's this about not bathing?'

I stopped and, turning to Rob, held him by the shoulders and replied with exaggerated patience.

'Cousin Rob, there is washing your arse in ice-melt rivers, and then there's bathing: do not confuse the two.'

'What's the difference?'

'One wrinkles your bum and shrinks your bollocks, but the other is a much warmer affair. I'm sure you'll find it pleasanter, and if it goes well you will find it very relieving.'

'Relieving! Relieving of what?'

'Tired muscles and certain kinds of congestion.'

'Congestion, congestion of what?'

I began walking, encouraged by the aroma of unguents and oils, sparking pleasant memories.

'How long is it since you lay with a woman, Rob?'

'Woman! What in the name of miracles is a woman?'

'Exactly. Now come in here.' I led my confused cousin into the comforting gloom of the steamy bathing rooms, to be met at the entrance by attendants. 'Here you are, strip off and they'll give you a robe, then follow me.'

Flanders followed me into the pool area where he had no difficulty in sliding into the warming waters, following the example set by me.

'Ahh! This is good, Robert, this is very good.'

Such bliss, such relaxation. I began to wonder when the next part of the therapy would begin, and my dick began to stir; I wondered where Sassie was, teasing doxy!

With the weight off his body and the warm waters working to relax his tired muscles it was not long before Rob started to snooze. I was close to following his example, when I heard a cry.

'*Mon Dieu!* Robert!'

I looked across the bath; my companion's eyes were open wide in astonishment.

'What?'

'There is a black woman behind you.'

There was indeed. I looked up to see the grinning teeth of my erstwhile companion beaming down on me. I reached up and she jumped into the bath, giving a delighted whoop, and near drowned me as she did so.

Flanders was nonplussed.

'What are you going to do with her, Robert?'

'I am going to continue my studies into the practices of Eros with this crazy creature. Why don't you do the same?'

'What! Sex with an African?'

'Indeed. Try it for yourself.'

'I don't know. I've never done it as a threesome before... and not in black.'

'You don't have to; you can have your own, look behind you.'

He looked back over his shoulder and his jaw dropped even further. Waiting behind him, in a sheer shift, and with the same toothy grin was the twin of my Sassie – a matched pair of women.

'*Mon Dieu*! Will she? With me! Jesu, what will Clementia say?'

'That!' said I, my voice muffled by being enveloped by black breasts, 'depends on what you tell her.'

'*Mon Dieu!*'

'Rob, stop cursing and take hold of her. God's treasures come in all shades, just be grateful.'

Sassie said something over her shoulder and the other girl slid down behind him and started to work on his neck with her hands.

'Jesu! She smells gorgeous.'

'Yes,' I replied, 'and tastes and feels the same... and you will find she is pink inside.'

'Pink, what do you mean?'

'Take her into your chamber and find out for yourself.'

There was a silence for a few moments.

'I think that I will... later. This is marvellous.'

'Enjoy it, you've worked for it.'

I looked at Sassie and pointed to Flanders' companion, she grinned knowing what I meant. 'Asha,' she informed me. I looked over her shoulder to tell Rob but I only caught a glimpse of two naked backsides; four sashaying orbs, two glistening brown and two starkly white, as they disappeared into the gloom of a side chamber.

'Where is your sister?' I asked Sassie. She rubbed her stomach and replied, 'No good.' So I said I was sorry and left it at that; women's problems are privy after all.

The servants retired discreetly leaving we battle-weary warriors to enjoy some time with gentleness and love. *God knows, we deserve that.*

As is the wont of fate, the good times are always followed by the bad and we enjoyed probably too many before the inevitable messengers arrived to spoil our idyll.

First, Argyros was announced, all smiles, all diplomacy, always skirting around the real reason for his visit.

I waited until he had run out of obfuscation before he came out with it.

'Is it true, my lord, that you were awaiting the appearance of the emperor's troops to garrison Antioch?'

'Aye! That would have been helpful if he had shown some interest.'

That remark worried Argyros; he pulled at his robes for a while, trying hard not to let his gaze fall upon Sassie. She was not quite naked, but being wet and wearing only the flimsiest of robes, was clearly a distraction for any man.

'Erm, your brother-in-law, named Stephen, I believe?'

'What of him? Toadspawn,' growled Rob, distracted from feeding his companion grapes, her hard nipples straining her sheer gown.

'Yes, Argyros, what of that cowardly toadspawn?'

'He entered the camp of the emperor at Philomelium, where he was coming through Cilicia on the way to Antioch to join you, my lord.'

'Alexios was on his way to Antioch?'

'Surely, my lord. He was three hundred miles away but he was coming to you. It was Stephen who prevented him.'

Rob suddenly lost interest in the twin peaks of Asha.

'What, in the name of all that is holy, do you mean, fellow?'

'The lord Stephen told the emperor that the city had fallen, that all were slaughtered, and that he and his companions had made a fortunate escape.'

That revelation was a real conversation-stopper.

We looked at each other in astonishment. Cowardice was one thing, lying to camouflage it quite another.

Rob spoke first.

'*Mon Dieu!* I should not have named him toadspawn, tis an insult to slimy creatures.'

'I suspect that the next time I see him will be an interesting occasion,' I forecast.

'The next time you meet your brother-in-law, I suspect that he will have a higher voice.'

'Ah yes. My sister will have prepared him to join the company of men like Taticius, I suppose.'

'If she lets him live.'

'I shall relieve him of his wretched life personally; he can face me in the lists.'

I turned to Argyros. 'You have understood this conversation, I believe?'

'Every word, my lord. It is, as you say, astonishing.'

'Then convey my words back to the emperor, and ask him for forgiveness for my family name.'

'I shall be sure to speak out on your behalf, my lord. The extent of Stephen's treachery will be made quite clear.'

'Thank you. Now you can answer my questions. Where is Stephen now?'

'He went on his way. The emperor gave him thanks, and money, and a ship to Italy; he thought him a hero.'

'He will soon know differently. Thank you, Argyros, I will deal with the matter upon my return to Normandy. Tell me, did the emperor not continue to Antioch, or at least send forth a scouting party to see the truth of it?'

The fellow shuffled and searched his library of diplomatic responses.

'No, my lord, of that I know nothing save that your countryman told a tale of complete annihilation, of a venture failed.'

'I see.' Although I did not, for surely one of the biggest cities in the East would have merited some curiosity. But I doubted there was much to be gained from badgering this envoy so I let the matter stew.

After the fellow left us I felt a numbness of spirit; treachery was surely the nadir of men's relationships, all else can be forgiven, but this... never.

Those were my final words on that episode. Rob, watching my face, had more sense than to comment. Then Sassie intervened and I had more immediate things to concern myself with.

Very observant was my ebony Venus, and knew ways to ease my distress. Later, in bed, I was scratching the palm of my right hand with Sassie's left nipple, when she giggled.

'What amuses thee, my dark volcano?'

My hand slid down her stomach and delved into her lips.

'My sister, she says that you are strange people. Oh!' She exclaimed gently as I found her pleasure bud.

All of Sassie's words came out as if they were noises of the wind, whispers, or the rustling of leaves. I was fascinated by her. Then my fingers got to work and she moaned.

'Why are we strange, Sassie?'

She opened her legs wide and cast back her head; the next time she spoke it was to the ceiling – in gasps.

'You all colours. Your head brown, white bodies.'

Yes,' I agreed, 'that must be very strange. Now what about him?' I asked, looking down to where her hand was grasping my throbbing dick.

She giggled again, and told the ceiling. 'He is red, he is ready, Sassie ready, my lord.'

There was nothing else for it. I turned and planted my hands either side of her shoulders, then felt her hands guide my hot end into her warm passage. I looked at her face as she bared her gleaming teeth, then she gasped as she thrust upwards. I withheld until she subsided and then slowly pressed him home until our pubic hair meshed. That was the signal for a brief thrashing about until we both surrendered and climaxed together.

A heady mixture were we, Africa and Normandy; both colourful and passionate, a kaleidos of love amid the deadly winds of war: what odd humours doth the gods possess.

It was well beyond next midday when the servant Erastos came into the sunny courtyard, all of a dither. We were at ease on couches, amid the fragrances of the herbs planted all around, playing a game with grapes, eating and practising at siege engines at the same time: we were attempting to toss a grape into our dusky friends' mouths – in a parabola, as if from a ballista. The penalty for missing was a forfeit, a glass of wine downed in one gulp. As the afternoon wore on the number of missiles finding their target diminished and the courtyard became slippery with grape seed and skins. Hunger grew conversely, from lack of sustenance.

Erastos interrupted our sport.

'There is bad news, my lord.'

'Uh! And is that not the nature of news, Erastos?'

'It might seem that way, my lord.'

'Tell me then.'

'Your messenger ship has come down from St Simeon. They are greatly afraid, there is plague in Antioch. Your captain of ships, he awaits outside with a report.'

'Shit! That's all we need.' Rob had taken to the quality of Alexios' hospitality, and was not pleased to have it ended so abruptly.

'Artus!' I shouted, 'come in, have a grape and tell me about the plague.'

Artus was as glum as I was merry. He was reluctant to spoil the mood, but needs must.

'There is plague in the city, my lord. Some suggest that it is because it there are still unburied corpses, and they have been seen rotting in the river. Our leaders have deserted the place; Bohemund has gone north and Raymond to the south and it is spreading... it has spread. We stayed in our stockade by the coast and made little contact with the city, but the Germans were not so fortunate.'

My ears pricked up at the mention of Germans.

'What Germans?'

'They sailed into the port directly from the north. They wanted to join Godfrey's contingent, but they all fell ill and died within days. Now the beaches are fouled; it is dreadful.'

'My God!' Rob's mood soon changed when this sunk into his wine-enriched brain.

'How many of them were there?'

'There were about fifteen hundred, my lord.'

'Jesu!' I was shocked. 'All warriors?'

'All knights, my lord...with horses.'

Artus sat twisting his goblet in his hands, reluctant to partake from it, as if the news was not yet at an end, so I prompted him.

'There's more?'

'Yes, my lord. The bishop, Adhémar... he's dead, and so is Philip de Bellême.'

I was sobered by that announcement.

'Philip?'

'I am afraid so, my lord, in his sleep, without suffering.'

'Where are Payne and Ragenaus?'

'They left the city and are coming down the sea road; everyone has left the city until the pestilence has gone. They will all return when it's safe to do so I am sure. Your chaplain came with us, he is at the harbour.'

'Pray God that they do.' *Oh no, Arnulf, my conscience. He had better not mention the subject of women else he find himself back on a boat to St Simeon.*

The mood darkened, and the light was fading in the sky – as if to match our spirits.

Sassie took me to bed early. She tried to understand my sadness and bring comfort to me in the dark, but for once she failed, my mind was elsewhere and not even this dark beauty could raise my ardour.

I awoke early the next morning, but remained in bed watching the woman's back rising and falling as she remained in deep sleep.

She was beautiful, and innocent. I wished at that moment that my life could be so uncomplicated, but it wasn't. I rose and gently pulled a cover over her shapely haunches. Dressing quietly I wandered outside into the strengthening light of the courtyard dawn.

Arnulf was already there.

'My lord, you have made it for Prime this morning.'

'Have I? Is it that early?'

'I'm afraid so, could you not sleep?'

'No. This adventure is getting messy again.'

'There is devil's work at play. Perhaps he thinks we are too close to success.'

'I do not think that we will have success unless we honour our promises and remained united. This unseemly land grab has not the scent of holiness about it. Nor do I like the stench of death in my nostrils, it is rank.'

'What are you going to do?'

'I do not know. Where are you holding Prime?'

'We'll do it here. We'll pray together if you like.'

'Yes, I'd like that, Arnulf. Pray that the Lord gives me strength.'

By the end of August we had received word that there were no more occurrences of plague so I thought it might be safe to go back to Antioch and see if any progress had been made in resolving the differences between Bohemund and Raymond. Raymond was not there and Bohemund was not interested, so I returned to Laodicea, leaving Rob behind to furnish me with regular reports. I was now uncertain what to do. Arnulf composed letters to be sent back to the pope, and the emperor, to explain the need for assistance in the promotion of the crusade; indeed, he suggested that Urban should make an appearance and lead us into Jerusalem himself.

Then Raymond decided to go and find himself another city to seize and use as a power base, and his gaze settled on Marrat an-Numan, just south-east of Jericho.

The Provençal leader, although not entirely respected by all, had two distinct advantages at this time, he still had the holy lance and many were strong in their belief that it was this relic that had played the major part in the victory at Antioch.

Rob was one who subscribed to this view and joined with him for a while, perhaps suffering from an excess of contrition over his recent adventuring in the pleasures of the flesh.

Raymond's other advantage lay in his treasury. He carried enormous wealth with him and he was not slow to use it.

So I played with Sassie, and played with the idea of going back home, then that made me glum because Tegwin and Sibyl entered that consideration. I was cool towards Sassie and scolded myself for it, she deserved better – meanwhile the crusaders enhanced their reputation for ruthlessness and cruelty.

Having no success in persuading Bohemund to share the ownership of Antioch, or indeed to do what they had agreed to do, hand it over to the emperor, Raymond made for Marrat and laid siege to it. Upon discovering this, Bohemund followed him and joined in the expedition. After some initial setbacks they succeeded in gaining the town and set about sacking the place. All Turks found in there were slaughtered without mercy and all of the wealth of the place grabbed without remorse of any kind.

I remained in Laodicea, much troubled by the news as it filtered down to me, and it took some persuasion to get me to go back to Antioch for a meeting.

I made my unhappiness known to Arnulf.

'I seem to be losing my friends, Arnulf. Are you contemplating leaving me any time soon?'

'I am not planning it so, Prince Robert, but on a venture such as this, our choice is limited to what the Lord wills.'

'Is it his will that Bohemund and Raymond are set on opposite courses?'

'If they forsake the Lord they will surely make wrong choices.'

'I know what Bohemund is about, his ambition is plain, and it was crafted before he left Apulia. But Raymond, what of his ambitions, Arnulf?'

'I know not, Prince Robert.'

'He has the lance, is that not a symbol of God's guidance?'

Arnulf gazed at me and pondered for a while before he answered.

'Ah yes, the lance.'

'Ah yes, Arnulf, the lance. Huh! You sound really convinced about *the lance*. I think not.'

'As you see fit to mention it, no, I'm not, and neither was Adhémar.'

'I know, he said it was in Constantinople. And you knew this?'

'Of course!'

'You let everyone believe otherwise!'

'It served a purpose.'

I was not really surprised by Arnulf's admission; the lance had been far too convenient – and far too useful – at the time.

'Arnulf, we are joined together in deceit but you will not deceive me in such matters again, will you?'

'No, my lord, never again. We need to trust each other if we are to get these scoundrels moving again. Besides, I never said that I believed it in the first place.'

'No, that's true. But isn't that the same as not telling the truth?'

'It might be argued that way, Prince Robert. Will you go to Antioch, one more time, and see if you can improve things?'

'I suppose so. If I don't go there I am leaving this place. I shall speak with them once more.'

Without much enthusiasm, and several days late, I set off for Antioch, arriving on 11 November to join the squabbling and the greedy, the opportunist and the pious, gathering there to agree the next move.

My mesnie was complete again as it could be on the beach at St Simeon. Payne and Ragenaus were there, but sadly no Aethilheard and no Philip; it did not help my mood. When we reached Antioch, we discovered that far from reaching any agreement, Raymond and Bohemund had invented a new argument for their amusement. Raymond had secured the major part of Marrat, but Bohemund's men had a strategic hold on a significant position in the city, so he would not yield to Raymond's claim to dominion over the ruined town. This was the mirror image of the situation in Antioch.

Godfrey, along with me and Rob, sought to settle the matter with Arnulf's help, but in the absence of the emperor, or indeed the pope, we lacked the authority to compel an agreement.

Seeing no end to the impasse, and continuing to lose interest in these petty princes' affairs, I told Godfrey, 'Until these two can agree then the crusade is mired in these sands, and without their armies we will not have sufficient numbers to take Jerusalem. You have no doubt questioned why we are here and why those two came along; Jerusalem seems to have slipped into their distant memories. I am going back to Laodicea to maintain communications with the emperor, and keep control of the fleets using the port. If anything new transpires, let me know.'

Godfrey did not contest that and I left him with his own thoughts, but it was obvious that without the help of either Bohemund and Raymond we could not hope to succeed in our mission and so without them it was pointless moving on.

I left Rob with Raymond. I told him, 'Be careful, he is losing credibility, and I would rather you attached your force to Godfrey. I judge him to be one of the few who retains a modicum of trust. But stay with Raymond for now and keep me well informed about his intentions and his doings.'

Then I went back to my maritime headquarters.

The squabbling had lost us another summer and another winter was certain to pass before there would be any prospect of an advance upon the Holy City of Jerusalem. To the Moslem observers this dichotomy in the Frankish performance, on the one hand a ruthless military efficiency and on the other a hopelessly divided leadership, must have been a source of puzzlement and frustration, as much as it was to me.

Then, as tides do, it began to turn against Raymond. Bohemund tired of his game and withdrew his men to Antioch, declaring that he would not move on Jerusalem. Raymond could not hold Marrat on his own, and withdrew into the desert. The bloodshed caused by the onslaught upon that place was now rendered unnecessary and valueless. In addition there was a growing volume of dissent among Raymond's followers. Distressed at the obvious venality of their leader, they called, 'We have the lance, why should we wait to advance upon Jerusalem?'

Raymond's lance had turned into a double-edged sword, one which could be used against him. He was forced to ask for another meeting of the leaders and we convened at Rugia, south of Antioch, on 4 January 1099.

I rode along the Orontes valley below the Jabal Ansariyah in the company of Payne and Ragenaus to find Rob's camp. It was part of Raymond's greater encampment but I needed to speak to him before visiting the Provençal leader.

Rob and Allen were present but I was surprised to find young Tancred, Bohemund's nephew, there as well.

'Tancred has joined us because he does not agree with his uncle Bohemund's position on Antioch,' explained Rob, 'and there is something else that involves us all that needs some consideration.'

'I see,' said I, 'what business is that?'

'Raymond is being pressed by his own followers to cease this nonsense with Bohemund and get off to Jerusalem immediately, so he has a new plan.' Rob hesitated a moment.

'I wasn't aware that he had a plan in the first place,' I put in helpfully.

'Well he has one now,' muttered Allen.

'Aye,' confirmed Rob, 'he wants to buy our loyalty. We have information that he intends to offer us money to come with him to Jerusalem.'

That remark puzzled me.

'*Come* with him? Is he our leader? But we are going anyway, or we were until he and Bohemund held the whole expedition up. Why does he think to pay us?'

Tancred entered the conversation.

'We believe that he is planning ahead. If he commands our loyalty, and Bohemund remains in Antioch's citadel, then Raymond intends to leave a garrison in the lower city and buy our support to make claim to the governorship of Jerusalem.'

Allen clarified that. 'Over Godfrey, do you see, Robert? Raymond believes that he can have dominion over Jerusalem, and Godfrey, if he has our support.'

'Yes, I see that, and the money will be useful. I have made arrangements for a quantity of supplies for the expedition, for which I have ceded control of the port of Laodicea to the emperor.'

Rob asked, 'What supplies, Robert?'

'More siege materiels. I am not camping outside of Jerusalem for six months.'

'Then why did we not use them at Antioch?' asked Tancred.

'Think on, young man,' I retorted tetchily, 'we were not planning to lay siege to anywhere except Jerusalem, until it was decided to starve the city of Antioch into submission.'

Allen agreed. 'True, Robert, but that's behind us and it is sound planning that you offer for Jerusalem.'

Tancred also concurred. 'This is why I am happy to accompany the Duke of Normandy: he thinks in straight lines.'

Rob said, 'This is no straight-line thinking, Tancred, this is as convoluted as it gets, but it is honest. So what do you want to do now, Robert?'

'Simple, take Raymond's money and get on with it.'

Tancred sniggered. 'Simple isn't it?'

Then we were gladdened when Godfrey turned up. We soon briefed him, and although he was anxious to safeguard his own interests he soon accepted our plan and we all agreed to present a united front to Raymond.

Godfrey explained. 'I am not short of funds, but if Raymond wants to support my purse I will take the money; in the name of God, of course.'

It only remained to agree upon an amount, or amounts, that we would settle on, before we went off to see Raymond and wait for him to make us an offer.

In the event we accepted his money. The old man had obviously lost himself in the complications of his scheme, because he actually paid Godfrey as much as he did me, notwithstanding that Godfrey was the only realistic alternative ruler of Jerusalem, and he still commanded thousands more men than I did. Given the past record of the Frankish princes in regard to promise-keeping, it was likely to be a waste of money, and I wondered if this new unity would last even before the funds were spent.

So, along with Godfrey, I received ten thousand solidi, Rob took six thousand, Tancred was pleased to receive five thousand, and other minor leaders, 'proportionally, according to their rank'.

Whereupon we agreed to recommence the journey to Jerusalem and the leaders, having agreed a schedule, went back to their camps to prepare for the final part of the journey.

When everyone was ready, I asked Rob to stay with Raymond.

'To keep an eye on him, Robert?' he chortled.

I sent Wulf's archers, most of my cavalry and my men-at-arms to join Godfrey. He, Allen and Tancred were to move southwards along the coastal road, separately from Raymond's force who were moving inland. They all set off on 13 January, Raymond leading his discontented army, who were probably as unconvinced of their purpose as at any time since they had left the shores of Europe. Bohemund was left to lord it over his new city, and the Emperor of the East was no doubt wondering what to do about it.

I watched as they rode off into the desert. Payne seemed a bit put out.

'What if they find a fight, my lord?'

'Frightened to miss another slaughter, are you?'

'Tis what we are here for,' added Ragenaus.

'Don't you want to see how your housekeepers are... keeping?'

That brought a smile to their faces: housekeeping! Their favourite sport.

'Oslac! My horse if you please, we are off to sea; Laodicea awaits. We will rendezvous with Count Raymond and Flanders further south.'

Sassie lay across my chest. In our fusion of colour she was sad. Although she did not entirely understand the reasons why, she nevertheless knew that great events were afoot and that I was deeply involved in them. And she was determined to make the most of the short time we had left together.

'Master,' she whispered softly in my left ear, 'will you return?'

I shifted a little and her right nipple scraped across my chest. I sniffed the scent of the oil in her black hair and enjoyed again the touch of her silken skin as she moved her right knee deep between my thighs.

She moved her left hand down my right side, and as it felt its way around my hips to grasp my right buttock, she nuzzled my balls with her knee. I hardened and her hand wandered around to the front and grasped my shaft. I thrust upwards in a gentle, involuntary movement. Then she curled her back as she brought her face down to gaze at the hard and reddened end. I had been a source of wonderment since the first time that she'd seen me naked, a bronzed head on creamy white shoulders and body; to her, I knew that I appeared as a multi-coloured apparition. It was only when I entered her that she knew that I was real, and now she wanted that pink shaft deep inside her.

She soon finished whetting her appetite, and when she had done with the tongue exploration she abruptly pushed herself up. Then, throwing her right leg over my hips and supporting herself with her hands on my chest, she gently yet firmly slid her wetted vagina down my shaft until she squashed my balls. Then, holding my gaze, she proceeded to suck and squeeze all of my juices deep into her eager body, only stopping when I cried out in ecstasy as my stomach exploded and I shot my life-liquid into her. Then she sought her own relief, seeking satisfaction in a frenzied attack with her hard bud against my bone, rubbing violently until with an orgasmic shout, enough to waken the harbour, she spasmed and collapsed upon my chest.

We slept as one until the first of the day's sunrays crept over our contented bodies through the bedchamber's high window slots.

11. The Journey Resumes.

Godfrey and the others arrived after a week of pleasant travel along the coast and I went into town to greet them.

Almost of necessity, *it is always thus on this escapade,* they brought mixed news with them.

'Your friend, Bohemund,' cried Godfrey as he reined in his tired horse, 'he hath the bulk of an elephant but the mind of a serpent.'

'What now?'

'He came after us to join in our holy quest.'

I looked behind Godfrey at the troops trailing in after him, but could see no sign of Bohemund.

'Indeed, Robert, you might well look,' said Allen angrily. 'The devious sod turned back not twenty miles since, he has returned to Antioch.'

'He's going to seize it?'

'Aye,' concurred Godfrey, 'and good riddance, I have had enough of him.'

'Oh well,' I responded, 'that's the end of that friendship. Shall we get on with it; there's no point in staying here... unless you want to take a ship back to Italy.'

Nobody did, but they might have dreamed about it that night, so I laid on a feast to keep their minds occupied, then stayed sober enough to give Sassie a fond farewell.

Late in the morning, I appeared by the harbour to meet with Argyros and the Duke of Cyprus, Philocales, who I'd met several times before; both representatives of the emperor – they were in a state of amusement.

I greeted them somewhat puzzled.

'Morning, good fellows. You appear in a happy mood this fine morning.'

'Indeed, Prince Robert. Good morning to you. We have observed that your seamen are strangers to horseback.'

I looked towards my men. They were lined up along the quayside ready to depart, archers ready mounted at the fore, followed by my cavalry, infantry and wagons at the back, but the middle section, where my seafarers where grouped, seemed to be ill at ease, and the motley collection of ponies they were mounted on were demonstrating a certain lack of confidence in their riders.

'Ah yes, indeed. At sea they are without equal and they have made their way from Norman shores to here, but now they must give up their ships and come with me to Jerusalem.'

All but one of my ships had finally given up the ghost, and they had been broken up on the shore. The usable timbers and ropes had been salvaged, and the light equipment packed onto wagons to accompany me overland. Heavy timbers, ironwork, and the like were packed into Matilda's Genoese cargo ships for onward transmission by sea. My last *knörr* was to travel to Cyprus where the captain would arrange for further supplies, including my remaining horses, to be moved along the coast nearer Jerusalem. At last things were moving again.

I wanted the talents of my seamen at my disposal, so a number of shipwrights and sail-makers, navigators and sailors, had been brought ashore with the intention of turning their skills with wood and ropes, mallets and chisels, to good use in the event of a siege. So, for now, they sat uneasily upon their new beastly companions, but a seaman's feet would be no match for the miles of desert that lay ahead.

'A very wise ploy, my lord.' Philocales was impressed, and another favourable report would be passed back to Alexios. No doubt – my reputation among the Byzantines was without equal among the other princes, *scurvy chancers that they were.*

I had one more thing on my mind before setting off, and came close to Philocales.

'I have a favour to ask of you, Duke Philocales.'

'Ask, Prince Robert, I shall do my best.'

'The girl, Sassie. I would be easier in my mind if I knew she would be well cared for. She has comforted and pleased me greatly.'

Argyros looked a little discomforted at this request and I noticed.

'What is wrong, Argyros? Is this request not possible?'

'Oh no, Prince Robert, it is entirely reasonable, the girl will be well cared for. In time we will find a suitable position for her and she should be content.'

'But?' I detected a hesitation.

'It's a question of her sister...'

'Oh yes, I haven't seen her this time, where is she? Safe I hope.'

'Erm, yes, she is safe, my lord... and the child.'

'What! There is a child?'

'Yes, my lord, a boy, just delivered. It is a very strange hue, lightly coloured, but with blue eyes.'

I was performing some calculations.

'Oh my God! My first visit?'

'Yes, my lord. Your young companion on that visit, it seems that he had a true aim.'

Jesus! Philip. I instructed him to leave her something to remember him by, and now he lives on... in Africa.

'Then she should be cared for too, with her sister. Will you see to it please, Argyros?'

'I will indeed, my lord, be assured. They will be housed and I am sure that we'll find a suitable household to place them with.'

'Thank you. Should I leave some money?'

'Certainly not, Prince Robert, we owe you more than that. Please do not consider it, the girls are in the care of the emperor.'

I rode off and joined my squire, waiting at the front of the column, but as I gave the signal to advance, and set off to Jerusalem, my thoughts were anything but warlike as we wound our way down the coast. *I wonder what she's named Philip's son; I wonder what old Roger Montgomerie would think if he knew that his youngest son had been delving into deepest Africa!* Then Sibyl entered my mind and the journey became pleasant once more.

The travel as I'd guessed proved painful to the feet of my erstwhile mariners.

'Why do you walk when you can ride?' I asked a limping sailor two days after we set off.

'Because it is a choice, my lord,' he replied. 'Blisters on my arse or blisters on my feet; I'm sharing them out today.'

'Have you no shoes, man?' I asked him.

'Aye, lord, but they are as new as this donkey is old, and I am suited to neither at the moment. I expect it to improve.'

'Good, we must go on. Ride when you can.'

Loyal and brave, they deserved better than we leaders were giving them.

We stopped near the town of Arqa. We were too far ahead of everyone else; being small in number we made better progress as my seamen's feet hardened to the march. Godfrey had dropped behind and of Raymond I knew naught; no riders reached me and I prayed that Flanders was safe – who knew what idiocy Raymond would try along the way.

Eventually Godfrey came up with his contingent and while we waited for Raymond he used the time to tell me more about Raymond's antics in Marrat-an-Numan.

'They slaughtered the lot, Robert,' Godfrey murmured, 'no mercy; and ransacked the city. It was unholy work.'

'He can answer for his actions in the highest court, Godfrey,' I responded, for truth to tell I could think of nothing else to say.

We spotted the dust on the horizon a couple of days later as Flanders' outriders appeared. He was in the vanguard, seeking out trouble for Raymond's mob following.

Despite the dust I spied Rob at the head of his column.

'Good morrow!' I cried when I recognised him, 'a fine day to meet up, Rob.'

'Fine day! Another poxy hot one. *Mon Dieu*, the desert shimmers like the ocean but not a drop to drink up here.'

'Are the hides of water not holding up?'

'The water diminishes inside; though they do not appear to leak, it still goes down.'

'Are they covered? Try to keep the sun off them. Anyway, where's Raymond?'

'Him! He's miles behind. He's broken his journey to scavenge along the way, a raid here, a slaughter there; the man possesses no direction in his mind or to his path. We might face the walls of Jerusalem together, only the two of us at this rate, Robert.'

'Bollocks! At least Godfrey is here; we will not wait for Raymond for more than another day.'

It was only near the end of the following afternoon when Raymond's dust was spotted on the horizon, so we waited for him, hopeful that we could gain some momentum come the morning.

The old sod was unrepentant when I spoke to him the next day, and he boasted of the sacking of Marrat-an-Numan.

'A great haul of booty and many Turks sent to their God,' was his view of things. He really was a venal object, so without further discussion I left him in his glory and headed up the long procession through the heat. Godfrey had by now tagged on to the end of the queue with his contingent and we were spread over several miles; a tempting target if the Turks could get themselves better organised, I thought.

I passed by the port of Arqa, but behind me Raymond made a different decision and on 14 February he laid siege to Arqa, dispatched a force to secure Tortosa, and then sent envoys to hold discussions with the emir of Tripoli.

There was a problem with Arqa. It was not prepared to join in the general mood of depression that existed in the wider Moslem world over the possibility of winning a fight with us. The place was heavily fortified and determined to resist. It was peopled by folk of all persuasions including Turks, Saracens, Arabs, Paulician Armenians and assorted pagans – none of whom were prepared to yield their town.

By the time the remainder of the army with Godfrey and Flanders arrived with me in March, Raymond was still outside the walls and several notable persons had been killed in fruitless attacks.

Then messengers brought news about Bohemund's latest treachery. It was as Godfrey explained.

'He came into Laodicea once we'd left, after saying he was going back to Antioch. I fear that he has taken Laodicea as well as Antioch. He may cause us some trouble with the emperor.'

I was well pissed off with the big arsehole by now, but needed to press on.

'Shit! We could do without that, but there is little we can do at the moment. Let's see if we can get Raymond to give up his new obsession of Arqa, and move on to Jerusalem.'

But, ironically, Raymond had achieved some successes and was not ready to move. The force sent to Tortosa gained the port by a subterfuge. They lit fires round the circumference of the port, thus fooling the garrison into thinking that a massive army had them surrounded. They fled and left behind warehouses full of supplies. Another small port nearby was also vacated when the Franks approached.

Soon Tripoli surrendered and hoisted Raymond's banner, although he did not enter the city. The ruler paid handsomely for the privilege of not being attacked, raided, raped or stripped of his possessions. This was costly to him but highly profitable to Raymond; he was becoming a very successful merchant adventurer in the area and the other leaders, me included, thought it time to reduce his ascendancy.

Arnulf held the key – *the lance story* – and was fortuitously presented with an opportunity to publicly debunk the whole fabrication.

In April, the visionary, Peter Bartholomew – finder of the lance – had come forward with some new visions. He claimed that he 'was instructed by God, to root out the disaffected in the ranks of the crusaders, and purify them.'

Raymond believed him, and by publicly supporting the ridiculous claims committed a serious blunder in his management of the venture. He antagonised almost everybody, especially those who had doubts about the lance from the beginning.

After some discussions I sent Arnulf in for the kill.

He stage-managed a confrontation with the unhinged Bartholomew and challenged his assertions by crafty argument. Arnulf was a skilled orator and a man not to be challenged on matters of credo. Then, despite his arguments being demolished by the well-prepared priest, Bartholomew would not back down, and foolishly demanded to be tested by God as to the truth of his visions.

All the leaders, save Raymond, quickly agreed to this and an ordeal by fire was arranged to help the visionary prove his status as 'the messenger of God.'

This was in no way the same as that ordeal which my beloved Tegwin was forced to endure when she was falsely accused of witchcraft; that was a political ploy that I'm still certain was engineered by my brother Henry. This, however, was easier to understand. Peter Bartholomew was preparing for another one of those 'it's all the fault of the women' madnesses, and Raymond was taking advantage of it to propagate his own ascendancy – I was prepared to tolerate neither, nor engage in any more foolishness which would slow down even further our already fractured progress towards Jerusalem, so my sympathy for the deluded Peter was slight.

A bed of fire was prepared and Bartholomew agreed to cross over it to demonstrate his protected status.

He did so on Good Friday, having prayed for three days beforehand, and with his holy lance clutched to his breast, he set off along the twelve paces of the fiercely burning track of olive branches: he was badly burned and died in agony twelve days later.

With Bartholomew's demise, I could see the beginning of the demise of Raymond's authority in the ranks of the Franks.

'God's works are truly a mystery, Payne, are they not?' I said at the graveside as we buried the cinders of belief.

'Indeed they are, my lord. Are we going to Jerusalem now?'

'Yes, of course, what else is there?'

'You said that a year ago, Robert,' added Allen.

'True, but we are a lot closer now,' said the uncertain Arnulf, who had awarded himself some penances in case he had sent an innocent man to a premature death.

'I shouldn't bother yourself about that, Arnulf,' I had told him. 'If you did penance for everybody who's died on this venture you'd be an old man before you finished.'

That remark only increased the furrows on his brow, but it cheered me up to say it – priests!

12. The Grand Treachery.

While we were busy worrying about lances, news came back from Jerusalem; things had altered, and there'd been a change of ownership. Travellers we encountered long the road were returning from there in a hurry, their pilgrimage cut short. Jerusalem was now in the hands of Fatimid Egyptians, and their ruler, Vizier al-Afdal. Following the demolition of Kerbogha's force at Antioch, they had felt confident enough to throw the Seljuk Turks out of the city and claim it for themselves.

I wondered if Bohemund's oddly contrived contact with those Egyptians outside Antioch had something to do with their actions, but as Bohemund was missing I couldn't question him over the affair. However, other rumours circulating among the travellers gave me food for thought.

The waters of Byzantine–Frankish relationships, already muddied, were thrown into maelstrom conditions by the arrival of ambassadors from Alexios. They asked for me and lost little time in stating their intent.

They come in pairs, do diplomats. This is no doubt a result of often only their heads being returned as an answer to their senders; with two the survivor can carry the message.

'Prince Robert,' began the tall cadaverous one, 'I am Panteleimon. My companion is Giannis,' he waved at the short, stout fellow standing behind him. 'His esteemed majesty, the emperor, sends his regards, and wishes that you clarify matters regarding the issue of Antioch.'

'My best wishes to his imperial majesty. You may tell him that I know as much as he does; however I will take you to see someone who might assist you in your mission.'

This was an opportunity to bring Raymond's chickens home to roost, and might provide some sport; I sent for Godfrey to meet me at Raymond's pavilion and invited the tall and the short to accompany me.

I arrived in time to hear Arnulf. He was engaged in a lively discussion with Bishop Peter of Narbonne about the significance of *Peter Incendiarius,* the flammable visionary: Bishop Peter was losing the argument but the pair had wandered so far into the arcane depths of religious theory that Raymond had nodded off.

When he was prodded awake the ambassadors were shown in. Arnulf and Peter gave rest to their tongues and hovered to see what it was that they wanted.

I joined them in similar curiosity and watched as Raymond, his eye showing signs of fatigue, quickly came under considerable pressure from the emperor's delegation.

After a few minutes I had heard enough and decided to take control of the situation. Raymond could not counter the arguments and was clearly floundering.

'Well now, good fellows,' I boomed in my best Bohmey voice, 'may I assist in this matter.' I stepped forward and took a position behind Raymond's chair; he fluttered a hand in my direction, giving over control immediately.

The ambassadors looked to Raymond for guidance, uncertain now: *who is leading?*

Raymond quickly seized the opportunity to pass the problem along, and taking me by the arm waved broadly at the Byzantines.

'Prince Robert knows Bohemund best, perhaps he can help you.'

Here's an opportunity to ask a few questions of the emperor and put down Raymond, and I'm not about to let it pass.

The pair bowed and Panteleimon re-introduced themselves for the benefit of the drama.

'My lord, it is an honour indeed to meet again the great warrior, Prince Robert. We have come directly from the emperor.'

'Yes, so you said.' I stared at the pair, weighing them up, it might have seemed an eternity, for they began to shuffle, *lost for words – some diplomats.*

'So... what do you want?'

I watched the uncertainty cross over the face of Panteleimon; I was not prepared to ease his distress.

Raymond stirred himself.

'It seems, Robert, that the emperor feels deprived of Antioch, and would like to enter Jerusalem at the head of our army.

However that might not be necessary as the new governor of Jerusalem has agreed to allow unarmed pilgrims into the city... if we keep the army away.'

I continued to glare at the fidgety envoys before speaking to them gently.

'Is this the emperor who failed to turn up at Nicaea? Who left us bereft of support at Antioch?'

Panteleimon felt he could answer that one, and stuttering replied, 'My lord, he did send you those boats to help at Nicaea, and as for attending himself it was not possible due to the affairs of state. Did you not receive supplies through Cyprus to help you at Antioch?'

'Yes, Panteleimon; some. Most of the supplies came from Normandy, and Genoa. What we received from you was late, poor quality, or short in the amount. We have not received one single horse from your emperor, and since Taticius left, not one soldier of his has served with us. Is that the support you refer to?'

The temperature in the tent was rising fast, but I was set on my course and no one felt inclined to hold me back, nor offer the perspiring diplomats as much as a sherbet.

I continued on a different tack.

'Where have you come from, Panteleimon?'

'What? Well, my lord, from Cyprus.'

'I see.' I waited, because I knew where they'd been before Cyprus. 'So you went there from...?' I left the question hanging in the air.

'From the emperor, in Constantinople!'

Panteleimon was now bereft of his diplomatic charm, stuttering his replies, which made me certain of the approaching denouement.

'I see. So you have not been to Jerusalem?'

'No, my lord, it is occupied.'

'Or Cairo?'

Their eyes fluttered and I knew that they had. The game was in the open now: Alexios had been in touch with the Fatimids. Why else their appearance in Bohemund's position back at Antioch?

'Cairo, my lord?'

'Cairo. Where you made an arrangement with al-Afdal to admit us as pilgrims only.'

'No, my lord, that was not us.'

'But you know of it?'

Usually quick-witted, as envoys need to be, but not on this occasion, Panteleimon and Giannis were reduced to an embarrassing silence.

The envoys had been trapped into a tacit admission that Alexios had indeed been in negotiation with the Egyptians: the end of trust had arrived.

I left Raymond's side and walked towards the exit. Pausing to look the visitors in the eye, I said quietly, 'If your emperor wants Antioch, he had better ensure that we have Jerusalem first. If there is to be no Christian occupation of the holy city, as seems to be his desire, then there will be no Christian occupation of Antioch... save by Normans. Carry this message very carefully, if you please.'

Godfrey, who had been watching silently with the others, turned to nudge Flanders in the ribs, and said none too quietly, 'Remind me, Rob, never to annoy your cousin. Those two have stained their pants and he frightens me.'

Tancred followed me out of the tent and we walked back to my camp together.

'Raymond did not seem very happy with your diplomacy, my lord.'

'He has no reason to be, he has much to ponder. When he works it out, he will realise that he's just been demolished as the expedition leader.'

'Hmm! How so, my lord? Explain further, if you please.'

'His lance has been held up to ridicule and now any loyalty to Alexios has been washed away by the emperor's own treachery. Raymond's siege of Arqa is stalled, and the Fatimids may or may not give him permission to enter Jerusalem. You may think of a worse position, but right now I would be hard pressed to invent one.'

'Phew!' I could hear Tancred's mind churning over. 'What next? What should I do, Prince Robert? What are you going to do? Did you plan this?'

'Questions, Tancred, questions! No, I did not plan it, but opportunity beckons at times, take it when it calls. You go and join Godfrey; he is steadfast in purpose and will be a good leader. I will try and get Raymond moving again, and it's time to bring Flanders back into my fold.'

My mind was unsettled; there were hidden games churning in this bloody mire. What was the price for easy entry into the holy city? The Fatimid Egyptians had thrown out the Seljuk Turks, but what if they united against us? Questions abounded, but answers had I none. I had no option, we must press on if I wanted to return to a land of the sane... and Sibyl, visions of her proud head entered mine. *I must finish this task and return to Italy, that's it! Come on, Robert, let us be about our work, the lady awaits.*

By the end of April we had sucked in sufficient goods, animals and supplies from the city of Tripoli and its surrounds to make any further delay ridiculous. Arqa still stood firm, Raymond's troops were becoming more discontented by the day, and some asked to join me.

The nexus of power had shifted. Godfrey and I were now regarded as the most likely to accomplish the mission, especially after we made a deal with the emir for port facilities.

We finally left the area of Tripoli, together, on 16 March 1099, bound for Jerusalem, only two hundred miles away. After some, probably painful, heart-searching, Raymond gave up his ambitions outside of Arqa and followed along behind. Bohemund became a distant memory.

The journey passed without major incident and it seems that discord and disagreement in leadership was not our sole preserve, the Moslem princes were exhibiting the same traits and there was no co-ordinated effort to prevent this inexorable progress towards our final goal.

Down the coast to Caesarea – where we spent four days to celebrate Pentecost – then on to Arsuf, where we turned, at last, inland towards the holy city.

The next significant stop was the town of Ramleh, a site of religious significance, as the place where St George was buried in the basilica named after him. It was here that a decision was taken that further established the primacy of the prince-leaders.

Godfrey was intent on emphasising the purpose of the crusade to all followers, so wanted to propose the creation of a new bishopric in the town, and gathered us together. It was a strange atmosphere. We were so close to Jerusalem, and it seemed almost impossible that there would be no further obstacles placed in our way, that neither the Turks nor the Egyptians would miss the opportunity to stop this miserable cavalcade in its tracks, so that we would come no nearer to the holy city than we were today. The atmosphere inside Godfrey's well-worn, raggedy pavilion was tense with anticipation as he began his speech.

'I have it in my heart that this place is so close to our journey's end, and so important in its historical significance to Christian belief, that we ought to proclaim its importance by establishing here a new bishop of Christ.'

Flanders was quick to support the idea.

'I agree. We are now so close to our goal that we should stop for a moment and take time to reflect on our just cause. If we can stand, and pray together for our final success, and mark this day by proclaiming a new bishop, we will surely be blessed and supported by God and ensure his eternal approval.'

There was silence; somehow the reference to how close we were to the end of our quest had imposed upon us a heavy reflection of the costs that we had borne so far: it seemed almost an anti-climax.

I concurred.

'I doubt there will be any disagreement on this subject, Godfrey. Have you a candidate in mind?'

It seemed that Godfrey had given the matter some thought because he came straight back with his response.

'I have, and you know him, Robert, or at least you know of him.'

Godfrey looked across at Arnulf and I thought for a moment that he was going to nominate my own confessor; tis him, I thought.

Then Godfrey spoke directly, 'Arnulf, you have with you a kindly priest by the name of Robert?'

Arnulf looked at me and grinned; he knew, *sod*.

'Indeed we have, my lord Godfrey. Robert of Rouen. Prince Robert knows him too.'

Tancred looked puzzled.

'Robert? Robert? Robert this and Robert that, have you northern men no imagination? What stoppage of the brain has you naming everyone in Normandy Robert?'

The contemplative silence was broken by Tancred's outburst, and the matter was sealed with much mirth and merriment, which was a condition that had been in short supply for many months.

Robert of Rouen was installed as Bishop of Ramleh, the second such fighting cleric after Peter of Albara; but he was not of Raymond's following, his moon was on the wane: Godfrey and all his Roberts were firmly in the ascendancy.

I brought my people together that night, those who had travelled with me in my mesnie and those who had remained in constant support of me, whether we moved together or were separated from time to time.

I knew that I needed their support one last time and so made a plea to focus them on the task ahead. Allen, Duke of Brittany; Robert of Flanders; my life-saving knights, Payne Peverel and Ragenaus the Saxon; and my chaplain, Arnulf. I spotted my new squire, Oslac, hovering just outside the flickering firelight and bade him come nearer.

'We are all in this enterprise together, Oslac. You will be close to me over the next few days, and because of that your life will be in peril; I attract perils: sit down with these good lords and hear what I have to say.'

He shuffled in and sat down at the edge of light with eyes wide open and mouth shut. If he wanted to attain knighthood he needed to know about the skills of leadership, and now was as good a time as any to begin. Allen offered him an encouraging grunt, an unusual and priceless acknowledgement, and the squire's jaw dropped a little.

'Soon we will reach our ultimate target and I want you to forget about how difficult it was to get here. That is in the past and we have learned many lessons along the paths of our journey. We should reach the holy city tomorrow or the next day and we will need to take some decisions. Firstly, and above all, there will be no siege: we do not have the time, we do not have the numbers, and there are rumours of an Egyptian army on its way. If the other leaders will not agree to this approach then I am minded to return to Normandy with the task incomplete. What say you?'

'It is perhaps, an early decision, Robert,' ventured Allen.

'Perhaps,' I replied, 'and one which I cannot make for you all. However you should be aware of what is in my mind; I will not lead you into annihilation. If, when you view the walls, you see a different solution, then tell me. I believe that Godfrey is of the same view as me, but if there is any procrastination among the leaders, if there is not an agreed plan, then I am not prepared to wait and fart about as we did before the walls of Antioch.'

'Then why did we, my lord?' All eyes turned to Oslac as he uttered the unutterable.

I smiled, Rob spluttered, and Arnulf cast his eyes to the heavens.

'Because we believed it was necessary, Oslac. That we should leave such a base for the Turks in our rear as we marched towards Jerusalem was, at the time, almost unthinkable. Now it's not the case.'

'No,' said Allen, 'now we know that they are terrified of us, they have tried to defeat us and failed, and now they are many miles behind and not a threat.'

'But we know naught of the Egyptian army. We are now so few in number, and there will be no help from the Byzantines; we are isolated. Only a quickly executed, coordinated plan has any hope of success. Of that I am certain.'

They looked at each other with varying degrees of expression; some puzzled, some intense, and some vacant, waiting for inspiration no doubt, until Flanders made up his mind.

'You will agree a plan with Godfrey, and if Raymond will not consent... we go home?'

'That's what I think.'

'Sad, my lord,' said Payne, 'I wanted to test my metal against Egyptian flesh.'

'And die a glorious death,' said Ragenaus.

'There is nothing glorious in dying for a lost cause, but there may be glory in finding another way. God gave us the wit to choose, do not insult his wisdom.'

'Is this another test, my lord?' asked Oslac.

'Perhaps,' I replied without enthusiasm, I'd had testing enough for one life.

Then Arnulf spoke. Perhaps his visions of success were measured against different outcomes than mine.

'Is there no hope that we can talk our way in, my prince?'

'You can try, good priest. Somehow I doubt it, they have no need or desire to let us in.'

'Very well, Robert.' Allen had made up his mind. 'We get in or go home; I've had enough of princely scheming. We cast our lot with Godfrey, he, at least, still believes that we are on God's holy mission.'

'Thank you, my friends; let us pray for our final success. Arnulf, lead us if you will.'

And so it was settled, all or nothing, God's will to prevail.

On 6 June 1099 we made camp within a day's march of the target; but many could not wait, and on the morning of the 7th, we were standing on the horizon before the city, watching as the sun rose over our shoulders to reveal the walls of Jerusalem.

13. The Walls of Jerusalem.

Day One: 7 June.

As the sun explored the earth with its godly light, we fell to the ground, raising praise to the heavens for the privilege of reaching this hallowed spot, and sharing in God's reflected glory. For us it was the culmination of three years of danger and privation, but today all of those memories fell away from our shoulders and we could feel the spirit of the Lord raise us up above all corporeal woes and earthly worries.

Arnulf turned to me and with tears in his eyes, proclaimed, 'If I should die now, Prince Robert, then I would die a happy man.'

I gazed at the city before me, its towers and walls, buildings seemingly piled on top of buildings, and lying below the Dome of the Rock the main prize – the Church of the Holy Sepulchre – the very place where Jesus had died.

As we gazed I was surprised to see Tancred riding towards us. He must have a message from Godfrey, I surmised.

'Prince Robert,' he greeted me as he dismounted, 'I have taken the first prize.' I was puzzled but he seemed quite emotional so I let him explain.

'I have taken Bethlehem, my flag flies over that most sacred place.'

'Godfrey let you loose did he?'

'Indeed, my lord,' he said with tears in his eyes.

To my surprise he was overcome. The young warrior was releasing all the pent-up emotions that he, and we, had kept inside for the past few months: I moved instinctively closer and stood shoulder to shoulder with my brother-in-arms.

Turning to Arnulf I said, 'Don't die yet, my happy friend, there is work still to be done, and no one wants you to escape it with an inconvenient death.'

But Arnulf's eyes had glazed over too. *God's bollocks*, I thought, *what company is this to seize a city*.

Then my attention was taken by other activity. Now we were witnessing the glint of metal as the agitated defenders lined up along the walls. They would know with certainty that the long approaching nightmare had at last appeared before them: we were outside the walls – and we wanted their city.

'How long will it take us to gain entry, Prince Robert?'

Arnulf had returned to earth.

'I do not know, my priest. Oslac, fetch the city map that Taticius gave me. We need to take stock of the defences and form a plan; perhaps you could ask God if he has a plan for us,' I added hopefully.

'I will, my prince, and I will count the days.'

Day Two: 8 June.

It was not long before we were petitioned by those coming to us for aid; these were the Christian citizens of Jerusalem, cast out by their rulers. They were given audience and what they had to say was to prove very useful.

Godfrey called a conference, and when we were assembled under a large awning, which looked remarkably like the salvage of a pavilion, he began with a briefing.

'The city is being cleared of Christians at the hands of a Fatimid governor named Iftikhar ad-Daulah. He is well prepared and has been reinforced by cavalry sent in by the Egyptian vizier, al-Afdal. He has also poisoned the wells around the area so we must be careful.'

I spoke next.

'You have seen the city; it has been here for two thousand years. The walls have been breached before, but each time they have been reinforced and entry made more difficult.'

Flanders commented, although not with any optimism.

'It reminds me of Antioch, except that the walls are higher and we are now fewer. By my reckoning, we have only thirteen hundred mounted and twelve thousand on foot bearing arms.'

I stood and faced the others, my mind set.

'I have no intention of spending another winter camping outside of another city, holy or not. There is no hope of laying siege to it, we have not the time. We have been unopposed on our approach so far, but it cannot be long before the Egyptians gather enough of an army to wipe us away.'

Godfrey supported me.

'Yes, as Prince Robert says, it's not the Turks that are our worry now, this is not their territory, and we have word that the Egyptian vizier, al-Afdal, is bringing a large army from the west. As you say, Robert, we do not know how long we have left before we'll be opposed in the field.'

'Then there is no question of a siege,' said Tancred, in support. It was remarkably similar to what we had faced at Antioch.

'None!' I replied.

'Then what?' voiced Rob, briefed beforehand to ask.

I nodded at Godfrey, because we had already decided, and gave my opinion.

'We have no choice: speed is the essence. We will attack forthwith at the most vulnerable parts of the wall and gain entry by mechanical means.' I gestured to a large sheet which had been unrolled by Payne: it was the plan of the city. 'Here,' I said, pointing to the stretch of wall to the north, between the Quadrangular Tower and St Stephen's Gate, 'this has been surveyed and we recommend that our forces are concentrated there. By the use of siege engines and ballistae we should force an entry over the wall at this point.'

Raymond suddenly opened his eye. He had been listening, although with the appearance of nodding off, and regarded the others balefully. He'd not been consulted, but we'd hatched a scheme whereby Raymond would contribute to the overall plan without knowing it – and he now fell into our trap.

'I,' he began, 'do not agree to this. I think that we should attack in more than one place at a time to split their defending forces.'

'An excellent strategy, Lord Raymond!' proclaimed Rob. He could flatter if he felt so inclined, and was one of the few who had maintained some kind of polite relationship with Raymond throughout. He'd been primed as the one who would arouse less suspicion of being manipulated in the French lord's mind.

'Where else do you suggest that we invest?' Rob drew his fish further into the net.

The old count drew himself up onto his feet, and crossing to the map prodded it with certainty on the spot that marked the Tower of David.

Godfrey caught my eye, and I suppressed a smirk, *the old sod has bought it.* That place had been ruled out as the most difficult place upon which to mount an attack, and now Raymond had agreed to waste his time there, while we attacked the place that offered the best prospects.

'Then we are agreed. Arnulf, if you would be so kind as to lead us in a prayer, before we part?'

Arnulf obliged. 'Oh Lord, make us worthy of this venture in your name. May we succeed in our sacred mission and bring peace to this land and truth to its citizens, vanquish the unbelievers and cast them off your sacred soil. Amen.'

While Arnulf was calling down the blessings of the Lord I pondered a more immediate problem, that of survival. Those who had arrived outside the holy city were the hardiest; any weaknesses in body or mind had culled those not utterly determined to reach this point.

This applied also to the remnants of those pilgrims travelling with us. The men, and particularly the women, having suffered as we had, were now fully incorporated into our organisation, providing such assistance as they could in order to release the soldiers from as many tasks as possible, so the camps were now run by them, leaving the troops to do what troops do.

I was particularly impressed by the determination of the women, some heavy with child and other with brats about their feet, who nevertheless were determined to remain useful for the greater good. I noted that the priests had become less vocal in their contempt for that sex, and whatever thoughts they harboured regarding the obvious sinful activities going on around them, they kept their mutterings to themselves. Such sin, as was available, played a part in maintaining morale, and as such, I thought, had a place in our holy wanderings and purpose; it was, after all, the pope's guarantee that all those who helped in this venture would receive the privilege of eternal salvation, however they fulfilled that task.

Then there was the question of water. With the water sources nearest the city being put out of use by the Egyptians, we were forced to send out armed patrols to find untainted sources. Some did not return and it was obvious that there were marauding patrols out and about.

We instituted protected-wagon foraging, using carts carrying animal skin containers to go out into the wilderness and find water.

Day Three: 9 June.

Then Raymond found a spring near the foot of Mount Zion and placed an armed guard around it. But it only filled at intervals and was soon exhausted, and there had been scuffles to draw upon its resources.

It being now the height of summer these measures, although a draw upon our meagre manpower, were essential if we were to survive and prosper, and meant that we were, as usual, fighting more than one battle at a time... with the Lord's help. Then it arrived – my messenger *knörr*, left languishing at Cyprus for the purpose, was off the coast and communications were restored.

14. Prayers Fulfilled.

The same day Godfrey and I held the first planning meeting where we gathered together our commanders, including my former fleet captain, Artus.

The grizzled old mariner seemed lost without the sea around him. Allen spotted him and laughed.

'Why are you here, lord of the seas? I see no ships.'

'No, Allen, you're correct and your eyesight does not fail you,' I replied. 'He is here for walls.'

'Walls?' asked the puzzled Breton, 'what walls?'

'Those walls yonder,' said Godfrey, pointing at Jerusalem. 'He's got to get us over them.'

'Oh! I see. With what, ships' rigging?'

Oh, Allen, you don't know how close you are.

I turned to bring another man forward.

'With this fellow here.' I gestured to a man watching from the back of Godfrey's pavilion. 'Come forward, Gaston.'

The man shuffled forward, not too keen to be held in the gaze of so many, I surmised.

'Artus, meet Gaston of Béarn. He is an engineer, an architect supreme, and has left the service of Raymond to join us here. Gaston, meet Artus, he has skills in masts and rigging, and methods of lifting objects. Together you will devise ways of scaling those walls and of building the devices we need to hurl objects over them. In short, you are to provide what we lacked at Antioch, and fashion for us the means of entry into the holy city.'

Artus and Gaston met with cordiality and went off for a quiet discussion.

Then with Godfrey I brought in our sergeants and explained to them the details of the impending assault.

Day Four: 10 June.

Godfrey had directed that we institute a daily briefing, where we could review progress and receive reports, and this morning saw the first.

Today the construction artificers would have the centre of attention as they explained how they were going to get us over the walls.

Artus spoke first.

'I have been shown sketches of some odd devices by Gaston, and I'm assured that he's made them work in the past. I'm certain that we could produce such devices here; however we have only the limited materiels that were in the ship you sent from Laodicea, my lord; we need more ropes, timber, nails, tools and such like. They are all at sea in your Genoese ships.'

'I know, Artus.' I turned to Godfrey. 'When we turned away from the sea at Arsuf we also left behind timbers we brought from Normandy and transferred at Laodicea to some Genoese ships. These are the makings of our ballistae and other siege devices. But as you know it's not safe to land there yet, and the fleet lies off the coast.'

'Fret not, Robert, we have found many local people who are only too eager to help, and they have offered to lead us to timber supplies and provide all the tools and nails that you require.'

'If Artus will go with this man here,' Godfrey gestured at a local, 'he knows where to obtain supplies until ours can be landed.'

'Yes, Artus, you and Gaston go with him and let me have your detailed plans by morning.'

Those two were easily satisfied and I hoped that all my problems would find solutions so quickly. They wandered away engrossed in discussions about levers, pivot points, load-bearing structures and blah de blah – things that normal men never even dream exist.

Later in the day we moved to our allotted positions; me and Godfrey in front of the northern wall while Raymond went off to confront the Tower of David. He didn't stay there very long; as soon as he realised it was altogether too strong to assault he moved further to a point opposite the Zion Gate on the south of the city.

We had now achieved the perfect positioning, splitting the defenders in half and leaving them to guess at where the main offensive would take place. Then we were left to wait as the machines of war began to take shape before the wall of Jerusalem. I wondered if the governor was regretting his decision to hold out against us, and then I wondered if he knew more about the rumoured Egyptian army than we did.

Whatever plans the Egyptians had, we pressed ahead with our own and the sites we had chosen were turned into construction sites, fit to mirror those famed in Egyptian legends when that nation built its pyramids. And they shared a connection – death.

As many men-at-arms were released into the charge of the artisans as were required. The rest were taken out of sight into a nearby valley to practise scaling walls. Mounted knights and archers meantime were on constant patrol to protect us while we worked towards the first assault.

Day Seven: 13 June.

The first sign of ill-discipline came when Tancred became impatient with my insistence on proper preparation and led an exploratory attack on the wall. He had some ladders fashioned, hoping to gain entry in the manner of climbing the walls of Antioch, but ignored the obvious difference, in that he would be opposed.

One foolhardy knight named Raimbold led the climb and when he reached the top, had his arm chopped off – so that idea was quickly abandoned.

I had a conversation with Tancred in which I invited him to adhere to his instructions or go and join Raymond: he stayed.

Day Eight: 14 June.

Frustration among Raymond's troops fermented rapidly. Three years to get here? – they wanted entry immediately, and some of his followers shifted to Godfrey's command, hoping for a better chance. Among them was another engineer, he had extensive experience of siege machines and went to work with my crew. Raymond employed one named William Embriaco in the same position, but he had not the overall experience of our builders and their progress was slower.

If there was ever any hope that the defenders had misinterpreted our activities outside the city it was now gone as those fearsome machines of war were now rising towards heaven, proclaiming our intentions for all to witness.

Day Eleven: 17 June.

On the 17th I received the news I had been waiting for from the Genoese fleet: they had occupied the port at Jaffa, and wanted an escort to bring the cargoes safely to Jerusalem.

Three squadrons of cavalry were despatched under Allen to bring up the much needed construction supplies.

The mission was mostly successful despite having to fight their way down to the port. They arrived safely... but when the soldiers met the sailors it quickly became an occasion for celebration and story-swapping. When the ships had been emptied and the cargo loaded onto wagons for the return journey, they gathered together for an all-night bacchanalia. When the dawn came it was with horror that they saw the port was blockaded by a Fatimid fleet.

With a clever tactical response, Allen persuaded the Genoese to abandon their vessels and travel with the supplies to Jerusalem. This was a blessing and brought more skilled seamen into the construction crews, but confirmed that the Fatimids were seriously moving against us: time was at a premium.

And still, Rob, assisted by local eager Christians, was bringing in wagonloads of timber from local sources and our work went ahead with renewed urgency. The two encampments were working at their fullest: braziers burning for the smiths to wrought iron and heat rivets; giant saws used by two men making mounds of sawdust; and the relentless hammering of wooden mallets on wooden pegs and joints, and metal hammers on metal fittings filled the air day and night – and the city defenders were forced to watch impotently from the wall.

Day Twenty-five: 1 July.

Nearing readiness, I called for Payne and Ragenaus.

'Let's go and visit Godfrey. Payne, find Tancred and invite him so that we may inspect our progress.'

We gathered together where my men were busy in the mayhem of our open-air workshops, and I waved my arms about proudly at the activities going on before us.

'This is how we prepare to assault a city, Tancred. Take note and learn.'

He watched, fascinated by the industry of the workers as I asked Godfrey about my seamen.

'I said they would be good, Godfrey, what do you think of my seamen now?'

'Three levels, Robert, three!' replied Godfrey, ignoring my pride and gazing at the assault castle rising above the ground, 'it looks like a *keep*... on wheels. We have used such towers before, like *Castle Malregard*, but not movable ones.'

'A ship in the desert, Godfrey,' I quipped.

'Quite,' replied Godfrey.

'It's quite open, my lord,' said Payne, looking at the uncovered ladders leading to the top, 'they'll be able to shoot arrows at us.'

'It's not quite finished. We'll add wattle shields and cover them with hide to control fire, and it'll be quite cosy inside.'

He seemed unconvinced and went for a walk around the contraption.

'Is that a drawbridge at the top, Prince Robert?' asked Tancred.

'Aye, tis really clever. It's a shielding wall until lowered, and then becomes a bridge.'

'Clever,' Ragenaus agreed, 'and the whole thing moves, you say, lord?'

'Yes, see the wheels; the whole thing is on a giant wagon.' Godfrey was more than pleased.

'Aye, Godfrey, the tower sits on top at present, but it will come apart and fit *into* the wagon so that we can rush it to different positions.'

I was more than pleased. This was good: *a giant portable castle keep, complete with drawbridge.*

'That's genius, and built in so short a time,' said Tancred.

'There is one problem,' said Godfrey. 'It needs flat ground to deploy it.'

'Ah, yes, of course. Fear not, we have thought of that too and I will explain later. What else have your blessed artisans produced?'

Godfrey led us along to those production areas under his control.

'Apart from your galloping tower, nothing new. We're assembling the various siege machines that you brought from Normandy.' He gestured at the busy workers. 'As you see, various ballistae. Those are onagers, they can fire giant arrows, but we'll use them to hurl parcels of rocks, they will scatter and spread over a wide area. The aiming is not exact but the effect will be killing over a wide area.'

'Local rocks, eh? Cheaper than arrows.'

'Aye, Robert! And mangonels, those over there, to throw even bigger rocks at them?'

'Big enough to reduce the walls over time.' All of this was familiar. Although I was by choice a cavalryman, the methods of siege warfare had been part of my education. It might be a bit tiresome, but today it was essential if we were not to become trapped against the front walls of Jerusalem in the way we almost were outside Antioch.

Godfrey's enthusiasm knew no bounds, and he was still droning on.

'Over time, yes, given time the walls can be reduced. Then we have this monstrous battering ram, it has a metal head and will be unstoppable... if we can get it running apace that is.'

I noted the piles of wattle shields lying about the place and gestured towards them.

'This is another idea,' Godfrey explained. 'All the men working to move the tower or move the ram forward will be protected by guardians carrying these shields. Like your layers fixed to the tower. They should deflect anything that the Fatimids can hurl at us.'

'This is all good, Godfrey, but time is the key: how soon can we begin?'

'Our progress has been rapid; at the present pace we should be able to begin an assault within a week.'

'Then we need to show Raymond these fearsome machines and discuss deployment and tactics.'

'Aye, Robert, and plenty to do if we are to start next week.'

'Jesu, my lord,' uttered Tancred as we walked off, 'this is a monstrous vision: such machines to crush men.'

'Aye, my brave one, but they are not new; they have come down through history. Some peoples, such as the Romans, who named them *onagers*, were skilled in their deployment.'

'And now us. They seem to be better than hemp ladders, my lord.'

I laughed. 'Let's hear no more of such foolishness, Tancred. I'm here to enter the city, and now I have the means, I will not be stopped. Now we'll go into yonder valley where there is more to see.'

I took the puzzled warrior to a place out of sight of the defenders on the wall. Here were dozens of wagons; some which had survived the journey, much repaired; some which we had bought or been gifted by disgruntled Christians; and some which had been cobbled together in strange ways.

Tancred gazed at this odd assemblage and turned to me with a questioning face.

'Aye, lad,' I grinned, 'this is a surprise for our reluctant hosts, and when the time is right you'll see how devious the mind of man can be when he contemplates the destruction of his enemies.'

'They are filled with pebbles, rocks, and planks, Prince Robert. What use is that?'

'And metals, and ladders, and timbers of strange purpose.' I pointed out those wagons and laughed, 'Think on, Tancred, what use would you put these devices to? Tell me when you have thought it through.'

We rode back to Godfrey's side, my companion silent throughout and I wondered if he would guess it right.

At the southern side of the city, reports came that Raymond's preparations were considerably less certain than at the north; Godfrey invited me along to see them.

His constructions lacked the essential skills shown by my mariners, especially in the use of rope and timber, and although the ground was more open, and unencumbered by the presence of a curtain wall, it had before the Zion Gate a deep ditch. Raymond needed to fill it in order to trundle his tower up the wall, but by now his followers were displaying a healthy lethargy when it came to dangerous work.

After some discussion he refused a visit from our architects to advise his artisans on improvements to his tower, saying, 'I have a fellow named Embriaco, the best there is.' I doubted that the ramshackle affair could be much bettered anyway, but then he solved the problem of the ditch through his own ingenuity.

He offered payment, at the rate of one penny for three stones, if his men would run up and throw them into the depression to level the dry moat. Unfortunately he lost a lot of the foolhardy, or hard up, to missiles coming at them from the battlements.

Day Thirty-two: 8 July

Almost a day of rest day for us. While Raymond's men earned some money hurling rocks we continued to improve our preparations, mostly in personal protection. We made wattle shields by the dozen, the groves for miles around were denuded of growth in pursuit of preserving lives – there would be many deaths come the final assault, but we needed as many men as possible over that damned wall.

Day Thirty-three: 9 July.

As it happened we were not going to be without help from God, for Arnulf had decided to enlist his aid and called upon as many as possible to join him in a procession around the enclosed city. It must have been knackering – it being a journey of several miles – so I prayed that it would have a positive outcome, although I suspected that the detailed preparations that I was engaged in might influence things more surely.

Day Thirty-seven: 13 July.

We pronounced ourselves ready on 13 July and hoped that the city governor, Iftikhar ad-Daulah, had observed our preparations accurately, and made his own accordingly.

    He would see that the south wall gave us the best prospects of success, especially now that Raymond had moved to the Zion Gate and filled in the dry moat; I prayed he believed that the engines being built outside the northern wall were a ruse, knowing that we would never get them past the curtain wall to attack the main wall proper. If, as we hoped, he was concentrating his defences at the south and had moved his resources to face Raymond, including his ballistae, then he had miscalculated.

Day Thirty-eight: 14 July.

On this day we pronounced that our machines were ready and we gathered our men, and numerous pilgrims, together for prayers and a final briefing. Afterwards the pilgrims were sent away to a nearby valley, and given instructions not to move or show themselves until they heard the sounds of our assault, which would begin at dawn on the morrow.

    I was standing next to Godfrey when the rag-bag collection of men, women and children had shuffled away out of our sight.

'Are there no fit men left among that lot who can help with the fight?' asked Allen.

'I'm afraid not,' I replied, 'although there are some women who would join us.'

'We can't have women alongside us, surely,' said Tancred, 'I would worry too much about their safety.'

'Indeed, young man,' agreed Godfrey, 'you have a proper attitude to women, unlike some.' He scowled in the direction of Arnulf and the little group of priests, feeling pleased with the last sermon, no doubt.

'Never mind all that. Gather round and we'll discuss the order of events for tomorrow. When we have done go back to your men and have them prepare their weapons and then get some rest; tomorrow will be busy.'

Godfrey led the briefing. It was good, he was an inspirational speaker and I could feel the tension rise in our midst. After all that had gone before we were ready, ready to commit ourselves to the glory and mercy of God. Come the dawn he would decide if we would return in triumph to our homelands, or perish here in this miserable desert dust, so sodden with the blood of centuries since the death of his son, Jesu.

Day Thirty-nine: 15 July

On the morning of the 15th the lightening sky revealed to us that ad-Daulah had indeed made the prayed-for blunder. The siege engines were no longer outside the wall where they had been the previous evening; during the night Godfrey had dismantled and moved them half a mile away – to the east of St Stephen's Gate. This was where the defences had been observed to be at their weakest; it was the only area of the wall where the ground sloped down towards it.

Here the ground was too rocky to dig a ditch, and, to counteract this, the defenders had constructed a low curtain wall a few paces in front of the main wall to prevent a direct assault. We had decided to remove this obstacle to allow us to move the siege tower directly against the final barrier of the city wall itself, and this is where the battle would commence.

Those mysterious wagons had been deployed and the various items they'd contained were now assembled in front of the wall; ballistae of all sizes and shapes, mangonels, catapults and the like by the dozen, each with a pile of pebbles or rocks heaped next to them.

The sun came up, the horns sounded, the men cheered and the artillerymen loosed off their first missiles – the Fatimids on the wall might well have wished they were somewhere else.

The first phase of the engagement was to achieve control of the killing ground in front of the wall. To this end, salvo after salvo of arrows and rocks were launched at the ramparts and into the web of narrow alleys immediately inside the wall, suppressing the activities of the defenders. I was in charge of this flattening deluge, assisted by Tancred, while Godfrey was responsible for the tower.

Meanwhile the battering ram in front of our new position, directed by Flanders, was ready to do its job. I watched as it set off, pushed from behind by a team of six horses in pairs, harnessed to a long pole between them. This provided the impetus, and with a dozen men on each side to control the excited animals the thing quickly ran out of control, leaving the men trailing in its wake as the terrified horses panicked. The speed of the assembly exceeded belief. It was fortunate that just as the horses began to trip and fall the monstrous ram crashed through the low curtain wall, casting it aside and making rubble of its blocks – hardly impeded, it struck the base of the main wall. It had gathered a frightening pace and could not have been stopped, so out of control it was. As it struck, the impact threw the horses in the air. I heard the screams from where I stood, as they were killed or maimed along with many men.

There was a silence – broken by the cries of men and those distressed animals still alive, and then a great cheer went up from our watching assault troops and chaos seized control of the day.

The Fatimids, in panic, poured oils over the wall and set fire to the wooden ram, forcing a retreat. The reaction of our local assault commander was to attempt to extinguish the flames, using up valuable water supplies, but I quickly put an end to that.

'Let it burn,' the command was sent, 'it will add to the confusion on the wall.' The stench of burning flesh was sickening as wounded horses and men perished in noisy agony beneath the walls of the holy city.

Then pioneer parties, under the protective cover of wattle shields, went forward to clear away the remaining rubble for Godfrey's assault tower. There were a few casualties but, mindful of our resources, I ordered a slow-down of our arrow deluge and left it to the ballistae to keep the defenders off the parapets – slings full of small pebbles saw to that.

Godfrey sent a message back. 'The ram is now an impediment, Robert, get rid of it.'

'Fire arrows, Wulf, get the ram burning afresh, it must go.'

Wulf looked at me as if I were mad but gave the orders and soon the ram was peppered with burning missiles. Then Godfrey sent forward more men under cover of the wattle shields and I ordered my barrage to stop.

I shouted to Payne. 'Go forward and see what they're up to.'

He ran off down the slope and quickly puffed his way back up.

'They're carrying pails of oil, my lord, to soak the remains of the ram. It will soon go when the liquid is afire.'

'Good idea,' I responded. 'What are the Egyptians doing, Payne? Look at them atop the wall; they're tipping pails of oil onto the ram.'

'No, my lord, it's water, now they're trying to put out the fire. They know what we are doing.'

'Tis a mummery: fire on, fire off.' Ragenaus burst out laughing and we joined in the manic raucous.

Then the Fatimids began to hang bundles of straw wrapped in rope, hoping to protect the masonry from further battering.

Acting quickly, Wulf's archers loosed more flaming arrows at the bundles and set them alight. It added to the confusion along the battlements. Men were diverted to try and extinguish the flames and perished under a hail of missiles.

Quickly the wooden watchtowers built on top of the stone walls were under threat from the flames, and those soldiers manning them were forced to retreat.

It was while the Fatimids were in such disarray regarding their burning policy that Godfrey was able to send in more ground-clearing parties. Under the protection of the artillery, now raining rocks on the heads of the shambolic Egyptians, they were able to continue clearing the approach of obstacles ready for the deployment of the siege tower.

All too soon I could see them falling back and demanded to know why.

'They've got a new weapon, Prince Robert,' Tancred shouted back to me. He had been down to see why progress had slowed.

'What is it?' I asked wearily. It had been an exhausting day and we still needed more work to be done to get that damned tower against the wall.

'Mallets, my lord, wooden mallets.'

'What about them?' My brain had heard too much noise and seen too much torn flesh to grasp a simple statement.

'They are wrapping mallets in cloth and tar, driving spikes into them and throwing them on to our men. The spikes penetrate flesh and timber and burn both horribly. I saw one fellow take one to the head, he ran around in a circle with his head afire until someone severed it from his body.'

'Merciful heaven,' I muttered, and then Tancred remembered his purpose.

'My lord Godfrey has called a halt to take stock; will you join him please, Prince Robert?'

'Indeed, I'll trot off now.'

The day lengthened into evening and then down came the dark. I heard complaints that we should start moving the tower but Godfrey and I had agreed that as we would only have one chance, everything needed to be right.

Tancred was one of the impatient ones and I told him straight.

'If we fail the first attempt it will take months to prepare another. We have not the materiels or the time; suppose the Egyptians send reinforcements? We haven't the strength to resist if we're caught out here in the open. No, my friend, we will succeed at the first try, or never.'

So when night came we used the cover of the darkness to further improve the uneven ground; a mixture of gravel, sand and soil was dumped all along the approach, then finally a smooth surface of planks placed down as a road for our tower.

We would be ready by dawn to launch the next phase of the attack.

We had suffered many casualties, despite efforts to minimise them, and the Fatimids were proving a determined and brave foe. Although many had fallen under our withering missile onslaught, they appeared to have recovered some order behind the wall and were now able to respond with some venom of their own.

Under cover of the dark, artisans had approached the low wall and demolished more of it block by block. Now there was a gap wide enough for the siege tower to pass by the stinking remnant of the smoking ram, but which would not be visible until the dawn light revealed it. We had lost a few men during the process from blindly shot arrows, but by returning a few in the night air we managed to suppress their sporadic attacks.

There would only be a few more horses in this attack. Some were needed to move the tower, or be used by commanders and messengers – otherwise this was a war of the artillery and infantry.

Day Forty: 16 July.

I was woken before dawn by noises; familiar ones at first, men coughing, the usual farting and cursing, then the rattle of cooking pots and the smell of smoke in the air. I went out of my tent to water the desert and see who was out and about their business, and then I realised that the background noise had not ceased all night, artisans were still making some final adjustments to their machines. The sound of blades being whetted resounded – today we would enter the holy city – today was our day come at last. Then the shouting began, insults from the wall, insults hurled back in a different language. What matter if the words were not understood, the tone of them was, and it was not friendship in the air.

Oslac came up to me with a tankard of wine and a bit of bread, with some grapes as a special treat. I thanked him.

'Are you ready, lad?' I asked.

'Yes, my lord. We're disappointed that the cavalry will not be needed this day.'

'Aye. The horses do badly at climbing ladders. But you will be needed as messengers, you understand that? It's vital that we keep control of the battlefield.'

'Yes, my lord, we will be swift as the wind.'

His eyes were bright with excitement. Hardly a youth, yet death excited him; such a strange thing, our business.

Then Arnulf paid a visit, or rather interrupted my thoughts.

'We will gain entry today, my lord.'

'Yes, Arnulf, that is our intention. How do you know?' I asked to humour him.

'You asked if God had a plan, Robert; he has. Remember how Jesu fasted for forty days and forty nights in the desert before he felt relief from the devil?'

I wondered where this was going.

'I remember.'

'Today is the fortieth day, and we shall be rid of Lucifer.'

Then the noses of warfare started up once more, horses clattering, machinery creaking, trumpets or horns somewhere, everywhere the creak of leather and the clank of metal, and then the first machine let off its deadly cargo, a shout of '*loose*,' the creak of wood and the thump of leather upon leather as the propelling arm struck the stop. The earth shook beneath me as the next shout of '*loose*' hurt my ears from a mangonel close by. The day was begun.

Ahead of me the remains of the battering ram were still smouldering, the smoke lending to the air of confusion. The defenders needed to hold the wall and now they would see that just out of arrow-shot Flanders had lined up his men with dozens of threatening ladders; it was a dangerous stretch of wall for the Egyptians.

It was difficult to hear anyone unless they were close by. I went to talk to Godfrey, to see who had been chosen to lead the first assault, when a shower of rocks came flying towards us. A knight standing next to Godfrey lost his head to a direct hit and I was showered with blood and earth thrown up, and then an arrow whizzed past my head. Oslac cursed and dragged me by the arm.

'Come, lord, move back.'

We prudently moved backwards to resume the conversation. Allen was assailing Godfrey's ears, demanding to be in the first attack, I would have supported him but Godfrey had someone of his own in mind and any argument came to a halt as we were again showered with rocks. One hit Allen on the helm and he fell, cursing.

Flanders shouted, 'Your banner, Robert, lower your banner.'

We had been targeted by the Fatimid commander.

'Payne, move away a little.' Then we stopped to finish our discussion and I received a blow on the shin as a reward.

The defenders would know by now that we had achieved our first objective: we had reached the base of the city wall and laid a roadway for the tower.

We waited for word from the throng of craftsmen gathered around the base of the tower. Godfrey, impatient, sent for Artus or Gaston to ask about the delay in moving.

Artus came puffing up to our position, red-faced and out of breath; a sailor's condition, I thought.

'That thing,' Godfrey pointed at Artus' contraption, 'should be rolling by now, we are wasting valuable ammunition.'

'I know, my lord, but there's too much ground to cover before the wheels find the plank road, they're sinking into the earth.'

A chorus of curses went up. 'Shit,' 'bollocks,' and other harsh words assailed the heavens as eyes rolled and Artus' rosy face deepened its colour.

'What're you going to do, captain?' I asked.

'I can do two things, my lord. Lengthen the road and widen the wheels, one or both.'

'How will you widen the wheels?' I asked, wondering why they weren't as wide as could be already.

'I can add another wheel to the axles, my lord, I wasn't certain that they'd take the strain at first but if we move it without troops inside I'm willing to try.'

'Adding planks to the road will be dangerous. Do we have enough, Robert?' I could see that Godfrey's usual calm demeanour was at stretching point and tried to calm him.

'Yes, but we can protect the road with shields and we have enough timber left. Let us prepare properly. Send to Raymond and tell him we are delayed; he is to maintain his efforts.'

'Very well, Robert.'

In the end I sent Oslac off to encourage Raymond while we watched the extra wheels being fitted. He returned all in a sweat with news from Raymond's position. To the south it had been a calamitous day. When he got there Raymond's operation had already faltered, as his men were facing the best prepared and most determined of ad-Daulah's defenders.

Because of the ground inside the wall being relatively clear of buildings and other obstacles, ad-Daulah had been able to deploy his ballistae to better effect. He could cover the ground outside the wall from close to the base to three hundred paces beyond – he had a perfect killing ground and used it to good effect.

The heavy mangonels, hurling rocks as big as a man's head, smashed down upon Raymond's men, shredding their wattle shields, while the lighter onagers, shot from the top of the wall, were able to cause carnage among the scattering infantry by peppering them with the smaller pebbles. When he attempted to move his rickety tower against the wall it was quickly smashed by the plummeting rocks and fire rendered it useless. Raymond's day was going badly with hundreds of casualties; his troops were demoralised and dispirited – but his sacrifices had improved our chance of success.

By midday, after a morning of thirst, dust and mind-numbing noise and heat, the defenders must have watched with dismay as Godfrey's tower commenced its inexorable crawl towards the base of the city wall. It was now crowned by a gleaming gold crucifix. Arnulf had created his own totem, and it was firmly fixed above our heads to lead us forward to God's victory.

Making the most of the prepared ground, the men at the base, fully protected by their wattle guards, advanced the tower. Unlike Raymond, we made no attempt to place men inside the tower, thus making it easier to shift.

The lighter missiles from the ramparts made no obstacle to progress – until the Fatimids deployed another weapon: Greek fire. This was a substance they could only deploy at close range but its effects were limited. Being of Byzantine origin, we knew of it, and its antidote; it failed when doused with vinegar and we had placed skins of that suppressant close to hand.

To our relief the tower rumbled along nicely until it came to rest against the base of the wall and the assault proper began.

First to enter the tower, through an avenue of shields, were archers. They climbed to the top level which was higher than the wall and began firing down on the defenders.

I watched with uncertainty as Godfrey led his men into the base of the tower. I could not afford to lose him in battle, he was a worthy commander, but he needed to lead from the front so I hadn't argued the point. Next entered the first of the fully armoured knights, sheltered by their shields and the wattle guards. First was Ludolf of Tournai and his brother Engelbert. They were to climb to the second level, which was at the same height as the top of the wall, and prepare to drop the bridge. When the bottom level had filled with supporting knights the pair would be ready to attack.

All the time I shuffled closer and closer, eager to join in, but I received warnings as rocks fell about me. Others were hurt, I heard a crack as one of Godfrey's knights took a blow to a leg; he collapsed with the bottom of the leg almost removed at the knee. I was dragged back by Oslac, braveheart. The noise was terrible, and after the weird silence of entering Antioch, something of a shock. Shouts; men screaming orders; men screaming hurt, hit by rocks hurtling at them from the wall; terrified horses added to the din and so did the sound of missiles hissing through the air, only heard after they'd passed by. There was a stench too, timbers fired by that abominable Greek fire were hard to extinguish and there was burning flesh and the stink of spilled guts; it was hard to keep a steady mind.

Truth to tell we were ill-prepared for this mayhem. The arrows and swords, the lances and charging horses in those previous encounters were little as compared to this arena of dreadful machines; we had not practised for this.

'Get back, Robert,' shouted Tancred, over the din, 'this is no place for a cavalryman.' Payne dragged me back, shoving Oslac out of the way to do it. One of our mangonels went off next to me and when the throwing arm struck the leather-padded restraining bar I thought my ears would burst. The things were mad, no wonder the Romans called them *bucking donkeys*, for when their load was released the whole thing jumped up into the air, then as their lethal loads arced towards the city the machines crashed back down to earth with a ground-shaking thud. Everybody was moving their lips but I heard naught for a while after that.

By now the top of the tower was in a state of confusion; the Greek fire had been suppressed by skins of vinegar taken up there for the purpose, but everywhere was smoke and flame, including the drawbridge. The wooden ramparts along the wall were also aflame and the defenders were forced away from the assault point. Then Godfrey dropped the bridge and out of the tower the assault began.

We could see Ludolf throw wattle shields upon the burning drawbridge, and then high above us he ran across at the head of his men to seize the ramparts.

'By God's glory we are in.'

Godfrey appeared on the battlements and waved a fist in triumph.

As soon as our waiting infantry saw Ludolf's banners raised atop the ramparts they charged forward cheering and shouting cries of triumph; with dozens of scaling ladders, too many to repulse, the invasion quickly became a rout. The defenders were completely overcome and began to run off in horror, knowing the fate that awaited them now that the wall and the city would soon belong to the warriors of the cross.

Soon the gates began to open and we lost control.

I watched helpless as every leader galloped forward to find the nearest ladder or gate and join the flood of avenging Franks pouring through, and then all the worst emotions of the invading army took over. All the frustrations, all the privations and losses, friends killed, everything that was bad that had happened to them over the previous three years was now laid on the heads of the Egyptians and a terrible revenge exacted.

My men had not been directly involved in the actual storming of the walls, instead my cavalry were held back as not needed. Wulf had employed his archers to pepper the battlements and what surviving foot soldiers I had, some six hundred of the thousand that left Rouen, had been deployed to support the artisans and artillery.

They wanted, quite naturally, to enter the city, but I restrained them with the promise of a grand cavalcade the following day, when we would march to the Church of the Holy Sepulchre.

In the event that became a fruitless promise when word filtered out of the city of a kind of madness that had beset the invading army. There were reports of slaughter, rapine and rape, and fires could be seen from our position opposite St Stephen's Gate. We heard cries and screams; it was hard to tell which came from men and which from women. I prayed for mercy within the holy city, but had a great unease in my stomach. The noises diminished throughout the night and it was quiet by the time dawn came. We slept but fitfully outside the walls of Jerusalem that night.

The next morning I sent in a patrol to gather information, but for three days this army of savages ran riot and none were spared.

Terrified Egyptians huddled on the roof of the Temple of Solomon but were dragged down and killed; they gathered on the Temple Mount begging for mercy, but were killed; the madness became endemic and soon anybody found, woman or child, and unfortunate Christians, were killed. The streets ran with blood and the rampaging lunatics began to trip over the headless corpses as they ran mindlessly through the gory streets.

Only ad-Daulah and his closest escaped. Using horses they made it to the Tower of David, where, leaving their mounts outside, they barricaded themselves in to await their fate.

Raymond found them first, scaling the walls only when the defenders had run off, and bartered their lives for possession of that citadel. His part in the assault was only the minimum, but he had by fate seized one of the most significant sites within the holy city.

When the madness subsided and we managed to regain control we gathered together at the Holy Sepulchre to give thanks to heaven for allowing us the blessed privilege of freeing the holy city from the loathsome grasp of the pagans, and the gift thereafter of eternal life in the presence of the Lord.

After which they began to gather the bodies from within the walls and I went to see what destruction had been wrought in the name of God. It was worse than any imagining.

Not only were bodies gathered, but also piles of hands alongside piles of heads, torsos with or without limbs, all piled into wagons to clear the streets. A trail of dripping blood, spilt intestines and slippery organs painted a grisly path that led from within through the gates and out towards pits dug for the purpose. In they went, people and parts, uncountable such were the numbers. When the digging of pits overcame the weary soldiers the flesh was piled up and burnt; Christian or Jew, Moslem or godless it mattered not, for they were dead: in the name of our God.

I found no triumph in that grim vision, and neither did any of those with me. As we returned to the peace of our camp some retched and spewed, for this was beyond comprehension; if this was a holy war, then what vision would an unholy confrontation present?

15. Christian Rule Restored.

On 18 July 1099, the leaders gathered to discuss the question of governing the city.

Raymond said that he wanted to be king, Godfrey wouldn't agree; the clerics said that the governor should be from the Church to replace the deceased former Patriarch, Simeon. I watched with Allen, Rob and Tancred as the leading proponents formed themselves into factions as different as oil and water supporting differing arguments.

We left in a short while and engaged in a much quieter and more considered discussion.

Flanders began.

'I'm totally pissed off. All this way and the twats start arguing about sharing out the spoils. The streets are stinking with blood and guts – and the flies; who'd want the place anyway? I'm for going home.'

I was still numbed, the consequences of the victory had shaken me and I wondered what glory there was in it.

'Well, as I see it the city had no king before we arrived, why should it have one now? All the Church has done is start the whole venture off and then stand back and watch. The emperor has been treacherous in his dealings. As far as I'm concerned they can get on with it. I've lost interest... I think that I might join you, dear cousin.'

Tancred said nothing and flicked at flies with a stick. Wulf and Payne sat back to back in the shade of a rare tree throwing stones at the same flies. Rob looked at Tancred.

'What about you, Tancred, what do you want to do?'

'Dunno... I've found lots of loot here, bloodstained gold. I might just go back to Antioch and see what Uncle Bohmey is up to.'

Rob snorted, 'You lack ambition, young man. Why don't you want to be a king?'

Tancred laughed at him.

'What! And be a target for an assassin? No thanks, kings do not have friends.'

I was deep in contemplation, but caught the end of that statement.

'Kings have no friends except that they send them to war, just like popes. If you want friends... keep a crown off your head, before you lose them both.'

'Both what?' Tancred wasn't always quick.

'The crown and the head that wears it,' was my rejoinder.

'We still need a solution,' said Rob. 'Who is to be governor?'

'It should be Godfrey,' said Tancred.

'Why does it matter to you?' asked Rob.

'It doesn't, it just seems to me that he is the best option... speaking as one who doesn't care, that is.'

'I agree on Godfrey,' I nodded, 'but why call him king?'

'True!' said Tancred, 'let's invent a new title for him.'

Rob looked at me with an odd glint in his eye.

'Strictly speaking, of course, the fact is that there's already a king among us; let's ask him to take the job.'

Tancred sniggered while I puzzled.

'King? What king? There's no sodding kings around here.'

The others looked at each other, then looking straight at me, chorused, 'Oh yes there is.'

I responded immediately, 'Oh no there bloody isn't. I've got a marriage to go to, and my kingdom, if I wanted it, is well away from this poxy abattoir in this fly-ridden wilderness.'

'That's a no, is it?'

'Yes, Rob, that's a no, not as long as I have a fart left in me, I would not join with this coven of unseemly ambition as long as I value my soul. Let's go and talk with Arnulf, I have an idea.'

We walked off, trailed by Peverel and Ragenaus. I noted how these two had left their youth in these bloody sands, it showed on their faces; hard, merciless eyes, gaunt skin etched with old men's lines, and I prayed there was a gentle flame still burning in their hearts, I prayed this would be their first and last such voyage of destruction.

Rob said to me, 'How do you know that she's waiting for you?'

'Because no one has said otherwise.'

'How old is she now?'

'Christ's miracles, Rob, she must be nineteen now.'

'*Mon Dieu!* And how old are you? Dear cousin?'

'Erm… forty-seven. Tell me, friend, do I look old?'

He turned and gazed at my shaven head, visible above my face as I had removed my helm.

'You look frightening; I wouldn't want to annoy you. Do you think her still to be a virgin?'

I unsheathed my sword and tried to see myself in its burnished Damascene steel. It was not a flattering image, distorted no doubt, but a strange goblin face stared back at me, dark below the eyes and pink, almost white above. What maiden would want to marry that?

'You're a nosy bugger today, Robert of Flanders.'

'Just curious, I don't want you to get your hopes up.'

'Listen, friend. Her father wants a queen for a daughter; her virginity will be the tightest citadel in Christendom.'

Nearby, and earwigging, Payne said to Ragenaus without regard for my dignity, 'Hear that, Saxon? Our leader's going to get the tightest fanny in Christendom.'

'God! What a thought. Did you see his African companions?'

'Yes, of course. What a prince,' he said admiringly, and then called to my twitching ears, 'my lord, I hope that I'm still as lively as you when I reach your age.'

'The way we are living you won't see thirty,' I responded.

'Cheerful bugger!' said Rob.

On 22 July, the council met to vote upon the issue.

Arnulf made a proposition and it received a unanimous approval, except from Raymond of course.

Godfrey was appointed Advocate of the Holy Sepulchre.

This implied, but did not exactly specify, a connection between the Church and the laity. Godfrey's first request was to Raymond, he was asked to hand over the Tower of David, but he refused and went off in a rage.

In an act of public defiance, Raymond turned the tower over to the newly created Bishop of Albara – his friend, Peter of Narbonne.

Peter, being a wise man, promptly handed the keys over to Godfrey, leaving Raymond well and truly out in the cold.

Raymond then decided to sample the waters of the river Jordan and set up camp at Jericho. Once he had gone, Godfrey made his first appointment and Arnulf of Chocques, my former chaplain, became the new Patriarch of Jerusalem.

I was not entirely happy with this, it seemed to place my chaplain alongside other, more ambitious men, and I consulted Flanders.

'Remember this, Rob, things that go around come around; just wait your turn and you can be king one day.'

'You are very wise, cousin. And your chaplain has risen beyond his ambitions.'

I giggled, 'Perhaps they might make something of this bugger's muddle after all, Rob.'

'They?' he queried.

'Aye, dear friend, *they*. I'm getting ready to leave, as soon as I have the energy.'

With the new patriarch came a new ruling philosophy and this was revealed in the period after 1 August when Arnulf was ceremonially installed. It was not to everyone's liking. Raymond, who came back for the event, considered Arnulf common: 'unfit by birth for high office,' he was heard to say. I wondered what the son of a carpenter would make of that, but nobody cared. Raymond's status had reached a new low and he was left to blether into his cups.

I spent the next two weeks relaxing in an olive grove to the north of the city. I found the stench of death in the city too much to tolerate and had remained in camp outside the walls. Today, the men of my mesnie were at swordplay – practise, practise and practise again – always my maxim for those who wished to survive on the battlefield.

Rob rode up and joined me, sitting leaned back against a tree.

'Your chaplain has turned odd, Robert,' said he, 'and something new has arisen.'

'I know, he was once a gentle priest, now he is pissing me off.'

'Heard his latest?' my cousin enquired.

'Another batty idea?'

'You might think so. You know those Christians of the eastern credo, that came back into the city, he has ordered they be thrown out from the Holy Sepulchre... says they're an insult to the true faith, or something.'

'All of them?'

'Seems so. Armenians, Copts, followers of Jacob, Nestorians... I haven't heard of most of them.'

'Alexios will not be pleased when word of this reaches his ears; he called us here to save all of these people.'

'Yes indeed, Robert. And he isn't going to be pleased when he hears that we haven't appointed a Byzantine priest as patriarch here.'

'Oh yes, that. Godfrey can deal with that, Constantinople is a long way off. Something new, you said.'

'Mmm! A good one. Remember how Arnulf demolished Raymond's miraculous lance cult?'

'Of course, old One-eye must have been desperate when he lost that unholy tussle, and now?'

'Well, Arnulf's found a bit of the cross.' Rob's smirk was wondrous to behold.

'He what? This might be a miracle too far, I think.'

'Some mysterious Syrian has led him to where a piece of the Cross of Jesus was buried.'

'How very fortuitous. A remarkable find, after all these years.'

'Yes it is. Unfortunately it's hidden in a gold and silver crucifix, so you can't actually see it... just believe it.'

'I see. What exactly is the purpose of this miracle?'

'Easy. He says that it proves that the Latin Church was meant to occupy this place because God has led him to the relic.'

I pondered a little before saying, 'Do you recall that he said how he knew that Raymond's lance was false?'

Rob thought for a bit.

'He said that Alexios had the real one, locked away in Constantinople.'

'Correct! So now he has a more powerful relic with which to challenge the right of the emperor to appoint bishops in the Holy Lands. Do you see the logic of it, dear cousin?'

''Tis a very clever piece of finding.'

'Very timely.'

'Indeed.'

It was clear that me and mine were the ones who had kept some grip upon reality; it seemed to be in short supply in this mad place. This was the final piece of lunacy and it set my mind at rest, I wanted no more to do with this mummery.

'Rob, I am going home. I have done enough of this crusading. It seems rather short of being the uplifting experience I'd expected.'

Flanders simply nodded and called for a flagon of wine.

'Fetch our captains,' he called, 'we're going to get pissed, and then go home.'

The command, and news of it, spread rapidly throughout my encampment and soon that forgotten emotion, jollity, rent the air with cries of joy, and the wine vendors descended upon us like the desert flies that had become our eternal companions.

During our celebrations news came from Rome. In an ironic quirk of fate, the instigator of this great undertaking, the despatch of thousands of souls to heaven before their time, had not lived to hear of the victory at Jerusalem. Pope Urban had died in Rome on 29 July, and the news of our sacred success had not reached him.

The next day, 6 August, I was forced to postpone my return to sanity. Tancred, who was patrolling along the seaboard, had sent word of a concentration of Fatimid forces at Ascelon, about fifty miles away on the coast.

Godfrey made swift preparations to move out of Jerusalem to confront the Egyptians on the plain; he believed that any enemies who fought in the open would be defeated by our cavalry. I thought that he lacked sense and that we had been too successful for our own good. I would not confront any enemies until I knew more about them, and I could choose the ground. Godfrey was not surprised when Raymond declined to join him, but he was when I refused to leave my camp.

I sent Allen to calm him.

'Tell him that this is scant information, and it leaves the city open to a ruse. I am certain that there's something to defend here, but I know not what awaits us in the desert.'

When Allen returned it was with Godfrey's response: 'Guard the gates and do not let Raymond in.'

Godfrey rode out on the 9th towards the coast and a rendezvous with Tancred at Ramleh, some twenty-two miles away. I sent Flanders to watch his doings. Within a day he sent back the worst news, after Tancred had briefed him and described in detail the force now gathered at Ascelon.

His message was thus. 'Al-Afdal has arrived with vengeance in mind and an army of some twenty thousand.' It consisted of Egyptian heavy cavalry and an array of North Africans including Bedouins, Berbers and Ethiopians – none of which peoples we had met in battle before.

Godfrey must have known immediately that to fail here would lead to complete annihilation; there would be no mercy shown to us or our Christian brethren in Jerusalem. Contained within that message was a desperate plea from Godfrey. Now more than ever, I was needed at the centre of the Frankish deployment.

Reacting swiftly and putting aside my distaste for the politics of religion or land disputes I gathered my troops together and went to confront Raymond.

'You can remain here now, and forever, or come with me and live a bit longer; choose now.'

Raymond, realising that any power grab he might have in mind would be short-lived if Godfrey was eliminated, gathered his men, and with his holy lance held ready he prepared to join me in the dash to Ramleh to join up with Godfrey.

We were ready by the late afternoon of 11 August, or almost.

'Is that the best horse I have left?' I gazed at the dismal creature prepared for my inspection.

'That! Duke Robert,' said Allen, 'is one of the best *we* have left, others are riding Turkish asses.'

'Oh,' I responded. I knew we no longer possessed any of our northern horses, but this came as a surprise. 'So is anybody riding camels, Allen?' I quipped.

'No, Robert, they offer no comfort and it's difficult to tell which way they're facing in the dark.'

'How so?' my curiosity stirred.

'Because they fart from both ends, my lord.' Payne had the last word and I left it there.

Setting off early the next morn, we numbered one thousand two hundred cavalry and nine thousand infantrymen, not forgetting Raymond's holy lance and Arnulf's sacred crucifix. According to Godfrey's reports that meant we'd have less than half the numbers of the enemy, but with Raymond's nail, Arnulf's splinter, and God's blessing, how could we fail?

Payne was riding alongside; there was a tatter of cloth attached to the end of his lance, the remains of the papal gonfalon. He posed an interesting question.

'When we have despatched the Egyptian army, my lord, who else will be coming to test our mettle?'

'I know not, Payne. Who else is there?'

'I know not, my lord, but perhaps God wants us to go on fighting until death claims us.'

'You're in a cheerful mood today, Payne.'

'Yes, my lord, that few days' rest has energised my spirits and now my sword longs for more foreign flesh.'

'Oh well, let us see the colour of Egyptian blood.'

Arriving near the sea after dark, we gathered for a detailed briefing from Tancred. In a valley, with the burning lamps hidden from the enemy's sight, Tancred scraped lines in the sand to show us the location of the Egyptian formations. While Godfrey, Raymond and the others looked on I could see that the battle formation was more or less chosen by our combined assets. I took the floor and explained.

'You see that Tancred has revealed how the enemy are formed up in camp along this ridge, with their commander here in the centre at the head of this valley?' I took Tancred's stick and touched his sand map. 'Our best hope is to do the unexpected.'

'We have come to expect that of you, Robert,' growled the war-weary Raymond, 'will you share your next unlikely event with us?'

'Yes, Raymond, if you will share your remaining cavalry with me.'

The old schemer looked at me with his single eye and grunted. More politician than soldier, he knew that his standing remained at an all-time low but he could see no profit in failure at this juncture.

'Very well, Robert, you have used your assets effectively up till now, I pray that God will guide your hand in this once more.'

With my diplomacy working well I saw no need to antagonise the grasping sod, so I thanked him and went on to explain my battle plan.

'It is very simple, my lords. As well as, hmm, Count Raymond's assets, I will employ two God-given factors – the night and surprise.'

They stared blankly at me, but there were no objections.

'I intend to form up here,' I traced a line in the sand about a mile away from the enemy lines. 'Godfrey, if you will form up on my left and Raymond on my right? Your infantry will lead, supported by what archers we have left and followed by what cavalry I shall leave you.'

'To what purpose is that, dear prince?' asked Godfrey.

'I intend to advance straight up this valley towards the Egyptian commander's position just before dawn and overrun it. Once I've moved off you will advance your troops and sweep through the enemy camp before they realise what is happening, and before full daylight. I expect them to be panicked and leaderless, so before they can get organised you must be in among them to strike them down.'

'How will you see your way, Robert?' asked the one-eyed leader.

'We've had moonlight these past few nights, and we have that valley to guide us. If you stay on the ridges on either side we will do very well, I believe.'

There was no disagreement, so in the absence of any other plan I gained their acceptance. I prayed that this would be the last battle, for I was heartily sick of the whole thing: tomorrow was all we had left in us: eternal life at dawn or sometime later, I cared not.

I prayed that the Egyptians had learned little from our earlier routing of the Turks. We deployed with Raymond on the right flank next to the sea and Godfrey on the left. Thus the infantry were evenly split, with the archers standing behind them in support. What few horses I left them would act as their pitiful reserve.

The cavalry, such as it was, contained the remaining fit horses. Some horseless knights elected to trot along behind, and I was grateful for their support. Then I made such hurried preparations as I could with the remainder of the night left to me.

It was not the best, but it was all we could muster. The dawn was about to reveal to me the next episode of my long and restless life.

In the dark we assembled. It was pointless trying to keep quiet, we could hear the infantry clumping and clanking, grumbling and stumbling its way past our horse-lines; they were on their way towards their own appointment. With the daylight would come death and disaster, or glory.

I mounted up in the centre, with what was left of my standards unseen in the dim desert dawn. We were restricted to three columns, because of the narrowness of the valley I could not deploy in my usual broad-fronted conroys in this action. I had Tancred commanding the right flank and Flanders to my left with Allen directly behind me as my first reserve. We all knew that our overriding, our single hope for victory lay in our first encounter. This was the surviving hard core cavalry of the Frankish army; if we lost, then all would be lost in the desert sands beneath us.

325

If, if, if, all was ifs. If Tancred had done his job well, then we knew exactly where the enemy forces lay, and crucially where al-Afdal's headquarters were, and I prayed that their superiority in numbers had blinded the Mussulmen once more to our discipline and efficiency.

'Are you ready?' I asked those near me.

'Aye, my lord,' they replied in gentle chorus.

'Then we will walk and trot as far as possible. This bag of bones possesses no more than a hundred paces of gallop.'

Taking advantage of the dark before dawn I moved slowly forward, passing through our still-deploying infantry and hoping that the Egyptians were feeling secure in their numbers. We could not tarry to be revealed by the rising sun. Suddenly we were trotting past dozens of outlying tents and curled-up bodies before ever they were aware of our presence; we had penetrated the dozing perimeter sentries without challenge; there was hope yet.

Now we made swift progress through the wakening troops as we closed rapidly on the Egyptian centre. I could hear the cries of surprised and dying men as those on my flanks exacted the ultimate price for carelessness. Then the sun cleared the eastern horizon and I was rewarded by heaven for my faith because the first rays caught something directly to my front and caused it to shine as brightly as a star. It was the famed golden globe, symbol of the Egyptian general and proof that Tancred had done his work precisely.

Screams behind told me that our infantry had reached the enemy encampment and many unsuspecting snoozers were now dying, in or outside their tents. The Fatimids were terrified to find that we were already in among them and hundreds died before they had time to lay hands upon their weapons.

It was the turn of al-Afdal's command base to find horror approaching along with the morning sun. The greatest opportunity possible had presented itself before me as I spied the personal standard of al-Afdal.

'That globe!' I shouted, and I lowered my lance to signal an immediate charge. I looked left and right as Payne and Ragenaus kicked their wretched animals into life and came alongside of me; a three-man conroy must needs suffice for this contest. Leaving the rest to follow in my wake I charged at that golden globe.

This was the time of madness, when those who judged their lives more precious than the cause would die, and those who would eagerly give their lives would live on, live to die another day.

'Now! For God!' Another shout rang out as my horse did its rickety best to gallop across the uneven sand.

Behind me, somehow, a ragged line formed across the widening valley and into an arrowhead; my steed, uninspired, closed with desperately slow speed upon the transfixed Fatimid headquarters. The standard guards stood firm to the last, I struck one with my thrown lance, the other attempted to run but I had my sword out and the final vision of that man, holding his leader's standard, was to be the tip of my sword driving into his chest before I snatched the golden orb from his dying hand.

Holding the captured symbol and turning, my feet touched the ground as the horse collapsed, the effort too much. I started to walk towards our infantrymen to show the proof of our victory when Oslac reined up beside me and leapt off. I gladly climbed on to his animal's back and prayed that it had a few more paces left in its tired bones. Raising the globe up high I heard the shout of acclaim ring out across the battlefield.

Seeing the Egyptian leadership collapse, Tancred and Flanders led their squadrons right and left and commenced the task of rolling up the Fatimids as they fled in defeat and terror. Allen took his reserve straight ahead, and, as was now the bloody custom, there was no mercy shown; those who had cast aside their weapons received the same savage sword blows and lances in their bodies as the ones who fought bravely to their death.

On the flanks Raymond and Godfrey sent their infantry in to complete the slaughter. Raymond even pursued the luckless Mussulmen into the sea, to drown, or die by the sword.

Al-Afdal had escaped along with only half his number and we found a great deal of gold and silver in his encampment, and yet the sun was barely above the horizon.

Once again the enemy had seriously underestimated us and paid dearly for their mistake.

Godfrey came galloping up all of a dither.

'Jesu, Robert!' he cried, 'that was brilliant; God bless you, my friend. You have the Egyptian's balls in hand I see.'

'Indeed, Godfrey, they are safely couched within my grasp. I think there may be tears in the eyes of al-Afdal today.'

He laughed and turned away to celebrate with his men. Another day dawned with sands stained red; a new kind of normal, it seemed.

Ragenaus was distracted. 'I thought that we were doomed today, my lord.'

'You were not alone, my friend,' I replied and lapsed into contemplation, conversation not being my desire at that moment.

Suddenly I came over dizzy and fell to my knees.

'My lord!' cried Oslac.

'Look, he's wounded,' said Ragenaus.

'Bring him under this tree,' ordered Payne.

'I'm all right, stop fussing,' I grumbled.

'Once we've attended to this gash on your leg. You're bleeding and it must be stopped.'

'Oh well, get on with it.' *Let them fuss, they have earned it; churlish it would be to stop them, besides, I feel tired*. I indulged in a little contemplation. *That fellow with the orb, he must have got a blow in before he died, brave man... but a pain in the arse...*

'He's sleeping,' said somebody.

Who? I thought *...There's too much to do.*

I awoke feeling someone bothering over my thigh.

'Watch where you place your hands... who are you?' I mumbled, feeling uncomfortable, and then tried to sit up. The fellow moved back in surprise. He was dressed in long robes and had the look of an Egyptian about him.

'Be quiet, Robert,' a voice commanded. I looked up, it was Allen.

'We found him in al-Afdal's tent, he is – was – Afdal's personal physician. He's agreed to treat you in order to retain his head.'

I looked at the wretched fellow. His eyes met mine in a kind of pleading. I thought that I should trust the man and gestured for him to carry on bothering... which he did, at the cost of some pain.

'Be careful, fellow,' I gasped, 'these are my best marrying legs.'

The gawping crowd surrounding me burst into laughter.

'Piss off, dogsbodies, there's little enough of them without losing chunks.'

'Lay still, my lord, let the man do his business.'

The large shadow of Payne cut off the sun and I thought to obey the concerned knight, lapsing into silent capitulation.

I must admit to being shocked by the ease of our victory, and how complete it became in so short a span. This would, of course, be seized upon and held up as justification, in the eyes of the clergy, for their claims of faith in their holy relics: God through his wisdom had revealed these relics to them as the corporeal truth of the justice of their cause.

It should have been cause for reflection. We had won by a fluke. Seen in the revealing light of the midday sun, the size of the battlefield and the extent of the Egyptian encampment, now destroyed, made our pitiful numbers seem absurd. How stupid, how reckless had we been to consider that victory would be possible in the face of such a numerous enemy; and the horses! If I had appeared in the lists of France or Germany riding such scraggy objects, I would have been laughed off the field.

With my wound dressed and me limping things were soon back to normal. As usual, after the military victory came the political shambles.

Raymond went to the locked gates of Ascelon and offered negotiations with the terrified citizens for their freedom. They were willing to treat until Godfrey turned up. Suspicious of Raymond's motives he barged in and broke up the tenuous trust that Raymond was nurturing with the city governor, so that he withdrew from the process – keeping the gates firmly locked.

This was an opportunity spurned to secure a valuable port and supply point for future use. It was enough for me, and when next we all met to discuss the future governance of Jerusalem I denied them the opportunity to speak before I had my say.

With Church and State sitting comfortably before me I stood and revealed my temper.

'All along in this venture there have been two enemies to cope with: the Mussulmen and your bloody ambitions. If you two – ' looking at Godfrey and Raymond – 'and Bohemund, had paid better heed to your promises and your duties, instead of trying to carve out new empires for yourselves, this campaign would have been better executed, more quickly and at less cost than you have brought upon us. As far as I'm concerned I am done here. You, Godfrey, can keep Jerusalem, and you, Raymond, can have the desert, and you –' I reserved my worst bile for my former chaplain, Arnulf – 'you can keep your best bishop's raiment, your dubious splinter, and your grand title, and pray – pray for forgiveness and for insight into your soul. You have mistaken your garments and your title for your being; they are not the same, and they can all be taken away from you. Pray, Arnulf, pray, and see if you can find some humility and Christian charity within you and perhaps you may save your soul.'

Then into the silence that I'd fashioned, I turned and spoke my parting words.

'My leg hurts, I am going to get married, and I am sending my people back home. There they can tell tales of bravery, treachery, and the values of self-serving opportunists: I pray that the rest of you will take measure of your souls.'

16. A Triumphant Return.

By the end of August, with my leg healing nicely, thanks to a new Byzantine *chirurgien* who had slapped some smelly unguents on it – my Egyptian having vanished one night, probably feeling anxious to retain his head – I was almost ready to leave. Ships were scarce and I decided to go back to Tripoli to try and get as many as possible over the sea from there. Of my remaining soldiers and supporters, not everyone wanted to return. Some quite liked the life of killing and booty, and went to find new fiefdoms to take over, or warlords to join. Godfrey and Arnulf thought they would best serve the Lord, and themselves, by remaining in Jerusalem. Raymond seemed uncertain as to his next move but within a few days he said that he would move back along the coast with me. That dismayed Godfrey, who would be left with fewer than three hundred knights to defend the city. I felt little sympathy for either; their ambitions had been exposed along the way. They had not even set off from France with pious thoughts in mind, their aims were territorial and Jerusalem was merely another target: a pox on them all, I thought. But I agreed that Raymond could accompany me on the journey back to Tripoli, knowing full well that he would be looking for new domains to seize, silly old man that he was.

Letters went to Matilda asking for help, and then just before we set off I received a message from Emperor Alexios. He asked to see me and said a galley was on its way to Tripoli to carry me back to Constantinople.

With only fifty knights, and only half of those others who set out from Rouen left, I had fewer than a thousand to care for now. All, however, were saved souls, who doubtless would find many earthly sins to indulge in for the rest of their lives knowing that their place in heaven was already secure. To ensure that the journey would be as comfortable as possible my shipwrights and other artisans set to work; wagons were crafted, horses, or anything with four legs, were procured and as many of us as possible rode on something, although as always most would walk, with their food riding alongside.

Along the way, most of those we came across, especially governors of towns and districts, were pleased to help us as we passed by – no doubt our reputation for ruthlessness helped in that regard – and the journey was largely uneventful until we reached Tripoli.

Here, an emissary from Alexios was waiting to greet me. It was my former adversary, Panteleimon the Embarrassed.

'Prince Robert.' The Greek bowed and fidgeted, uncertain of his reception. He nodded at Raymond, who ignored the man.

'Oh! It's you, Panteleimon. How is the emperor?'

'He is fine, and in awe of your achievements, Prince Robert.'

'He is? Then perhaps he might have joined us.'

'Indeed, Prince Robert, he sees that, and wishes me to express his disappointment in not being able to make the journey.'

'I see. I take it that his attachment to the Egyptians is at an end?'

Panteleimon hesitated a little. Being a diplomat was never easy, but sometimes, just sometimes, there could be room for a little honesty.

'The emperor has borders with these Fatimids... You understand, Prince Robert, we need to maintain a certain degree of understanding with them.'

'Of course, wars are started over misunderstandings, are they not?'

'Indeed, my lord. The emperor has a high regard for you personally, Prince Robert. I am to offer you one more task and to issue an invitation.'

'A task? And an invitation. Which will I enjoy the most, dear ambassador?'

'If you enjoy the first you might enjoy the other even more.'

'Ho-ho! Tell me about the task so that I might judge the value of the invitation.'

'It concerns the port of Laodicea... and Bohemund.'

He left that hanging, hoping, no doubt, that I would fill the space for him.

'Ah! You want him out? No doubt you want me to persuade him?'

'A small matter that perhaps you could attend to along your way, Prince Robert.'

'Then there will be a price, dear Panteleimon. We are short of ships; I had hoped to send some of my people off to Cyprus and on to Italy. If we give you Laodicea, can you take them to Brindisi?'

'Most assuredly. I will arrange it personally, my lord.'

'Good. The invitation?'

'My lord, it would give the emperor great pleasure to receive you in Constantinople and to offer you his personal tribute over your tremendous achievements in the name of Christendom. In his view no one has done more.'

This was an invitation I could not turn down. A chance to meet once more, this time to question Alexios, to hear what reasons he would offer for his desultory attachment to supporting our venture and let him speak for himself.

'Very well. Please convey my thanks to Emperor Alexios, and tell him it would be my pleasure to accept. I look forward to it, thank you.'

'My lord, is there anything that I can do for you?'

'Yes, we will furnish you with a list of supplies, if you will oblige?'

'My pleasure.'

'Then ships, if you please, to take most of my people over to Italy when we are done at Laodicea. They will divest themselves of all unnecessary baggage and I expect them to be provided with new horses over the sea to ease their journey home.'

'It shall be done, Prince Robert; new mounts will be made available over the water as required. Anything else?'

'Not at the moment, I'll let you know if I think of anything. Now, consider Laodicea the emperor's.'

The Greek was happier now than when we met, and sent off messages to Constantinople and Cyprus on my behalf. Being victorious was developing some quite welcome attention, I thought. Raymond scowled and said naught; I doubted that ships were in his mind.

We continued to Jebeleh, a place some fourteen miles south of Laodicea, and sent envoys ahead to determine the situation.

Within a day I received a clandestine deputation of citizens from Laodicea, and held a council with Panteleimon and Raymond. Raymond then revealed his intentions; he was not going to return to his homeland and was determined to carve out some new dominion for himself. He offered to garrison Laodicea, 'on behalf of the emperor.' An offer which the Laodiceans accepted and Panteleimon could hardly argue against.

We drafted an offer to Bohemund, which was basically, 'leave peaceably.' He accepted the offer and retreated to Antioch.

I did not meet him again, but he was another whom I did not wish to. I had lost too many true friends; Aethilheard, young Philip, those of my soldiers who we would not bring back, to concern myself with those who had proved false. And Bohemund was on the latter list.

I asked Panteleimon about this.

'Are you happy to leave Bohemund in Antioch?'

The diplomat replied cautiously, 'For the moment only. When the time is right he will be asked to move on.'

'Alexios is determined to regain the city then?'

He said naught, but his eyes revealed that the tenure of Antioch by Bohemund would be at the emperor's discretion.

Raymond, however, spoke openly and revealed his feelings.

'It should have been my domain to rule, on behalf of the emperor. I have assured Panteleimon that it will become so when the time is right.'

I stared at the ageing count, certain that the politics of Asia Minor no longer held any interest for me. *The old bugger; he has had this in mind since the day we left the Antioch all those months ago: none of this is what I came here to do.*

'Well then,' I said, 'I hope that your plan goes according to your wishes. I am leaving as soon as we enter the port.' Turning away from Raymond I asked Panteleimon, 'What ships have we at our disposal?'

We marched into Laodicea and were received with great celebration by the citizens. Raymond assumed his duties as the governor and Panteleimon was pleased to welcome Rob and me on board the finest Byzantine ship for the voyage to Constantinople.

I took a mesnie of twenty with me, leaving everyone else to be herded onto other vessels bound for Cyprus, then on to Italy, grateful for not having to walk back home from here.

I knew that there were many others, pilgrims, who had survived the perilous journey but would receive no assistance, and who set off back the way they came, on foot. They were likely to get home in the condition that they set off; penniless. Any wealth that they'd accumulated during their great adventure disappeared as water in the desert, on expenses such as hostelries, food, travelling tithes and taxes and simple robberies: I suspected that very few would find that eternal life was won at a profit.

Leaving harbour, the ship turned towards Constantinople. Fame I had, but like the penniless pilgrims, I had not fortune either and thoughts turned to home. Tegwin, my children. If Sibyl was still waiting for me, how would Tegwin view it? What if I could not pay my brother, King William Rufus, the surety I owed him for Normandy? It seemed that as the troubles of Palestine sank beneath the horizon behind, the troubles of Normandy were fast rising above the one ahead.

I slept the sleep of weariness the first night. The motion of the ship proved no barrier to the arms of Morpheus, and the lack of sand and soldiers seemed to have calmed my mind, at least until I awakened the following day.

Being attended by Oslac as if it were normal circumstances, I took the food he offered on to the open deck and breathed in the clean air, the first air unsullied by blood that I'd inhaled for the last three years, it seemed. I went forward to meet the oncoming sea and stood at the prow of the ship, listening to the rhythm of the oars. I suddenly felt tired again, the relief of last night's slumber gone in an instant. I was exhausted and overcome with guilt at having nothing to do.

Slowly I pulled my mail coat over my head and cast it into the ocean, then the leather gambon followed it and I stood near naked, gazing into the cleansing sea as it parted before our bows. Soon I was mesmerised and became dizzy, collapsing onto the deck. I had only the faintest memory of voices, Ragenaus, Payne, still there, around me as I was carried back to a bunk and placed gently into it... and drifted off.

I had but fitful rest on the thousand-mile voyage. During the day I worried about Sibyl. When first I saw my reflection in a Spanish mirror placed in my tiny cabin, it was difficult to reconcile the image reflected with my own expectations. The face and head were of a stranger; bronzed, except where he had shaved and his skin was a shade lighter. The sharp blue eyes stared out from lean and cruel cheeks – sparse of fat, but they matched the body, which carried only muscle.

I tilted the glass to survey that hardened torso. Below a patch of dark skin at my throat the skin was white, in stark contrast to my head and I wondered, *God! How shall she love a sight such as this? The head of an eagle and the body of a corpse – wait! Did not Sassie find it amusing? What if Sibyl finds me funny because I am... an old man. Made so by three years of war – and scarred.* I looked down at my leg, which added to the wreckage. *Not amusing any more, not attractive any more. She is only nineteen, what would she want with this decrepit old vessel?*

I sighed and spoke out loud, 'Well, it's all I've got, she can take it or leave it. I trust that she will be honest.'

Oslac poked his head around the curtain.

'You said something, my lord?'

'Aye, son, I did. Do not get too attached to the idea of a marriage feast... yet! We have signed no documents, made no promises.'

'Oh!' My young knight was disappointed. A squire no longer, as with all of those who came along with me from Rouen, he had aged, grown up, got harder, but with no youngsters to take to my side as squires, when I had knighted him he asked to stay, which was pleasing. Now I had disappointed him. He had been looking forward to a good wedding, and to seeing Sibyl. Told of her beauty by others no doubt, he knew that she'd be a feast for the eyes.

'I pray that you will not be deprived of that pleasure, Oslac,' I said, reading his thoughts.

He said nothing, but I expected that he'd have some gossip to share when he left me.

The nights brought no rest from doubt; instead, visions intruded into my sleep. Now the movement of the ship was disturbing but even more so were the disturbances in my head. Unsettling visions: heads with staring eyes floated in a dark red sky where vultures circled and rotting, fly-blown flesh floated into view then disappeared into flames. Dreams that had no purpose but confusion, where the body of an infant was impaled by a crucifix and where a screaming woman was transfixed by a lance thrust deep into her precious part; skeletons that laughed and vomited blood from toothy grins. Dreams that drifted in and out of my head, they rose to the surface and sunk back into the depths of my being with the dawn.

Many were the restless nights, the cries and the thrashing about in my bunk, which I, a soldier of Christ, suffered during the two-week voyage back to sanity. I was not alone in this as the insanities of the past three years worked themselves out of the minds of my men. I met, or rather bumped into Payne one night out on the open deck; he was hanging over the side, feeding the fishes with the contents of his stomach.

'Sorry,' I said, 'it is dizzying up here at times. Are you not well, Payne?' I asked when I recognised him.

'No, my lord, down below there are dark things in my mind. I prefer it up here, but my innards rebel.'

'Yes, I find it so.'

We stood in silence watching the wonders of the earth. The motion of the ship was not so bad, once the mind had steadied, and I was fascinated by the sights around me; there were many more at sea than most folk knew about. The prow cast aside the waters and it teemed with turbulence, forming itself into a trail which disappeared behind us, then, when the oars dipped into the waves, sparkles of light appeared and then faded as I watched. No one could explain this, and to lift my eyes above the sea was to see the heavens alive with sparkly lights, as if mirroring those of the waters beneath them. There were many things at sea without explanation. God's plan, too, was without explanation, I thought on nights such as this.

Payne was speaking to me. 'Is it true, lord?'

'What?' I responded, ignorant of his question.

'That the emperor, my lord, is pleased with our endeavours.'

'I believe so. This ship is quite a clue as to his regard towards us, is it not?'

'Then why are there no other princes of the north aboard, my lord?' I turned, Ragenaus too was sleepless.

'You must have chosen the right lord to serve, scurvy Saxon.'

Payne and Ragenaus, ever jesting with each other. I knew that they would die for each other; no finer friendship had I witnessed these past three years.

'True, Norman lout, so why did he pick you?'

'A family matter,' was Payne's response.

'Will your wedding be a family matter, my lord?' Payne turned his attention to me.

'Wedding? If there be a wedding, it will be a family affair; most weddings are, after the politics of it are agreed.'

'What politics would there be so far away from Normandy, my lord? Surely you can marry just for love? What else is involved?'

'Payne, dear Payne, you lack imaginings in this matter. Believe me, if I wed in Italy the waves of it will be felt in Normandy...and England, long before any wine is drunk.'

There was a commotion behind me and Oslac rushed to the rail to feed the fishes: doing very well tonight were the inhabitants of the deep.

'I'm sorry, my lord, I hadn't realised you'd risen from your bed. Should I bring you some breakfast?'

'Calm yourself, Oslac, tis only the middle of the night. We have come up to enjoy the night-time air, have we not, Ragenaus?'

I turned to see the Saxon now hanging over the rail. At least the rowers found it amusing; the conquerors of Islam feeding the fish: what a blemish on our fearsome reputation.

The welcome back to Constantinople was impressive. Alexios had made it known that my contribution to the success of the crusade was of the highest merit, and so the city turned out to provide the very best of celebrations in my honour.

The sight of the city, with the looming bulk of the Hagia Sofia dominating the skyline and the flags and banners waving from the shore spurred me and I suddenly cheered up, chattering like a child and catching the excitement of all on board; perhaps I was my former self once more.

The ship came into the imperial harbour at the side of the emperor's Boukoleon Palace and I stood proudly on the deck. Everything I wore was new, save my sword, it had almost been hurled overboard with the rest of my arms but, not been to hand at the time, was saved from a watery grave. The new clothing had been waiting for me when we boarded. The emperor had gone to much trouble to provide cloth of the best, but in the Norman style; craftsmen had copied mail coats for me and my men, and we shone in the bright sunlight – it was as if God himself was beaming down his approval.

Again the city walls were overwhelming. When first approached by land they had been impressive, but here, with the sparkling sea lapping at their feet, they towered over us, the battlements alive with watching soldiers and waving citizens.

Flanders remarked, 'I would not like to lay siege to this place, Robert. Tis beyond imagining.'

'I do not want to lay siege to a sandcastle, dear Rob, and that is well within my imagining.'

I spotted Taticius; he was at the centre of a guard drawn up on the steps leading from the waterside. A new silver nose reflected the sun's rays.

He strode up the ornate bridge laid between ship and shore once our vessel had been secured to the steps.

'Welcome, Prince Robert,' he beamed as he held out his hand. 'His imperial majesty, Emperor Alexios awaits you in the Church of the Holy Wisdom. There will be a triumph, in the old style, and a service of thanksgiving to celebrate your great achievements.'

Rob nudged me. 'I didn't get up there on my last visit, Robert. We seem to be more welcome this time. And a triumph? I thought that was reserved for returning generals.' He gestured towards the crest of the hill. The Hagia Sophia had been visible for miles across the sea as we approached the city, but now the dome of this remarkable structure was hidden behind the buildings of the waterside palace.

'No, dear cousin, but last time we were a doubtful asset; this time the emperor knows who his true friends are. And a triumph is a grand procession for returning victors, Rob, and that's us.'

'Aye, Robert, and Bohemund is not one of them.' I nodded. A sad disappointment the giant had turned out to be – but was he any worse than the other graspers? I thought not.

Passing through the grand watergate we were invited to mount finely caparisoned horses.

'We're riding, Taticius?' I called to the Greek. 'We walked through the gardens last time.'

He came close to me and said quietly, if nasally, 'This time, lord, the emperor knows your worth.' He hesitated and I gestured for him to continue. 'I should make you aware, my lord, that the emperor is not in the best of health at present, you may find him... altered, since you met him last.'

'Thank you, Taticius, for that confidence; I shall be aware of it. Now, pray tell me, good general, why are these horses wearing boots?'

Rob coughed and sniggered a little. 'I was going to ask about that, Robert. Are these what imperial horses wear, Taticius?'

The general grinned. 'Not normally, Count Flanders, but we are going to a celebration at the Hagia Sophia, and the way is steep from here. The horses are wearing Roman hippo-sandals to help them make their way on the cobbles.'

340

'Oh!' commented my cousin. 'So we can add this oddity to the tales we'll have to tell when we get back home.'

'Tales, Rob? I doubt if half the tales we have to tell when we return will be believed; and hippo-sandals will not be the most bizarre, I am sure.'

We came out of the palace grounds through a wall gate, higher up the hill than the watergate, to be greeted by thousands of cheering folk. As foretold, the way wound steeply up the hill towards the Hippodrome. By the time we reached the walls of the ancient Roman building the throngs had grown thicker and louder until we entered a passageway between imperial guards holding back the joyous spectators.

As we approached the great church door, Taticius leaned closer, and making himself heard above the tumult, told me what would happen.

'After the service of thanksgiving, Prince Robert,' he said, 'there will be a private reception in the palace. When you enter the cathedral, walk to the front and the emperor will greet you, but there will be no public conversations; do you understand, my lord?'

'I understand perfectly, good Taticius. I have some things of a privy nature which I wish only the emperor to hear.'

He gazed at me with a grin. 'I'm certain that what you have to say, Prince Robert, will not be far removed from what I have said already.'

Hm! I think that I have a friend at court, if I am not mistaken.

Truth to tell, the occasion had more glory about it than the realities of the bloody plains that we had left behind, as if the one had nothing to do with the other. But now the moment took over and we were swept along in a fever of mindless joy to match that which sent us off to Palestine in the first instance.

I did feel a bit special, dressed for the part of the returning hero, glorious in survival and forgetful of the dead. Attired in shiny metals, we were, but with surcoats of white, bearing the red cross of Jesu. Before us, priests in fine robes bearing crucifixes waited while we dismounted and formed into an orderly column. I thought to unsheathe my sword, the one I had won the Egyptian orb with, and lifted it aloft by the blade – as a symbol of the cross of the Lord – and the noisy acclaim reached new heights.

Taticius, between Rob and I, led us towards the towering doors.

Loudly he told us, 'These are the imperial gates. You are honoured to enter through them, my lords, but you should leave your arms at the door.'

I turned to Payne and Ragenaus, holding my tattered emblems.

'Give your lances and swords to Oslac, he will remain here.'

The squire was downcast until Taticius intervened.

'Prince Robert, was this young warrior with you at Jerusalem?' I nodded. 'Then he should accompany you within.'

He snapped his fingers and the weapons were taken from Oslac and the smile returned to his face.

'They will be held safe for you,' said the general kindly. The lad was obviously overawed; I suspected it was only the beginning of that condition.

Passing through these exclusive gates we saw before us a second entrance into the church proper. Above the door was a mosaic of striking richness and texture, and at our feet a threshold of shining marble: such richness. Taticius saw me looking on high.

'That is Christ the Redeemer, Prince Robert, and the figure kneeling beside him is symbolic of the emperor.' He no longer needed to shout now we were inside the first door, the tumult from without had been silenced to our ears. I looked through the inner door. Inside it was thick with smoke – incense from the choking thuribles – and there seemed to be an army of acolytes, all busy trying to outdo each other in the production of fumes. Passing through the door the enormity of the place was overwhelming, and it was full to overflowing with a congregation; of the great and good, I supposed. And candles, candles everywhere; in hands, in sconces dangling from the roof in huge frames, a roof so high as to be out of sight. Halfway up the walls I could just make out myriad heads peering over the galleries; they were at least the height of twenty men above me. And it was hot.

342

'Jesu, Robert,' uttered Rob in amazement, 'if this be heaven, how hot is hell?'

'I hope not to find out, dear Rob,' I responded as we progressed up an alley between priests and lords towards a great throne.

'Stand here, Prince Robert, if you please,' instructed my guide. I stopped in the middle and heard my followers being guided to the sides to sit in the front row of the congregation. It gave me time to take a good look at the figure sitting in splendour on the imperial throne of Byzantium.

He seemed to favour gold, did Alexios Komnenus. From hat to shoes, all was gold, a contrast set against his black, curly beard and his dark eyes examining me from beneath black brows. He raised an imperious hand and Taticius whispered, 'Go now, Prince Robert, approach.'

I went forth. Fully twenty paces I needed to reach the bottom of the dais upon which was the throne of the Christian Emperor of the East.

He stood up and seemed to tower over me before he came down the steps towards me, smiling, and holding out a hand. I managed a stiff little bow. He spoke in Greek, and I would have struggled, but I heard the reassuring tones of Taticius behind me.

'The emperor bids you and your companions welcome, Prince Robert. He says that he finds it difficult to find the words to express his admiration for the exploits of you and your men during the long, difficult, and successful campaign now behind you.'

'Tell the emperor that he is most gracious, and he can be assured of our loyalty in this matter. We would welcome the opportunity to relate to his imperial majesty the full tale of our endeavours.'

Alexios watched my face as the message was conveyed to him. I was certain that he'd understood it perfectly the first time, but diplomacy has its ways, so I waited for the response.

The voice of Taticius filled my ear from behind as he relayed the emperor's answer.

'He agrees, Prince Robert. As soon as he can escape from all of this theatre, you will find him at leisure in surroundings more suitable for sensible conversation.'

'I am grateful, imperial majesty.'

Taticius took me by the elbow and we found our places next to my men in the front of the congregation. Then the priests, bishops, patriarchs and the metropolitan, the senior churchman of Constantinople, took over our world and we were treated to seemingly endless liturgic rites and singing until I could hardly breathe in the fog-closeted world of the great church. Thankful to escape, eventually we were returned to the noise of the multitude as we made our ear-deafening way back down the incline to the welcome gate of the imperial palace.

It was well into the evening when we found ourselves safely within the Boukoleon Palace walls, and within the confines of a grand villa set aside for guests.

'How very peaceful,' said Rob, 'after all that smoke and noise.'

'I have never seen gardens like these,' ventured Ragenaus. 'Are they usual in the East?'

We gazed at the sight, and took in the aromas of the plants. They were in raised beds, hanging in baskets from overhead trellises, and overflowing from huge pots placed all around on the ground, and there were trees of strange appearance, some with oddly shaped fruits suspended from their trimmed branches.

'Only in the palaces of an emperor,' I informed him, 'so make the most of it while we're here. I doubt these flowers would grow in the chill of Normandy. And that was holy smoke, Rob; be blessed.'

'Blessed! My lungs need air, not blessed suffocation.'

Soon an officer came with an escort to take me to Alexios. I motioned for Rob, Ragenaus and Payne to stay close to me, and we set off through the palace gardens to see the emperor, away from the high ceremonial that had surrounded him today.

In the quiet of a reception chamber we found a feast laid out: wine, sweetmeats and fruit, with other delicacies that had long been denied us. It seemed almost an excess for we lean warriors.

'Don't eat too much,' I cautioned, 'it will be rich pickings for a tight stomach; just take some time.'

They were hard pressed to obey, but being disciplined kept to my advice while we waited for Alexios.

Shortly there was a wafting of fine silks as the first of Alexios' advisors came into the chamber – closely followed by the emperor himself.

'Robert of Normandy, and Robert of Flanders, how nice to greet you away from all that flummery.'

Now, in privy, he needed no interpreter, and his honesty pleased me.

'I'm pleased to get out of all those robes; they're so heavy in this heat. Now, Robert.' He took my hands in his, and looking me straight in the eye, said, 'If we can be straight and honest it will save some time, do you agree?'

I nodded, although I was surprised at his opening. I had been expecting some convoluted diplomatic exchanges before ever I got near to saying my piece. I was also reminded of Taticius' warning; out of his robes, hat, gold and other decorations, the man did appear unwell; I wondered for how long, and if, this illness had affected his behaviours and judgement during the past three years. It was worth bearing in mind, I thought before replying.

'Certainly, majesty, I prefer honest dealings.'

Rob agreed. 'We have had enough of negotiating with clouds this past year; you can be straight with us, majesty.'

'Good! That's the way. Robert, I need to know the truth about the situation in Jerusalem. My agents tell me that Godfrey has little to hold the city with... pray give me your assessment.'

I thought that I would clarify answers to some questions of my own before I answered this seemingly friendly potentate.

'Do you understand that we're aware you were in contact with the Egyptians?'

'Yes, I do. But are you are aware that I was trying to negotiate access to the holy city, without that siege and bloody capture?'

I looked at Rob – this was new, we had not known that before.

'No! But your diplomats did not make that clear,' I said defiantly.

'Sometimes it is better if they only know what I want them to know. They can be confined and tortured, and sometimes there is more than one diplomat in the field. I needed to test Cairo, to see how attached they were to the Seljuks. But the attack by the Egyptian Fatimids upon the fleet at Jaffa warned me that they had, or have, their own agenda.'

'I see.' I watched him carefully, but behind his sad eyes I could detect no duplicity. 'So you did not brief them about our numbers... or dispositions.'

Alexios smiled in his beard, and his eyes crinkled.

'Robert!' he chided. 'To confirm what they already knew by counting you across the desert is no great transfer of knowledge... but it is a useful way of appearing helpful. I told them nothing of your dispositions, because I knew nothing, and apparently neither did al-Afdal: I have given nothing of use to the Fatimids, nor could I. Think about it.'

Rob nodded.

'It's true, you knew nothing more than spies in the camp or eyes in the desert could have known, and as for tactics... only Robert knows those, and he only tells us at the last moment.'

'That's not quite true,' I bridled. 'I can only know what to do when *I* know what the enemy has in mind.'

Alexios held out a hand saying, 'Diplomacy, my friends, has rules of its own, and only rarely does the appearance resemble the truth that lies beneath.' He looked at me closely before he spoke again, carefully weighing his words it seemed. 'I know that you considered Bohemund a friend, but I suggest, if I may, that what passed between the Egyptians and your Norman friend outside Antioch had more to do with them occupying Jerusalem before you got there than anything I did.'

'You think he made some kind of accord with them?'

'It is possible that he agreed to leave the western Mediterranean to them while he controlled the east from Antioch.

Remember his father, Robert Guiscard, invaded my lands long before now. Bohemund is still there, is he not?'

'He is,' I confirmed, 'and it is long past when I considered him a friend, imperial majesty.'

'Then he's had the best of us, Prince Robert: he has fooled us all.'

Rob was more upset at the notion of being used by Bohemund than was I, but then that particular worm had been ousted from my head a long time ago.

Alexios, seeing this, held out a hand to each of us and we took it without hesitation. Thus we made a friendship possible – at least until the next diplomatic exigency came along.

'Now,' said Alexios, 'tell me more about Antioch.'

We gave Alexios our considered view about the actions, both political and military, before and after the siege of Antioch, although Alexios had been receiving detailed contemporary reports and was more interested in analysing the present situation rather than the past.

It was after a prolonged discussion that Rob finally realised something and burst out with the pithy comment, 'It seems that we left Antioch, and then returned to find the situation had not altered. Bohemund sits inside and Raymond waits impatiently outside the gate: it's as if the journey to Jerusalem was just an interlude.'

'It was a costly interlude,' I put in.

'It still is,' responded Alexios, 'Raymond does not come cheap.'

I looked at Alexios.

'You're paying Raymond?'

'Well, yes. If I want the city returned to my fold, it will cost me somehow.'

'Raymond is not a cheap whore,' muttered Rob, 'but no doubt you'll get your money back one day. Bohemund cannot hide inside forever.'

'No,' replied the emperor, 'but it suits me to have a Christian residing in the place if it keeps the Seljuks out. Prince or whore, it serves the same purpose.'

I laughed at that.

'Is pragmatism a quality required of emperors?'

Alexios didn't seem upset by the remark, recognising the truth in it.

'Emperors have a responsibility to care for their empires. I occasionally have princes to entertain, and whatever the appearance of it, I have to negotiate with that in mind.'

'I understand, majesty. I had not meant it against yourself, if anything I meant it against me. I like not the means and methods of governing, it all confuses me.'

'I recognise that, but we are born into what we are. I can envy the shipwrights and the potters the comfort of their lives.'

It was Rob's turn to laugh.

'Hah! They might envy yours, majesty, except for one thing.'

'Careful, majesty, Flanders is about to speak wisely,' I cautioned with a wry grin.

'Well,' said Rob, 'I meant that carpenters and masons live in this fabulous palace, but it matters not to them whose head wears the crown; they will go on living here.'

It was Alexios' turn to laugh.

'Except for one thing, Robert of Flanders. If the Turks find their way in here the carpenter might find his head on a spike... next to mine.'

Alexios turned aside the matter of politics for a moment.

'I wondered if I might ask you something. Prince Robert, would you consider entering my service? Your great-grandfather did. And your father too, Count Robert.' This remark was addressed to Rob, whose father had indeed served for a while when returning from a Jerusalem pilgrimage some years earlier.

'Your status would be of the highest, and your family's. Perhaps they would like to join the masons and carpenters in this grand palace?'

Rob looked at me and we shook our heads in unison. He responded for both of us.

'That is indeed an honour, imperial majesty; it means a lot to be thought of so highly. But we came here for a purpose, and it is now fulfilled. We had not thought of gain; not riches, nor land, and my cousin has a marriage in mind.'

I confirmed it. 'No, imperial majesty, for one thing I've gained beyond the purpose of this venture is the certainty that I miss my family and my land. They have been neglected too long and my earnest wish is to return to them as soon as possible.'

'I understand, my lords, I understand. There is however one other thing that you can do for me.' He waved his arm and officials entered with two small chests. Placing his hands upon them, Alexios said, 'In here is a small token of our appreciation. You have been the most loyal to the cause of myself and Christendom, and for that you deserve a reward. Prince Robert, if you will permit, I wish to offer you a wedding gift. And you, Robert of Flanders, a holy relic; you should also find enough money in there to build a church to house it. Accept these now, and later do me the honour of a public ceremony in which I shall make a presentation, and pay tribute to your wondrous work... what do you say?'

We accepted with grace. Although I had found the public acclaim somewhat oppressive and didn't want much more of it, I was happy to go along with Alexios' need for a hero, or heroes.

There was time to fill. I was anxious to reopen relations with Sibyl, if she was still willing, but it was a matter of etiquette that we stayed and enjoyed the impending ceremony. Meantime my young knights were beginning to wonder exactly what limits, if any, would be placed upon the emperor's hospitality.

As it happened there weren't many and the happy lads wandered about the palace each day with a vacant grin on their faces – in between feasts and other public engagements. They gained weight, and always retired early each night to enjoy their well-earned rest – but hardly slept a wink.

There had been much competition in the imperial household to bed the young men and two of these contrived encounters resulted in permanent unions. One of my knights and one of Flanders' enamoured asked permission to leave service and join the emperor's staff, which we were pleased to give consent to:

it would do no harm to have a presence in Constantinople; it might prove useful at some point in the future.

The small chests proved to be very large in value and were full of silver coins, but they were diminished by a further gift of gold and silver ornaments that we received at the awaited ceremony. It was a very formal affair which took place in that wonderful room overlooking the Bosporus. I think that the emperor knew of my aversion to pomp and the guests were limited to a few of his key officials and carefully chosen foreign diplomats. Alexios was kind enough to mention that the gifts 'might please a lady,' so I assumed that much of the gift was to honour the, as yet, unarranged wedding; I already knew that I had sufficient in coin to enable me to reclaim my duchy from my brother, William Rufus.

With the approach of November we were advised to make our departure if we wished to proceed by sea to Italy. So, with memories and treasure chests full, we left behind that glorious city and set sail for Brindisi, from whence I had departed at Easter 1097, some two and a half years earlier. The journey was made safer by a passage up the Saronic Gulf, to cross the isthmus over to the sea of Corinth, thus avoiding the difficult Peloponnesian peninsular navigation: we arrived in Brindisi in the second week of November with the sea already turning into the dull and grey of approaching winter.

There had been moments of reflection along the way. Rob had begun to fret about things at home, about his wife, Clementia of Burgundy, and their son, Baldwin, who would be six years old by now.

I was reviving doubts about my forthcoming marriage – or rather courtship: there was no guarantee of a marriage.

'Do you think I'm mad, Rob?' I asked as we gazed at the grey Ionian sea. Summer was over, our campaign was over, the world had become an anti-climax, and we were feeling dispirited.

'No more a madman than any of us, dear cousin,' he replied. 'Why do you ask?'

'I wonder how much has changed since we left Brindisi, or rather how much have *we* changed. Will Sibyl recognise me?'

'I doubt it, but that is not the worry, whether she *likes* you is the concern now.'

We concentrated on the grey waves rolling away behind the stern for a while, and then Rob said, 'Why a marriage, Robert? Are you so smitten? What about Tegwin?'

'Tegwin is safe, her position is safe; she is the mother of the first prince of all Wales and the future earl of Northumbria. William cares for her and the boys, I've had letters telling me so through Matilda, but I cannot marry her and she understands that. She is of the North Welsh in a fractured country. A son of mine can help to unite Wales and bring it together through a good marriage. The Norman–Welsh dynasty my father desired.'

'Marriage to whom?'

'Someone suitable from the southern kingdom. My father had a member of the Tewdwr family in mind, but the king, Rhys, was killed and I know not the current situation there.'

'So what will a marriage to Sibyl do if Wales is to come into England's domain through Tegwin's womb?'

'Think on it, Rob, think on it. My marriage will turn Sibyl into a duchess, who would be the queen-in-waiting. Rufus will never produce a child, and we're agreed that I am the heir to the crown. And if I die before William, a son of mine through a suitable marriage will be heir to England's crown.'

'Ah, dear cousin, how simple. It is good to be back in the friendly uncomplicated world of Norman politics.'

'Yes, it puts into perspective the pleasant world of crusading does it not?'

'Not!'

It seemed that the grey skies and the grey seas presaged the familiar grey world of northern Europe and the political murk that we were used to inhabiting: it cheered us not a jot.

Brindisi, always on the alert for any aggression from the sea, would have seen our sails appear on the horizon, and when we neared then my banners, replaced in Constantinople, would have been seen flying from the masts. By the time we were alongside the jetty the place was descended upon by those anxious to see for themselves the heroes of Jerusalem. It wasn't Constantinople, but it was excitement enough for the locals, and we homebound travellers.

Some of my followers, who had already crossed directly from Cyprus but not moved on, were among those risking a wetting by crowding onto the narrow wooden walkway. Soon a path was cleared and we were able to make our way to the end, where firm earth and a gathering of officials were waiting for us. Welcomes made, boring speeches listened to, and new horses mounted, soon a grand procession was formed and I followed an escort through the town.

Calling across to Flanders, I shouted, 'This is better; a proper horse under my arse, proper rain and proper cold... the desert heat seems a long way behind us.'

'Aye, cousin. Tis good to feel solid earth beneath the solid feet of a good horse; it makes one feel nearer to home, I think.'

The following morning we were treated to a breakfast feast. The food on this side of the Mediterranean was already proving beyond our expectations, and we had missed early prayers, but the clergy turned up in droves to bless us and our food before ever we got our teeth into it.

I had my closest with me on one table; Rob, Ragenaus, Payne, and young Oslac. I intended that they should stay with me and all the others, hovering and reluctant to go back home, would be given a purse, put on their horses and despatched northwards. This next episode of my life was going to be as privy as I could make it. Success or failure, it was not going to be a public event.

'Do you think, Saxon,' joked Payne, 'that you will keep your food inside you today?'

'One sight of it is enough, Norman glutton. Have you had enough of life at sea?'

'Sea and sand, Ragi, enough for a lifetime.' Payne dropped his voice to a whisper. 'Do you see those two over there?' He pointed at two giggling girls.

'I have. Do you think that they would?'

'They have that appearance. Will you ask, or should I?'

'You ask Prince Robert, I shall commence negotiations.'

'I heard, you unquiet hounds, go on, get on with it. I shall wait till midday; if you're not here you can find your own way up to Conversano.'

That was the fastest exit I'd witnessed for a long time, as the panting dogs went off to try their luck.

The fifty miles up the coast were interrupted by a succession of welcomes, with each town or village turning out to cheer the saviours of the Saviour's city. Payne and Ragenaus caught up at the second village. They were quiet, but smiled a lot. Oslac refused to talk to them for a few hours until curiosity overcame him, then I heard some intense whispering, accompanied by oohs and ahhs, as the lad was given a blow-by-blow account of Italian hospitality.

Crucifixes were held high outside the churches and people fell to their knees in prayer and thanksgiving. Some called us *miracle-bringers,* and asked for assistance with their personal problems.

'They think that we are miracle-workers, Robert,' said Rob, hearing the pleas.

'Well, it's not me,' said I, 'it must be those bones that you brought from Constantinople.'

'How do they know I've got bones?'

'It must be the way you're sitting on your horse.'

'What?' Rob's long-standing and biggest failure had always been his lack of ready humour.

We arrived at Conversano in the dark, at the end of the second tedious day, along streets still lined with crowds and lit by rushes, and then with great relief we disappeared from public view into the peace of Goffredo's palace.

'That was a long day,' said Rob as he dismounted.

'True. I don't think I could manage another one of those feasts tonight, could you?'

'Not me, I want to go to bed, especially one that does not rise and fall all night.'

I smiled at that remark. Ships are fine for getting about but their passage is not always an even one, but I'd suddenly been reminded of my favourite sort of bed.

'Yes, cousin, and floor that keeps still when you piss,' I quipped.

'A seaman's life is not for me.'

There was a call from the shadows as Count Goffredo came into view.

'Prince Robert, welcome back, thank God you are safe.'

He grasped me around the shoulders and hugged me. I had been a bit uncertain up till then, but this was the welcome of a man who was still expecting me to marry his daughter, and Rob might have gained the same idea as he watched.

I turned to him and said to Goffredo, 'This is my cousin, Robert of Flanders, a great warrior.'

'Indeed, I have heard of your exploits, all of Christendom has heard of the two Roberts now.' He came close to me and spoke gently. 'I overheard your remarks about your journey today, and we will not think it amiss if you go straight to your chambers and rest, then we can hear your stories in the morning.'

'That is most civilised of you, Count Goffredo, I think that we will take up the offer... can we be assured that our people will be taken care of?'

'You may rest assured, Prince Robert; all will be taken care of on your behalf.'

'Thank you, Count Goffredo, and the Lady Sibyl?'

'She has concerns for you; she values you highly and wishes to meet when you are rested.'

'Oh! She still wishes to see me?'

'Above all, Prince Robert, above all. She has not rested since you left, her prayers were well rewarded, and she is now praying in gratitude for your return.'

'So I might speak to her again?'

'She would die if you did not. There is only one prince for my daughter; she has set her mind on it.'

'I am much cheered. You do not think my appearance will put her off, Count Goffredo?'

'Your appearance will not keep her *off,* my prince. Your appearance matches your reputation; she could not feel safer in any man's embrace.'

'Oh!' This was all I could manage, but my heart leapt at the word *embrace;* now, there was a word to go to bed on – but then I thought of something.

'How does she know what my appearance is, good Count?'

He smiled. 'She thought to find out for herself, Robert. She was at the quayside when you landed, so is well aware of your appearance.'

'I see. Where is she now?'

'In her chambers; she needed to ride hard to get here before you.'

'This is a determined creature that you have raised, Count Goffredo.'

'Indeed, Prince Robert, and one that needs a gentle bridle, if I may say so.'

He was grinning widely now and I joined him, feeling much, much better. I was looking forward to renewing my acquaintance with this young woman.

'I have some experience in the matter of gentle bridles, Goffredo.'

'I am aware of that, Prince Robert. Go now, and may God bring you peace. You deserve it above all others.'

I slept but fitfully until the early hours of the morning when exhaustion overcame my turbulent mind; then I slept deeply until well past midday, the gloomy skies ensuring that my rest was not prematurely disturbed – and I missed Prime.

When I stirred, Oslac came into the chamber. Although now a knight he was still performing the duties of a squire, as the army had run out of young men to train. He bade me a 'good morning, my lord'.

'Mornin', Oslac; is it Prime already?'

'Err, I'm afraid you've missed today's Prime, my lord... and today's Sext.'

It took a minute to penetrate my brain that it was already past midday.

'Bollocks!'

'Yes my lord. The servants have a bath waiting for you.'

'Do I smell?'

'Yes, and the lady Sibyl has been seen about the palace.'

'Shit! Where's the bath, and find me decent clothes to wear, my good knight, I have some courting to do.'

I was not usually one to primp and preen, but I was willing to make an exception on this occasion, and it made a nice change to wear the silken gown over the top of other soft linen and cotton clothes.

That matters had been carefully considered was evident in the embellishments of the clothing, which bore discreet references to the crusade; there was a red crucifix upon the white cloth which now adorned my chest. I felt different; better, as Oslac picked and primped at me.

'You look splendid, my lord. A proper prince,' he added proudly as he pushed me out the chamber and led me off to one of Count Goffredo's opulent reception rooms.

In the darkening afternoon it was already lit by oil lamps and enlivened by a warming fire. There were not many in the room. Goffredo was sitting by the fire in a tall chair, and sitting opposite him was a stately young woman clad in fine silk, her beautiful face and cascading brown hair reflecting the dancing flames. She was impassive and examined me boldly, as I returned the examining gaze.

There was no need for introductions; we already knew each other. The only thing that bothered me – *such uncertainty* – did what she was seeing match that which she'd seen three years ago and, *and*, did she still like the view. For my part I saw that her beauty could be overwhelming, and an explanation as to why nobody had dared to ask for her hand in marriage. She was too much of a good thing – it might be a burden.

Goffredo stood up and came to greet me.

'Prince Robert, you are rested I trust?'

'Indeed, and quite alive now. I hope that I was not rude last night, Count, but I would have made a poor guest.'

'Not at all! Not at all, our concern is your welfare. Now!' he turned towards his daughter, 'you remember the lady Sibyl?'

'Of course,' I replied softly, 'it seems that she has grown more beautiful as I have grown ugly.'

The lady cast her eyes down but a smile played about those glorious lips. Goffredo took me about the shoulders and led me over to a buffet.

'You must be hungry, Prince Robert, let us see if we can tempt you.' He signalled to a servant. 'Pour Prince Robert a goblet of wine.'

The fellow went to do as bidden but was interrupted by a gentle female command from behind me.

'Leave that. You may go now; I'll see to that.'

The servant left, and on some unseen signal all of Sibyl's ladies, except one, left at the same time.

Sibyl left the fireside and crossed to the buffet. She avoided eye contact with me but she knew I was watching her every move, and listening to her every sound; she moved gracefully, her limbs caused a noise like a soft sigh as they moved within the silk encasements of her dress. With delicate movements she poured the wine and came close to me with the goblet clasped tightly in cupped hands.

She was almost within touching distance when at last she lifted her gaze and looked into my eyes.

We were evenly matched for height, and with a level gaze I felt a kick deep inside my stomach. *Olive! Her eyes are olive; I had not remembered, my God she is flawless... her skin.*

'Hallo, Prince Roberto... my lord.'

I did not notice at the time but the *my lord* which came from Sibyl was separated deliberately from the *Roberto.*

It was a message, but it was closely followed by another when she turned to Goffredo and said, 'I think that we shall manage now, Father. Perhaps my prince Roberto would appreciate some calm after the storms he has endured of late.'

Count Goffredo took the hint, and saying that he would return later, left us together in the firelight. She moved very close and the smell of her penetrated my mind, releasing long repressed emotions.

'Well,' she whispered, her breath caressing my nostrils, 'you have taken your time.'

'Ahh! Yes, my lady, not through choice I assure you.'

Sibyl sat down and indicated that I should take her father's chair. We looked at each other and laughed. There was not going to be much jousting, that she had made up her mind was evident; thoughts crackled fit to drown the wood in the brazier: there was going to be a wedding.

Sibyl spoke gently to the girl remaining in the room and she brought a selection of food from the buffet, placed it on small tables at our sides and topped up our wine glasses before sitting discreetly to one side.

'Thank you, Maria,' said Sibyl, graciously.

'My lady,' the girl responded.

She was also a beauty and I thanked her.

'Thank you, Maria.'

'My lord.'

There was a pause while we wondered how to proceed; the flames were useful to gaze into.

My doubts about how I would be received had faded into memory and I felt a burgeoning confidence. I sighed, quite deeply, and Sibyl looked at me closely.

'Is there a problem, my prince?'

I looked at her and grinned.

'No. But that is the problem; I am not used to such contentment.'

'Oh. That is strange.'

I was gradually sinking into the depths of her eyes. She knew that, and made no attempt to disguise her interest in me, boldly we were testing each other.

'We have heard many stories from the Holy Land... if only half are true then you have had a remarkable journey. Everyone speaks of your valour; everyone speaks of your deeds as a bold warrior.'

Her voice was mesmeric. Even without the exotic accent, her words held no discords.

'I expect... Some of the things are not fit for a lady to hear of, I fear.'

'I expect that I will survive.' This was telling me that she was determined to be told – regardless. I frowned, *she really wouldn't want to hear everything*, and then she backed off. 'If you would rather not talk about such things?'

'Perhaps I will find it easier to find some humour to tell you about. Perhaps tell you about some heroes, or places?'

'That would be interesting. I know, tell me about Constantinople.'

'Ah! Now there's a place...'

We talked well into the evening. I told her about one-eyed Raymond, and the metal-nosed eunuch. Sibyl told me about her life at Conversano, and her favourite focus – her horses. She was building up a stud, and was anxious to show it me as soon as possible.

Sometimes we just sat enjoying the silence, watching each other; sometimes a nervous burst of laughter broke into the silence for no reason. Then Goffredo returned and brought some of his household, and local *personages,* to meet me, now known as *the conquering hero.* The room became raucous and the flow of praise became tedious, and I almost wished for the quiet of the battlefield, until I was rescued by the most observant in the hall.

Sibyl gave me a laden glance, lifted her eyebrows, and after paying her respects, left. The room darkened and I immediately felt deprived, but managed to concentrate sufficient to answer questions and tell stories, and not appear rude. But without the lady, the social occasion was winding down and I was pleased when Goffredo, attentive to duty, spotted my eyes glazing over and politely shepherded his other guests out of the room, and then asked me to talk awhile.

Goffredo's man filled up our goblets and we sat down in front of the fire. I was, truth to tell, feeling drowsy by now – as Goffredo could see – so he did not detain me very much longer.

'You had a long conversation with Sibyl, my prince.'

'I did, and we intend to repeat the pleasure. Could you resist calling me *prince* so often, Count Goffredo?'

He laughed and we became a little easier together.

'I could do without the *count*, Robert.'

'Of course. There is something about her, do you not agree, Goffredo? She is a very special woman, very agreeable and easy to get along with.'

'No, she's not,' he responded quickly, and a shadow fell across his face. 'Most men cannot get near her. You are honoured this night, most men struggle to get a *good morning* out of her.'

I wondered if Goffredo had gone too far in his description of his daughter's aloofness.

'Is that true? Have there been no others to interest her in the last three years then?'

'The only balls that have interested Sibyl in the past three years have been the ones dangling at the back of her stallions.'

We both laughed at that, pleased that the evening had gone so well.

'Robert, she has changed much in the past three years, she is now impossibly beautiful, but one thing that hasn't changed is her opinion of you. She liked you from the very first and even if you had returned the most ordinary of men, I believe that she would still have been pleased to see you.'

I had a little moment of panic in my breast, *this thing has a speed of its own, yet I fear to involve her in my affairs.*

'How much does she know about Norman, em, about English affairs?'

'She is well informed. Matilda visits occasionally. Yes, she is well informed.'

Matilda! Still lurking in my background – still my guardian angel. I laughed.

'The Contessa Matilda, my good friend. Is she due here?'

'There's the matter of a new pope, she might be distracted by that.'

'*Might*? There'll be no *might*.'

'Yes, Pope Paschal II will need all the support he can attract in these first few weeks of his tenure, I am sure.'

I was both excited and tired at one and the same time.

'Would you think me rude if I retired, Goffredo?'

'Not at all, I understand. Perhaps a few days here will find you refreshed after your wars?'

'Is that an invitation?'

'If you do not stay awhile, Robert, I am a dead father – believe me.'

'You think that some time spent here would be worthwhile?'

'I am certain of it. She has waited for you. Take the opportunity, Robert, you'll not find a better one.'

'I think I know it. Then I should stay, do some wooing – thank you, Goffredo.'

So stay I did, and spent the time with Sibyl. Sometimes we rode down through fertile fields and olive groves to the coast at Polignano a Mare, where the wild winds blew in from the sea; it made for dramatic visions of my loved one as she rode along the edge of the sandy shoreline, horses splashing in the surf, her clothes blowing wildly as her hair tumbled about her head. I came close to pressing my ardour on more than one occasion, but I feared that it would spoil things, so kept my passion under strict control.

Then we had a discussion, that inevitable discussion, the one that needed to take place before we progressed any further. So it was on one of those wild days, while watching the seas tumble and the birds delight in their flight, that she raised the matter of Tegwin.

The other wild one: still in my thoughts, as if Sibyl knew. I could tell she had something on her mind even before we rode out, and I watched as she wrestled with it, deciding how to begin. I think that I knew what it would be before she uttered a word; but kept quiet until she was ready.

'Roberto, *mio tesoro.*'

Yes, my treasure?'

The mewing of the seabirds and the crashing of the waters on to the rocks gave an unsettling accompaniment to the unsettled expression on her face.

'If we marry –' here I saw the first moment of doubt cross her usually serene features – 'when we marry,' she corrected herself, 'what will happen to your woman, Tegwin?'

I dismounted and beckoned Oslac to take my horse. I offered my hand to Sibyl and without a word she slid off her steed and grasped it. Oslac took her horse and retired with the two to the shelter of the sand dunes. We walked down to the water's edge where I turned and held her by the waist. We were now at the stage when all the curtains had fallen away and our eyes held each other in an open and honest gaze – there was no way forward except honesty.

'These seas remind me of her, she is a wild one... as much as you are not, my treasure; but you are both deep. What do you expect me to do about her, the mother of my sons?'

She loosed her hold and bent down to pick up a pebble, then threw it at a seagull. It nearly hit the soaring creature.

'Oh!' she cried, 'I did not mean that.' And she grasped me once more around the waist. 'I could have killed it, Roberto,' she said into my shoulder.

'I think that I have had enough of killing, my treasure.'

I took a few moments to think, and she gave me time; we were becoming very settled with each other.

Then she said, 'When I am the Duchess of Normandy, I might not think it seemly to my dignity to share my bedchamber with another.'

'No, Sibyl, I can see that. What would you have me do?'

'You are the lord, you tell me.'

I laughed and pulled her close, and then I pushed her to arm's length and smiling said, 'Neatly turned, *mio tesoro*, you will make a fine diplomat.' She grinned openly at me and my stomach thrilled, wanting possession of her.

'Then my decision is that Tegwin shall remain in England until Richard becomes the first Prince of Wales, whereupon she shall become his guardian and advisor in some suitable place. You will be my duchess and rule with me from Rouen. You need never meet her.'

She turned away from me and gazed at the turbulent waters again, thinking. Then I felt her grasp tighten as she came to a decision and held me tight. She turned and fixed me with those commanding olive eyes.

'I want to meet her, Roberto, this woman who shares your love. I will either love her or loathe her, but either way I shall meet her.'

'Oh,' I said weakly, 'if that is your wish.'

'It is.'

The she pulled me close and wrapped her lips around mine, and her tongue became active, and the fabric of my breeches began to stretch.

As the days rolled by, my tormented dreams – those visions of hell – were gradually replaced. Instead came the tortures of frustration, just as disturbing, if not as violent.

Weeks turned into months and even the midwinter gloom went by unnoticed; that is, until the inevitable conversation took place.

Just after Christmas, on 6 January 1100, Epiphany day, we found ourselves suddenly alone in our favourite chamber – everyone else had disappeared for no obvious reason, so we were in our favourite chairs, in front of our favourite fire, with our favourite friend.

'Roberto,' she said gently, 'my thighs are on fire, I think I want you.'

'Sibyl,' I replied, 'my shaft is throbbing fit to burst and my balls are full, I know I want you.'

'Well, what are you going to do about it?' she asked.

'Will you marry me, my lady?' I asked.

'Yes, my lord,' was the answer.

So the matter was settled, and on 18 March 1100, the feast day of St Cyril of Jerusalem, we were married in the newly built Cathedral Church of St Benedict at Conversano.

It was grand, well attended, noisy and smoky, and lots of people said lots of things, mostly lost in the air as far as we were concerned. We were so close to being one with each other that all the efforts of all of those present determined to make an impression on the occasion were lost.

Faces kept coming up and saying things; some I understood, some I only smiled politely at, all I wished would go away and let my bride and I escape into the privacy of our own world.

Then there was the wedding feast, and I am certain that only the very best of wine and food was presented, but the taste was lost on me, and Sibyl only picked at her platter, and neither of us drank much, except a sip at the calls for toasts – of which there many.

Eventually, our smiles became painted on, and Goffredo, being an attentive host, and seeing our distress, stood up to make his giving-away address; not that he had any choice in the matter, the bride had made all the decisions, and who was I to complain.

So, red-faced and overly effusive, the father handed over the well-being of his daughter, now a duchess, and an intriguing chest, presumably a dowry, into the keeping of the bloody-handed foreigner whom they had invited into their world, and amen to that, I thought.

'How soon can we get away, my duchess?' I whispered.

'Very soon, my duke,' she replied and poked me to my feet.

This was the moment I had given no thought to whatsoever; I was to respond to Goffredo's gracious speech: *Jesu! Think of something nice to say.* I looked down and saw Sibyl, radiant, but that started a disturbance in my pants and I cast about for something else to concentrate on.

I thanked the count for the chest. As curious as I was, it remained closed; impolite, I thought, to open the thing. I thanked him for his daughter, and then the only thing that came to mind was the part that my absent friend, Matilda, had played in bringing us together… So I said a few words about that, then a few words about the generosity of Goffredo, then a few words about the loyalty of my friends, those fearless warriors sitting at the long table down the middle of the hall, trying to put their hands were they should not upon the lady guests, who wished they would succeed, but were pretending that they did not. I could see lots of things from the top table which I should not, presumably.

Then Sibyl pulled at the back of my silk shirt and I sat down – speech finished – presumably.

'We can go now, *mio tesoro.*' So I stood up again, unaided, and handed up my bride. The real business of the day was about to commence. We left the hall to a crescendo of cheers and much banging on the tables.

The bedding of newly-weds, especially such an important couple, was often considered a public – or at least a semi-public affair – but not in this case. The crowd of giggling girls and curious men who followed us up to the bedchamber were firmly rebuffed at the door when the statuesque bride turned on them and with one withering glance sent them packing.

'There,' she said, 'they'll have to use their imaginations.'

'Will I?'

She turned away from the door and said simply, 'No.'

Crossing the room she stood in front of me and grasped my face between her hands. She enveloped my mouth with her lips open and slid her tongue on to mine. We grappled thus for an age before she disengaged and we stood gasping for breath, our noses touching, sharing the air, and then she moved her hands down to my hips and slid over them until she had my buttocks firmly in her grasp.

'*Quanto tempo ho aspettato questo momento, Roberto mio,*' and then she pulled my groin into hers. I was bursting my breeches, of that she could have no doubt.

'Yes, Sibyl, I've been waiting an eternity too.'

Releasing her grip she turned and, thrusting her buttocks into my groin, commanded, 'Get me out of this gown.'

With trembling fingers I carefully undid each and every button down the length of her back, so slowly that she began to tremble with impatience. My hands reached the bottom button and then slid around the top of her hips to feel her flat stomach – before they commenced a journey up her front.

As they reached her breasts they paused, and then, with the fullness of them in my palms I teased her nipples, squeezing them between my first and middle fingers, and began to gently knead the tumescent tips until she groaned. My mouth was at work on the back of her neck, my tongue tracing the base of her hairline, and she shuddered.

Moving my hands further up I uncovered her shoulders, then gently teased the upper part of her wedding gown away, my thumbs tugging the silken cloth all the way down her smooth arms until the top of the gown fell off and her body was completely exposed above her hips.

We were both entering the madness stage as she turned and pushed me away so that I sat on the bed. Turning away once more she took the folds of her gown, still around her hips, and with her back to me she eased the waistline downwards, pushing it to the ground, bending as it slid, offering a view that no man had seen before. Then turning to face me again she displayed herself, naked and vulnerable, but smiling, letting my eyes play across her smooth and unblemished flesh. Then, reaching up behind her head – raising her breasts – she loosed the golden net holding up her hair, which shining crown fell down around her shoulders and made a perfect frame for her perfect face.

I quickly kicked off my fine leather wedding shoes and dragged off the silken wedding shirt, which was cast away somewhere over my head. I bent forward to push my breeches down and breathed in the scent of her hair-framed valley. With my fingers I eased the breeches over my heels and delayed standing upright so that I could nip the curly hair below her tight, muscled belly with my teeth. She gasped again, 'Roberto,' and I stood upright, with only my hardened shaft keeping our bellies apart. Simultaneously we wrapped our arms around each other to hold each other tight. She spun us about, falling backwards onto the ample bed. As we were locked together I fell with her and banged my knees on the side rail; no matter, the thing in our heads was urgent, her knees were apart and posed no barrier as I pushed up with my hands and brought our tongues back into play, without thought or guidance my shaft entered her and she pulled me in with her hands around my backside. Joined after all this time and with all reason gone, my climax came too soon but as the urgency faded there came the first command.

'I have not finished, *mio amore*, too soon, it is too soon.'

My head was alongside hers, so our ears were nuzzling. I raised my head so I could look into her eyes and breathed my reply into her nostrils.

'Sorry, my love, but that has been too long in the making. Let me take care of you.'

'Roberto.'

'Yes, my love.'

'Can we move? My feet are in mid-air and my back hurts.'

'Sorry, I didn't want to leave you.'

'Then let's make full use of the bed and we can start again, can't we?'

'We can.' I moved to one side and he slipped out, causing her to frown but I soon had her completely on the bed and we resumed our exploration. She was remarkably clear about what she wanted. This was a pleasant surprise, no falseness about this woman; our future together was becoming more certain with every moment.

Lying alongside nuzzling her right ear, I placed my right hand on her knee, her legs parted again and my fingers began their journey down the inside of her thigh. She trembled and sighed.

'Ahh!'

Then I felt her downy hair on the back of my hand as I moved to engage her mouth. Her lips opened and our tongues touched: that spark again, thrilling, travelling into my tongue and inside my chest, through my belly and straight to the end of my dick. She turned half towards me and grasped that fire-filled organ, her legs opened completely and my forefinger fell in between her nether lips and touched her hardened nub.

Throwing back her head she made a noise without a word in it.

'You have knowledge of this little friend?' I asked mischievously, half expecting her to deny it.

'Sì, she has been all that I can trust... until now.'

I engaged her tongue again and then began to tease her nipples with my mouth, plucking at those hard buds as I stroked that other hard place between her legs. She began to thrust as the motion brought her back into eagerness, she grasped and pulled at my dick and I had no option but to mount and enter her once more.

This time I had control of my urgencies and began to work him back and forth, taking care to replace my stroking finger with the grinding of my member, pressing her nub with my bone and making certain she could feel every movement. It did not take long, she being ready for it, and as she bucked to match my squirming thrust she cried out my name.

'Ro... ob... ert...o! Ahh! Give it, Roberto, give it,' the rampant princess commanded and I obeyed, with our bones clashing and our bodies drenched in common fluids we rose up in exaltation... the stomach-twisting, mind-blanking crescendo before descending once more into calm.

It was a while before either of us spoke, content to caress and kiss each other in a gentle fashion, at peace with the world and at rest with each other.

'I think that I like this, Roberto.'

'Good, perhaps we can become experts together, Sibyl.'

'It might take a lot of practice, my love,' she responded.

'– And we can make it last as long as you want. It will take a lot of practice to get it right though, have you got time for that, *mio tesoro?*'

'All the time in the world. Now, let me inspect this thing of yours, he seems to be full of life, my lord, and I want some.'

'That's not a problem.' And we set about our practising with renewed enthusiasm.

Later, during a period of rest, the sound of merriment below penetrated the chamber; I regained my senses and raised myself up on one elbow to gaze at the sleeping back of my stunning new wife.

My God! I'm married, and look at what I'm married to... she must be the most perfect creature in the whole of Christendom. Three years was never too long to wait for the privilege of wedding my Sibyl... I think I shall die happy, although I would like some more of this.

I traced a gentle finger down her back and she stirred. When I reached the valley at the top of her buttocks she moved her head, and when my hand slid into the gap at the top of her thighs she groaned, then spoke.

'Roberto! You are awake?'

'Yes, my love... Sibyl!'

'*Sì*, yes?'

'Did I hurt you?'

'Hurt me? Oh no, not that, you did not.'

'It was your first time, it might hurt.'

She shifted on the bed to turn towards me. Tracing the lines of my face with a finger, she smiled, her olive orbs penetrating deep into my mind.

'I have ridden numerous stallions, Roberto *mio*, but I have not been ridden, and riding stallions has made your entry a painless event. *Capisci?*'

'*Sì, capisco*, my treasure.'

'Treasure?'

'*Sì, mio tesoro.*'

She slid her hand down the bed until she found something interesting.

'Is this my treasure then?'

'*Sì, è il tuo cornucopia, mio amore.*'

'Ohh! Then prove it, my Norman warrior, let us see how plenty your horn is.'

She lay back on the bed and we engaged in a bout of tongue wrestling before it all became too much and we were forced to join together once more. This time Sibyl took the lead, and rising up straddled me with her legs; long lovely legs. She sat with her hands on my chest and looked down and giggled, 'Look, Roberto, we are sharing one dick.'

I glanced down; my shaft did indeed appear to sprout out of both our hair mounds.

'He needs the dark, my love; he works best in the dark.'

'Then dark he shall have, I have a dark place waiting.'

Lifting herself up a little she took hold of the searching serpent and parted her damp lips with him, drawing him along her groove until he felt the entry he had been searching for, she paused to let him see the beginning of his journey, and then, slowly, ever so slowly, eased her hips down so that he moved ever deeper inside until I felt her sit on my balls.

'I will do this,' she said, 'you stay still.' She moved herself up and down stroking my shaft, teasing, sucking, hardening it more. Now and then she examined my face to see what effect she was having, it was wonderful but I could not last very long like this, and she knew it. When she could see my time approaching she began to buck vigorously and her jiggling breasts added more excitement to my already tested restraint so that I lost control and arched up to meet her. That did it, the thrusting cast me over the cliff and I filled her with spasm after spasm, triggering off her climax as we went together into a shapeless aftermath of wet tremors.

The idyll continued in Conversano. I found it easy to fit into her life, the count was building a reputation in the development of the stud and Sibyl played a leading part in the breeding programme. She was a very direct lady, which comes from not lacking confidence, I believe, and she asked me quite soon after the wedding if I would assist her.

'Are these the horses that you would like to ride, my lord? To war, that is.'

'Aye, my lady, would that I had a few more of these in my stables at home. But we did have problems with similar beasts in the East.'

'How so?'

'Anatolia was too high and arid, then Antioch was too wet, and the road through Palestine to Jerusalem was too hot. Then of course we could not feed them properly or regularly. Solve those problems and you will have a universal beast, light of my life.'

She stared at me to see if I was jesting, then as I grinned broke into her stomach-thrilling smile.

'I am quite sore down here,' I said, as her smile awoke *him*, I cupped my parts and grinned.

She tossed her hair, freeing it from the bands she wore while riding. 'Me too, *tesoro*, my parts tingle all the time. I find myself thinking about *it* most of the time.'

'Taking your thoughts off horses, is it?'

'Not altogether, Roberto. Let's see if we can find a string of the finest to take with us to our new home in Normandy, should we, my randy stallion?'

'Normandy! Home?' That diverted my thoughts away from my stirring dick. 'I suppose we should think about it now the spring weather will soon be upon us, my sweet – time to prepare.'

'Gladly. How many wagons shall I have for my gowns, my lord?'

I looked at her to see if she was now the one jesting, but she wasn't, although she was still smiling. I said nothing in reply to her query, but it sparked a new concern in me, *why was that remark not a jest?* I changed the subject.

'There's been another missive from Matilda.'

'I know, you're going to tell me about it, *si*?'

'We can read it together, yes.'

As we wandered up the path from the stables she took me by the hand and halted, looking into my eyes.

'Was it like that for men, Roberto... the hardships?'

I paused as the memories of the dry, wet, cold, and blood entered again into my head.

'Yes, Sibyl, and for the women, and the children. Soldiers and pilgrims alike. All suffered the same.'

I could see pain on my lady's face and wished that I could have told a different tale. She placed her arms around my waist.

'You still cry out at night, my love, and thrash about the bed.'

'I'm sorry, *tesoro*, sometimes I am back there, it seems.'

'Don't worry, Roberto, my lord, I'll be with you and watch over you. These dreams will fade with time, but remember that my love is set to grow, of that I am certain.'

How my heart soared with that remark. *If Sibyl is my reward for the past three years of privation, then I have truly entered God's kingdom long before I reach his heaven.*

Later in the year we made the decision to set off on the long journey north, intending to spend some time with the chief conspirator of the plot that brought us together, my friend Matilda of Tuscany.

First, of course, there was a grand sending-off banquet. The feast was excellent, but we both got quite merry and left early, so inflamed had our passions become, fed by too much red wine.

Then came the sending-off of the wardrobe on wheels.

I did not believe her when she said, 'Three wagons, Roberto, I cannot fit into less than three.'

I stood gazing at this impressive convoy, gathered together outside Goffredo's main gate ready to go. 'Why so many, *mio tesoro?*'

She gave me one of those disparaging *why do you waste your breath?* looks and replied, 'Because I am a duchess, no?'

'Of course, what else? Because you are a duchess, yes,' I responded, for want of anything else to say, so we set off with as many wagons as an army might require to journey to Jerusalem.

I confess to being a little apprehensive as we neared Canossa. I wondered how I would react to seeing Matilda once more, or indeed how she would react at seeing me now married and out of her own calculations. Well, this was her idea, I thought, and distracted myself from any idea of a repeat of *that* emotional entanglement by trying to persuade Sibyl that taking her wagons up the tortuous path to Matilda's castle was not a good idea. In the end I instructed the wagon master to set off northwards and we would catch him up later. I knew that the climb up to the ridge would convince my love of the wisdom of that decision, but I had to endure a morning of disapproval from my decidedly sniffy bride.

Matilda was standing in splendour at her keep gate, attended by her impressive guard in their colourful uniforms, ready to greet us. I thought she'd decided on a strictly formal approach to welcoming us, but any coolness disappeared when she held out her hands to help me endure what could have been a difficult meeting.

'Prince Robert,' she said, 'I knew that you two would make a handsome pair, how pleased I am that my judgement was so good. Welcome, Sibyl, *duchessa*, you look splendid in that riding attire, would that I could wear clothes of such distinction.'

I began to answer but quickly found myself sidelined as the ladies decided this was to be a meeting to discuss fashion, rather than politics or religion or the status of a new duchess in a foreign land. So apart from a brief handshake and a nod, Matilda left me in the hands of her castellan as the pair went off to discuss hats, gowns, and ladies attire in general.

A generous buffet had been provided and Matilda's hall was filled with her closest friends and allies, nobles and knights, and civic dignitaries. They'd all been gathered, it seemed, to get at me and question me about my last battle outside of Jerusalem; it was the last thing I wanted and quite early on I caught Matilda's eye. There it was, that spark; not dead but restrained. She knew how to read me, did the lady, and soon brought Sibyl over to extract us from the melee and we made our way out of the hall.

Soon the noise was left behind and we found ourselves panting from the exertion of climbing to the top of the castle and into Matilda's privy chambers.

Now she dropped the pretence and grabbed me by the waist for a warm hug.

'Now you see, dear prince, why you should trust my judgement in all things.' She turned towards Sibyl. 'Come, my dear, give me some comfort, I have kept this proud prince for you. Have I chosen well?'

Sibyl came across and joined in the hugging. I was quite enjoying this, and then as if by signal we stood apart and the ladies giggled a little.

Matilda gazed at Sibyl. 'I have known this lady since she was fifteen, and now she is fully blossomed, do you not agree, Robert?'

'Indeed, I am most fortunate.'

Sibyl shuffled a little and smiled, and I detected a blush on her cheek, but most people lost some confidence when confronted by the indomitable Contessa Matilda.

I looked at Matilda while Sibyl struggled to find some kind words in reply. The lady was in her middle fifties now, some wrinkles certainly, but her own skin was still radiant, as if the light of her soul still found its way to the surface – I could easily have taken her into my arms once more if I gave way to my instincts, such was the power of our old connection. *Stop that, Robert!*

'Is it that long since first you met, my ladies?' I found some words.

'Indeed,' responded Matilda, 'and I needed to fight my way through the crowd of suitors, waiting to be graced by an interview with this haughty lady.' She laughed, and the haughty lady laughed with her.

'Yes, my lady, there was a long queue, but not many got to the front.'

'So I hear, and all of those who did left disappointed, dear Sibyl.'

'Yes, my lady, I knew I would have to wait for the right one.'

'And was the wait worth it?'

Sibyl looked at me with that look, the one that I could fall into.

'Steady on, ladies, I'm still here.'

'Never mind him,' said Matilda, 'is he worth the wait?'

'Yes, my lady, everything you told me, and more. He was well worth the wait.'

'Then care for him, my child, care for him.'

Later, in the familiar comfort of Matilda's guest chamber, I lay back on the enormous plateau of the carved bed listening to the chatter coming from an ante-chamber, where Sibyl, Maria and Sibyl's other companion, Claudia, were laughing and giggling at the silly events of the day. There was much splashing of water, and tempting aromas crept across the air. I detected some movement in my groin and prayed that the preparations did not last too long for I

374

intended to give the lady, my wife, some strenuous attention once her attendants had gone.

Oslac treated me to one of his harrumphs outside the elaborately carved wooden door; he had not yet discovered the more normal knock when not faced by our usual northern curtain.

'Come in, Oslac,' I commanded, and he wandered in, followed by a pair of servants carrying trays.

'We've been given your food to lay out, my lord,' said Oslac, his eyes searching for the real reason for his attentive visit, but she was still in the dressing chamber and he would be disappointed.

'They can place the food on the side table and then you may leave us. I'll see you in the morning for sword practice.'

Disappointed but dutiful he waited until the food and wine was placed as ordered, and then left with Matilda's servants, the object of his desire still hidden from view.

'What was that, Roberto?' The desired one called from behind the door, slightly ajar as it was.

'Some food, *tesoro*.'

'Good. It is your turn for the bath, *mio amore*. I have sent the girls away so you will be in my hands only, my lord.'

Oh joy, her hands – always a joyful mistress were the hands of the girl with the unflawed skin; always eager to have a handful of Roberto's dangling parts were the hands of the flawless one.

I started to drag off my tunic as I crossed the chamber. Leaning against the doorframe to rid myself of my boots, I looked at my beloved.

She was standing by the tub, filled afresh with steaming waters, and perfumed. She wore a flimsy epitoga, lit from behind by the setting sun. Her face was in shadow but the curves of her body stood in silhouette, save where the dark shadow of her triangle of hair was emphasised by the tantalising gap at the top of her thighs.

Her eyes left my face and travelled down my body, pausing to take in the sight of my thick arms and chest, before they too paused at the top of my thighs.

She giggled, holding a hand over her mouth before saying, unconvincingly, 'First, the bath, my lord, then the practising, *mio tesoro.*'

'If you wish, wicked duchess, but I can have both, can I not?'

'*Sì.* Off with those breeches, my lord, if you please.'

'I please,' I said and dropped my drawers.

'Sit down quick before I change my mind.'

I obeyed. *The longer we wait the better will be the joining together.*

I lay back and she started by lathering my head with oils. Leaving that she began on my shoulders, my favourite indulgence, at which she was very good.

'Roberto,' she asked in a manner that I had come across before, it was usually a prelude to an intimate question, 'you have let your hair grow since you returned from Palestine.'

'Mm, it would have held too much wildlife when we were at war.'

'Well, it is coming out grey, did you know?'

'No. Does it bother you?'

'No.' She paused. 'Some might suggest that I had married an old man, but I know different, you are the one I'm proud of, and love dearly.'

'Who says that I'm an old man?'

'Those who have not seen you as I have, like this, a naked warrior.' Her hands slid down off my shoulders and tried to take hold of my stomach, but there was naught there but muscle. Nor could all of the wedding feasts in Christendom have settled any fat on those rock-hard places since my arrival back in the lands of plenty.

She had her chin on my left shoulder, breathing steadily into my ear. I sensed that her hands were not going to remain where they were and began to harden below the waterline. Sure enough she began to explore. Her fingers tugged at my nether hair, and then her right hand grasped my cock while the other took the weight of my balls, feeling them.

'Roberto,' she whispered, her chin over the front of my shoulder so that she could reach my dangling bits, 'do you think

376

there might be another son in here... or two?' She twiddled my balls between her fingers.

'Well, we'd better see if we can get him, or them, out of there and into a place where they can grow, had we not?' I said, and lifted her arms over my shoulders. Leaning forward and grasping her by the elbows I stood up so she was draped across my back like a hempen sack of corn as I stepped out of the wooden tub and carried her through to the bedchamber: squealing with delight, she was.

Reaching the bed I turned and she slid off my back to stand on the bed. In turning I was blessed by the vision of her nether hair in my face. Grasping her by the buttocks I pulled her into me so that I could smell her privy parts. Her garment was wet, and although it hid little I wanted rid of it, sensing this she took her hands off my shoulders, and reaching down, pulled the flimsy drape up and over her head. I nuzzled into her hair and pulled a strand with my teeth.

'Oh, Roberto, *mio amore*. I want my baby now.' Her command was my wish and I was rewarded when, bending her knees and squatting down she opened her legs unto my gaze. I was as hard as a smithy's hammer now, and rampant, as grasping her by the waist I pulled her towards the edge of the bed and onto my tingling dick. She seemed nearer to completion than was I and I took but a few strokes to come near losing my reason.

She had her head back now, and with her eyes rolling towards the ceiling she cried out, 'Roberto! Give me a William, give me your son.'

The meaning of that cry only partially penetrated my head but her passion was in control now. Pushing my toes firmly against the floor I pressed and penetrated as deeply as I could. With Sibyl's legs wrapped firmly around my back, heels digging into my bones, I strived as commanded as she shouted, 'Give me a son. I–want–a–King–William–the–third... *now*.' Bucking with each gasping word she had us both dissolving into chaos at the same time, and I was reduced to a trembling jelly as my stomach exploded and I fell forward on top of her.

As my senses returned I found her heels still dug into my back while mine were pointing at the ceiling. It was not very comfortable and I grunted as I tried to move. Then Sibyl spoke.

'You are quite heavy, my lord.'

'And you, my love, are a raging fire.'

I found the floor with my feet and we both made our way to the top of the bed to sit with our backs propped up by the ample supply of pillows. I had an arm around her shoulders and she nuzzled into my chest. A hand wandered down to my balls and she squeezed gently.

'Empty, my lord; I have the best of you now.'

'Uhh! What was that about a William, my treasure? Where did that come from?'

'I always wanted a William, and it fits, yes? Your father is gone, and your family needs a new William to take the place of your brother when he goes?'

'My brother is still with us, my love.'

'Sì. But if there is no heir then he will have to declare one?'

'Sì. I suppose so. Even so, it's nice trying to make a new William, is it not, my love?'

Sometimes the days were not so nice. Matilda's courier network was working hard to keep the flow of information moving, and we were receiving regular notes.

In the north the storm clouds were gathering. During my absence William Rufus had exercised free rein over both England and Normandy, and had brought Maine under control, something in which I'd not been entirely successful, or entirely interested.

But Henry had been busy about his own business, building up an alternative power base among those lords disaffected by Rufus' behaviours and demands – but to what purpose?

William Rufus had proved a vexatious ruler. Through his tax demands he had annoyed all landholders, including the Church, and through his licentious behaviours had undermined his already poor reputation with the clergy: in short he was not very popular.

When news of my successes in the Holy Land was received in Normandy and England, Henry apparently became extremely agitated, and furthermore did not seem to welcome the news of my marriage. He would know well enough that through the treasures bestowed upon me by Alexios, and now Sibyl's dowry, I had more than sufficient to repay the mortgage held against Normandy that I owed Rufus.

Henry's hopes of ruling either Normandy, or England – the main prize – were thus ended. He had not married and although he'd made a sport of bedding women, and had produced more than two dozen bastards, none of them would be considered by Church or State as suitable rulers. Whatever Henry's hopes for the future had been, they were now a diminishing prospect.

Matilda was pleased to see that her plot for me had met with such outstanding success, so much so that in early July we were still enjoying the countryside around the Valle dei Quattro Castelli, near Modena, when the worst of news came to us.

While out riding from the castle at Canossa we spotted half a dozen riders in the distance. Reining in, I shielded my eyes from the sunlight to see better.

Our escort became agitated, not knowing who they were, and we not a very warlike band: besides me we had only Oslac and a knight from Goffredo's household, together with two of Sibyl's ladies and one of her brothers. We all rode together now and Maria had developed eyes for Oslac: the tall blond Saxon had her so besotted that Sibyl had warned the maiden, 'Be careful that you see the red moon each month; you won't be able to travel with me if you are with child.'

Now Sibyl asked me, 'What is it, my love?'

'I'm not certain, but that leading rider seems familiar to me, the way he sits; I wonder what they want.'

'Does it matter, Roberto? They are heading towards Canossa Castle anyway; I expect Matilda can manage without us.'

'Yes, she usually does, but there's something about that rider. Ah well. Come on, let's go down to the river and water the horses.'

'Race you!'

'Huh! Let's see about that.'

We galloped off down the hill, followed by our guardians, to a place along a sparse stream where water would collect and we could care for the horses. We made it back to Canossa later in the afternoon to find Matilda waiting in the bailey – together with the rider we had seen earlier.

'Edgar! God's miracles, tis Eddy.'

I leapt off my mount and embraced my old friend.

'What on earth are you doing here? You're too late for our marriage! Here, meet my wife Sibyl.'

I was excited, and Sibyl was curious, but both Matilda and Edgar were oddly serious. Sibyl held out a hand and dipped as Edgar kissed it lightly.

'My lady,' he said graciously. I watched and saw that when he raised his eyes he was troubled. Sibyl looked at Matilda and found the same worried expression.

She turned to me and I knew that something was wrong.

'Sibyl! Matilda! What's wrong? Eddy, why are you here?'

I stood silently, now knowing that Edgar's presence was not going to be for welcome reasons.

'It's your son Richard, Robby. I have brought bad news.'

I straightened up.

'Tell me!' I commanded.

'There has been an incident in the New Forest, near Winchester, a stray arrow it is said. He is dead, Robert.'

'Oh God! Tegwin! William?'

'They are safe, Robby. I have taken them to your cousin, William De Mortain at Launceston Castle.'

'Cousin William? Launceston? What's afoot, Edgar?'

'I am not certain. Let's go inside and I'll tell you all I know.'

Matilda led the way into her stronghold as I questioned Eddy.

'How long ago did this happen, dear friend?'

'Some five weeks ago, at the beginning of May. I came as soon as I could.'

'You did right, my friend, thank for your efforts.'

I turned to Sibyl. 'Know this, if things had been different this man would have been King of the English; he is a Saxon prince and his sister was Queen of Scotland until she died.'

She took his hand and settled her gaze upon him, saying in her sultry voice, 'You must tell us more, Prince Edgar, you have disturbed my Roberto.'

Our Italian and Norman companions followed us to the castle. Matilda, seeing my distress, had an arm about my waist as we walked across the bailey. Edgar fell in alongside of Sibyl, they had taken to each other immediately: any friend of mine...

To an observer those two may have sounded a little odd. Edgar's use of the Norman language, delivered in a Northumbrian patois with its own peculiar vowels, competed with Sibyl's attempts in her richly accented Southern Italian voice. It was likely that nobody from Normandy would have understood much of the conversation, but these two needed to, and so stumbled along with good grace.

When we were settled in Matilda's privy chamber I came out with all the questions racing around my head. I was composed now and determined to discover as much about the situation as possible before deciding on a course of action.

'So why Launceston? Where is that place?'

'It belongs to William de Mortain, as Earl of Cornwall. It sits in the middle of a desolate land far to the west, but is close to the Celtic Sea, and passage across to Wales.'

Matilda issued a command and maps were brought.

'But why did you take them there?'

'It was King William's command. He has suspicions that all is not well in the kingdom and that Henry is stirring up dissent.'

'But what has that to do with Tegwin and my sons?'

'Henry has started his own Welsh family connections. Remember when Rhys ap Tewdwr was killed, Henry took his daughter, Nest, under his protection? She is rumoured to have produced a child by him.'

'Well, he's shagged everyone else that goes near him.' I felt a chill run down my spine. 'Wales! Shite! Is he set on forming his own Welsh dynasty? You say that William Rufus is concerned?'

'Yes, Robby, which is why your son William and Tegwin have been moved away from Henry's grasp.'

'Tegwin's brother, Angawdd! Where is he?'

'With them, ever loyal, but he can't be in two places at once. He remained with Tegwin when Richard went off on the hunt.'

'So what happened?'

'It's said that it was a careless shot by a French knight, who's taken refuge in the Priory of St Pancras near Lewes.'

'French! That's strange, what is known of this man?'

'Nothing! I can find out nothing, everyone in the hunting party has gone away... scattered across the lands and the sea.'

'This smells of some control, it needs some thought.'

The others in the room had heard what Edgar had to say but may not have completely understood the meaning. Matilda was well experienced in unravelling complex issues and was first to ask a question.

'Is Sibyl aware of these issues, Robert?'

I nodded. 'We have no secrets, Matilda.'

'As it should be.' She turned to Sibyl. 'You know that Robert had two sons by his Tegwin... a Welshwoman?'

'Sì, a princess from the north.'

'And his father wanted a child of that union to begin a Welsh–Norman dynasty through marriage to a child of the South Welsh king?'

'Sì, Roberto has told me all.'

Matilda turned to me.

'So what has this to do with Henry? Where's the profit in it for him?'

'If he wipes out a union through my blood, and creates one with his, his son could become the first prince of all Wales.'

Edgar added another piece of information.

'Henry has married Nest off to one of his men, Gerald of Windsor. Henry has the privilege of Nest in his bed and Gerald is appointed Constable of Pembroke to keep him happy.'

'Pembroke?' I reached for the map that Matilda had ordered. 'Show me Launceston, Edgar.'

Edgar pointed out that place on the map and I traced a finger across the Celtic Sea to Pembroke.

'By God he has installed Nest opposite my Tegwin, across the sea.'

'Your brother has strange habits, Robert. He trades women for advantage? I like him not.' Matilda spoke her mind.

Sibyl became even more puzzled. She had listened carefully throughout but my last comment totally threw her.

'Sorry, my lord, I cannot make sense of this, why would Henry care who is Prince of Wales?'

Edgar stirred and looked at me, I nodded: *tell them*.

'It would only matter if Henry were to be King of England... if he wanted a united England and Wales for his realm.'

Sibyl replied, still puzzled.

'But he is not the king, Roberto. You told me that if William dies he leaves the crown to you. Why will this benefit Henry?'

I looked at my beloved Sibyl through worried eyes and sighed.

'It would only benefit him if both me, and my brother William, were to be removed.'

Matilda had seen it before, this long-range planning – it takes a labyrinthine mind to conceive such a plot, and an equally diverse one to recognise it.

'Clever!' she remarked, 'very clever; you had better see to your guard, dear Robert, your brother has rolled some dice for your destiny.'

It was as clear as day. Henry had lain like a serpent in the grass for long enough, now he had bared his fangs and tested them on my flesh. First blood to the sleeping scholar.

I looked at Sibyl and she knew straight away.

'Andiamo al nord... sì?'

'Yes, my treasure, we should go north.'

We made such preparations as we could. Sibyl's brother William was left with the task of catching up with our heavy baggage to bring it on after us, and we left Canossa, with a small escort, in the last week of July 1100.

Along the way Edgar entertained us with stories from the north. After King Malcolm and Edgar's sister, Queen Margaret, had died, there had been a bout of bloody struggling to seize the throne. He had been commissioned by King William to ensure that the Scottish crown went to a head which suited William's purposes, and Edgar himself had been in some bloody sword-work in carrying out his commission. Truth to tell, Sibyl found it less than amusing and I was too distracted to pay proper heed. I could question him later, no doubt.

By the middle of August we had covered almost five hundred and fifty miles and were near Bourges when we were met on the road by riders coming out of Alençon, still some two hundred miles away.

Their captain caused some consternation when he made straight for me and was almost met by Oslac's blade in his heart.

'Stay!' I commanded, 'I know this man… Speak, Captain Marellus, what ills have you brought to us?'

These were knights of Robert de Bellême, the departed Philip's elder brother and once my closest friend. They were accompanied by a knight in the colours of Stephen of Blois; they brought news that transcended that which Edgar had transported to Canossa.

'An evil deed, Prince Robert. King William is fallen; an arrow has taken his life.'

Edgar called out. 'The game has begun, Robby, tis worse than we feared; you are all that stands between Henry and the crown of England.'

The captain, hearing this, became agitated and seemed fearful of telling me more, but I demanded to be told.

'My lord, Henry has been crowned already, blessed at Westminster by the Bishop of London; he is the King of England.'

I felt the blood drain from my face and I shivered.

'He has usurped the crown. Who has helped him in this foul deed?'

The captain pointed out Stephen's man. 'My lord, he has an invitation, lodgings await you at Blois. I have the full details in a letter from my lord, Bellême. Perhaps you can read it as we travel?'

'I will try,' I responded, knowing that my reading skills were not the best. 'Eddy, read this missive for me.' I passed the scroll to the Saxon, and listened as he recited a tale of treachery.

It reminded me of another such tale and I called to Marellus.

'Are Stephen and my sister at Blois?'

'No, my lord, the invitation is from the constable, and I do not know where the lady Adela is... nor Lord Stephen.'

'I would like to speak with Count Stephen; we have some unfinished business to discuss with that warrior.' I turned to Sibyl; this was not the welcome I had in mind for the new Duchess of Normandy.

'My love, we have come from the light once more into the darkness of treachery. My eldest son, dead; the king of England, dead; how can this all be an unplanned disaster? It seems that Henry has been too conveniently placed to witness such events without having a hand in them, and in an indecent haste to pronounce himself king. By what twist of logic does he declare himself above me in succession? – Yet he is ordained, by Holy Church ordained, by God's authority ordained!'

I gazed helplessly at Sibyl. The shock on her face must have matched my own and for once she had naught to say, this was beyond flippant responses.

'I must take counsel. We go on to Alençon where I can take time to think matters through. Oh, Sibyl, this is not what I wanted for you, please forgive me.'

The remark sparked her into life.

'Do not be silly, Roberto, if this is my life then I have chosen it, and you. Let us go together – we practise together, do we not? Let us face perils together, and all will be well.'

What a woman. Thank you, Lord, but what web are you weaving for me now?

From the dark of Palestine into the light of Constantinople, then into the stellar radiance of my Sibyl; now I was staring into the gloom once more. *What reward for my efforts is this, dear Lord?*

To be continued.

If you've enjoyed this book, please leave a review on Amazon or your other provider and accept the heartfelt thanks of the author; and perhaps those others who might be as entertained as you were.

Then watch out for the continuing story of Robert's remarkable life in the last book of this trilogy.

Book Three – The Renegade Son.

If you have questions for the author, please leave them on the Q & A section of Robert's website and Austin will endeavour to answer them very soon.

www.waywardprinceproductions.co.uk